# THE EXTINCTS

## FLIGHT OF THE MAMMOTH

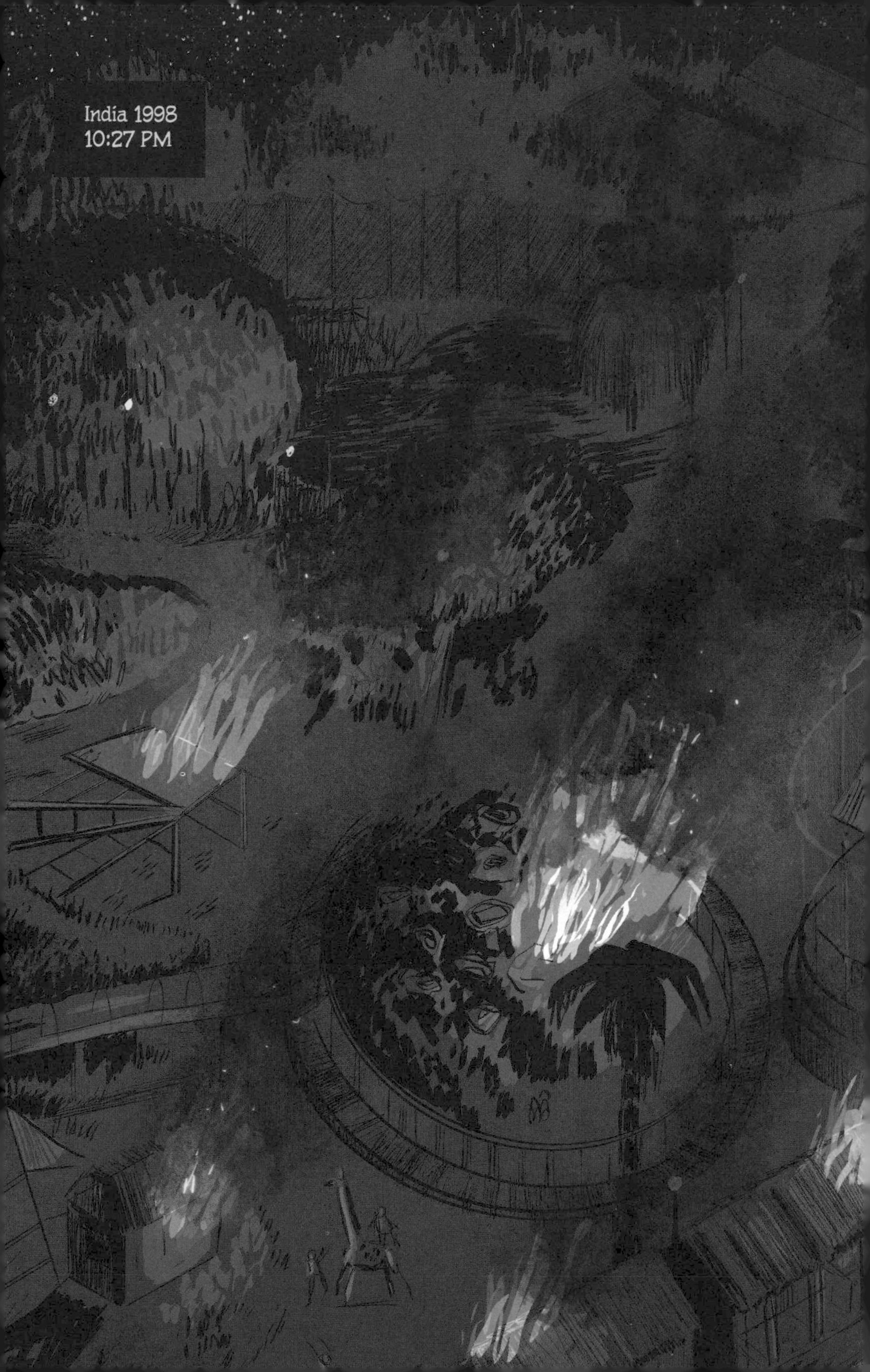
India 1998
10:27 PM

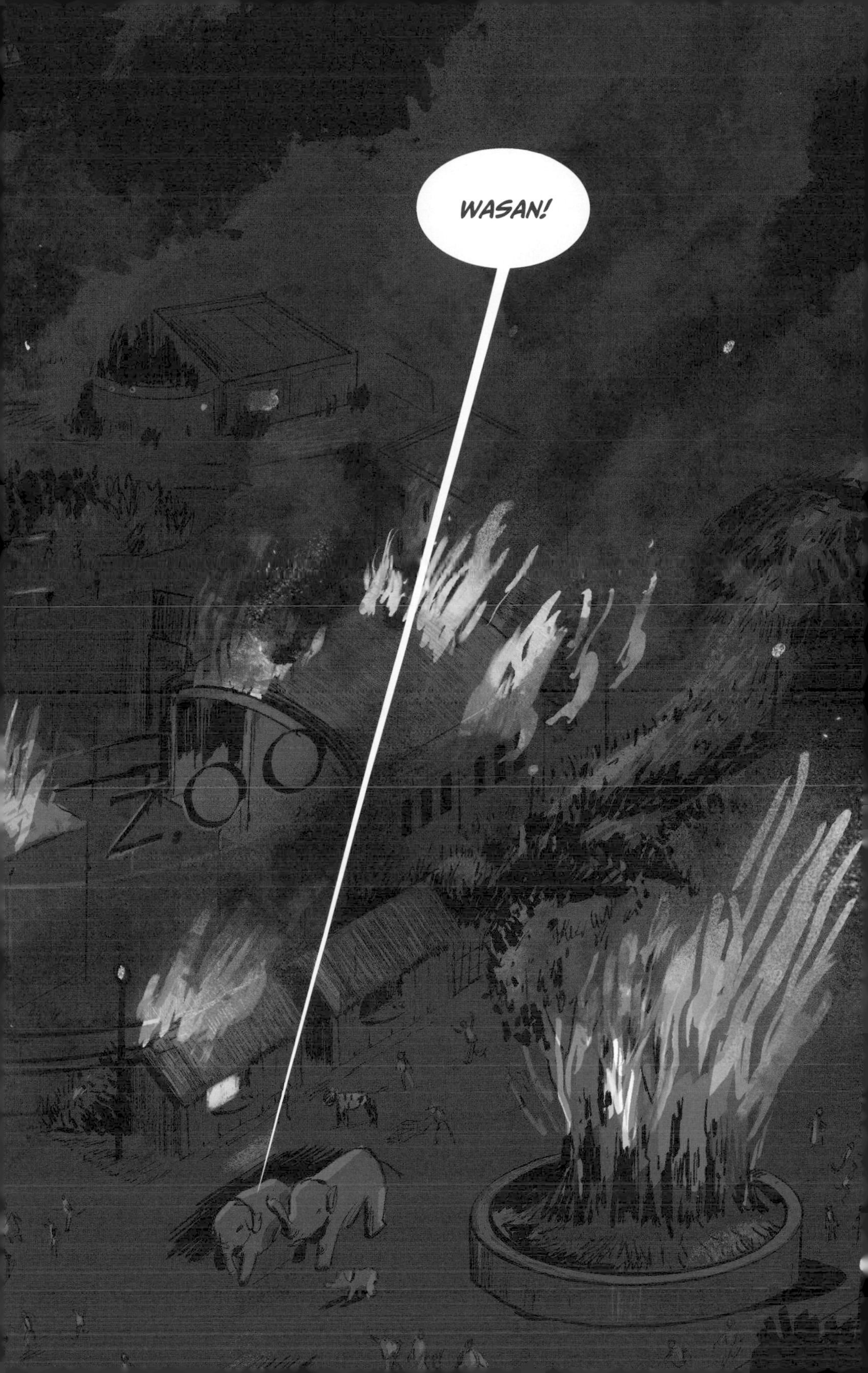
WASAN!

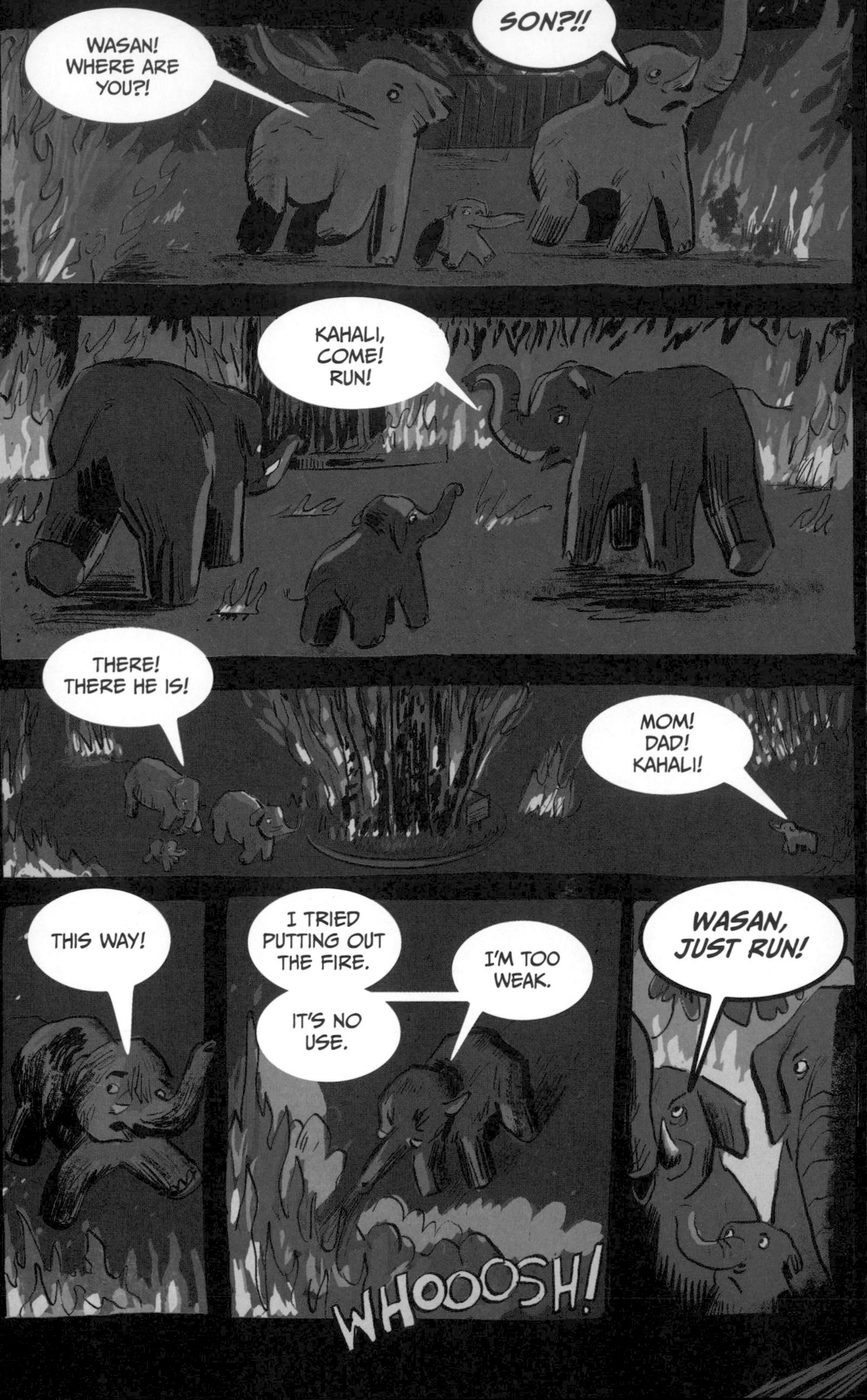
WASAN! WHERE ARE YOU?!
SON?!!
KAHALI, COME! RUN!
THERE! THERE HE IS!
MOM! DAD! KAHALI!
THIS WAY!
I TRIED PUTTING OUT THE FIRE.
IT'S NO USE.
I'M TOO WEAK.
WHOOOOSH!
WASAN, JUST RUN!

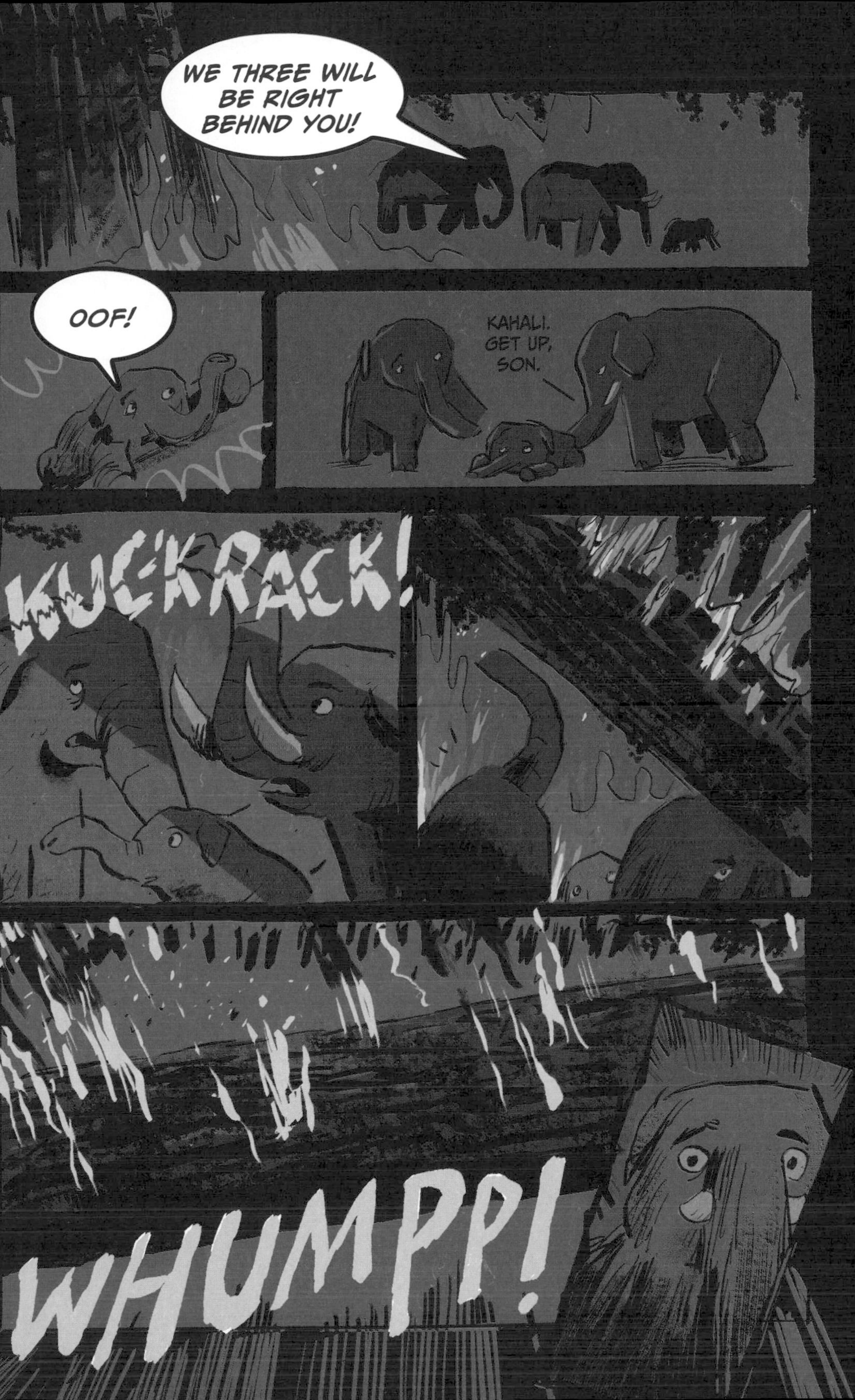
WE THREE WILL BE RIGHT BEHIND YOU!
OOF!
KAHALI. GET UP, SON.
KUCKRACK!
WHUMPP!

AMULET BOOKS AND

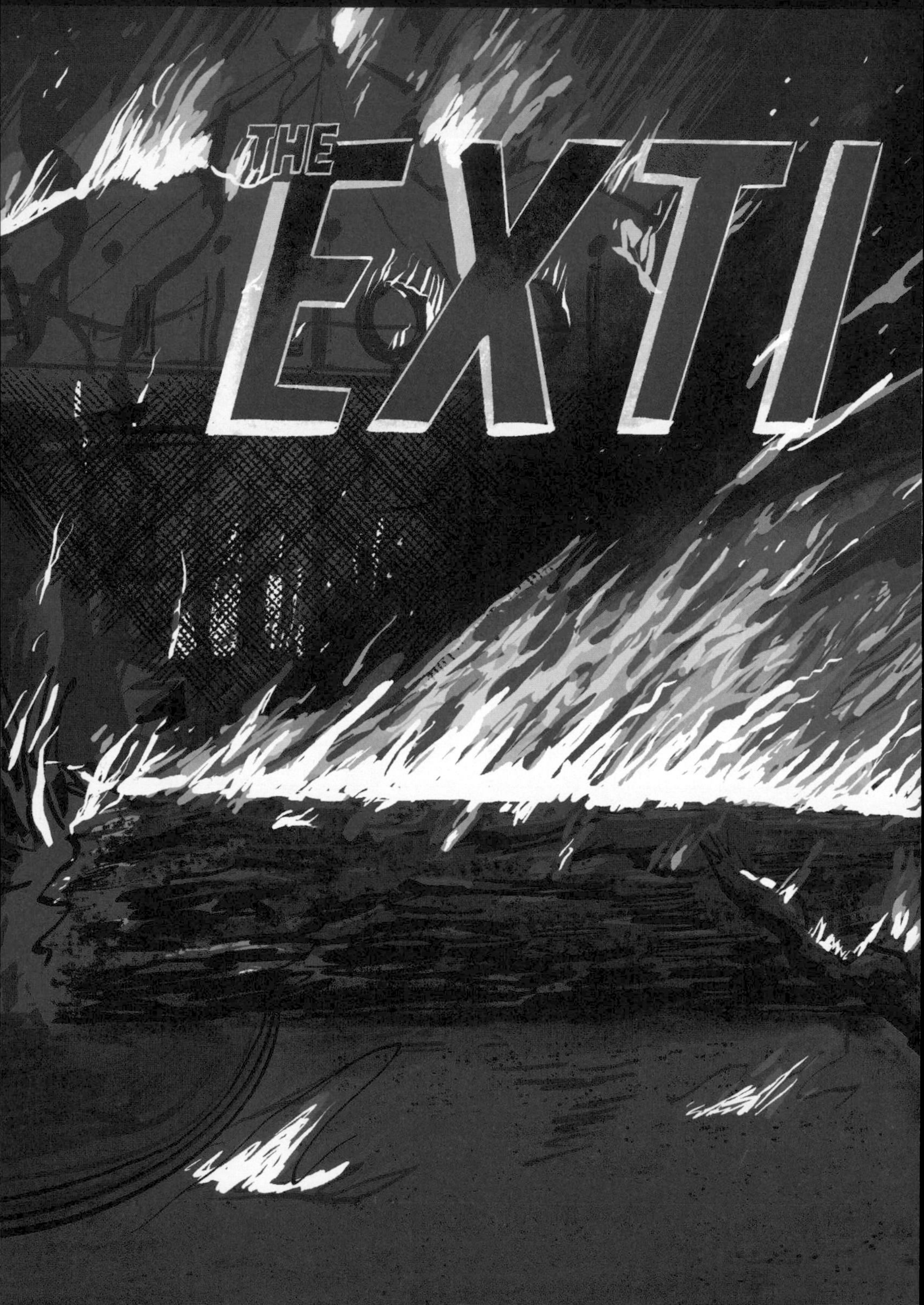
THE
EXTI

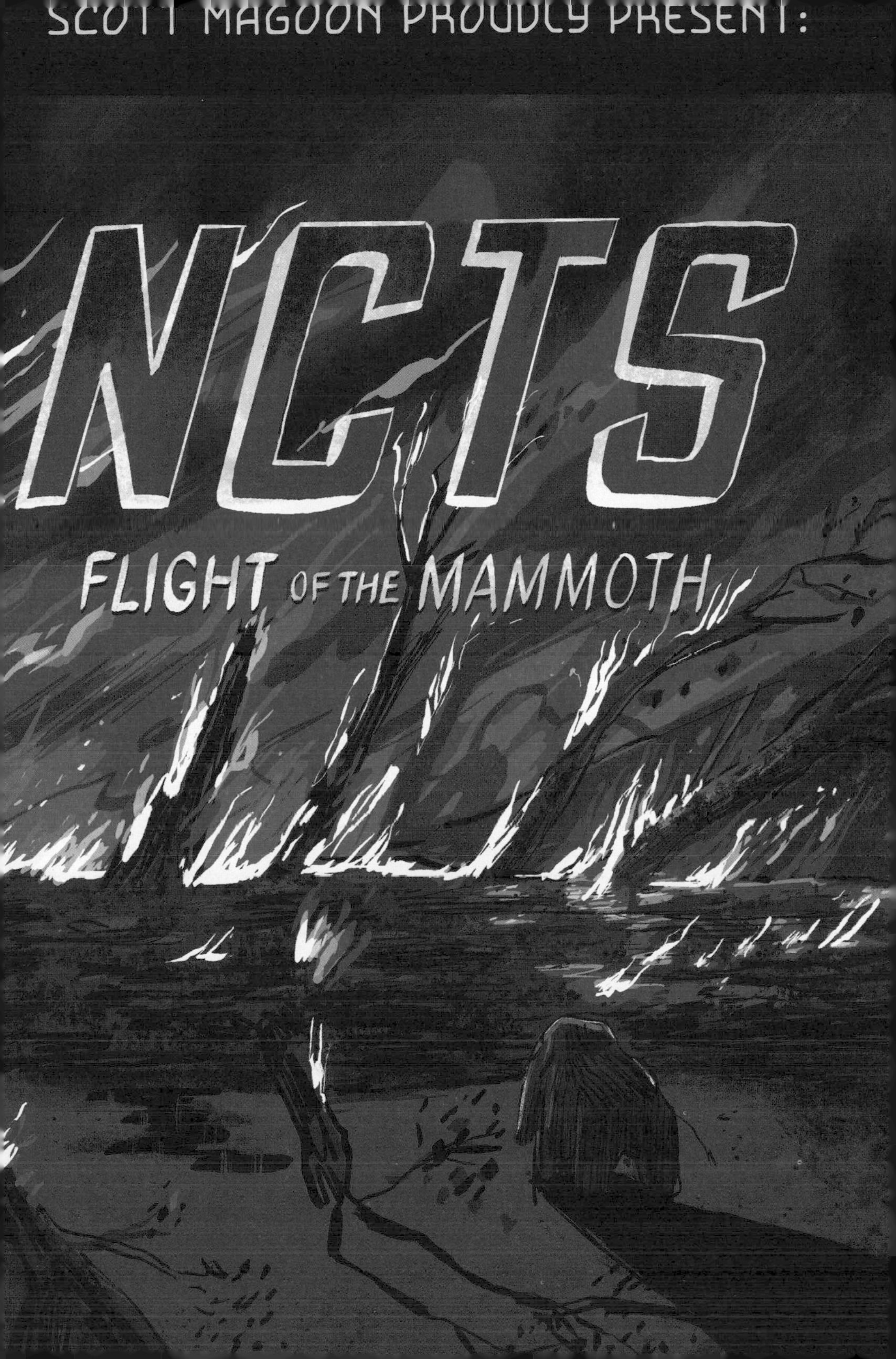
SCOTT MAGOON PROUDLY PRESENT:
NCTS
FLIGHT OF THE MAMMOTH

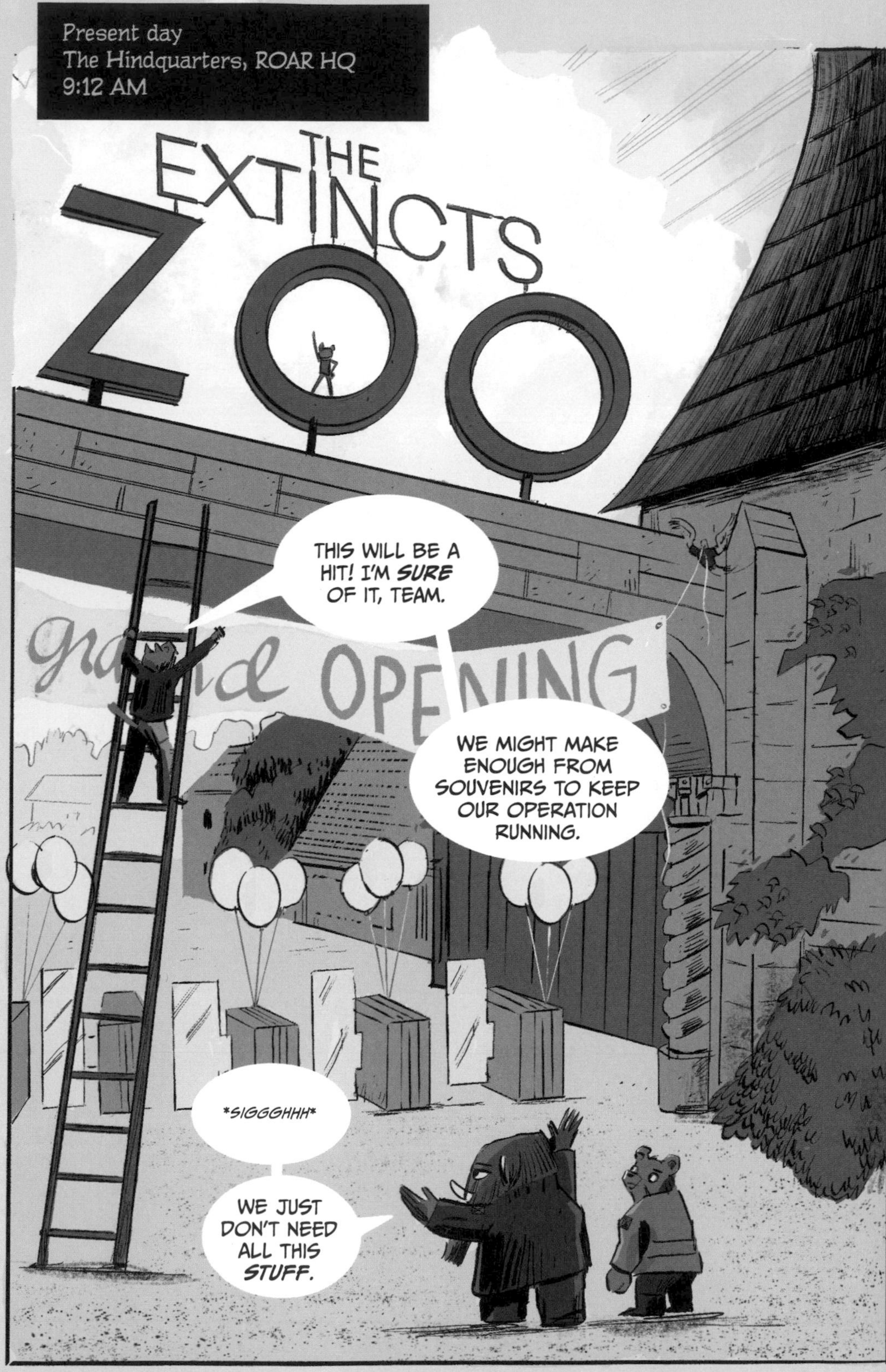
Present day
The Hindquarters, ROAR HQ
9:12 AM
THE EXTINCTS ZOO
grand OPENING
THIS WILL BE A HIT! I'M *SURE* OF IT, TEAM.
WE MIGHT MAKE ENOUGH FROM SOUVENIRS TO KEEP OUR OPERATION RUNNING.
*SIGGGHHH*
WE JUST DON'T NEED ALL THIS *STUFF*.

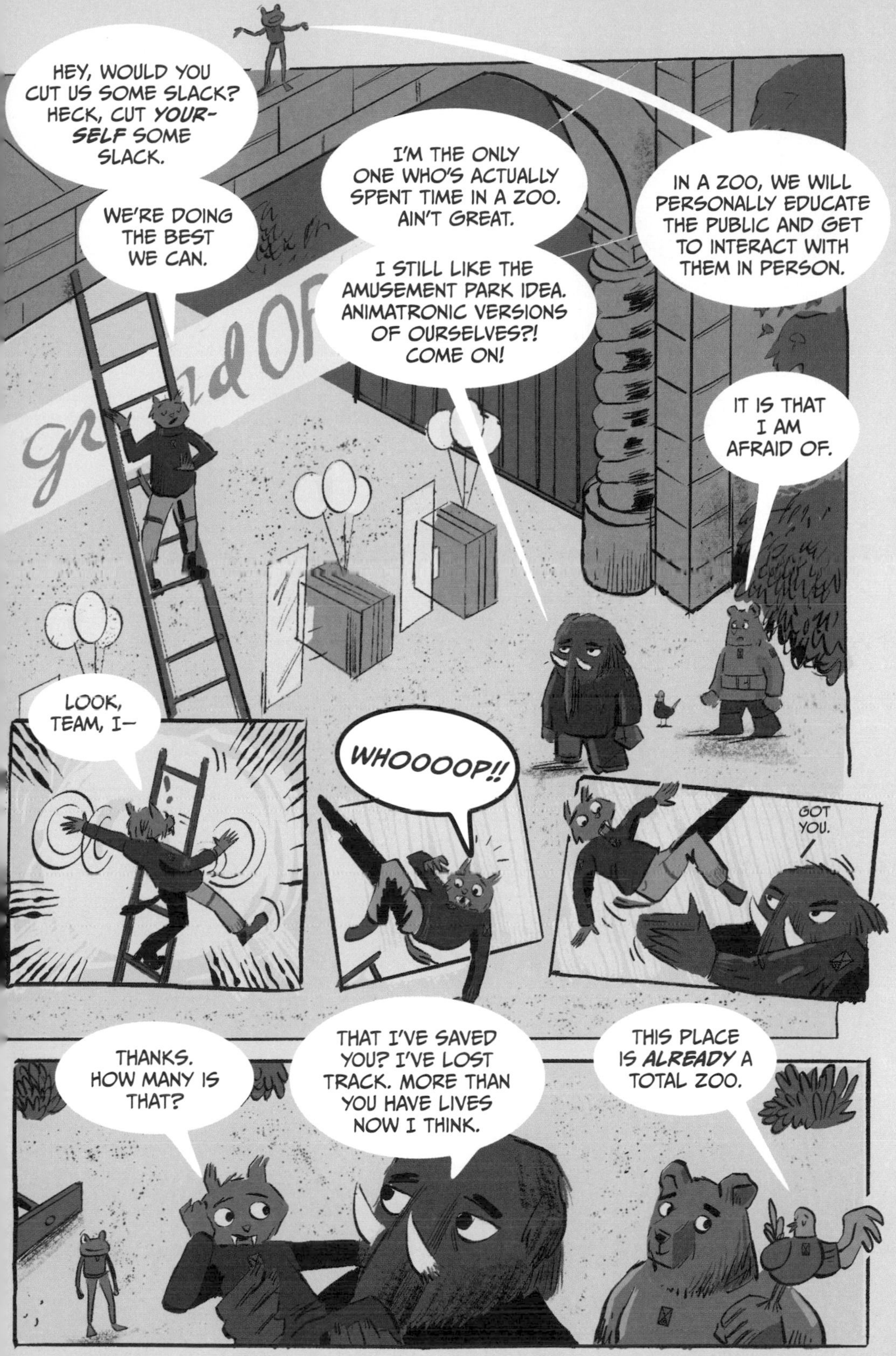
HEY, WOULD YOU CUT US SOME SLACK? HECK, CUT *YOURSELF* SOME SLACK.
WE'RE DOING THE BEST WE CAN.
I'M THE ONLY ONE WHO'S ACTUALLY SPENT TIME IN A ZOO. AIN'T GREAT.
I STILL LIKE THE AMUSEMENT PARK IDEA. ANIMATRONIC VERSIONS OF OURSELVES?! COME ON!
IN A ZOO, WE WILL PERSONALLY EDUCATE THE PUBLIC AND GET TO INTERACT WITH THEM IN PERSON.
IT IS THAT I AM AFRAID OF.
LOOK, TEAM, I—
WHOOOOP!!
GOT YOU.
THANKS. HOW MANY IS THAT?
THAT I'VE SAVED YOU? I'VE LOST TRACK. MORE THAN YOU HAVE LIVES NOW I THINK.
THIS PLACE IS *ALREADY* A TOTAL ZOO.

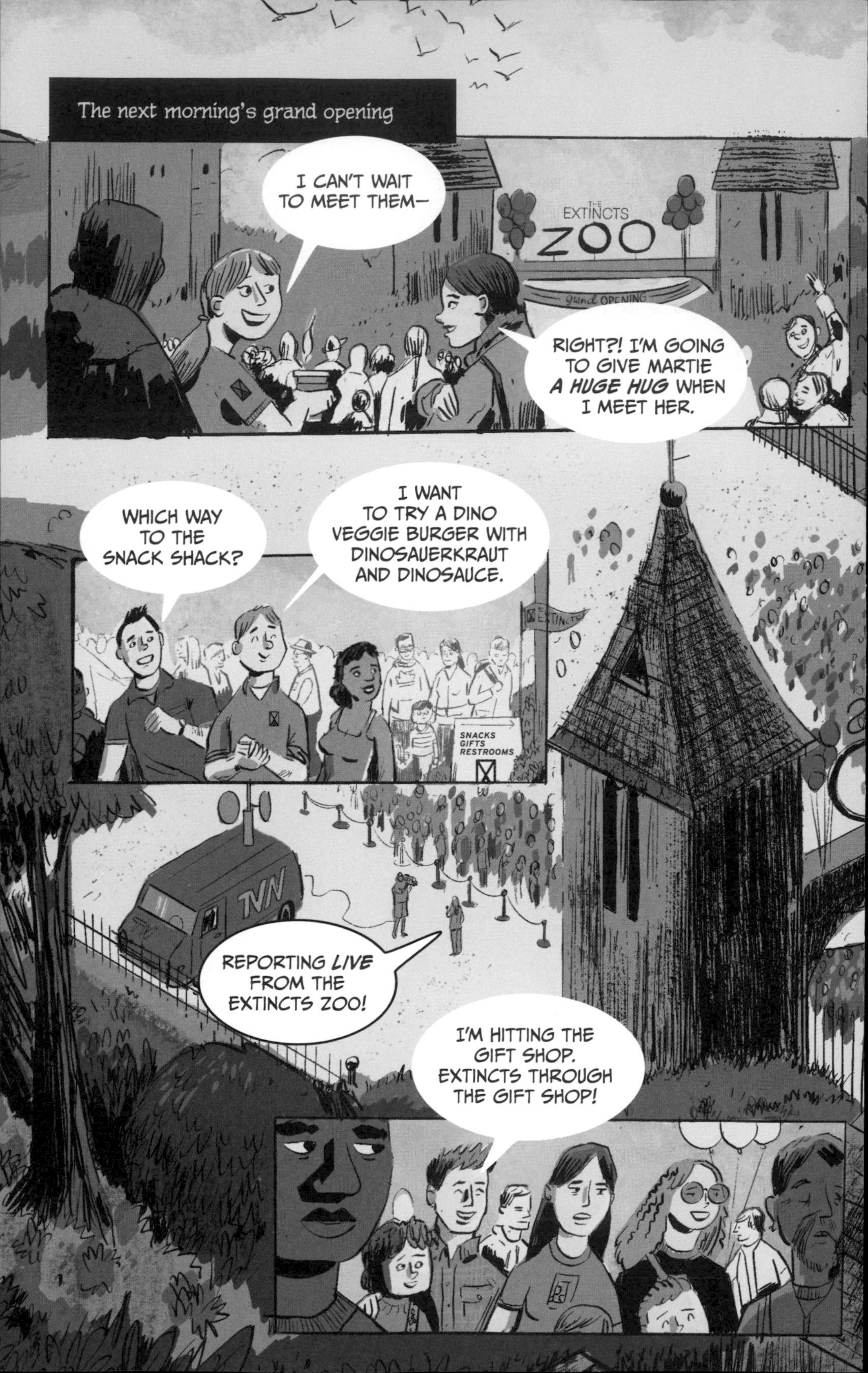
The next morning's grand opening
THE EXTINCTS ZOO
grand OPENING
I CAN'T WAIT TO MEET THEM—
RIGHT?! I'M GOING TO GIVE MARTIE *A HUGE HUG* WHEN I MEET HER.
WHICH WAY TO THE SNACK SHACK?
I WANT TO TRY A DINO VEGGIE BURGER WITH DINOSAUERKRAUT AND DINOSAUCE.
SNACKS
GIFTS
RESTROOMS
TVN
REPORTING *LIVE* FROM THE EXTINCTS ZOO!
I'M HITTING THE GIFT SHOP. EXTINCTS THROUGH THE GIFT SHOP!

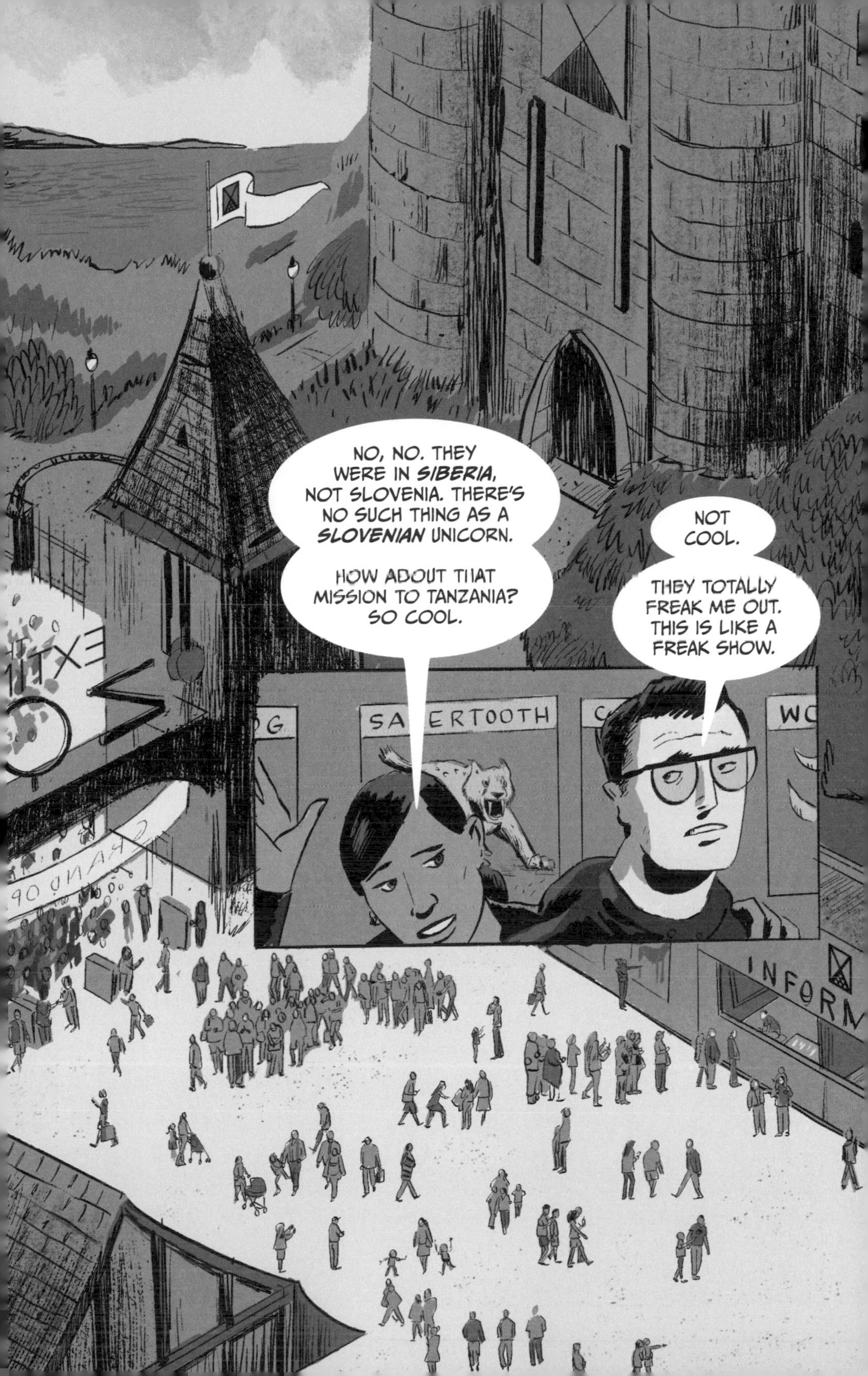
NO, NO. THEY WERE IN *SIBERIA*, NOT SLOVENIA. THERE'S NO SUCH THING AS A *SLOVENIAN* UNICORN.
HOW ABOUT THAT MISSION TO TANZANIA? SO COOL.
NOT COOL.
THEY TOTALLY FREAK ME OUT. THIS IS LIKE A FREAK SHOW.

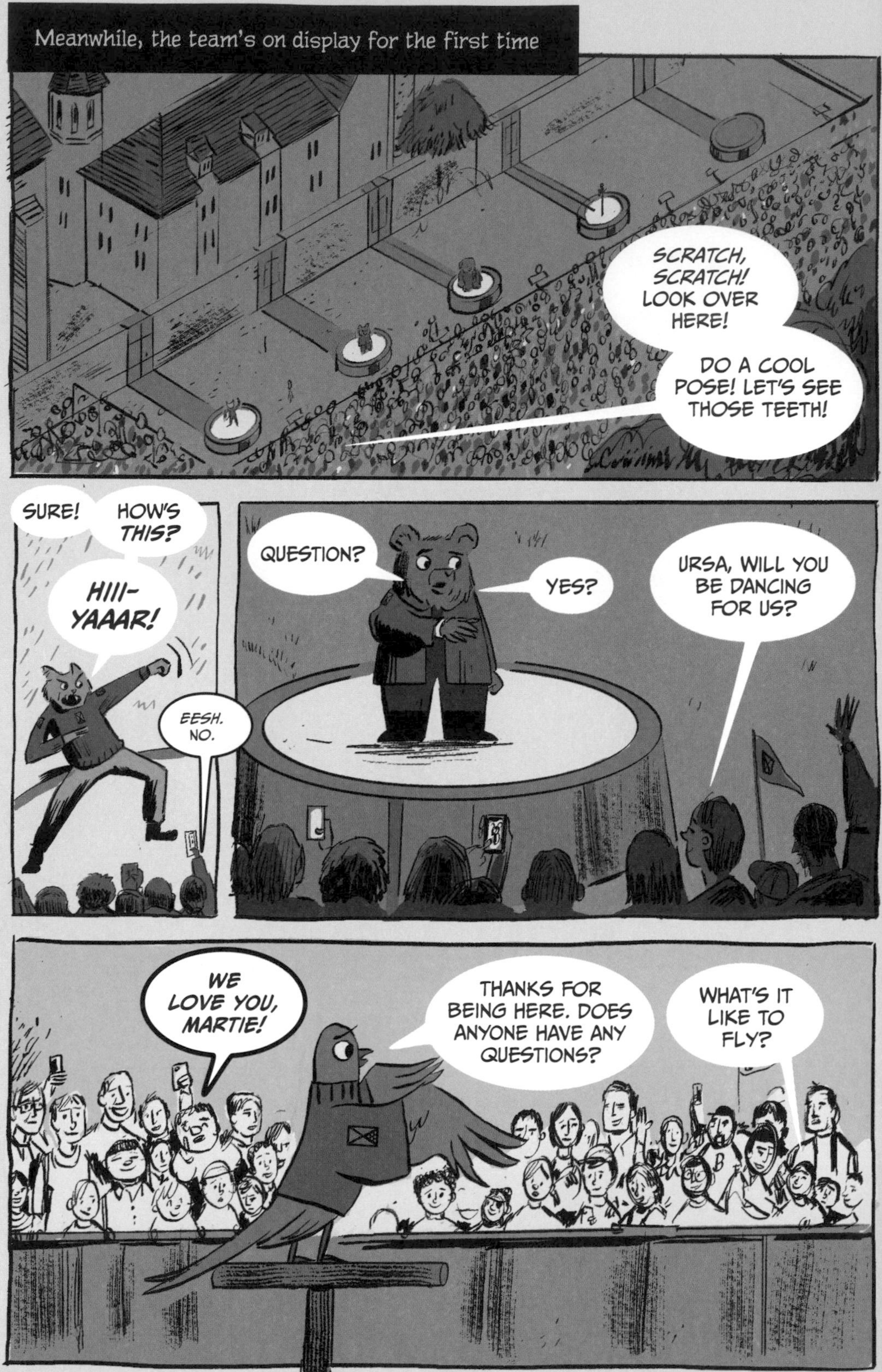
Meanwhile, the team's on display for the first time
SCRATCH, SCRATCH! LOOK OVER HERE!
DO A COOL POSE! LET'S SEE THOSE TEETH!
SURE!
HOW'S THIS?
HIII-YAAAR!
EESH. NO.
QUESTION?
YES?
URSA, WILL YOU BE DANCING FOR US?
WE LOVE YOU, MARTIE!
THANKS FOR BEING HERE. DOES ANYONE HAVE ANY QUESTIONS?
WHAT'S IT LIKE TO FLY?

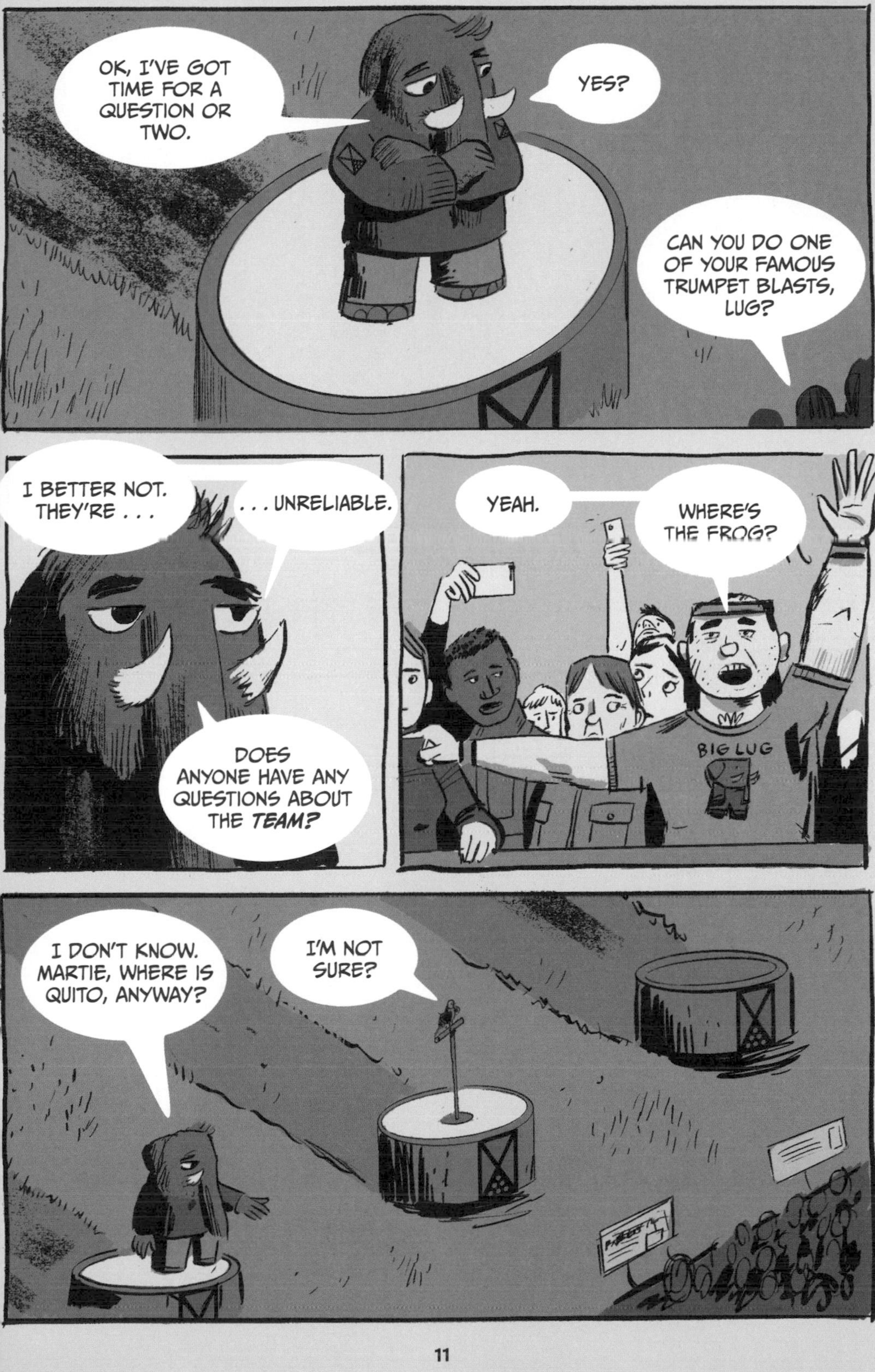
OK, I'VE GOT TIME FOR A QUESTION OR TWO.
YES?
CAN YOU DO ONE OF YOUR FAMOUS TRUMPET BLASTS, LUG?
I BETTER NOT. THEY'RE . . .
. . . UNRELIABLE.
DOES ANYONE HAVE ANY QUESTIONS ABOUT THE *TEAM?*
YEAH.
WHERE'S THE FROG?
BIG LUG
I DON'T KNOW. MARTIE, WHERE IS QUITO, ANYWAY?
I'M NOT SURE?

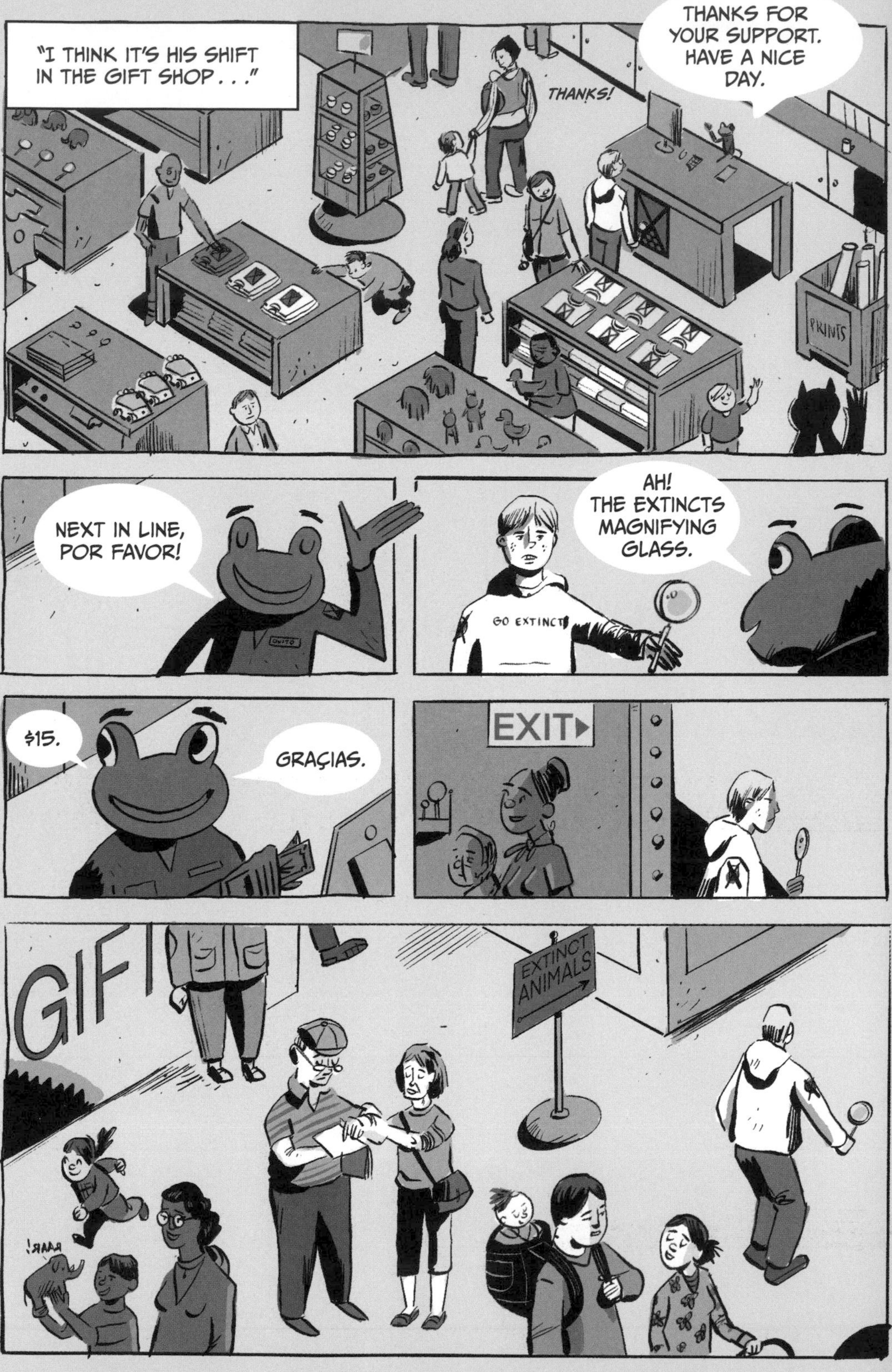
"I THINK IT'S HIS SHIFT IN THE GIFT SHOP . . ."
THANKS!
THANKS FOR YOUR SUPPORT. HAVE A NICE DAY.
PRINTS
NEXT IN LINE, POR FAVOR!
AH! THE EXTINCTS MAGNIFYING GLASS.
GO EXTINCT
$15.
GRAÇIAS.
EXIT
GIFT
EXTINCT ANIMALS
RAAR!

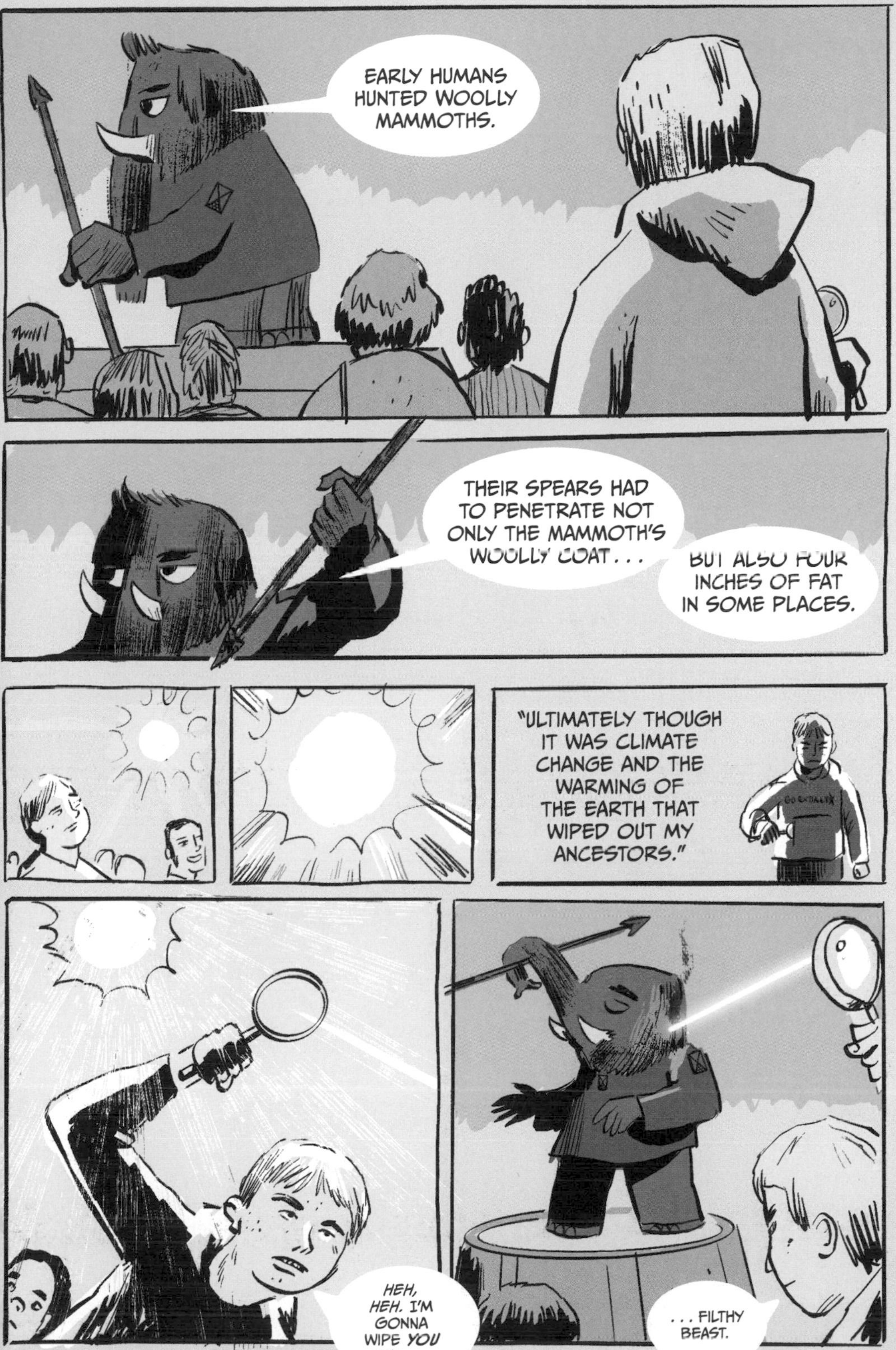
EARLY HUMANS HUNTED WOOLLY MAMMOTHS.
THEIR SPEARS HAD TO PENETRATE NOT ONLY THE MAMMOTH'S WOOLLY COAT . . .
BUT ALSO FOUR INCHES OF FAT IN SOME PLACES.
"ULTIMATELY THOUGH IT WAS CLIMATE CHANGE AND THE WARMING OF THE EARTH THAT WIPED OUT MY ANCESTORS."
HEH, HEH. I'M GONNA WIPE *YOU* OUT . . .
. . . FILTHY BEAST.

How glass focuses light, see page 152

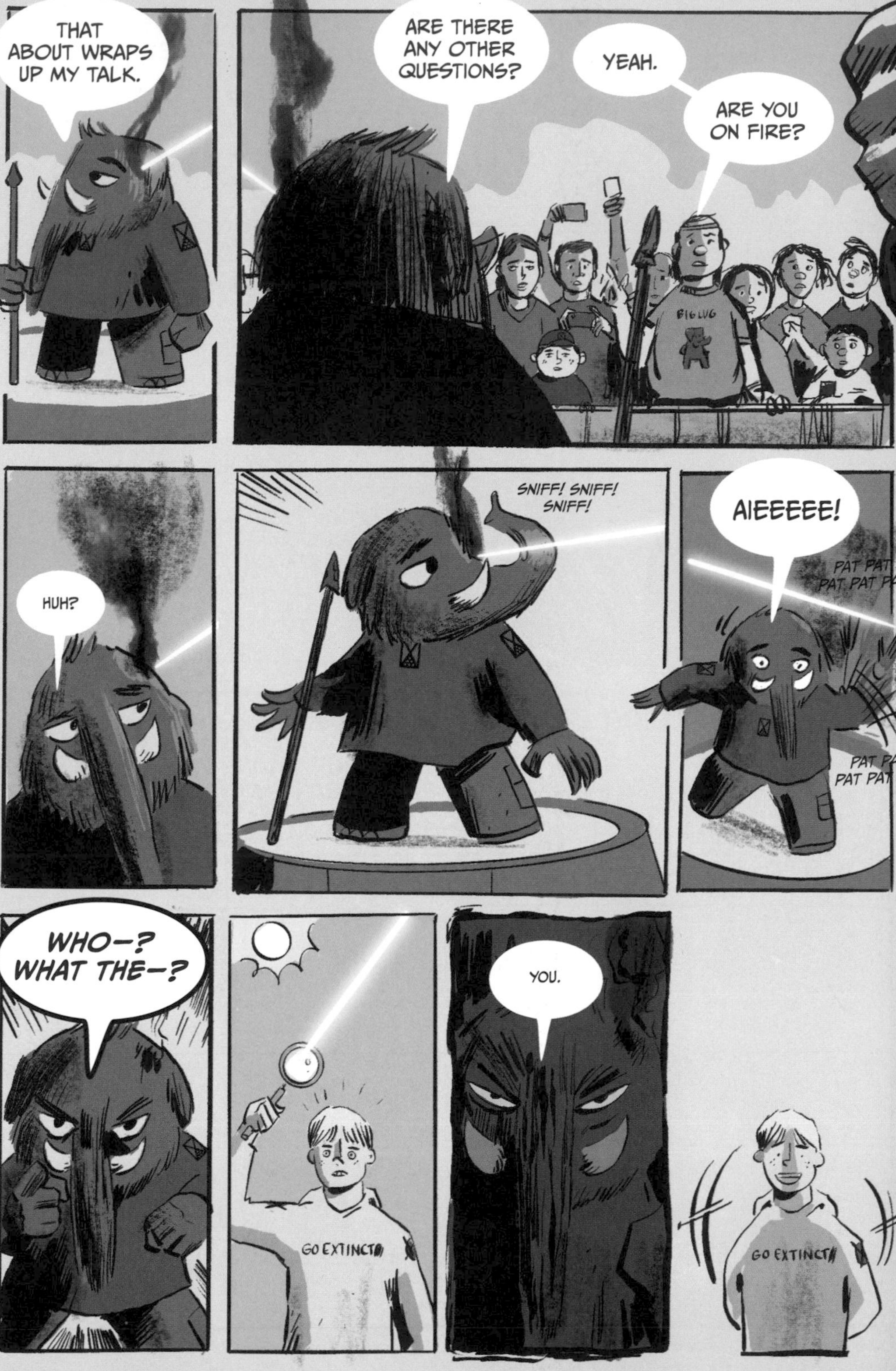
THAT ABOUT WRAPS UP MY TALK.
ARE THERE ANY OTHER QUESTIONS?
YEAH.
ARE YOU ON FIRE?
BIG LUG
HUH?
SNIFF! SNIFF! SNIFF!
AIEEEEE!
PAT PAT PAT PAT PA
PAT PA PAT PAT
WHO-? WHAT THE-?
GO EXTINCT
YOU.
GO EXTINCT

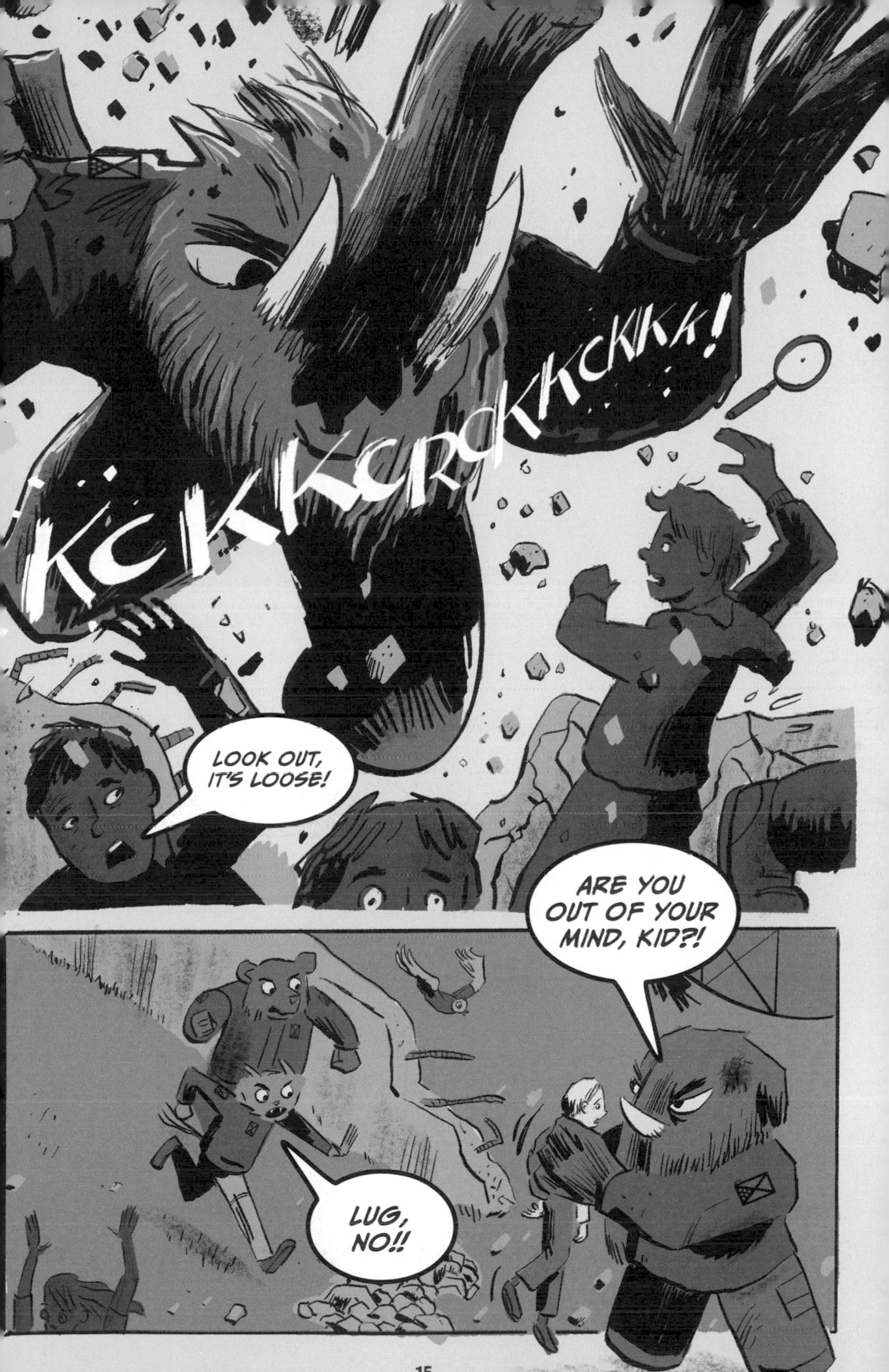
KCKKKCRCKKKCKKKK!
LOOK OUT, IT'S LOOSE!
ARE YOU OUT OF YOUR MIND, KID?!
LUG, NO!!

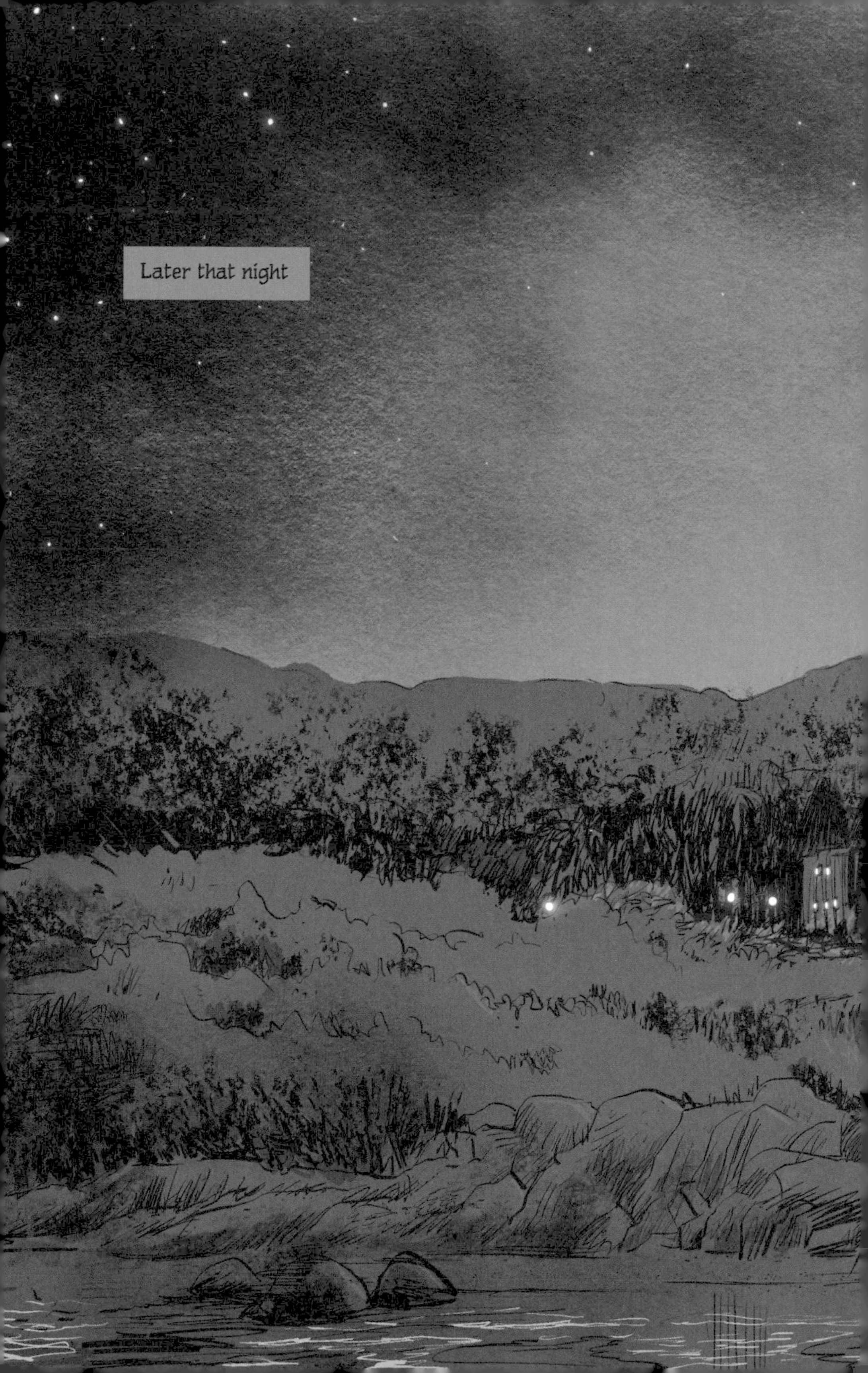
Later that night

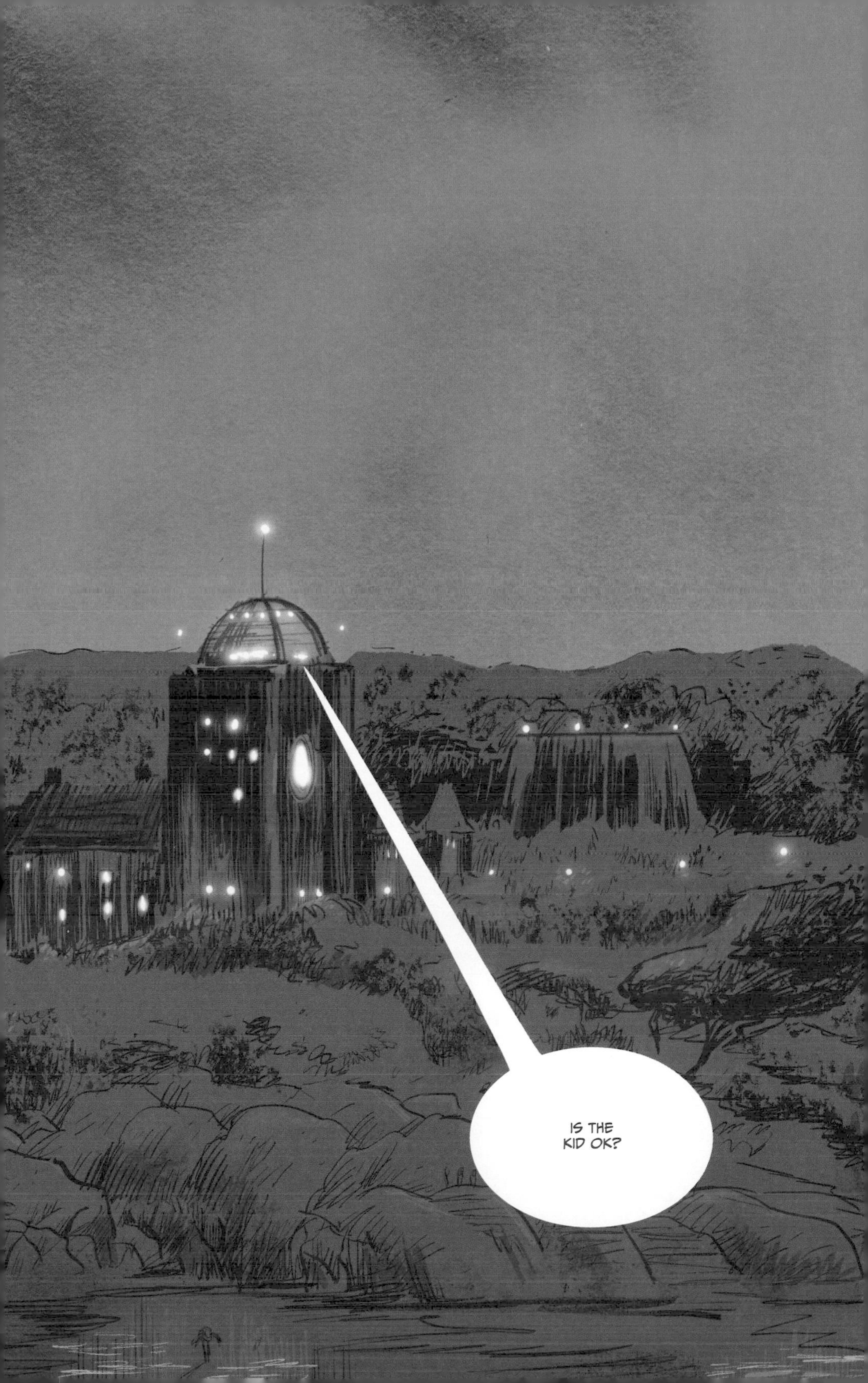
IS THE KID OK?

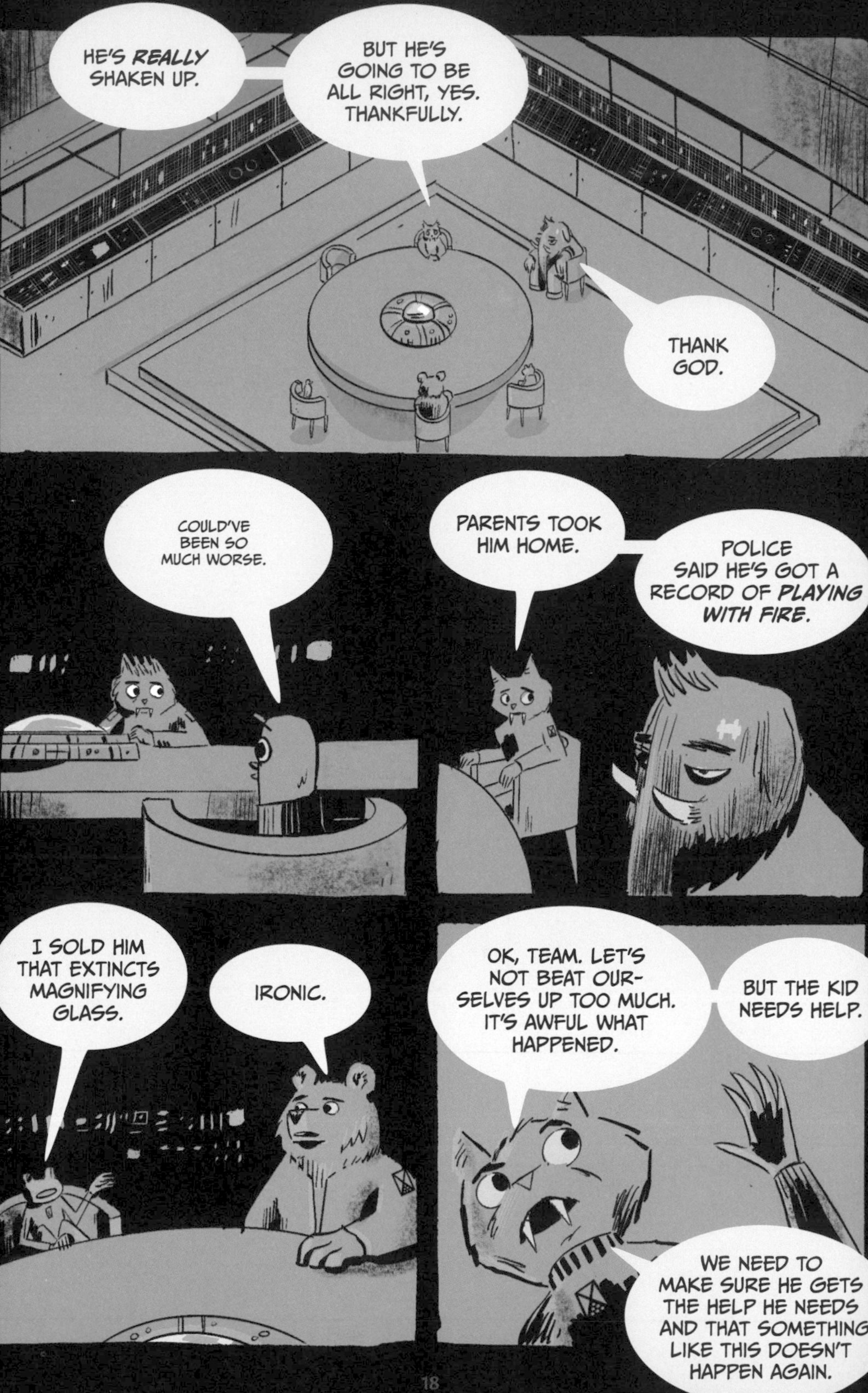
HE'S REALLY SHAKEN UP.
BUT HE'S GOING TO BE ALL RIGHT, YES. THANKFULLY.
THANK GOD.
COULD'VE BEEN SO MUCH WORSE.
PARENTS TOOK HIM HOME.
POLICE SAID HE'S GOT A RECORD OF PLAYING WITH FIRE.
I SOLD HIM THAT EXTINCTS MAGNIFYING GLASS.
IRONIC.
OK, TEAM. LET'S NOT BEAT OURSELVES UP TOO MUCH. IT'S AWFUL WHAT HAPPENED.
BUT THE KID NEEDS HELP.
WE NEED TO MAKE SURE HE GETS THE HELP HE NEEDS AND THAT SOMETHING LIKE THIS DOESN'T HAPPEN AGAIN.

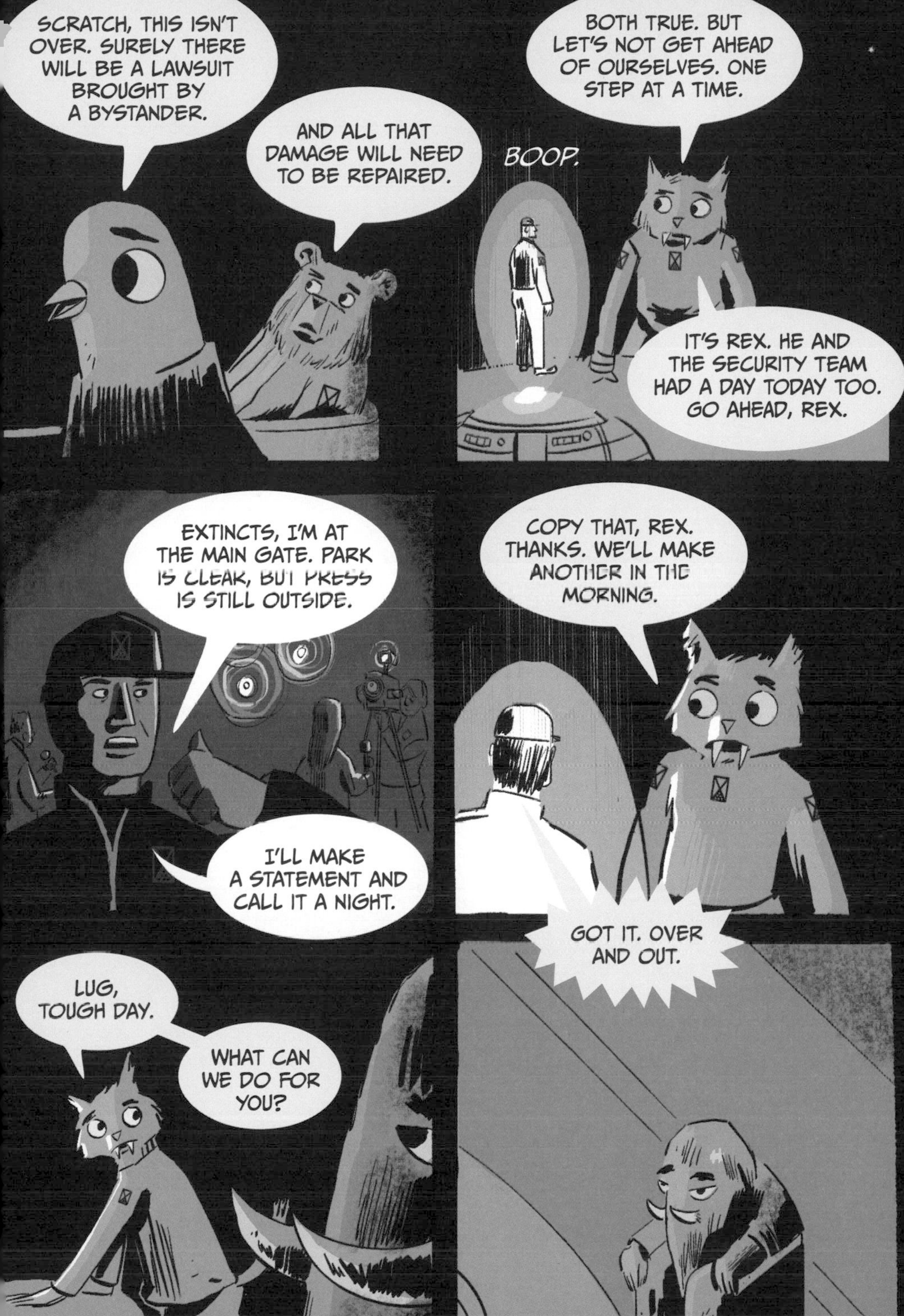
SCRATCH, THIS ISN'T OVER. SURELY THERE WILL BE A LAWSUIT BROUGHT BY A BYSTANDER.
AND ALL THAT DAMAGE WILL NEED TO BE REPAIRED.
BOTH TRUE. BUT LET'S NOT GET AHEAD OF OURSELVES. ONE STEP AT A TIME.
BOOP.
IT'S REX. HE AND THE SECURITY TEAM HAD A DAY TODAY TOO. GO AHEAD, REX.
EXTINCTS, I'M AT THE MAIN GATE. PARK IS CLEAR, BUT PRESS IS STILL OUTSIDE.
I'LL MAKE A STATEMENT AND CALL IT A NIGHT.
COPY THAT, REX. THANKS. WE'LL MAKE ANOTHER IN THE MORNING.
GOT IT. OVER AND OUT.
LUG, TOUGH DAY.
WHAT CAN WE DO FOR YOU?

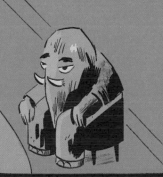

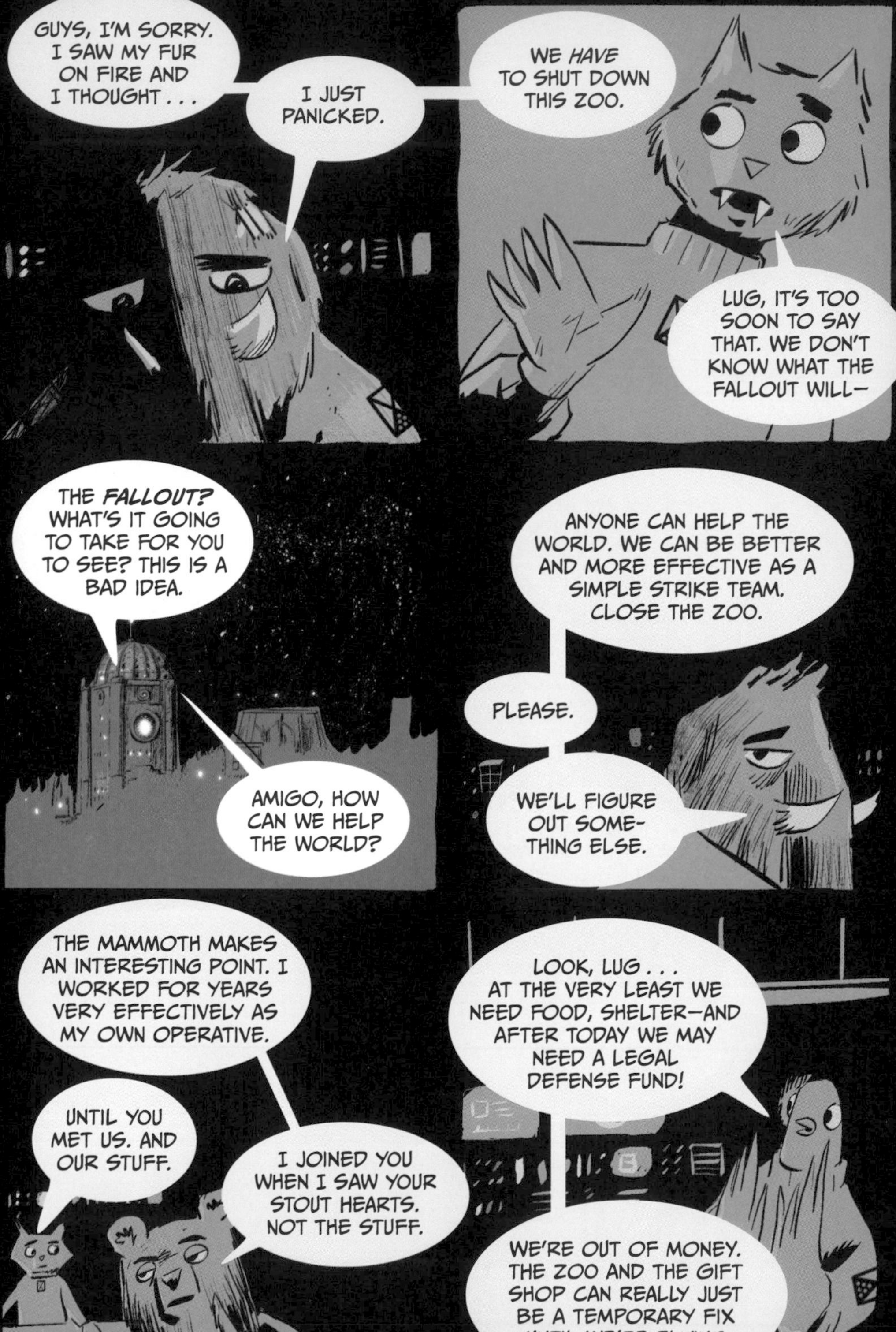
GUYS, I'M SORRY. I SAW MY FUR ON FIRE AND I THOUGHT . . .
I JUST PANICKED.
WE *HAVE* TO SHUT DOWN THIS ZOO.
LUG, IT'S TOO SOON TO SAY THAT. WE DON'T KNOW WHAT THE FALLOUT WILL—
THE *FALLOUT?* WHAT'S IT GOING TO TAKE FOR YOU TO SEE? THIS IS A BAD IDEA.
AMIGO, HOW CAN WE HELP THE WORLD?
ANYONE CAN HELP THE WORLD. WE CAN BE BETTER AND MORE EFFECTIVE AS A SIMPLE STRIKE TEAM. CLOSE THE ZOO.
PLEASE.
WE'LL FIGURE OUT SOME-THING ELSE.
THE MAMMOTH MAKES AN INTERESTING POINT. I WORKED FOR YEARS VERY EFFECTIVELY AS MY OWN OPERATIVE.
UNTIL YOU MET US. AND OUR STUFF.
I JOINED YOU WHEN I SAW YOUR STOUT HEARTS. NOT THE STUFF.
LOOK, LUG . . . AT THE VERY LEAST WE NEED FOOD, SHELTER—AND AFTER TODAY WE MAY NEED A LEGAL DEFENSE FUND!
WE'RE OUT OF MONEY. THE ZOO AND THE GIFT SHOP CAN REALLY JUST BE A TEMPORARY FIX UNTIL WE'RE FLYING HIGH AGAIN.

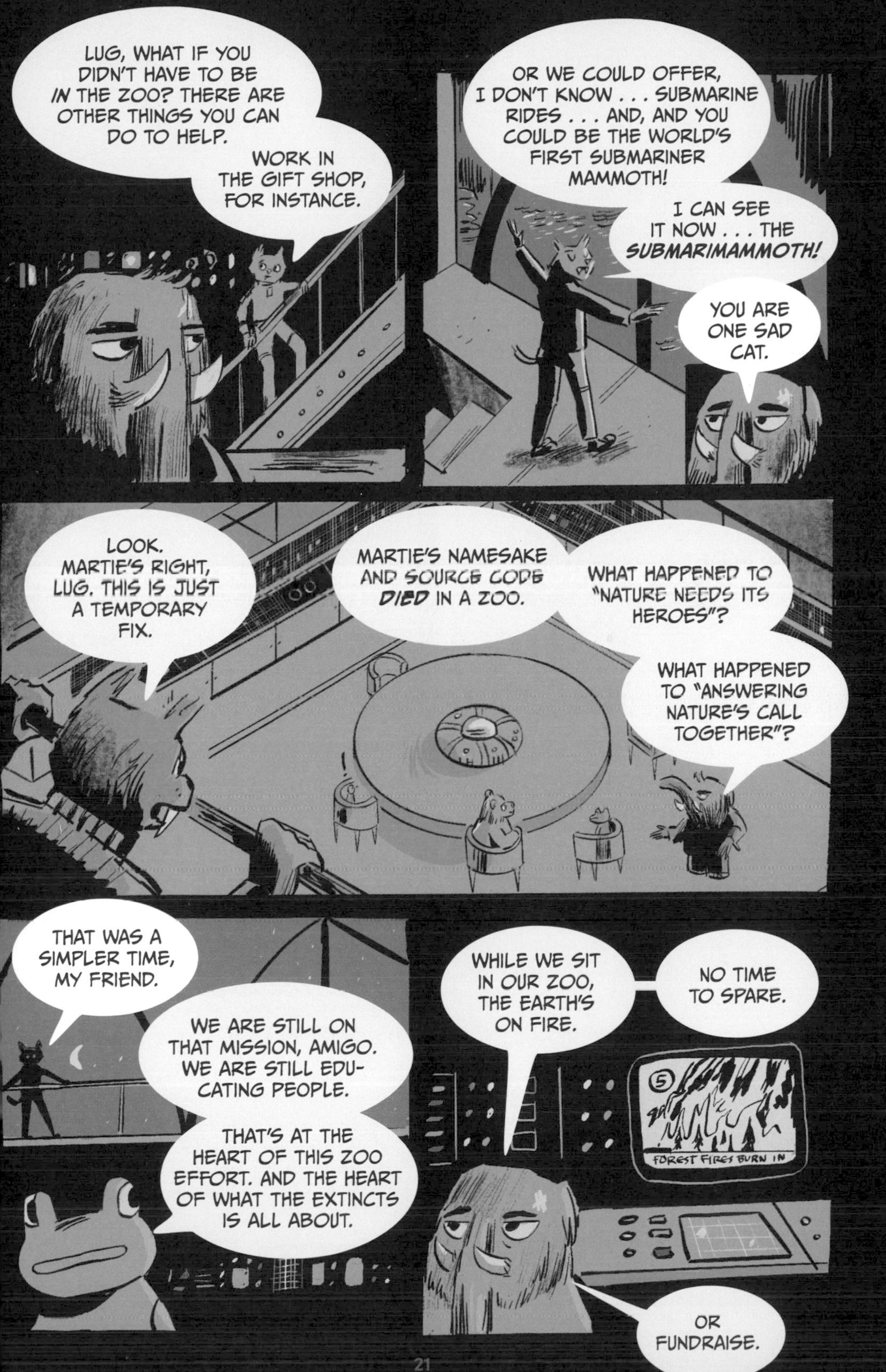
LUG, WHAT IF YOU DIDN'T HAVE TO BE *IN* THE ZOO? THERE ARE OTHER THINGS YOU CAN DO TO HELP.
WORK IN THE GIFT SHOP, FOR INSTANCE.
OR WE COULD OFFER, I DON'T KNOW . . . SUBMARINE RIDES . . . AND, AND YOU COULD BE THE WORLD'S FIRST SUBMARINER MAMMOTH!
I CAN SEE IT NOW . . . THE ***SUBMARIMAMMOTH!***
YOU ARE ONE SAD CAT.
LOOK. MARTIE'S RIGHT, LUG. THIS IS JUST A TEMPORARY FIX.
MARTIE'S NAMESAKE AND SOURCE CODE ***DIED*** IN A ZOO.
WHAT HAPPENED TO "NATURE NEEDS ITS HEROES"?
WHAT HAPPENED TO "ANSWERING NATURE'S CALL TOGETHER"?
THAT WAS A SIMPLER TIME, MY FRIEND.
WE ARE STILL ON THAT MISSION, AMIGO. WE ARE STILL EDU-CATING PEOPLE.
THAT'S AT THE HEART OF THIS ZOO EFFORT. AND THE HEART OF WHAT THE EXTINCTS IS ALL ABOUT.
WHILE WE SIT IN OUR ZOO, THE EARTH'S ON FIRE.
NO TIME TO SPARE.
5
FOREST FIRES BURN IN
OR FUNDRAISE.

LOOK.

EACH DOT ON THIS MAP REPRESENTS AN ACTIVE WILDFIRE.

WATCH THIS NEWS STORY FROM YESTERDAY IN CALIFORNIA.

BREAKING NEWS
WILDFIRES RAGING ACROSS WEST
5

"... MASSIVE FOREST FIRES ARE BURNING ACROSS CALIFORNIA AT THIS HOUR. FUELED BY WINDS, THE FIRES SPREAD QUICKLY TO BONE-DRY DROUGHT CONDITIONS TO OVER 300 SQUARE MILES ..."

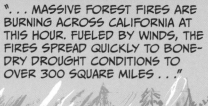

BREAKING NEWS
WILDFIRES RAGING ACROSS WEST
CHANNEL 5

"... OFFICIALS ORDERED MANDATORY EVACUATIONS OF THOUSANDS OF HOMES BUT NOT EVERYONE'S LEFT, CREATING CHALLENGES FOR LOCAL LAW ENFORCEMENT TO IMPOSE ..."

WE'RE STAYIN'!

BREAKING NEWS
WILDFIRES RAGING ACROSS WEST
CHANNEL 5

"ROAD CLOSURES HAVE FOLLOWED, WITH MILES OF STATE AND LOCAL ROADS SHUT DOWN BECAUSE OF THE DANGER POSED TO MOTORISTS."

"... ANIMALS HAVE BEEN SEEN FLEEING THE FIRE, SOME WITH SINGED PAWS OR AFLAME THEMSELVES ..."

HE'S GOING TO BE OK.

BREAKING NEWS
WILDFIRES RAGING ACROSS WEST
CH 5

"... WITH FIRES POPPING UP SO RAPIDLY, STATE AND LOCAL INVESTIGATORS ARE LOOKING AT THE POSSIBILITY OF A SERIAL ARSONIST AT WORK."

BREAKING NEWS
WILDFIRES RAGING ACROSS WEST
CH 5

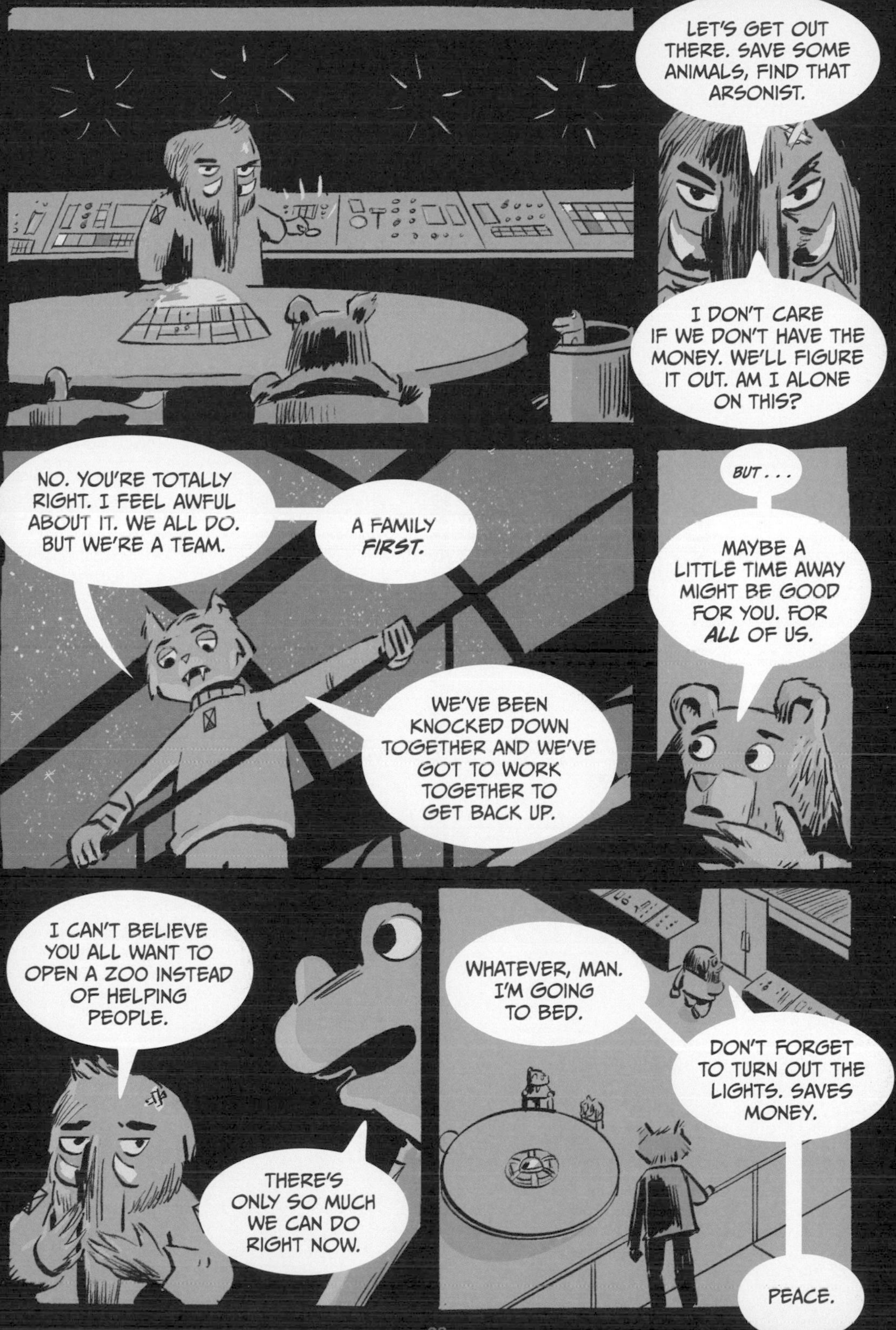
LET'S GET OUT THERE. SAVE SOME ANIMALS, FIND THAT ARSONIST.
I DON'T CARE IF WE DON'T HAVE THE MONEY. WE'LL FIGURE IT OUT. AM I ALONE ON THIS?
NO. YOU'RE TOTALLY RIGHT. I FEEL AWFUL ABOUT IT. WE ALL DO. BUT WE'RE A TEAM.
A FAMILY *FIRST.*
WE'VE BEEN KNOCKED DOWN TOGETHER AND WE'VE GOT TO WORK TOGETHER TO GET BACK UP.
BUT . . .
MAYBE A LITTLE TIME AWAY MIGHT BE GOOD FOR YOU. FOR *ALL* OF US.
I CAN'T BELIEVE YOU ALL WANT TO OPEN A ZOO INSTEAD OF HELPING PEOPLE.
THERE'S ONLY SO MUCH WE CAN DO RIGHT NOW.
WHATEVER, MAN. I'M GOING TO BED.
DON'T FORGET TO TURN OUT THE LIGHTS. SAVES MONEY.
PEACE.

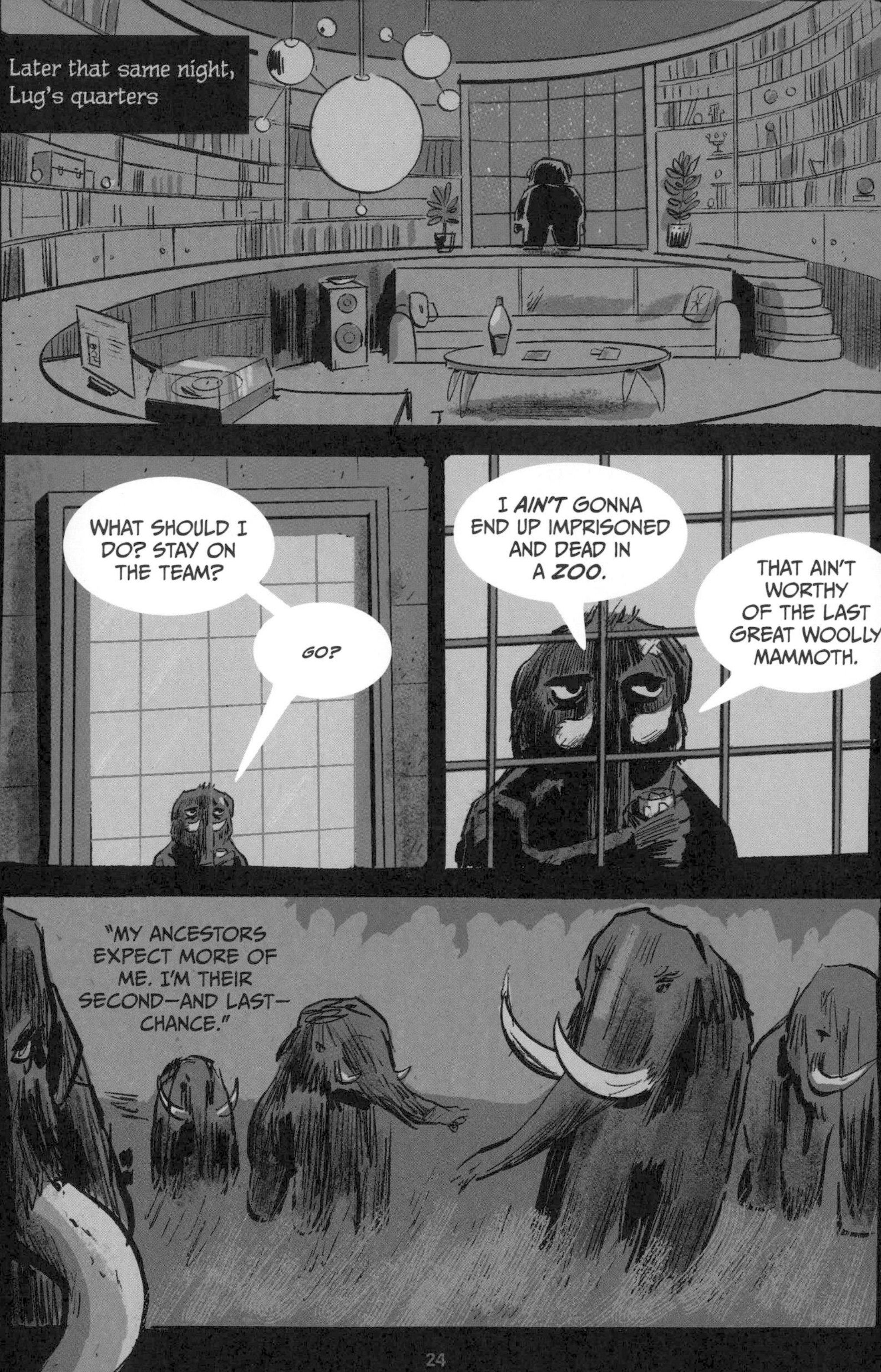
Later that same night, Lug's quarters
WHAT SHOULD I DO? STAY ON THE TEAM?
GO?
I AIN'T GONNA END UP IMPRISONED AND DEAD IN A ZOO.
THAT AIN'T WORTHY OF THE LAST GREAT WOOLLY MAMMOTH.
"MY ANCESTORS EXPECT MORE OF ME. I'M THEIR SECOND—AND LAST—CHANCE."

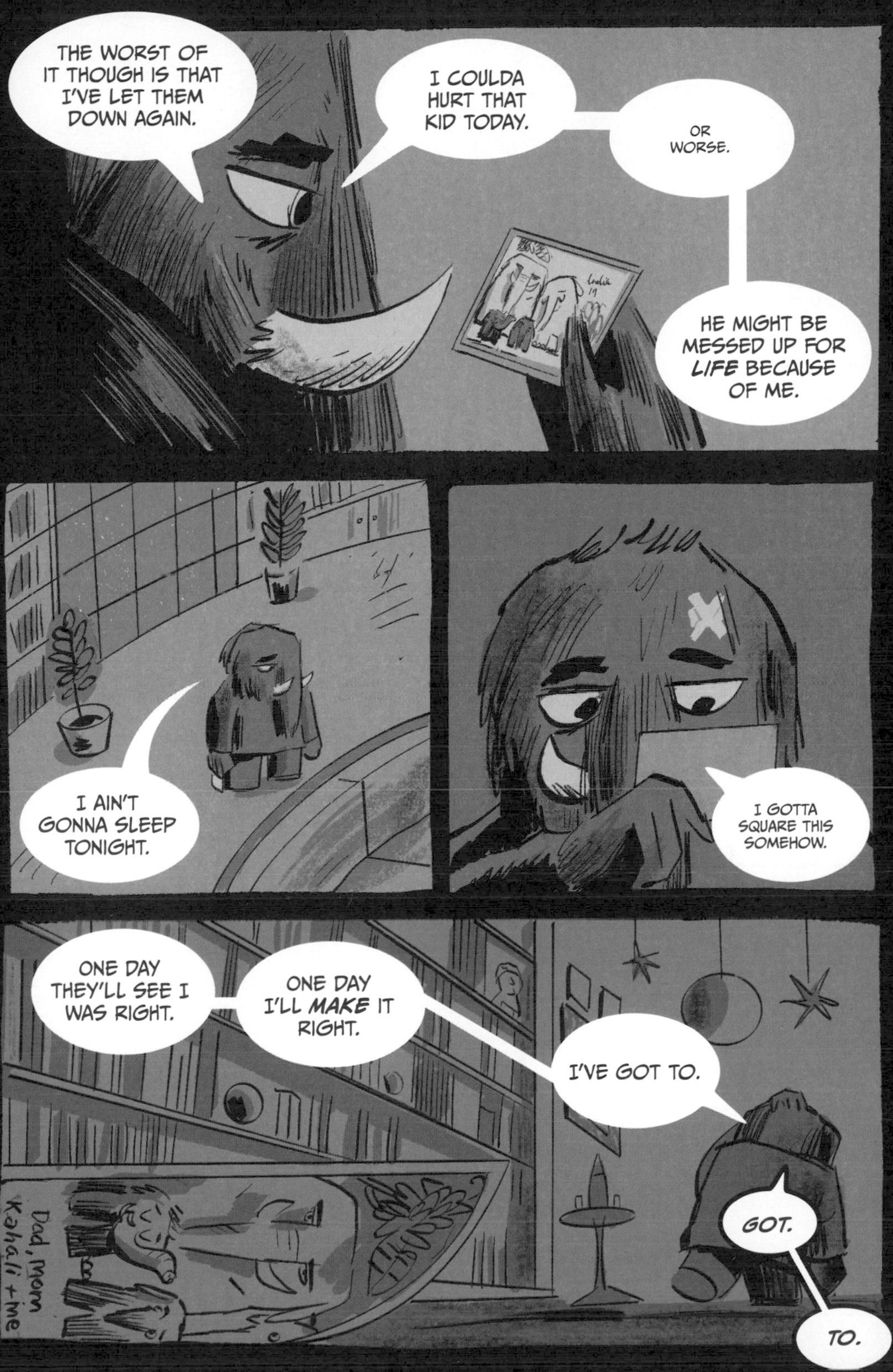
THE WORST OF IT THOUGH IS THAT I'VE LET THEM DOWN AGAIN.
I COULDA HURT THAT KID TODAY.
OR WORSE.
HE MIGHT BE MESSED UP FOR *LIFE* BECAUSE OF ME.
I AIN'T GONNA SLEEP TONIGHT.
I GOTTA SQUARE THIS SOMEHOW.
ONE DAY THEY'LL SEE I WAS RIGHT.
ONE DAY I'LL *MAKE* IT RIGHT.
I'VE GOT TO.
*GOT.*
*TO.*
Dad, Mom Kahali + me

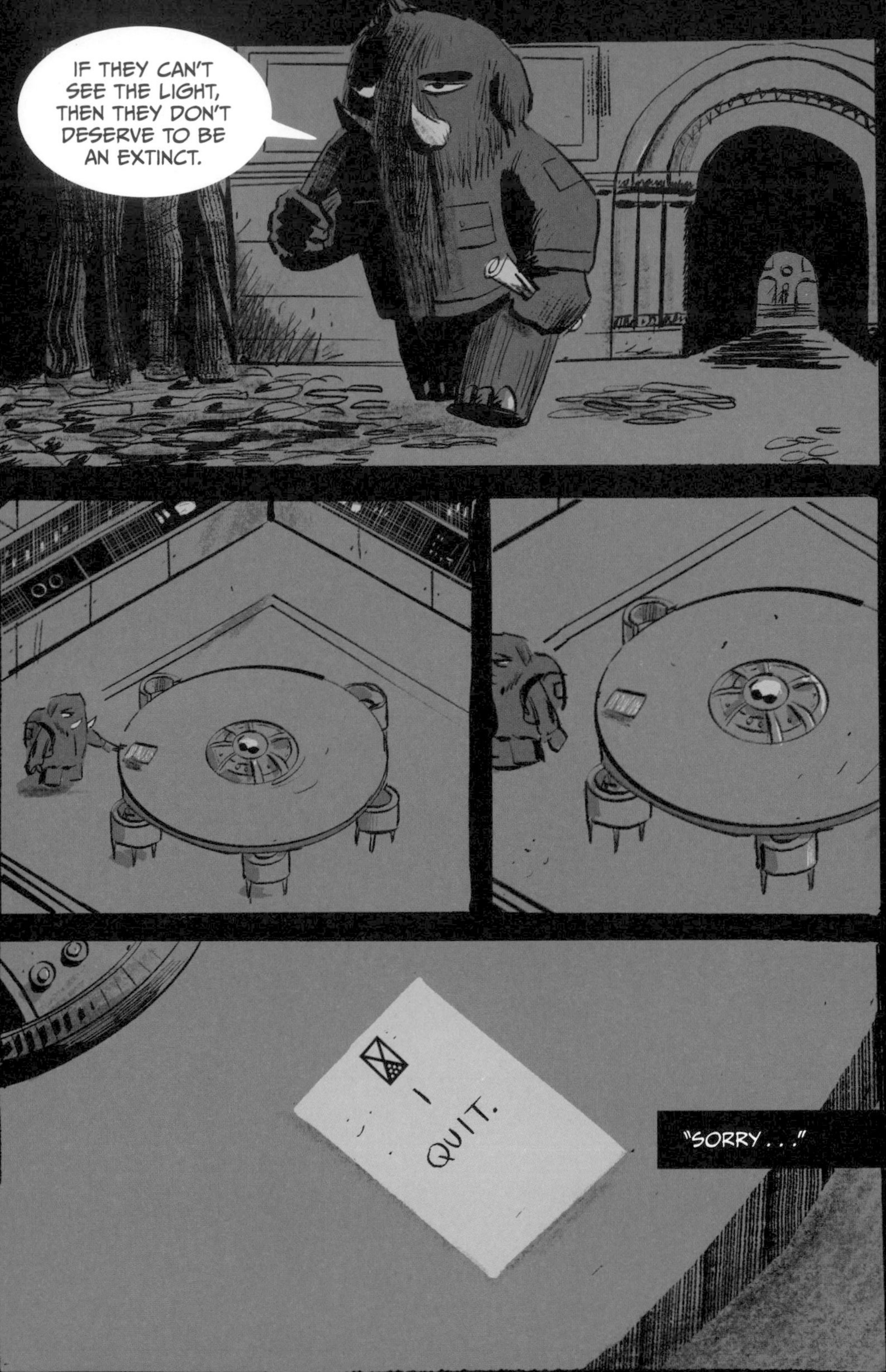
IF THEY CAN'T SEE THE LIGHT, THEN THEY DON'T DESERVE TO BE AN EXTINCT.
I QUIT.
"SORRY . . ."

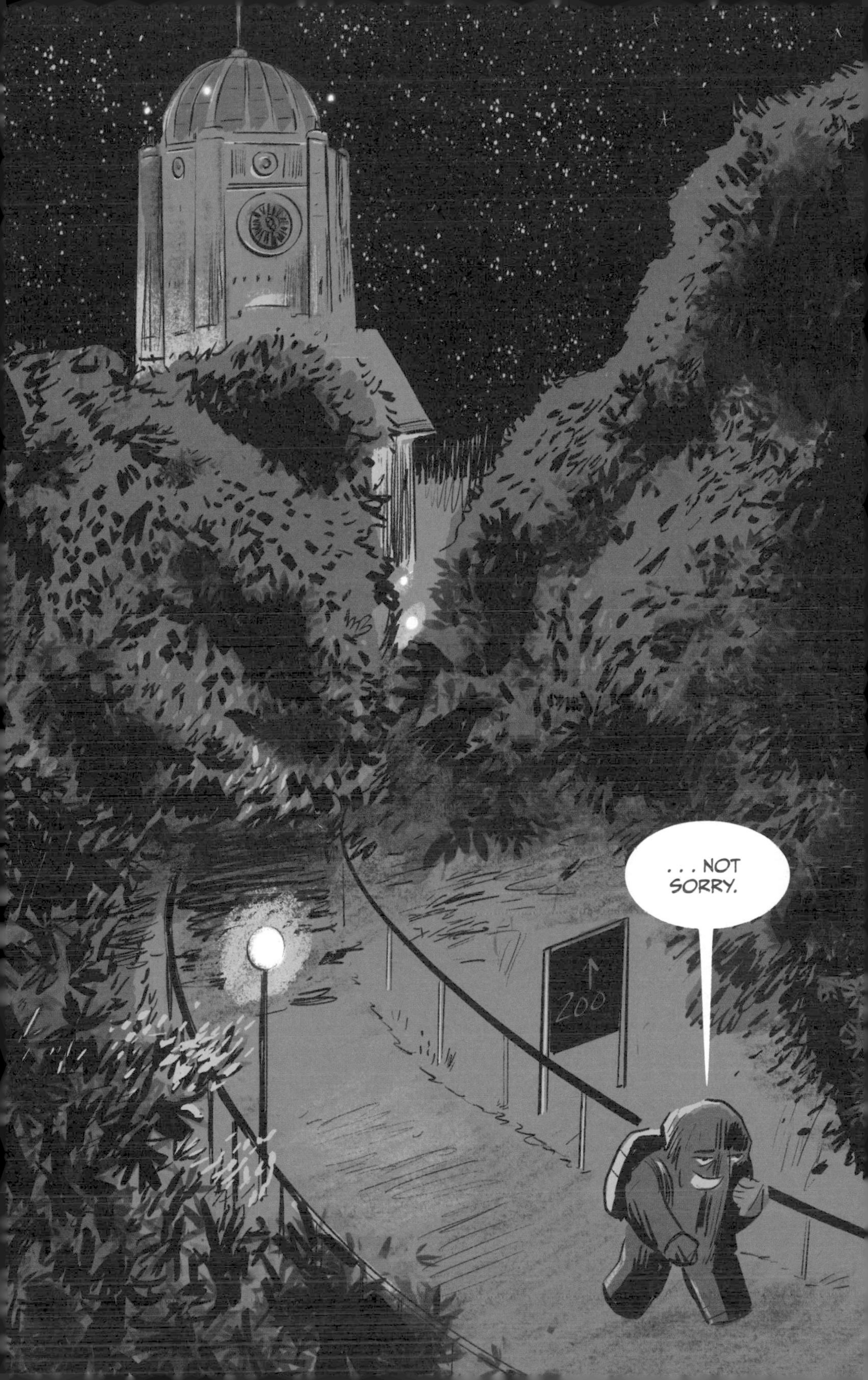
. . . NOT SORRY.
ZOO

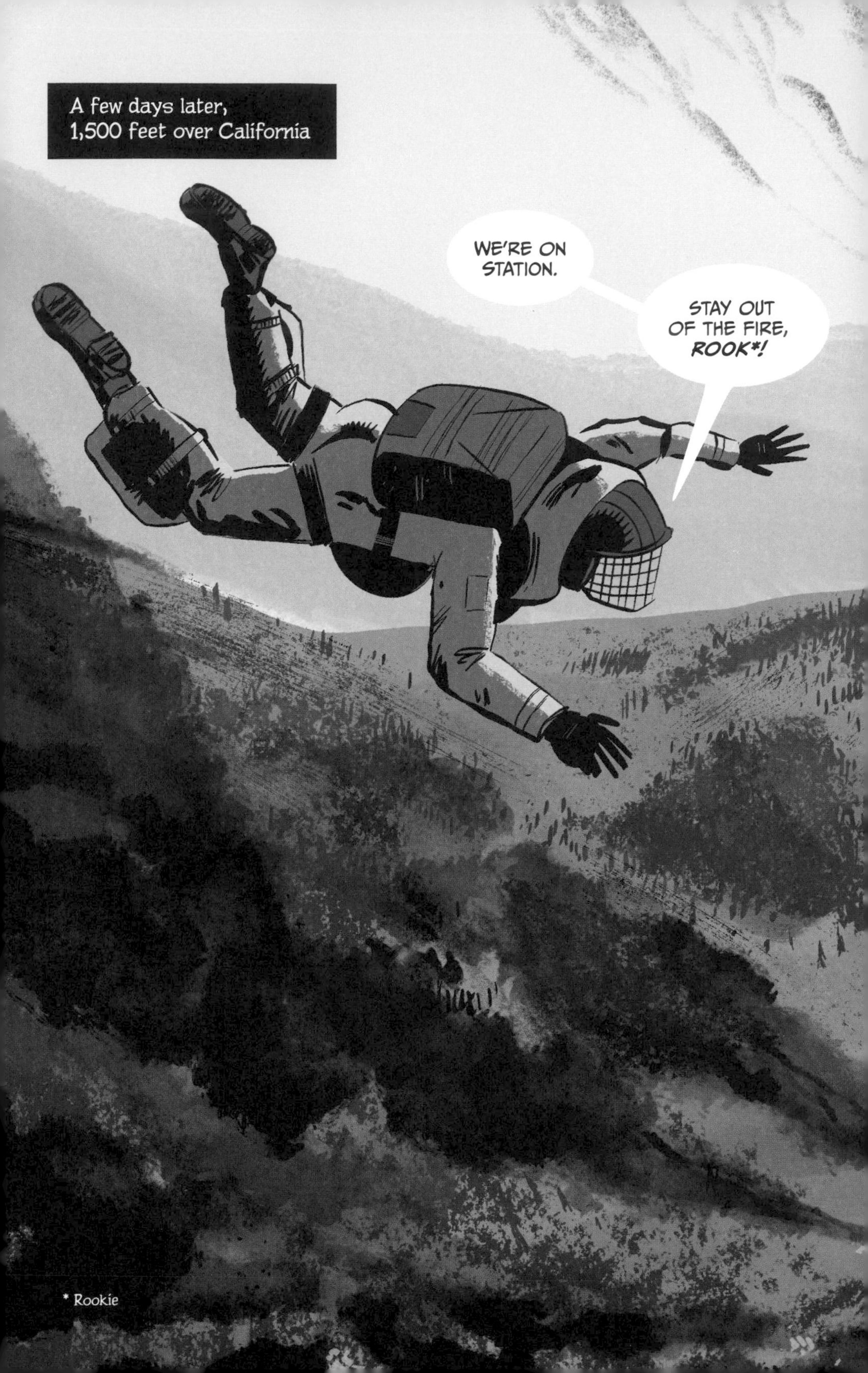
A few days later,
1,500 feet over California
WE'RE ON STATION.
STAY OUT OF THE FIRE, *ROOK**!

* Rookie

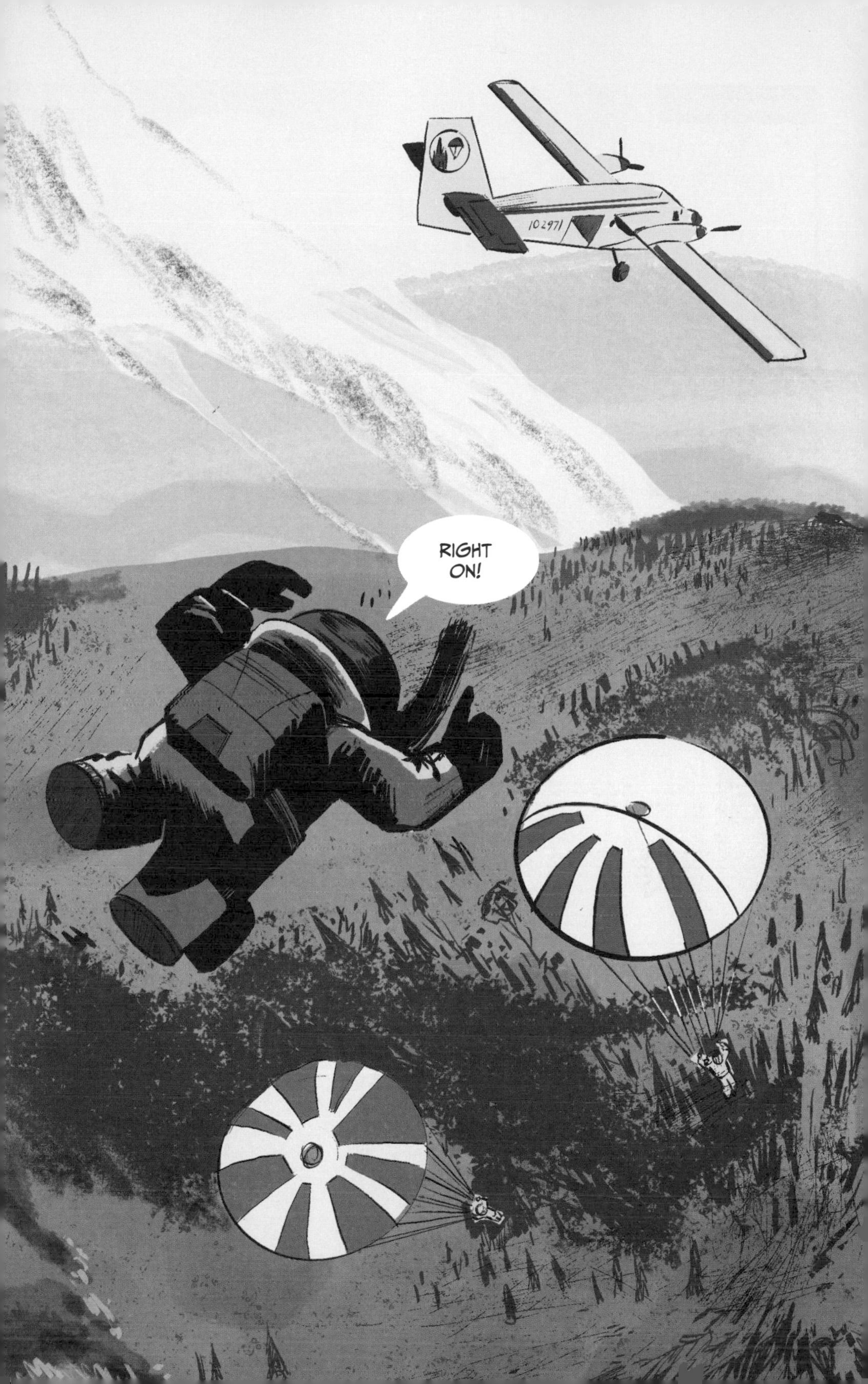
10297I
RIGHT ON!

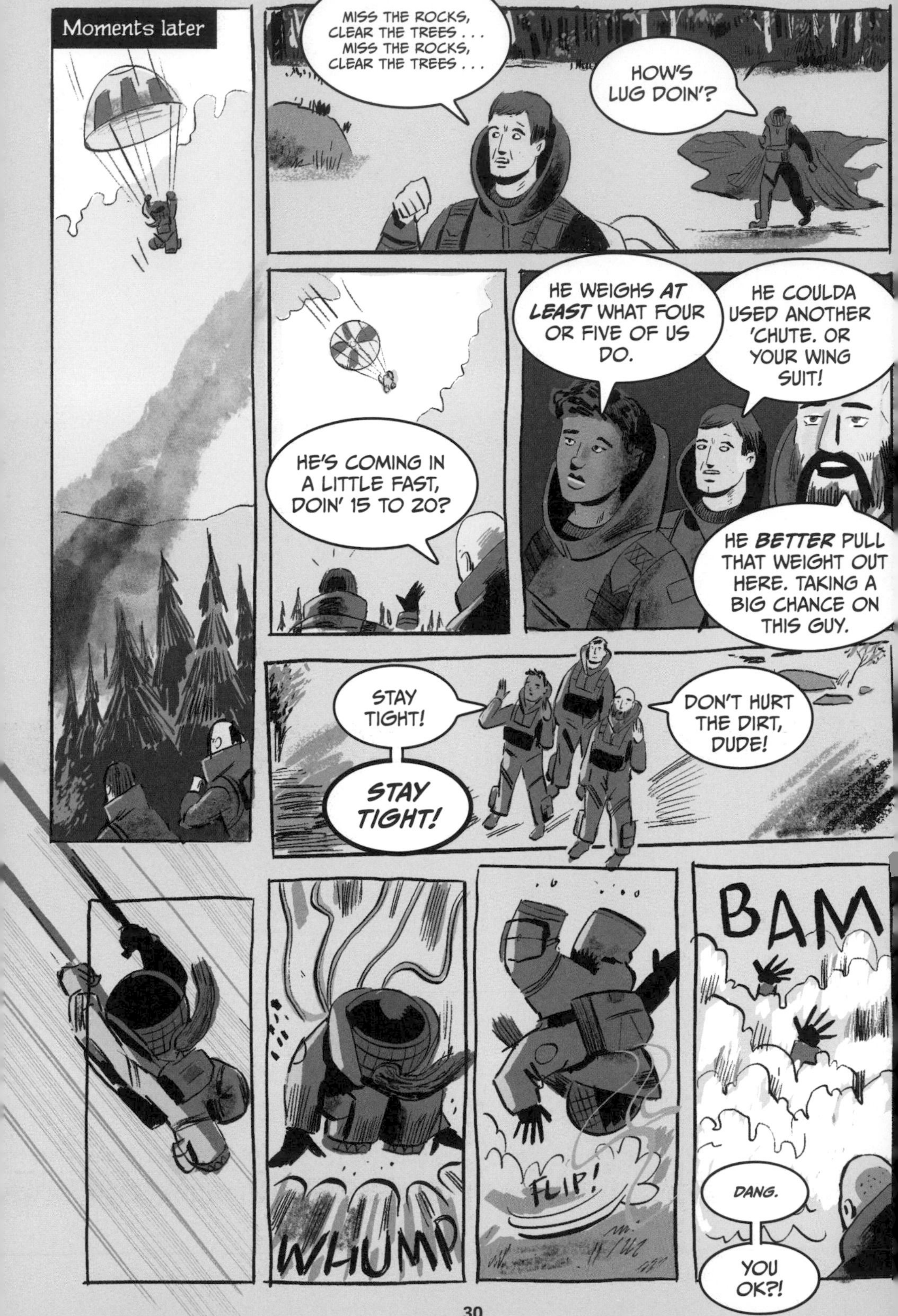
Moments later
MISS THE ROCKS, CLEAR THE TREES . . . MISS THE ROCKS, CLEAR THE TREES . . .
HOW'S LUG DOIN'?
HE'S COMING IN A LITTLE FAST, DOIN' 15 TO 20?
HE WEIGHS AT LEAST WHAT FOUR OR FIVE OF US DO.
HE COULDA USED ANOTHER 'CHUTE. OR YOUR WING SUIT!
HE BETTER PULL THAT WEIGHT OUT HERE. TAKING A BIG CHANCE ON THIS GUY.
STAY TIGHT!
STAY TIGHT!
DON'T HURT THE DIRT, DUDE!
WHUMP
FLIP!
BAM
DANG.
YOU OK?!

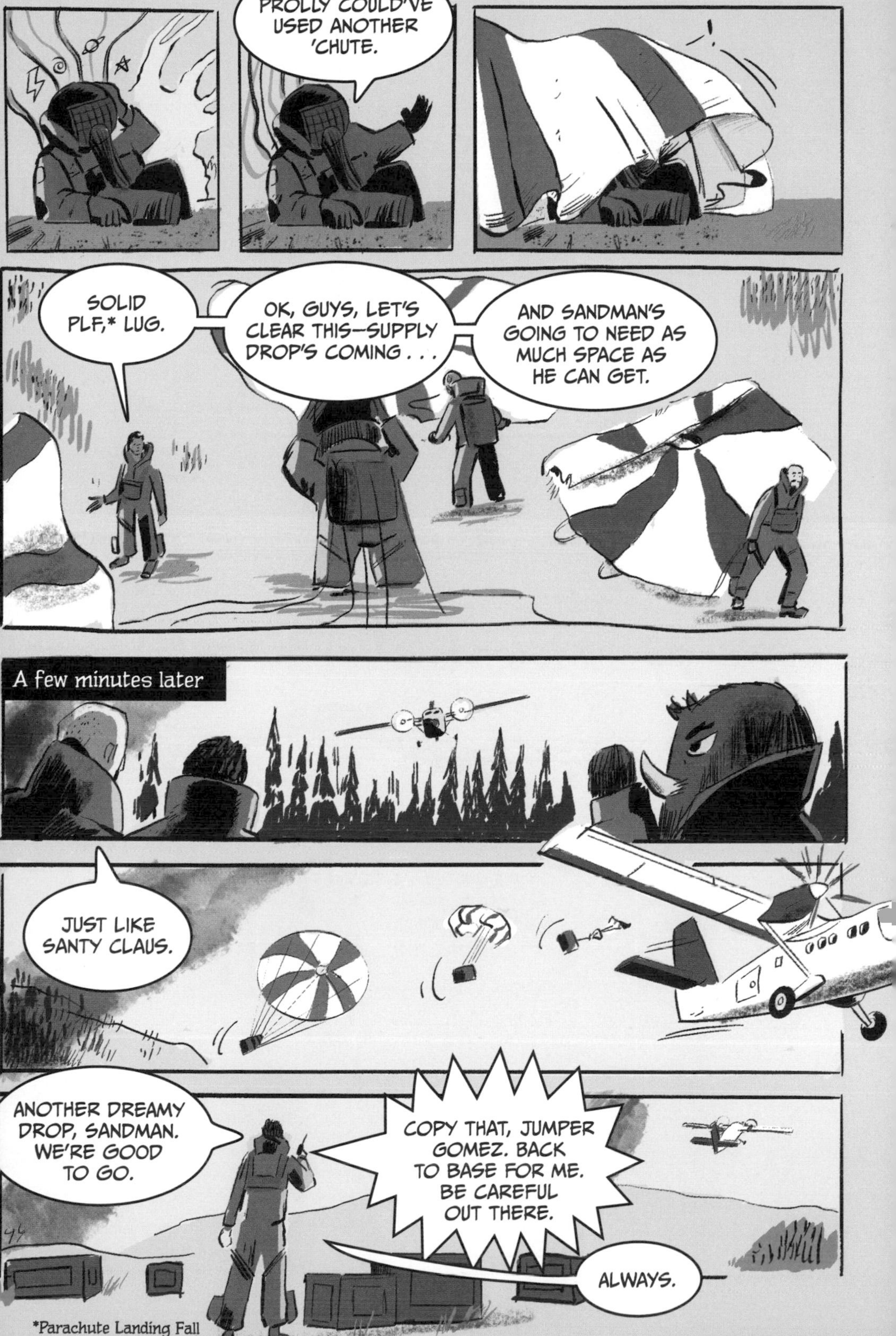
PROLLY COULD'VE USED ANOTHER 'CHUTE.
SOLID PLF,* LUG.
OK, GUYS, LET'S CLEAR THIS—SUPPLY DROP'S COMING . . .
AND SANDMAN'S GOING TO NEED AS MUCH SPACE AS HE CAN GET.
A few minutes later
JUST LIKE SANTY CLAUS.
ANOTHER DREAMY DROP, SANDMAN. WE'RE GOOD TO GO.
COPY THAT, JUMPER GOMEZ. BACK TO BASE FOR ME. BE CAREFUL OUT THERE.
ALWAYS.

*Parachute Landing Fall

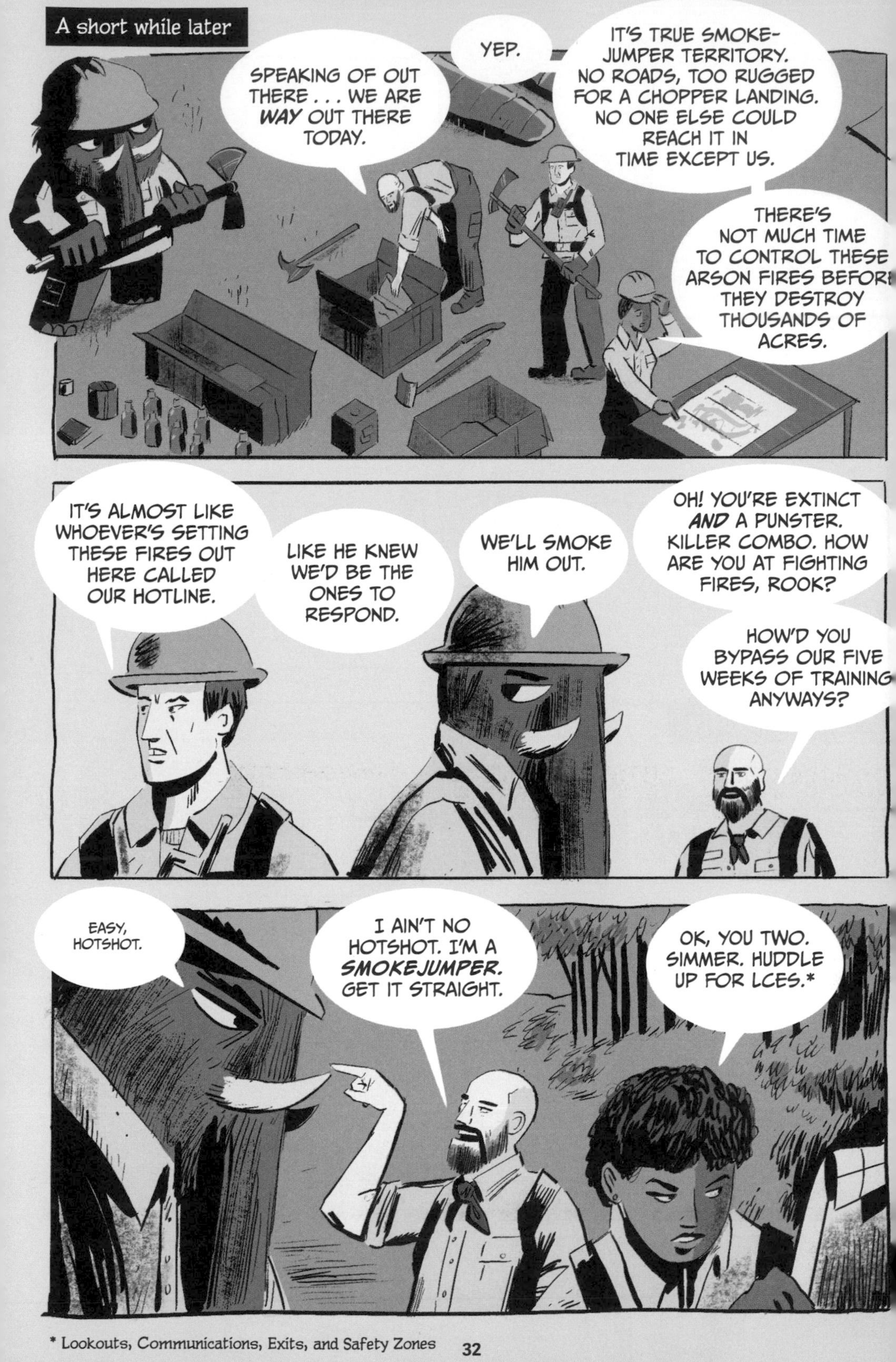
A short while later
SPEAKING OF OUT THERE . . . WE ARE *WAY* OUT THERE TODAY.
YEP.
IT'S TRUE SMOKE-JUMPER TERRITORY. NO ROADS, TOO RUGGED FOR A CHOPPER LANDING. NO ONE ELSE COULD REACH IT IN TIME EXCEPT US.
THERE'S NOT MUCH TIME TO CONTROL THESE ARSON FIRES BEFORE THEY DESTROY THOUSANDS OF ACRES.
IT'S ALMOST LIKE WHOEVER'S SETTING THESE FIRES OUT HERE CALLED OUR HOTLINE.
LIKE HE KNEW WE'D BE THE ONES TO RESPOND.
WE'LL SMOKE HIM OUT.
OH! YOU'RE EXTINCT *AND* A PUNSTER. KILLER COMBO. HOW ARE YOU AT FIGHTING FIRES, ROOK?
HOW'D YOU BYPASS OUR FIVE WEEKS OF TRAINING ANYWAYS?
EASY, HOTSHOT.
I AIN'T NO HOTSHOT. I'M A ***SMOKEJUMPER.*** GET IT STRAIGHT.
OK, YOU TWO. SIMMER. HUDDLE UP FOR LCES.*

* Lookouts, Communications, Exits, and Safety Zones

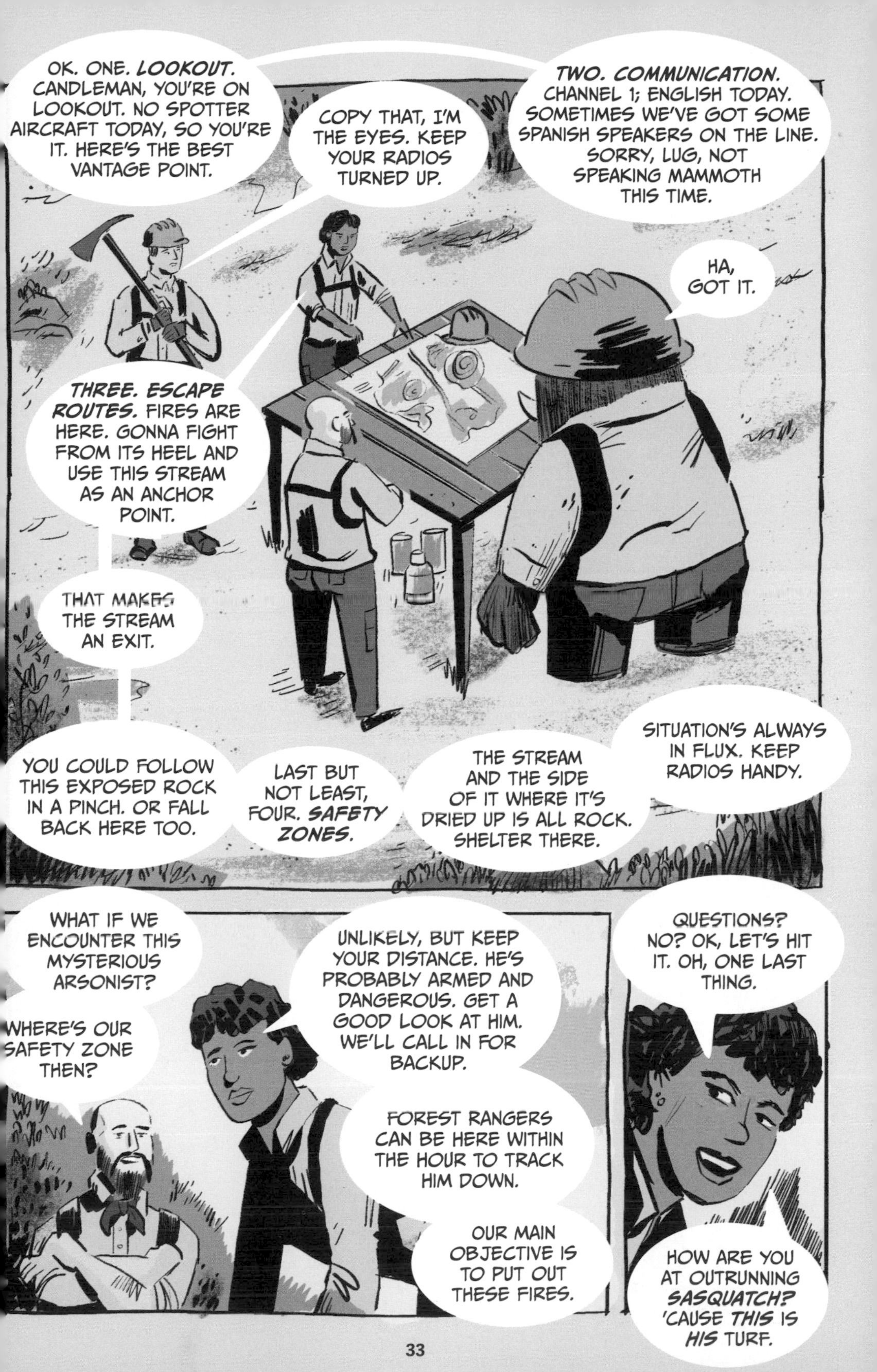
OK. ONE. *LOOKOUT.* CANDLEMAN, YOU'RE ON LOOKOUT. NO SPOTTER AIRCRAFT TODAY, SO YOU'RE IT. HERE'S THE BEST VANTAGE POINT.
COPY THAT, I'M THE EYES. KEEP YOUR RADIOS TURNED UP.
*TWO. COMMUNICATION.* CHANNEL 1; ENGLISH TODAY. SOMETIMES WE'VE GOT SOME SPANISH SPEAKERS ON THE LINE. SORRY, LUG, NOT SPEAKING MAMMOTH THIS TIME.
HA, GOT IT.
*THREE. ESCAPE ROUTES.* FIRES ARE HERE. GONNA FIGHT FROM ITS HEEL AND USE THIS STREAM AS AN ANCHOR POINT.
THAT MAKES THE STREAM AN EXIT.
YOU COULD FOLLOW THIS EXPOSED ROCK IN A PINCH. OR FALL BACK HERE TOO.
LAST BUT NOT LEAST, FOUR. *SAFETY ZONES.*
THE STREAM AND THE SIDE OF IT WHERE IT'S DRIED UP IS ALL ROCK. SHELTER THERE.
SITUATION'S ALWAYS IN FLUX. KEEP RADIOS HANDY.
WHAT IF WE ENCOUNTER THIS MYSTERIOUS ARSONIST?
WHERE'S OUR SAFETY ZONE THEN?
UNLIKELY, BUT KEEP YOUR DISTANCE. HE'S PROBABLY ARMED AND DANGEROUS. GET A GOOD LOOK AT HIM. WE'LL CALL IN FOR BACKUP.
FOREST RANGERS CAN BE HERE WITHIN THE HOUR TO TRACK HIM DOWN.
OUR MAIN OBJECTIVE IS TO PUT OUT THESE FIRES.
QUESTIONS? NO? OK, LET'S HIT IT. OH, ONE LAST THING.
HOW ARE YOU AT OUTRUNNING *SASQUATCH?* 'CAUSE *THIS* IS *HIS* TURF.

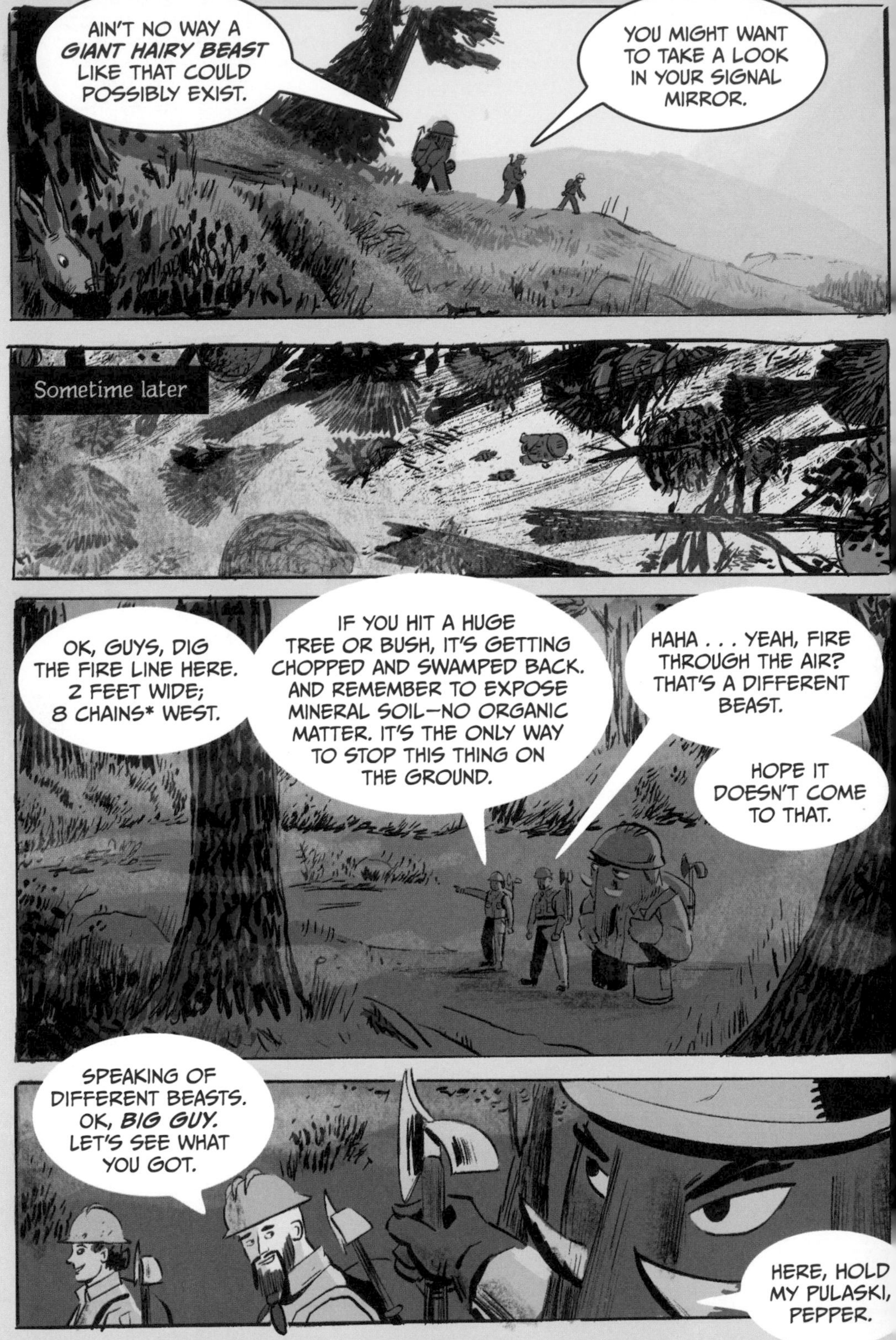
AIN'T NO WAY A GIANT HAIRY BEAST LIKE THAT COULD POSSIBLY EXIST.
YOU MIGHT WANT TO TAKE A LOOK IN YOUR SIGNAL MIRROR.
Sometime later
OK, GUYS, DIG THE FIRE LINE HERE. 2 FEET WIDE; 8 CHAINS* WEST.
IF YOU HIT A HUGE TREE OR BUSH, IT'S GETTING CHOPPED AND SWAMPED BACK. AND REMEMBER TO EXPOSE MINERAL SOIL—NO ORGANIC MATTER. IT'S THE ONLY WAY TO STOP THIS THING ON THE GROUND.
HAHA . . . YEAH, FIRE THROUGH THE AIR? THAT'S A DIFFERENT BEAST.
HOPE IT DOESN'T COME TO THAT.
SPEAKING OF DIFFERENT BEASTS. OK, BIG GUY. LET'S SEE WHAT YOU GOT.
HERE, HOLD MY PULASKI, PEPPER.

* A unit of measure; 1 chain equals 66 feet.

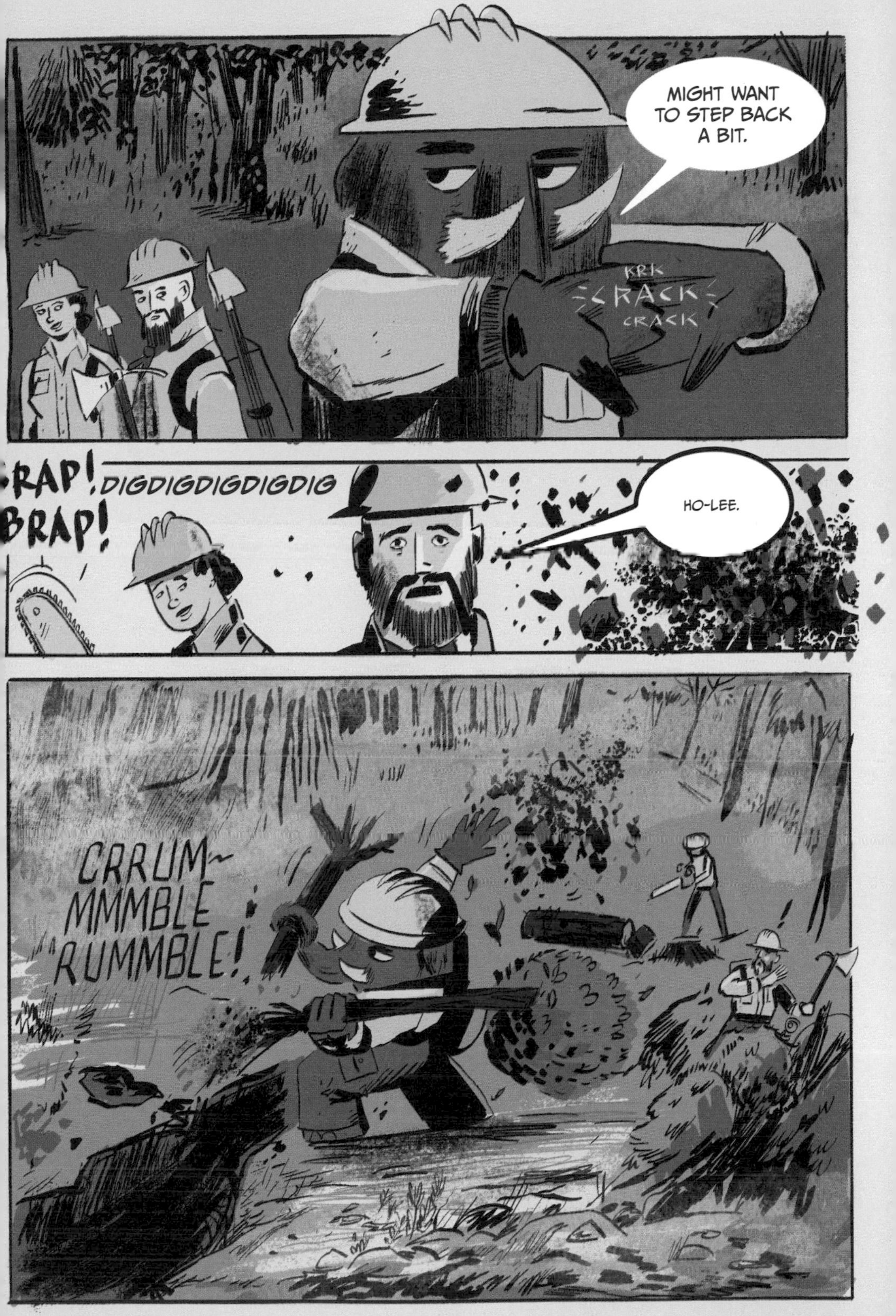
MIGHT WANT TO STEP BACK A BIT.
KRK CRACK CRACK
RAP! BRAP!
DIGDIGDIGDIGDIG
HO-LEE.
CRRUM MMMBLE RUMMBLE!

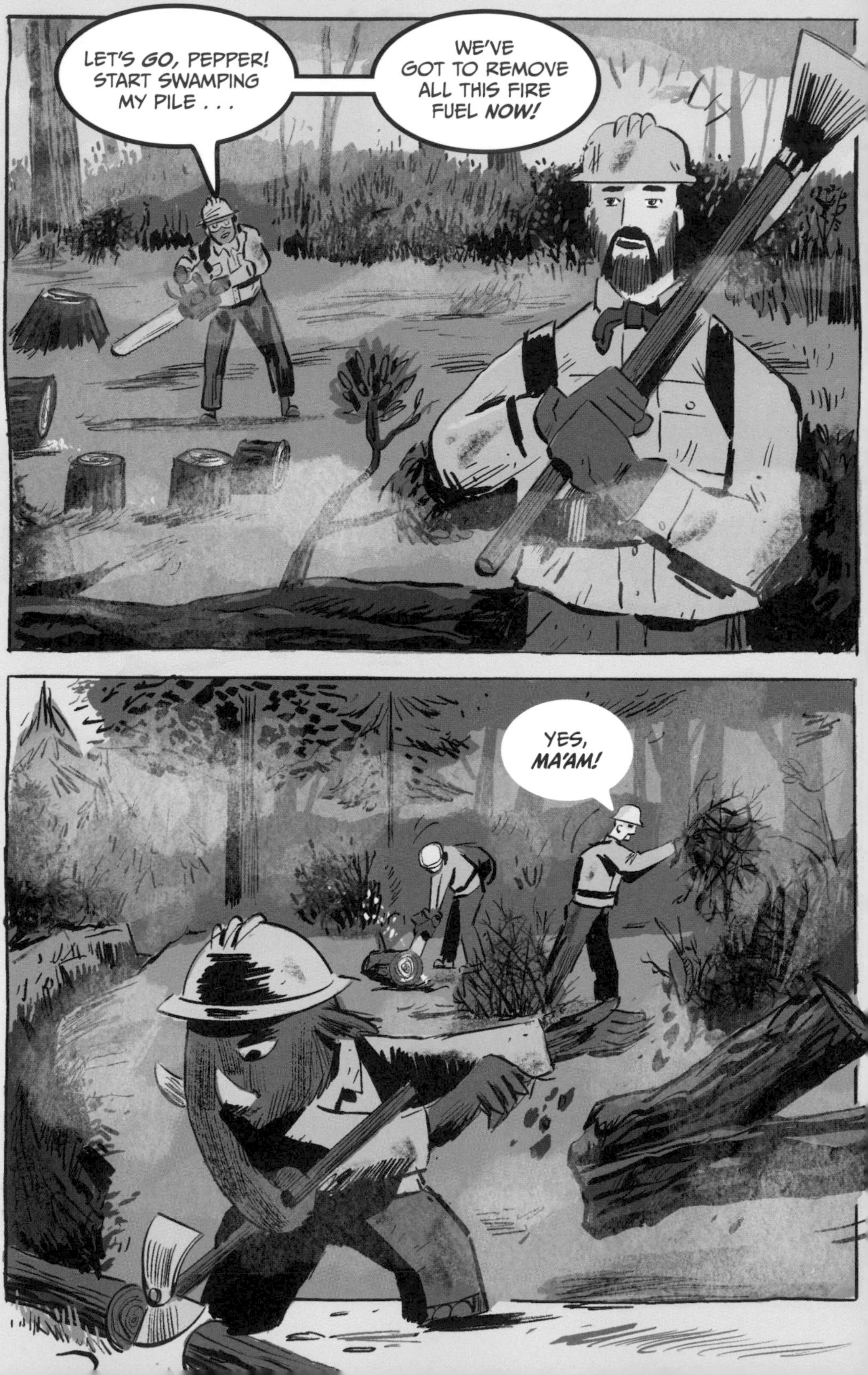
LET'S GO, PEPPER! START SWAMPING MY PILE . . .
WE'VE GOT TO REMOVE ALL THIS FIRE FUEL NOW!
YES, MA'AM!

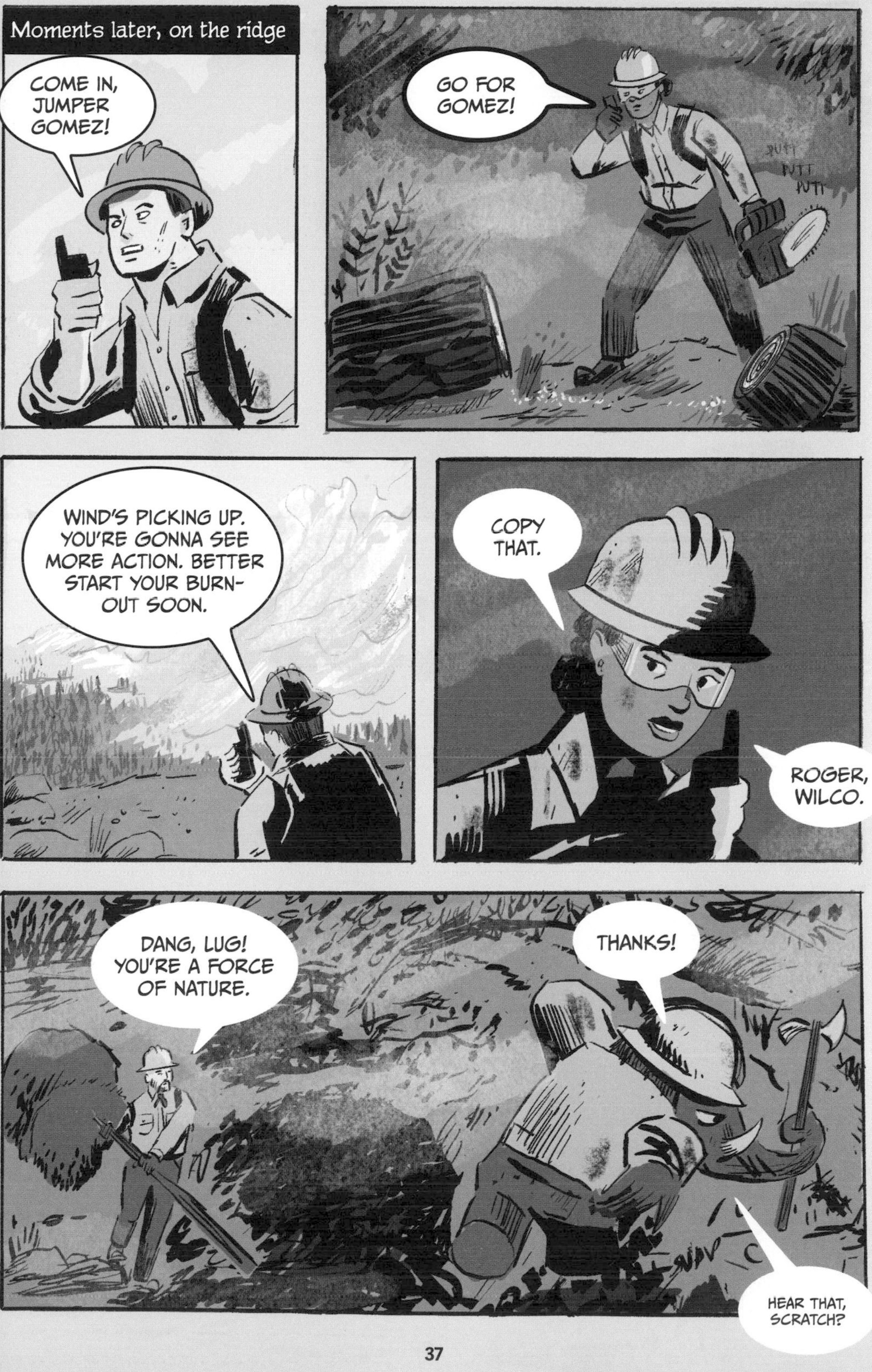
Moments later, on the ridge
COME IN, JUMPER GOMEZ!
GO FOR GOMEZ!
PUTT PUTT PUTT
WIND'S PICKING UP. YOU'RE GONNA SEE MORE ACTION. BETTER START YOUR BURN-OUT SOON.
COPY THAT.
ROGER, WILCO.
DANG, LUG! YOU'RE A FORCE OF NATURE.
THANKS!
HEAR THAT, SCRATCH?

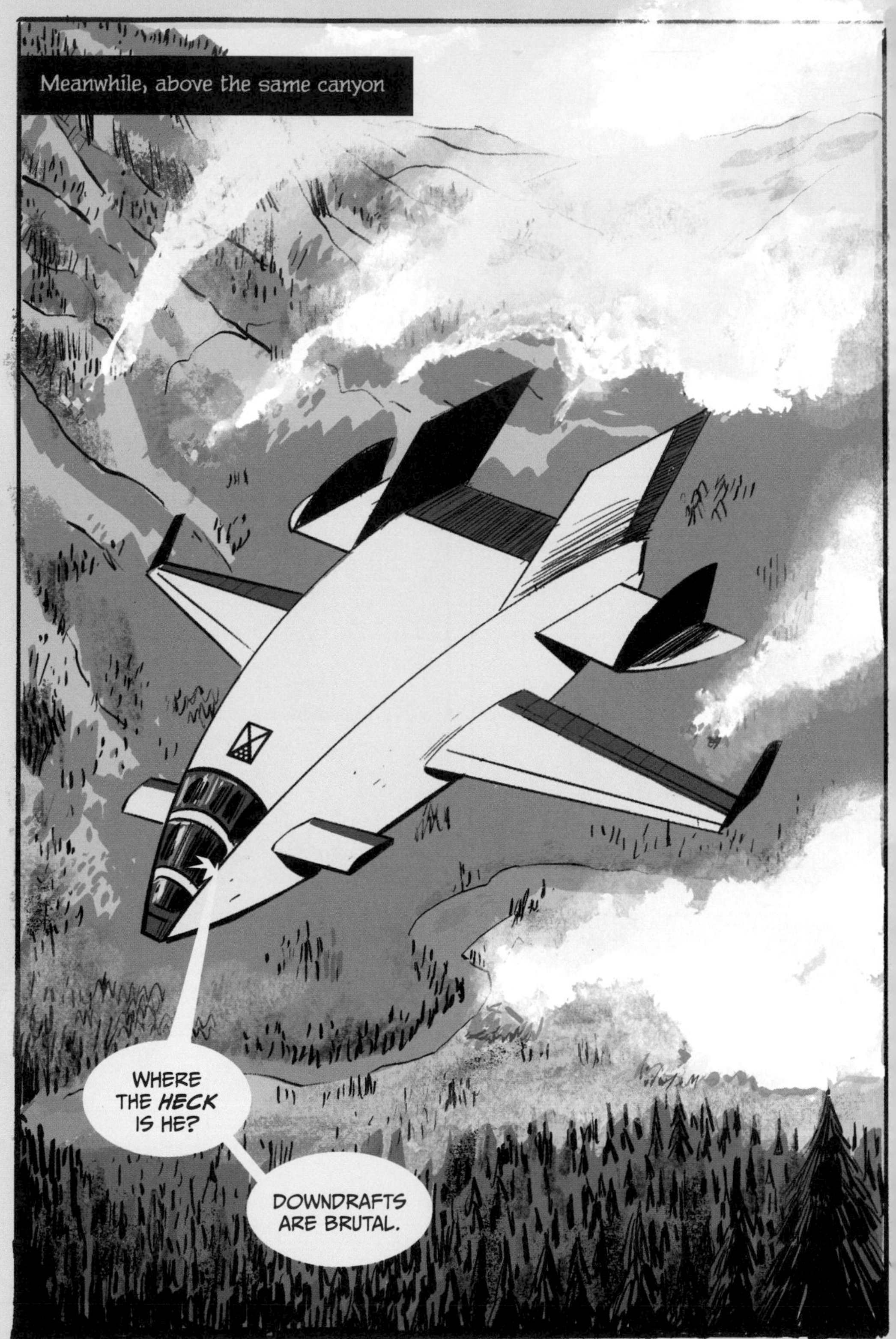
Meanwhile, above the same canyon
WHERE THE *HECK* IS HE?
DOWNDRAFTS ARE BRUTAL.

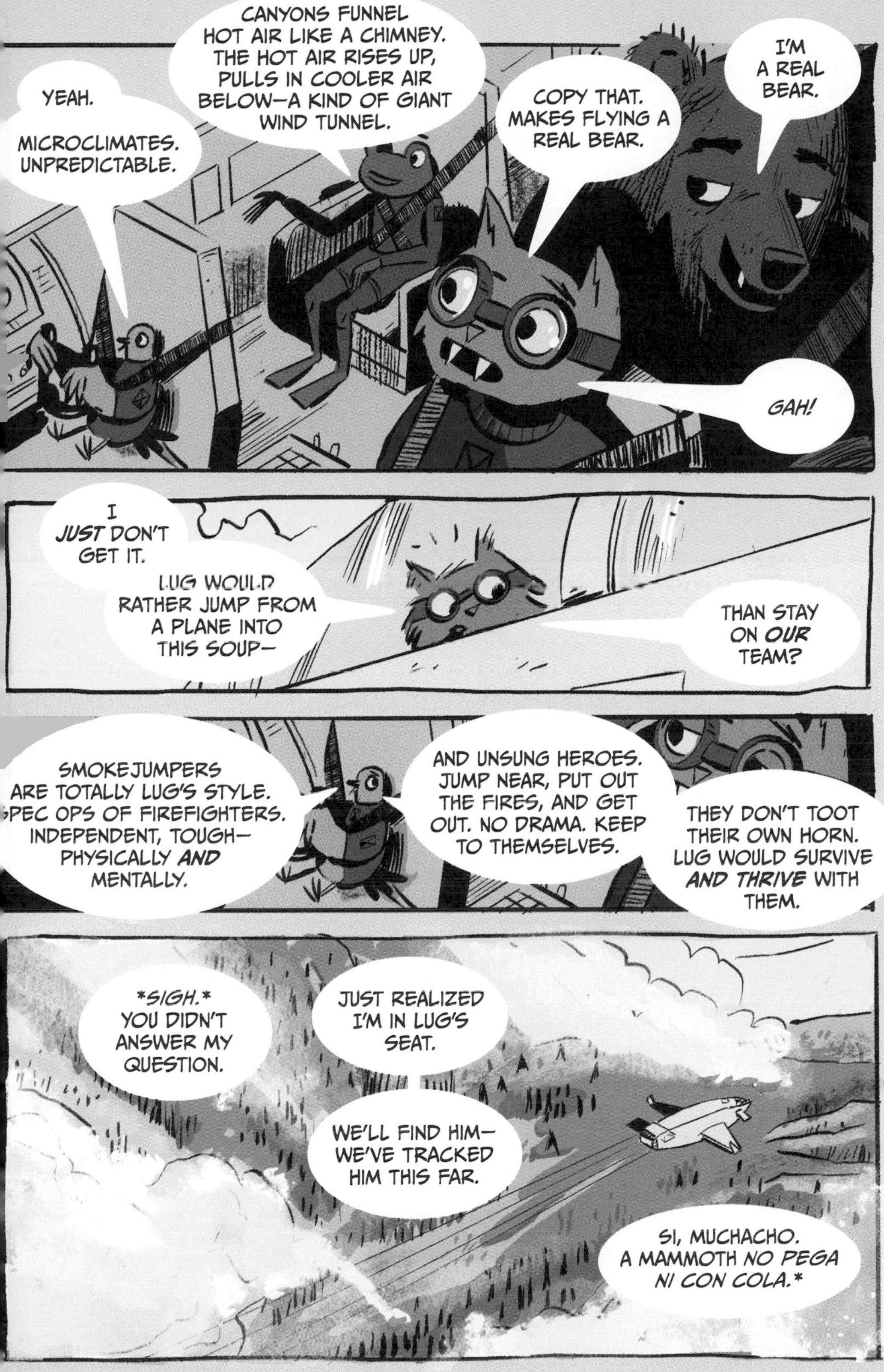
CANYONS FUNNEL HOT AIR LIKE A CHIMNEY. THE HOT AIR RISES UP, PULLS IN COOLER AIR BELOW—A KIND OF GIANT WIND TUNNEL.
YEAH.
MICROCLIMATES. UNPREDICTABLE.
COPY THAT. MAKES FLYING A REAL BEAR.
I'M A REAL BEAR.
GAH!
I JUST DON'T GET IT.
LUG WOULD RATHER JUMP FROM A PLANE INTO THIS SOUP—
THAN STAY ON OUR TEAM?
SMOKEJUMPERS ARE TOTALLY LUG'S STYLE. SPEC OPS OF FIREFIGHTERS. INDEPENDENT, TOUGH—PHYSICALLY AND MENTALLY.
AND UNSUNG HEROES. JUMP NEAR, PUT OUT THE FIRES, AND GET OUT. NO DRAMA. KEEP TO THEMSELVES.
THEY DON'T TOOT THEIR OWN HORN. LUG WOULD SURVIVE AND THRIVE WITH THEM.
*SIGH.* YOU DIDN'T ANSWER MY QUESTION.
JUST REALIZED I'M IN LUG'S SEAT.
WE'LL FIND HIM—WE'VE TRACKED HIM THIS FAR.
SI, MUCHACHO. A MAMMOTH NO PEGA NI CON COLA.*

*Sticks out

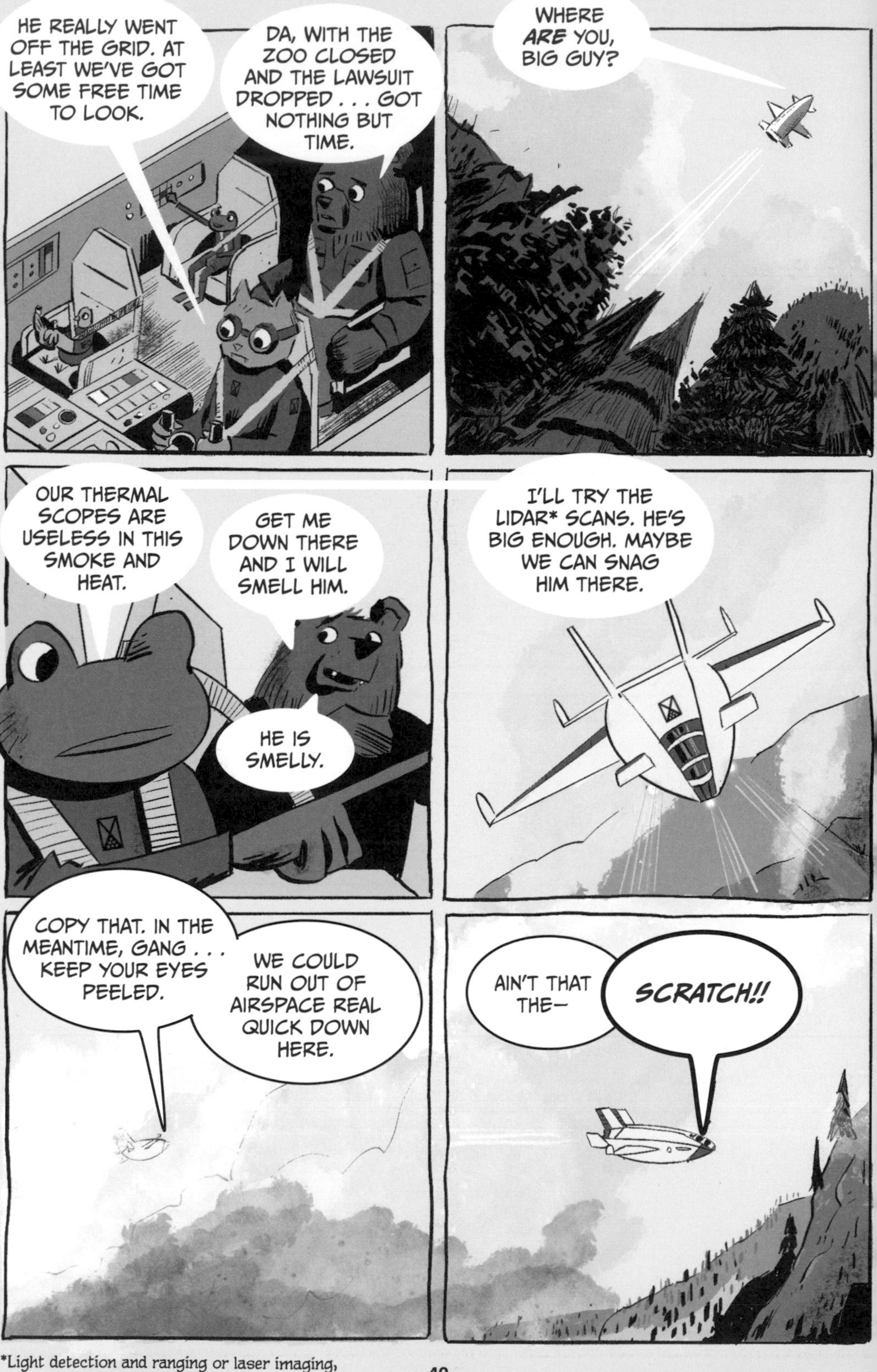
HE REALLY WENT OFF THE GRID. AT LEAST WE'VE GOT SOME FREE TIME TO LOOK.
DA, WITH THE ZOO CLOSED AND THE LAWSUIT DROPPED . . . GOT NOTHING BUT TIME.
WHERE ARE YOU, BIG GUY?
OUR THERMAL SCOPES ARE USELESS IN THIS SMOKE AND HEAT.
GET ME DOWN THERE AND I WILL SMELL HIM.
HE IS SMELLY.
I'LL TRY THE LIDAR* SCANS. HE'S BIG ENOUGH. MAYBE WE CAN SNAG HIM THERE.
COPY THAT. IN THE MEANTIME, GANG . . . KEEP YOUR EYES PEELED.
WE COULD RUN OUT OF AIRSPACE REAL QUICK DOWN HERE.
AIN'T THAT THE—
SCRATCH!!

*Light detection and ranging or laser imaging, detection, and ranging

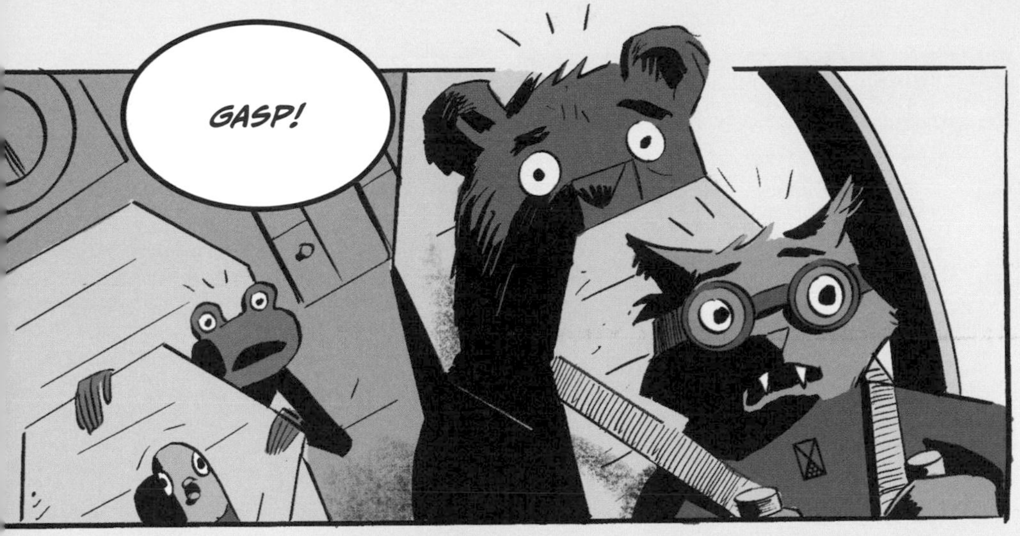
GASP!

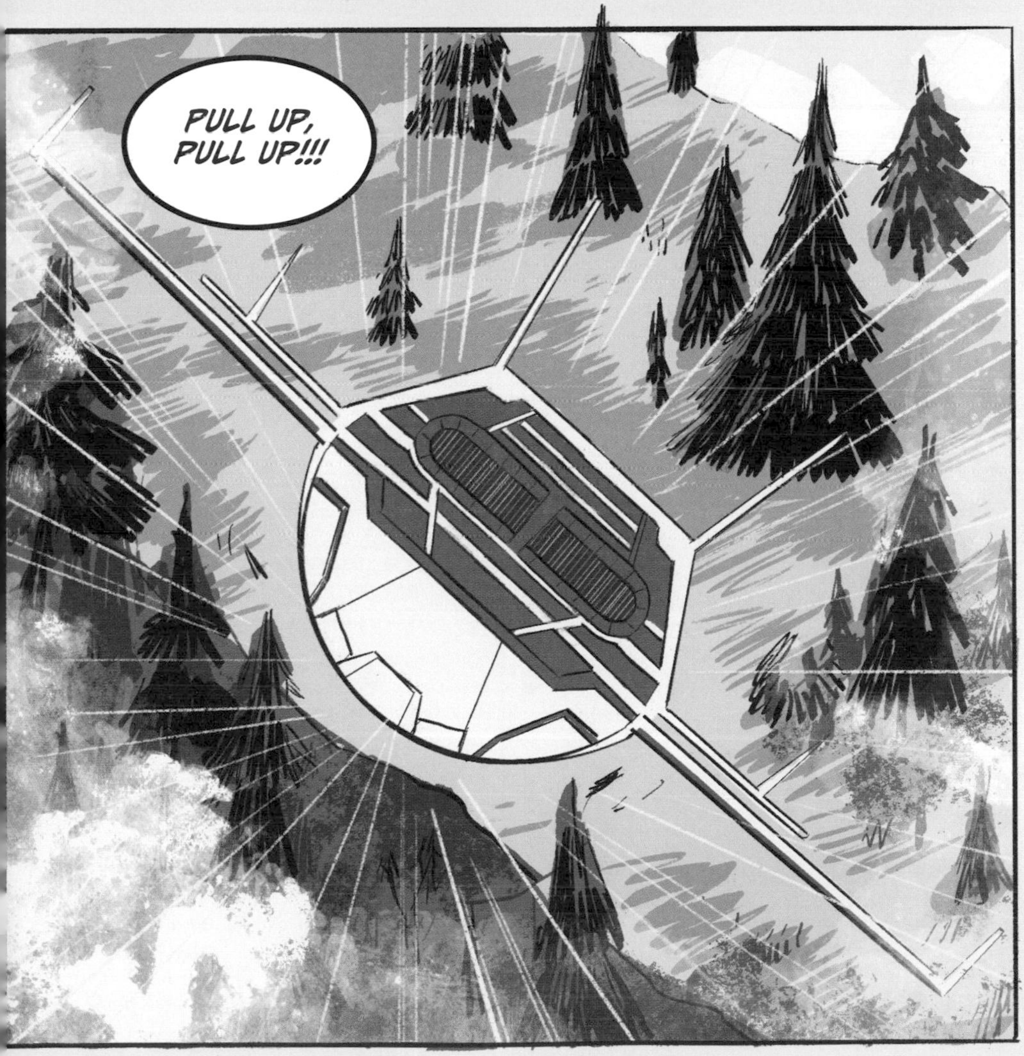
PULL UP,
PULL UP!!!

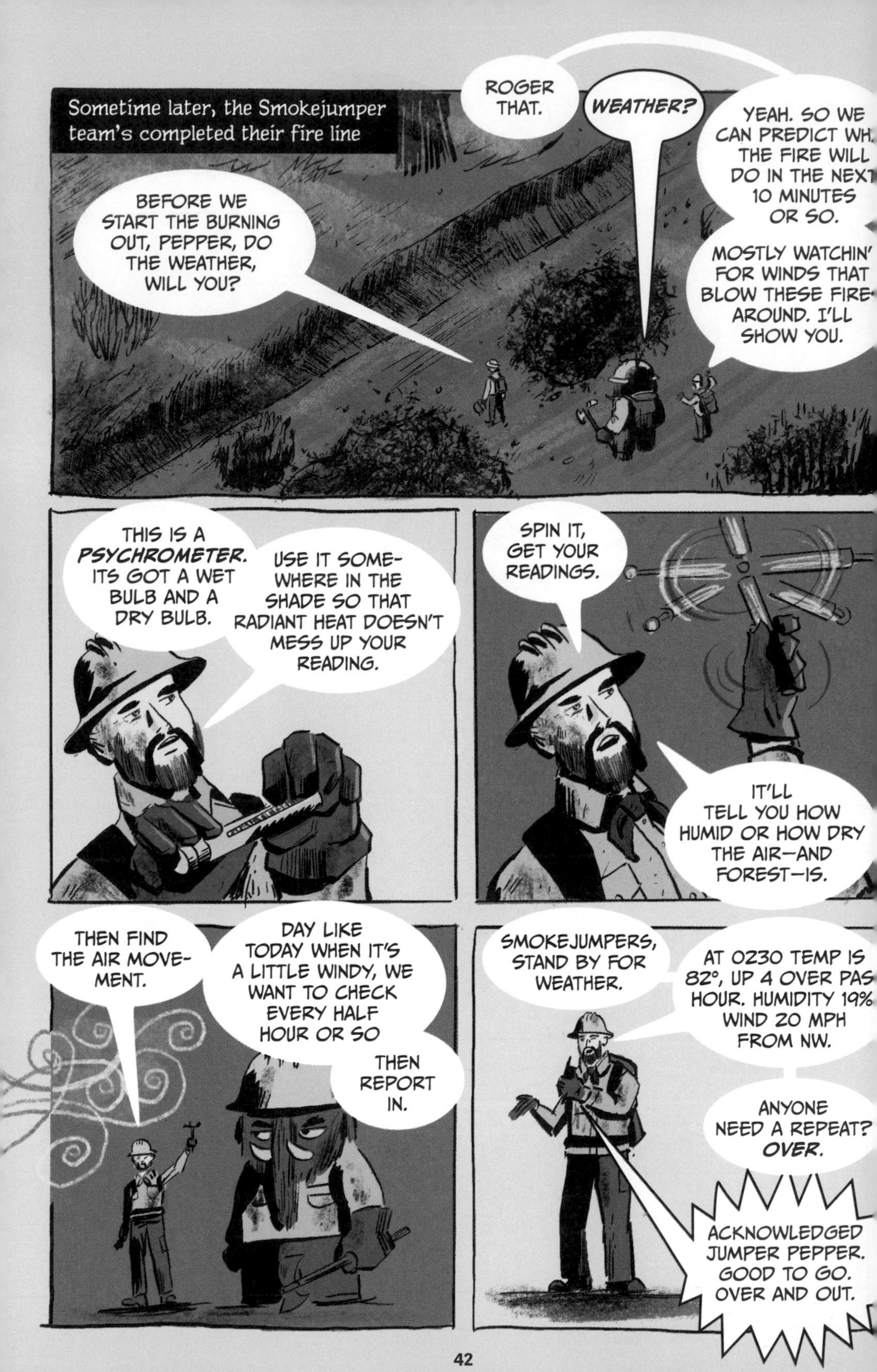
Sometime later, the Smokejumper team's completed their fire line
BEFORE WE START THE BURNING OUT, PEPPER, DO THE WEATHER, WILL YOU?
ROGER THAT.
WEATHER?
YEAH. SO WE CAN PREDICT WH THE FIRE WILL DO IN THE NEXT 10 MINUTES OR SO.
MOSTLY WATCHIN' FOR WINDS THAT BLOW THESE FIRE AROUND. I'LL SHOW YOU.
THIS IS A PSYCHROMETER. ITS GOT A WET BULB AND A DRY BULB.
USE IT SOMEWHERE IN THE SHADE SO THAT RADIANT HEAT DOESN'T MESS UP YOUR READING.
SPIN IT, GET YOUR READINGS.
IT'LL TELL YOU HOW HUMID OR HOW DRY THE AIR—AND FOREST—IS.
THEN FIND THE AIR MOVEMENT.
DAY LIKE TODAY WHEN IT'S A LITTLE WINDY, WE WANT TO CHECK EVERY HALF HOUR OR SO
THEN REPORT IN.
SMOKEJUMPERS, STAND BY FOR WEATHER.
AT 0230 TEMP IS 82°, UP 4 OVER PAS HOUR. HUMIDITY 19% WIND 20 MPH FROM NW.
ANYONE NEED A REPEAT? OVER.
ACKNOWLEDGED JUMPER PEPPER. GOOD TO GO. OVER AND OUT.

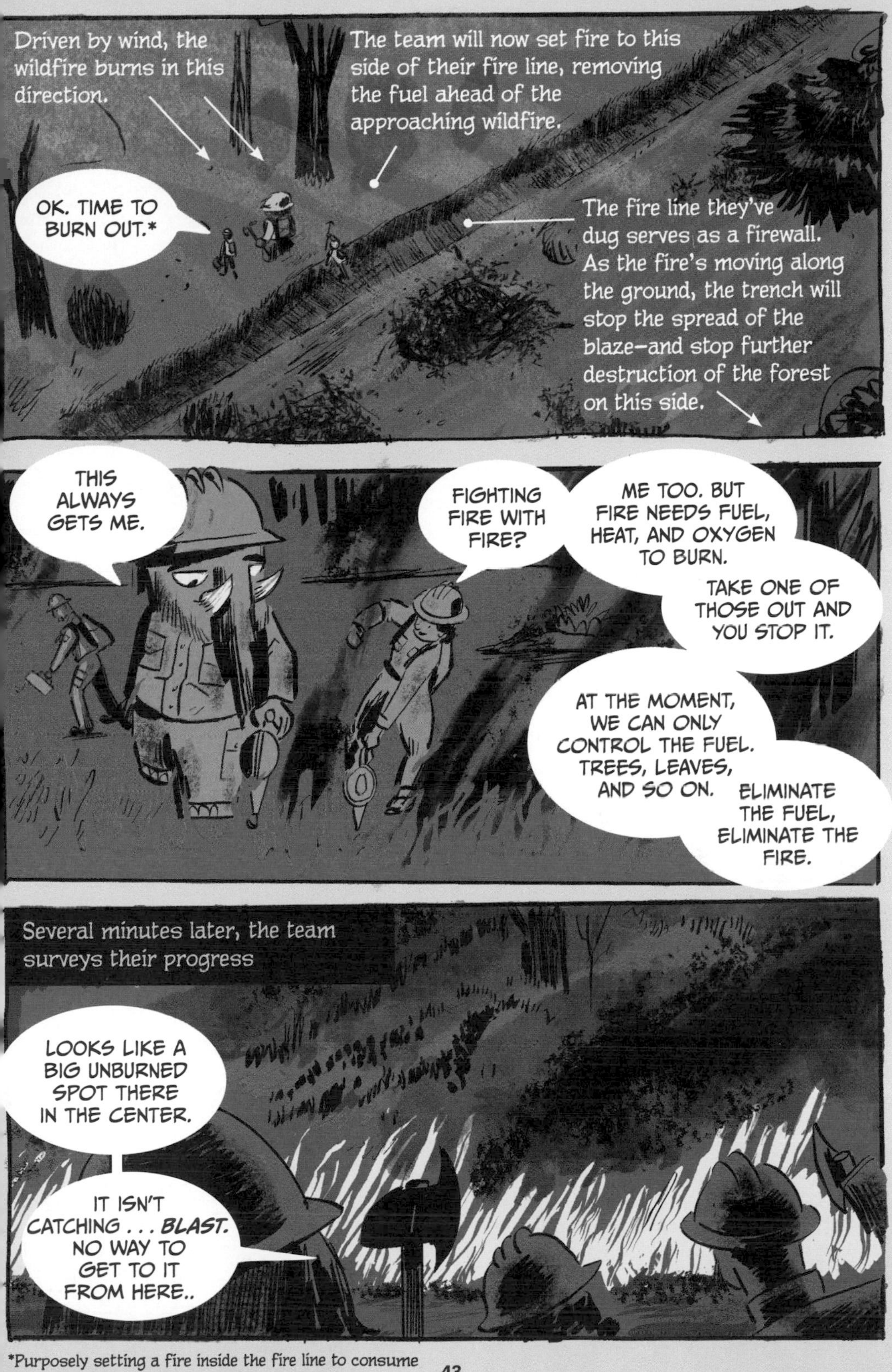
Driven by wind, the wildfire burns in this direction.
The team will now set fire to this side of their fire line, removing the fuel ahead of the approaching wildfire.
OK. TIME TO BURN OUT.*
The fire line they've dug serves as a firewall. As the fire's moving along the ground, the trench will stop the spread of the blaze—and stop further destruction of the forest on this side.
THIS ALWAYS GETS ME.
FIGHTING FIRE WITH FIRE?
ME TOO. BUT FIRE NEEDS FUEL, HEAT, AND OXYGEN TO BURN.
TAKE ONE OF THOSE OUT AND YOU STOP IT.
AT THE MOMENT, WE CAN ONLY CONTROL THE FUEL. TREES, LEAVES, AND SO ON.
ELIMINATE THE FUEL, ELIMINATE THE FIRE.
Several minutes later, the team surveys their progress
LOOKS LIKE A BIG UNBURNED SPOT THERE IN THE CENTER.
IT ISN'T CATCHING . . . *BLAST.* NO WAY TO GET TO IT FROM HERE..

*Purposely setting a fire inside the fire line to consume fuel between the fire line and the burning fire.

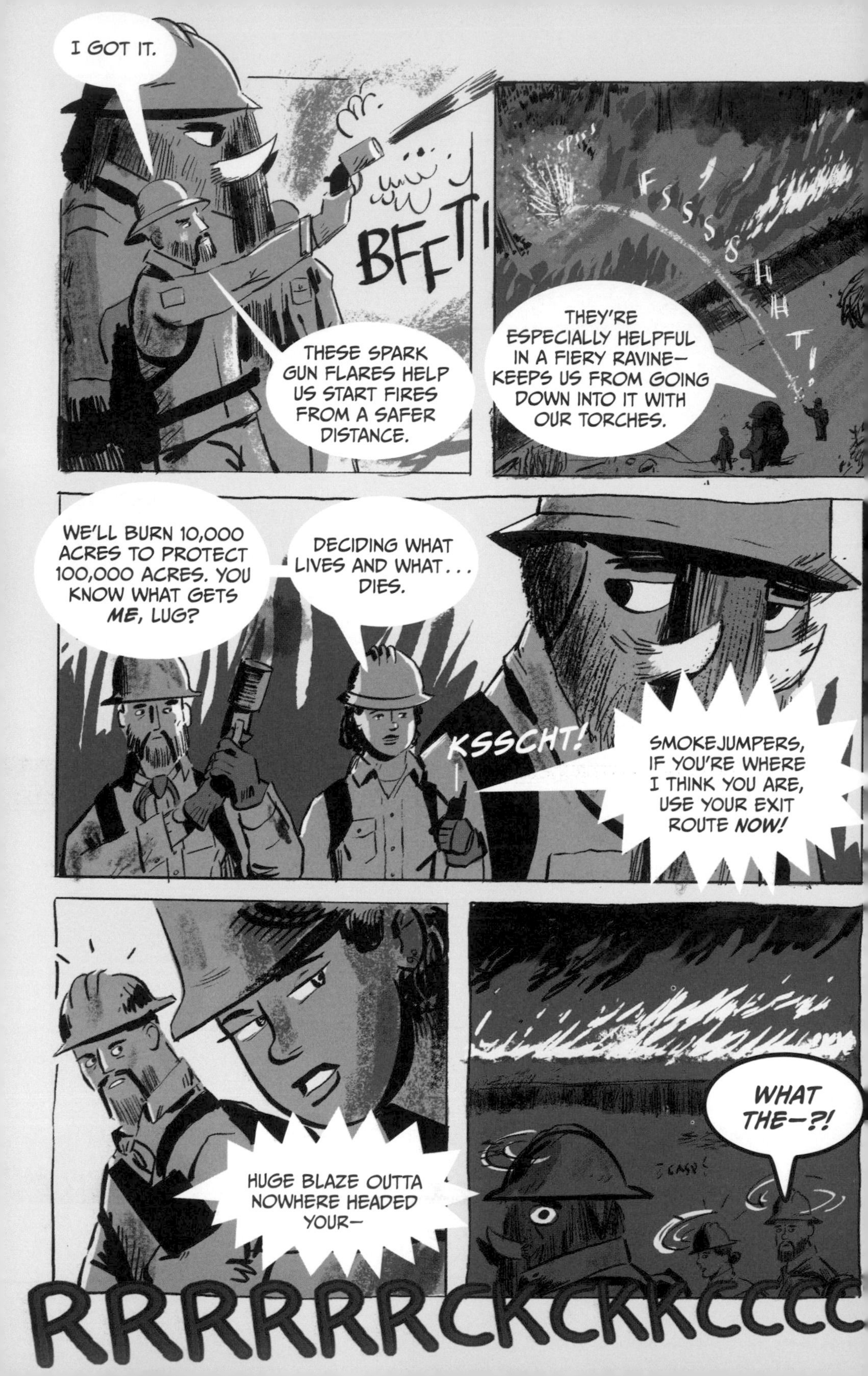
I GOT IT.
BFFT!
THESE SPARK GUN FLARES HELP US START FIRES FROM A SAFER DISTANCE.
FSSSSHHT!
THEY'RE ESPECIALLY HELPFUL IN A FIERY RAVINE— KEEPS US FROM GOING DOWN INTO IT WITH OUR TORCHES.
WE'LL BURN 10,000 ACRES TO PROTECT 100,000 ACRES. YOU KNOW WHAT GETS *ME*, LUG?
DECIDING WHAT LIVES AND WHAT . . . DIES.
KSSCHT!
SMOKEJUMPERS, IF YOU'RE WHERE I THINK YOU ARE, USE YOUR EXIT ROUTE *NOW!*
HUGE BLAZE OUTTA NOWHERE HEADED YOUR—
*WHAT THE—?!*
RRRRRRCKCKRKCCCC

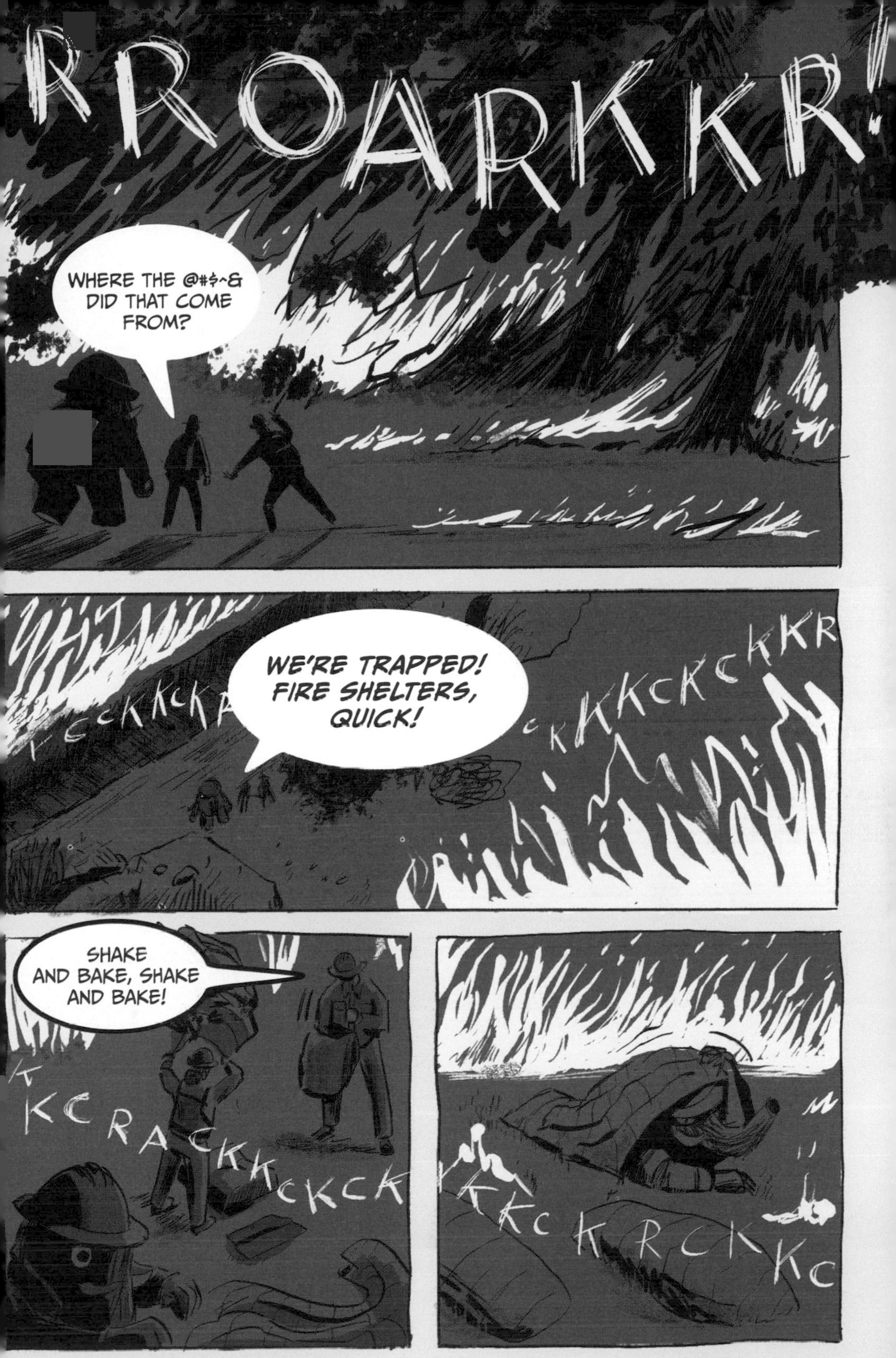
RROARKKR!
WHERE THE @#$~& DID THAT COME FROM?
WE'RE TRAPPED! FIRE SHELTERS, QUICK!
SHAKE AND BAKE, SHAKE AND BAKE!

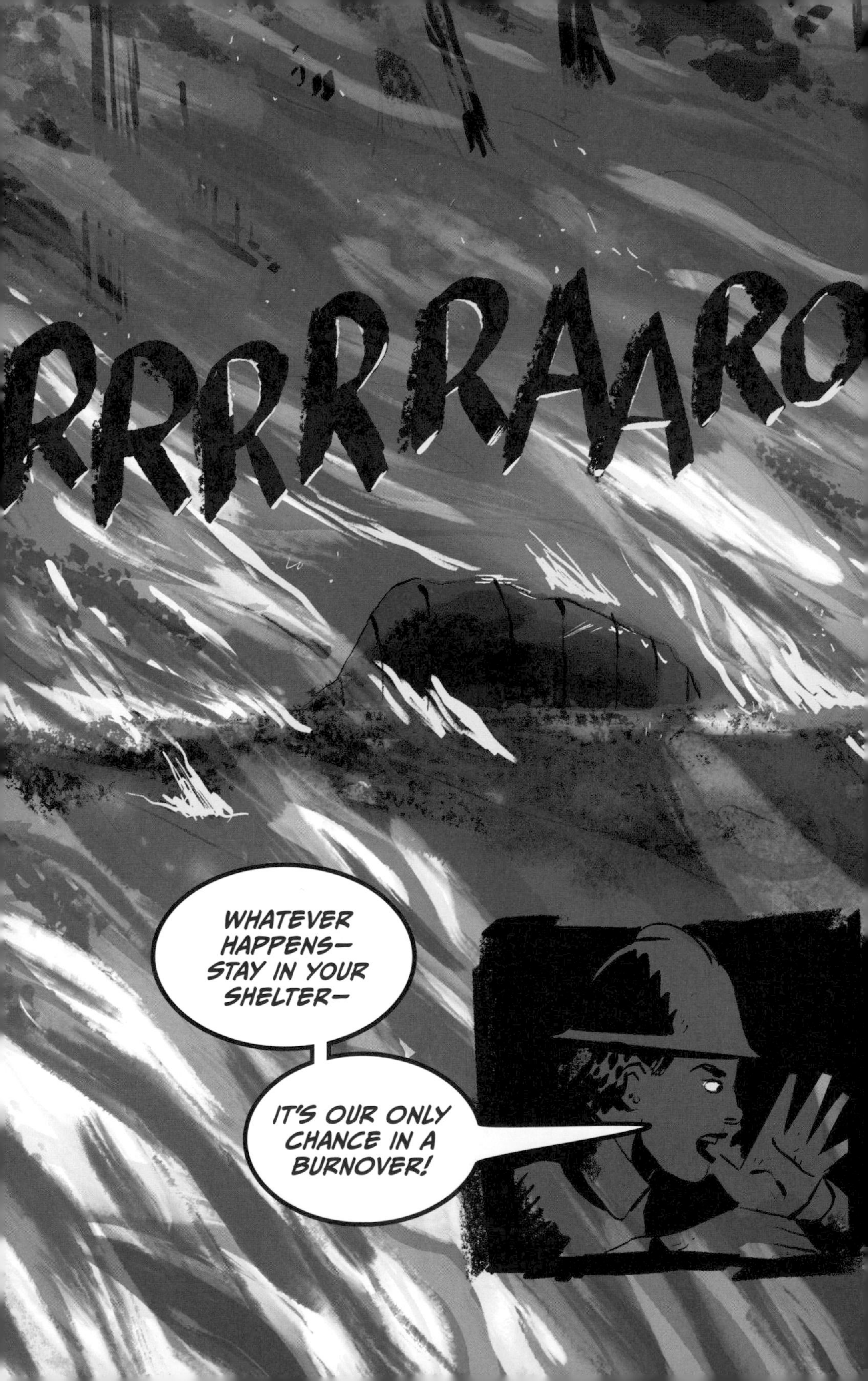
RRRRRAARO
WHATEVER HAPPENS— STAY IN YOUR SHELTER—
IT'S OUR ONLY CHANCE IN A BURNOVER!

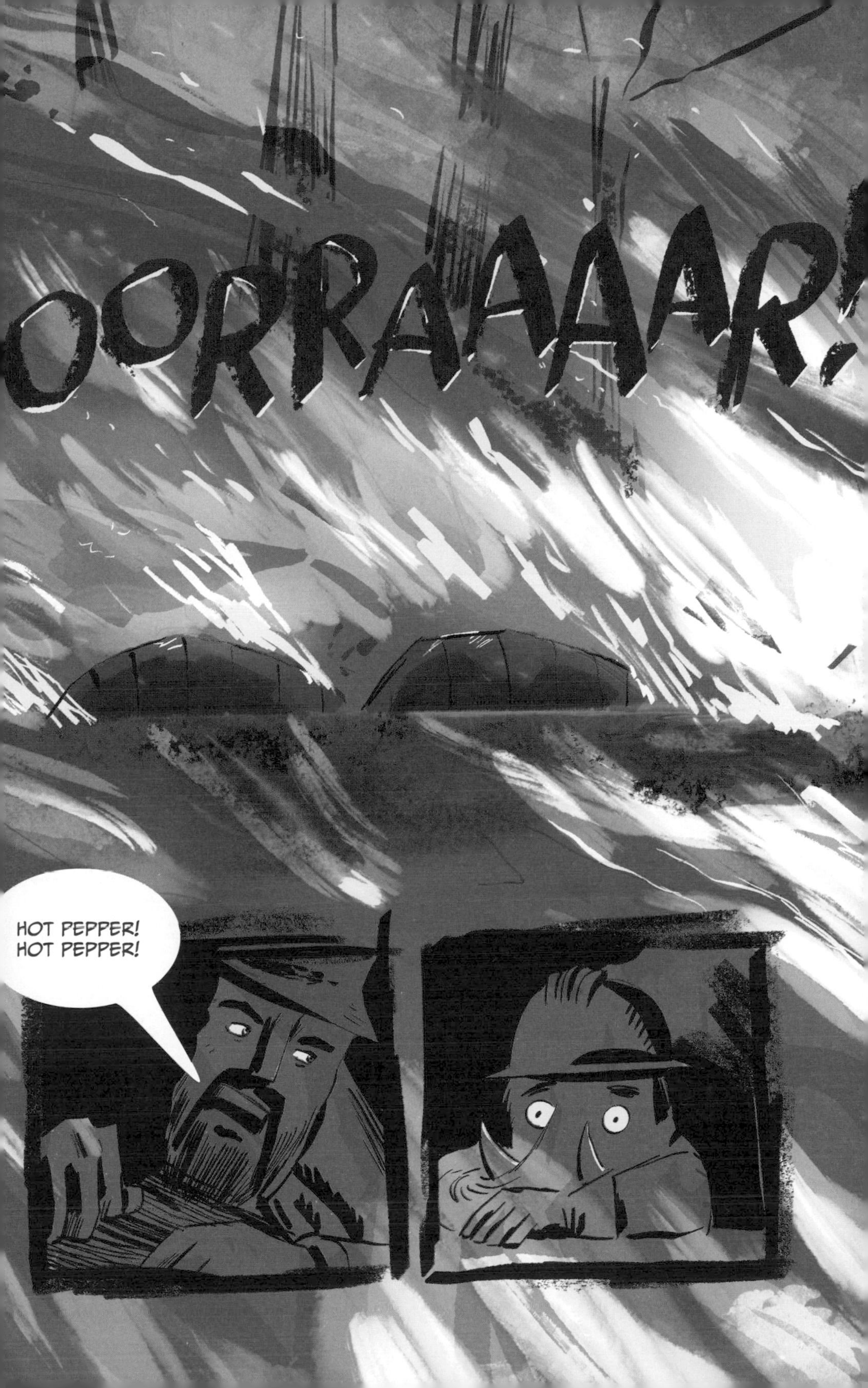
OORRAAAAR!
HOT PEPPER! HOT PEPPER!

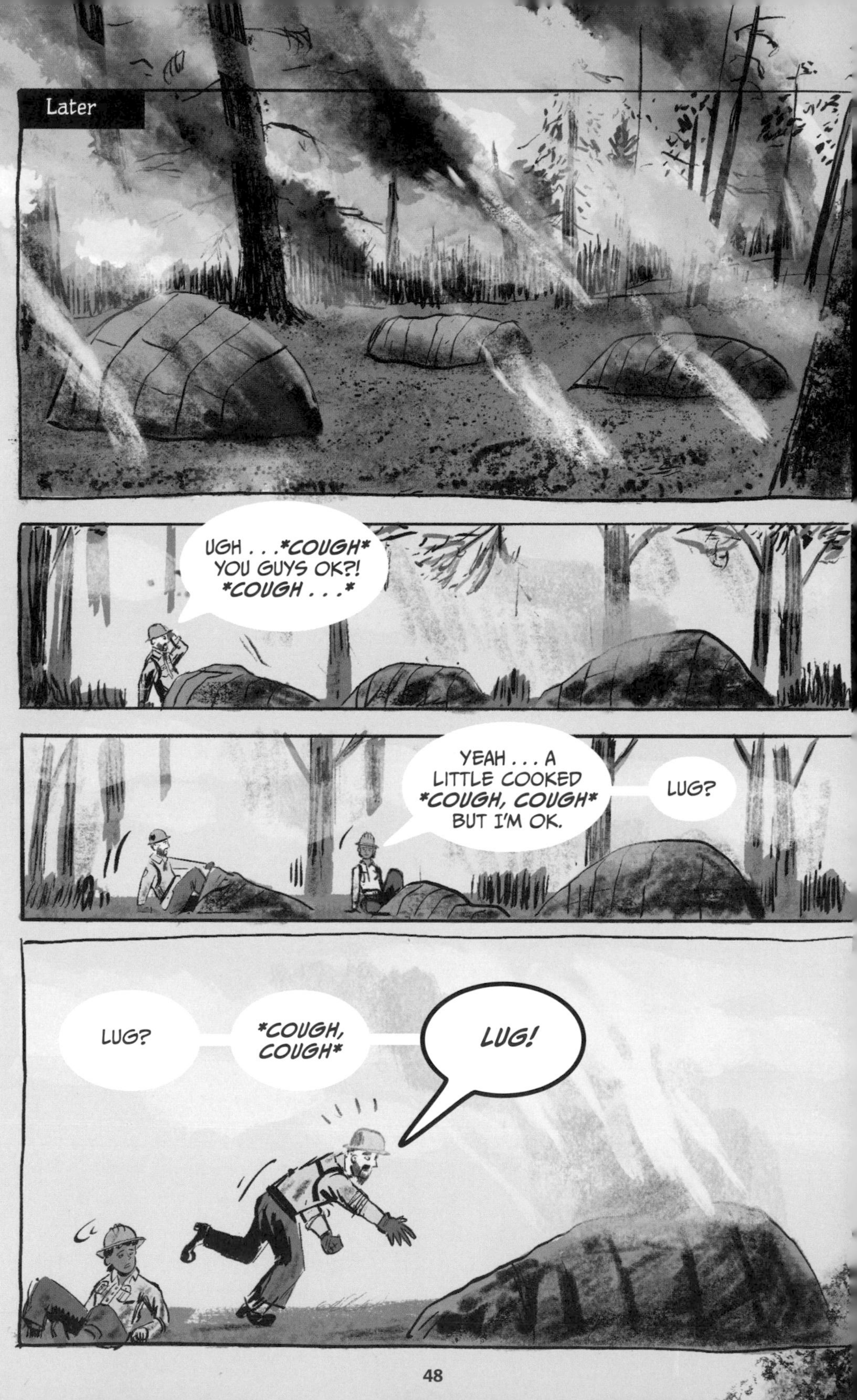
Later
UGH . . .*COUGH* YOU GUYS OK?! *COUGH . . .*
YEAH . . . A LITTLE COOKED *COUGH, COUGH* BUT I'M OK.
LUG?
LUG?
*COUGH, COUGH*
LUG!

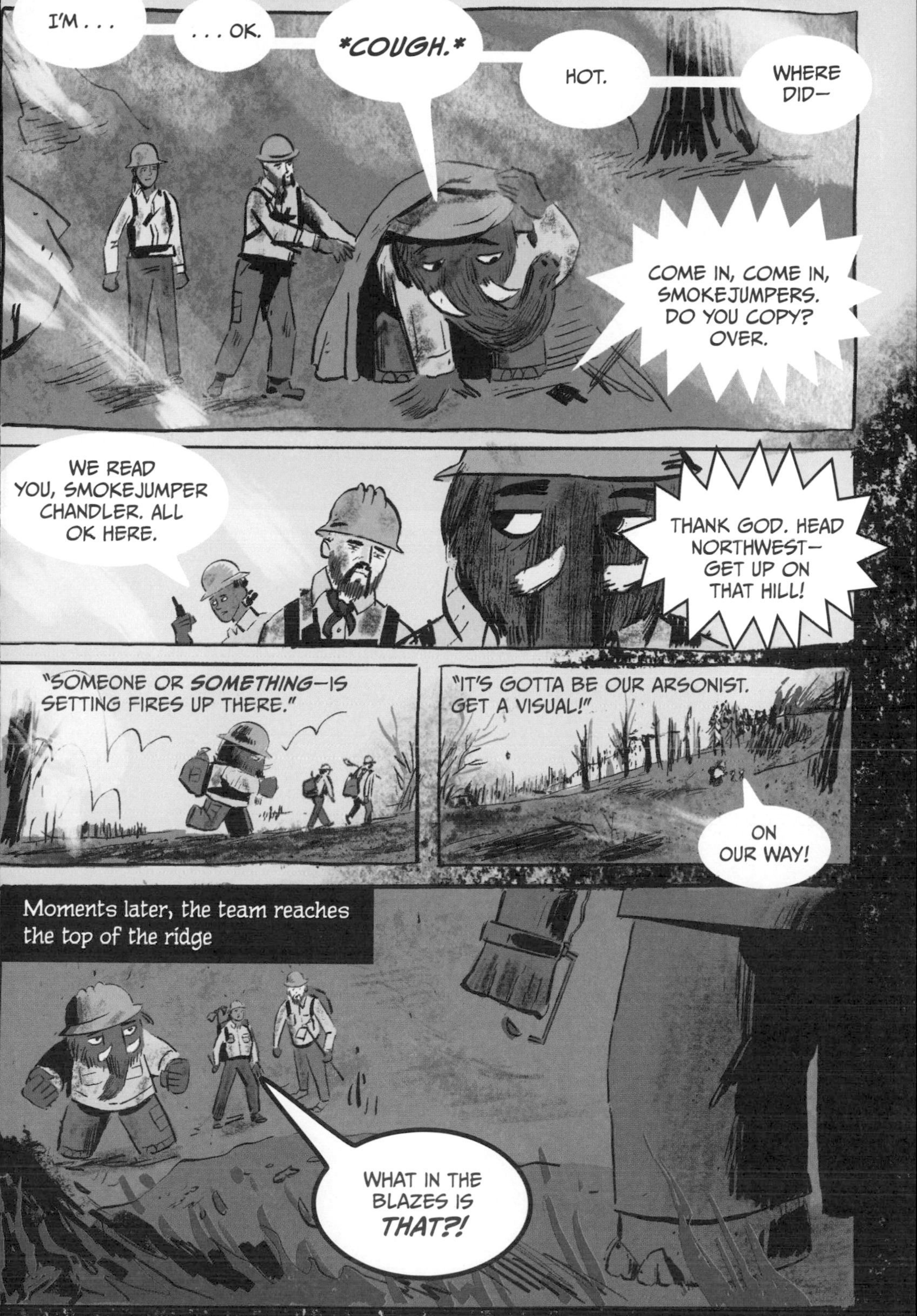
I'M . . .
. . . OK.
*COUGH.*
HOT.
WHERE DID—
COME IN, COME IN, SMOKEJUMPERS. DO YOU COPY? OVER.
WE READ YOU, SMOKEJUMPER CHANDLER. ALL OK HERE.
THANK GOD. HEAD NORTHWEST— GET UP ON THAT HILL!
"SOMEONE OR SOMETHING—IS SETTING FIRES UP THERE."
"IT'S GOTTA BE OUR ARSONIST. GET A VISUAL!"
ON OUR WAY!
Moments later, the team reaches the top of the ridge
WHAT IN THE BLAZES IS THAT?!

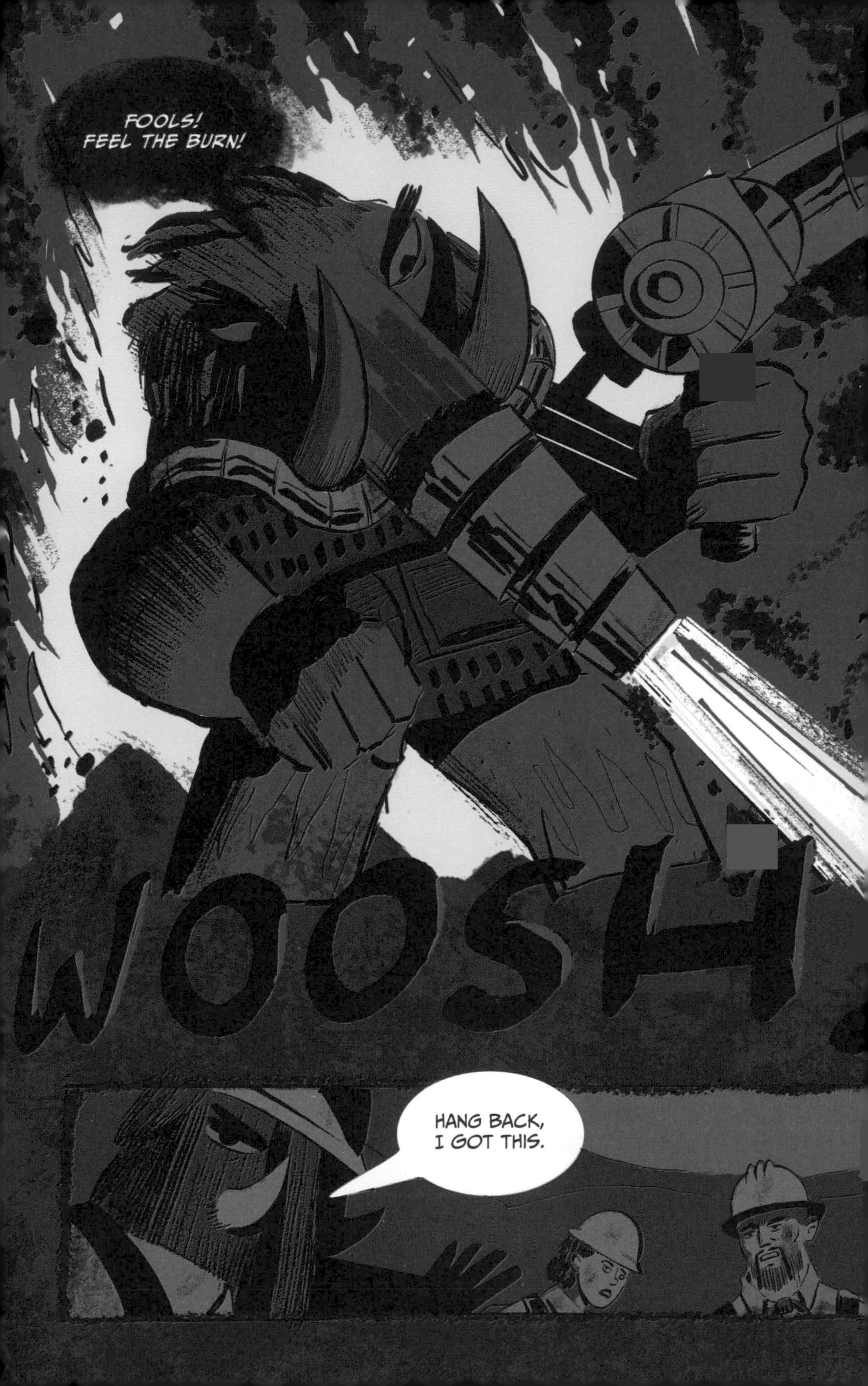
FOOLS! FEEL THE BURN!
WOOSH
HANG BACK, I GOT THIS.

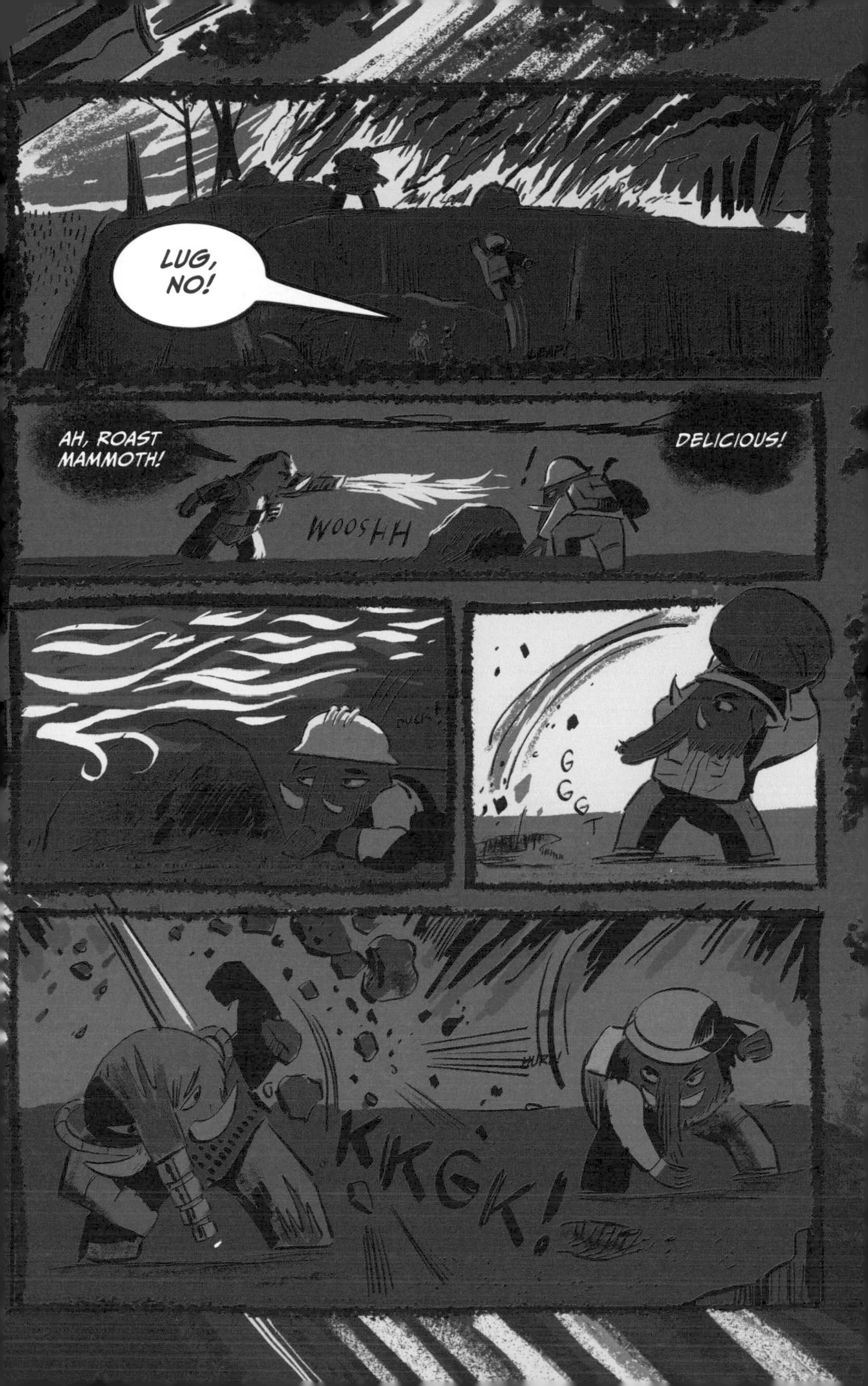
LUG, NO!
AH, ROAST MAMMOTH!
DELICIOUS!
WOOSHH
DUCK!
GGGT
KKGK!

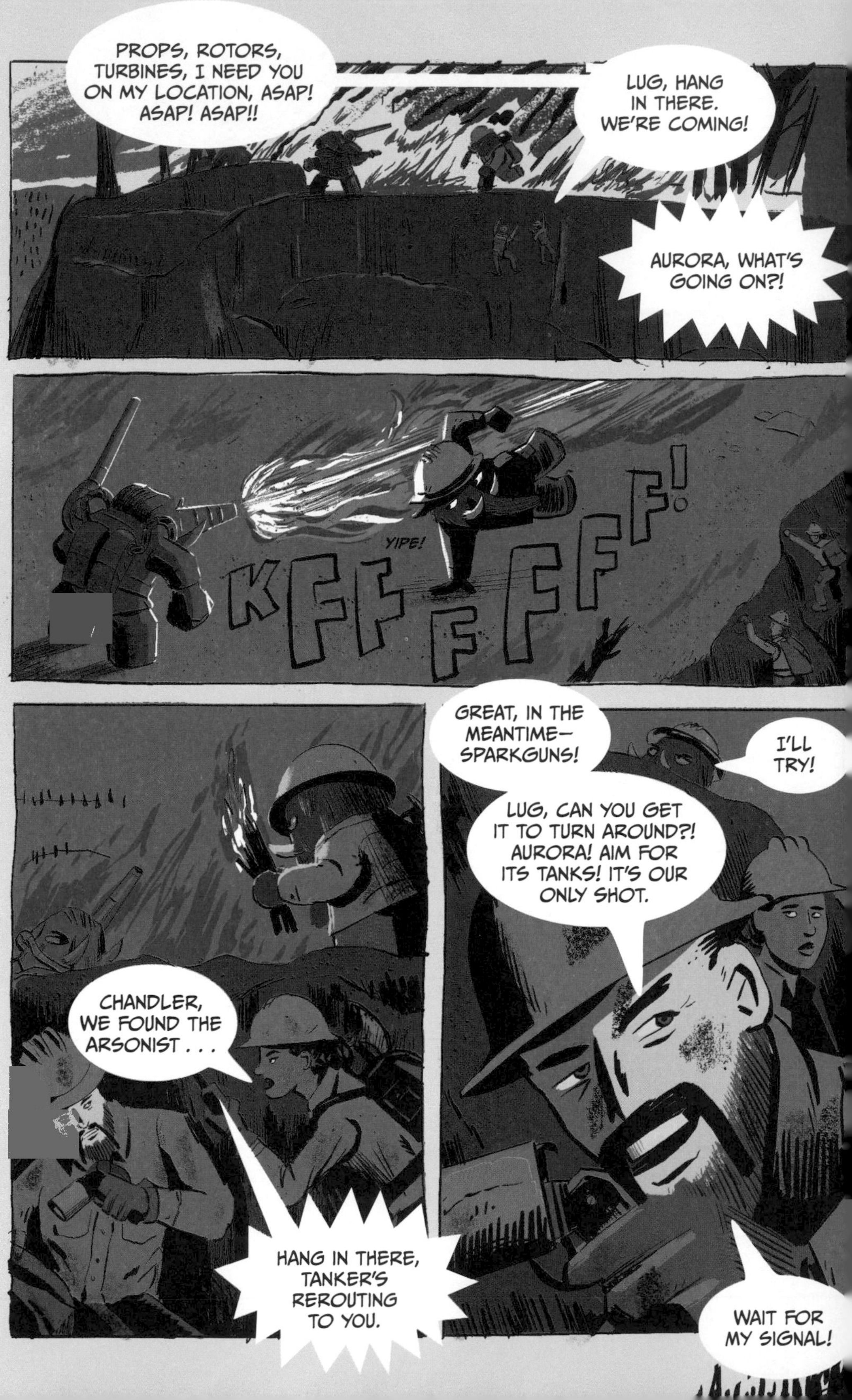
PROPS, ROTORS, TURBINES, I NEED YOU ON MY LOCATION, ASAP! ASAP! ASAP!!
LUG, HANG IN THERE. WE'RE COMING!
AURORA, WHAT'S GOING ON?!
YIPE!
KFFFFFFF!
CHANDLER, WE FOUND THE ARSONIST . . .
HANG IN THERE, TANKER'S REROUTING TO YOU.
GREAT, IN THE MEANTIME— SPARKGUNS!
I'LL TRY!
LUG, CAN YOU GET IT TO TURN AROUND?! AURORA! AIM FOR ITS TANKS! IT'S OUR ONLY SHOT.
WAIT FOR MY SIGNAL!

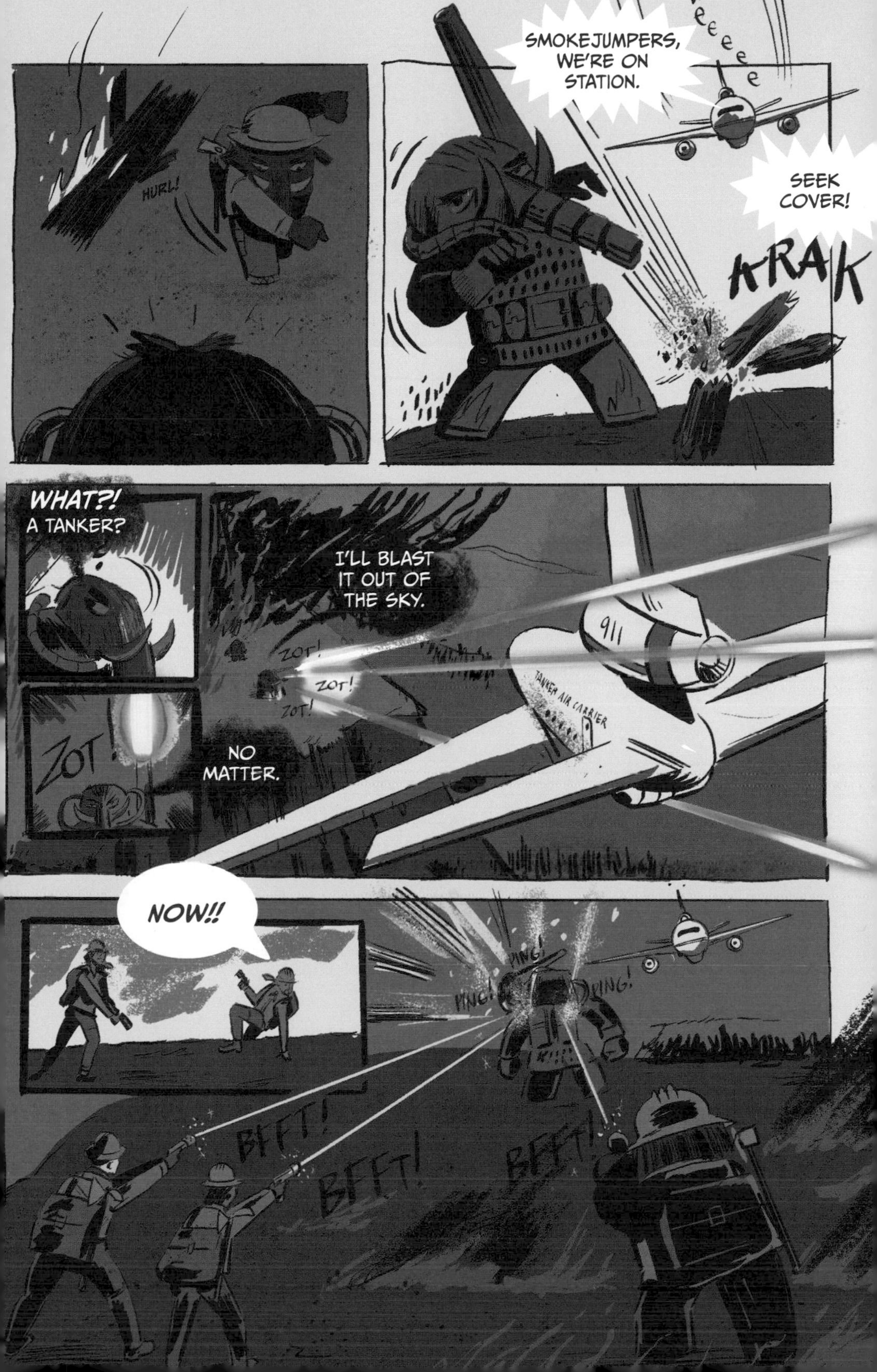
HURL!
SMOKEJUMPERS, WE'RE ON STATION.
Weeeee
SEEK COVER!
KRAK
WHAT?! A TANKER?
I'LL BLAST IT OUT OF THE SKY.
ZOT!
ZOT!
ZOT!
911
TANKER AIR CARRIER
ZOT!
NO MATTER.
NOW!!
PING!
PING!
PING!
BFFT!
BFFT!
BFFT!

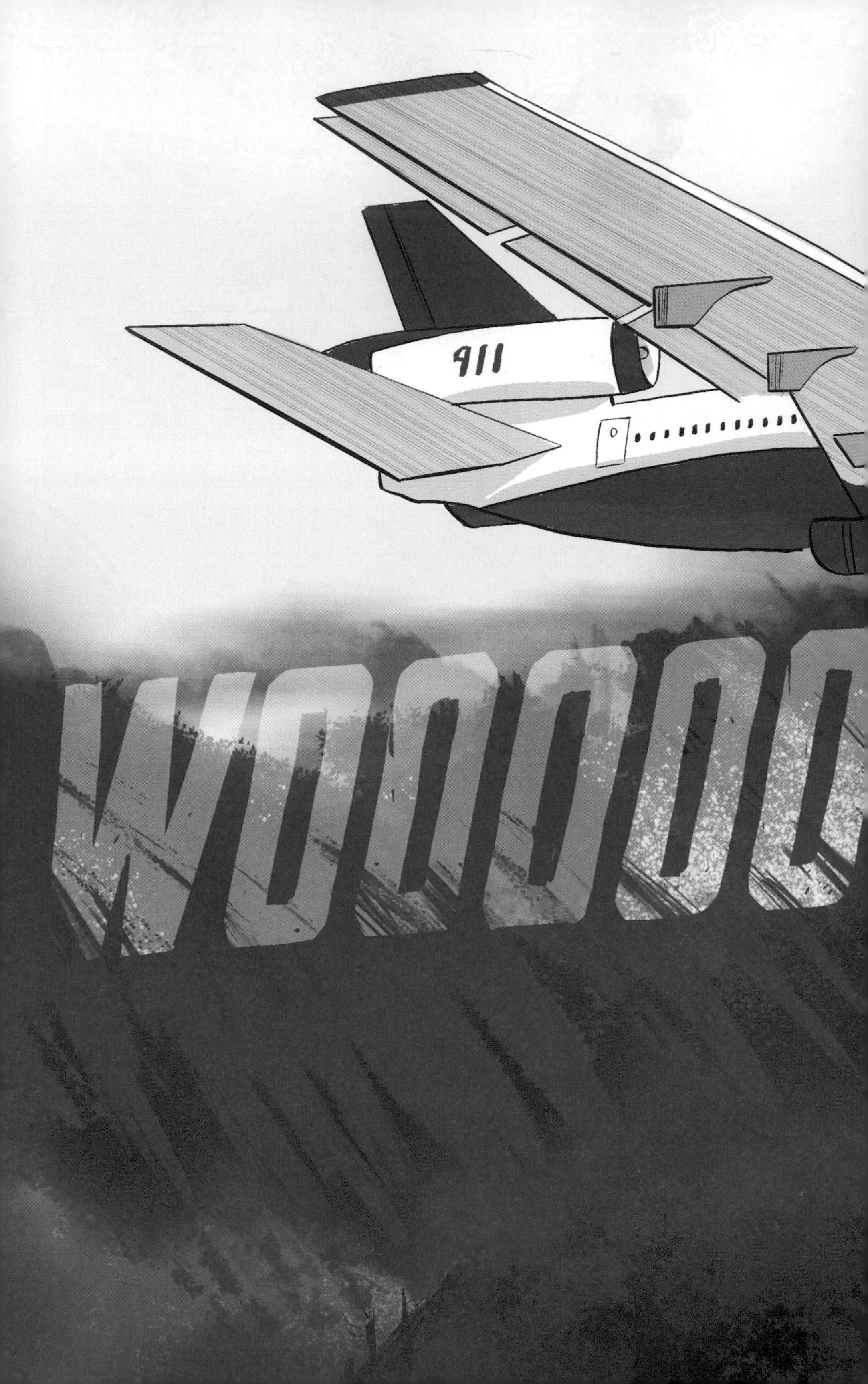
911
WOOOOO

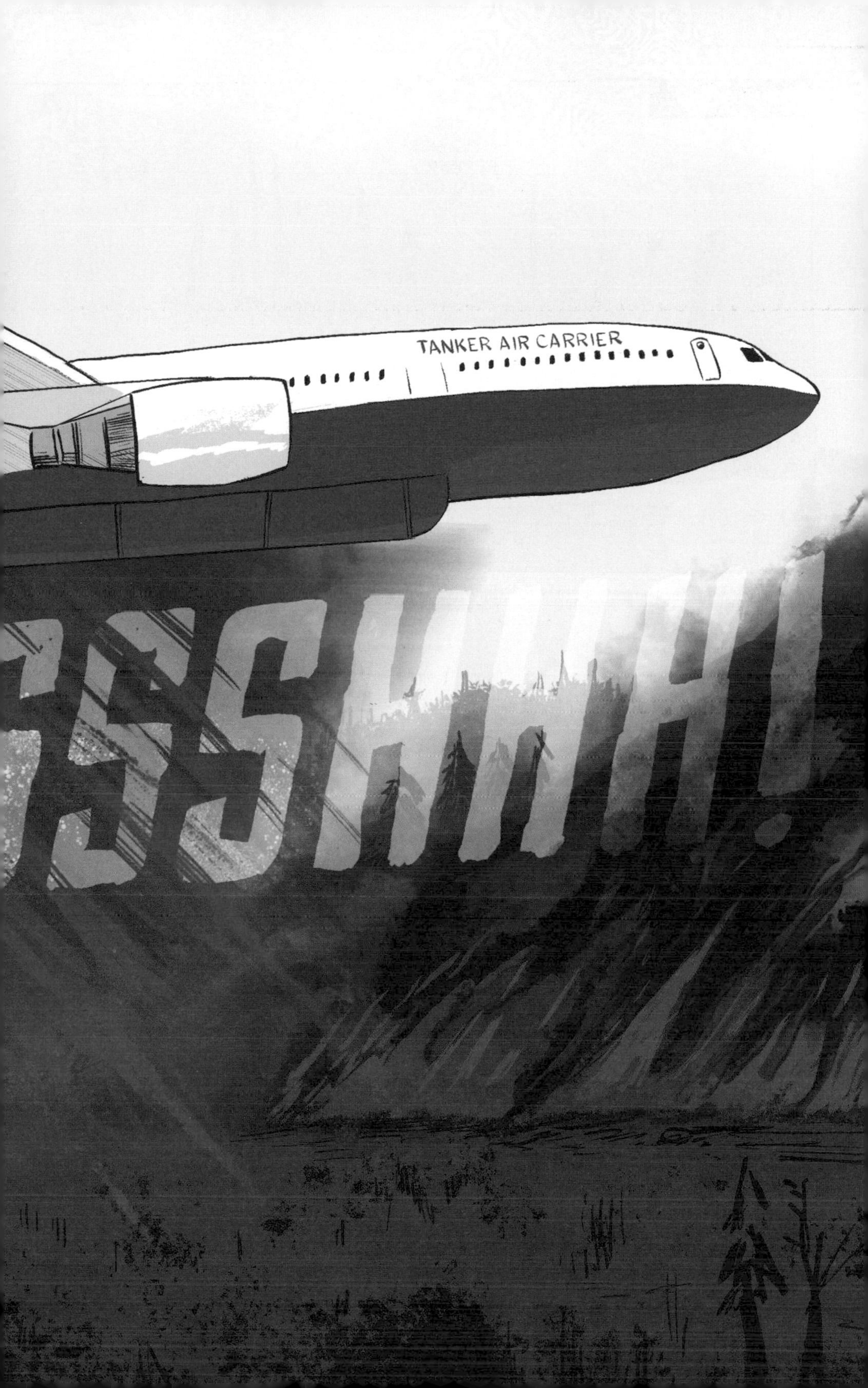
TANKER AIR CARRIER
SSHHH!

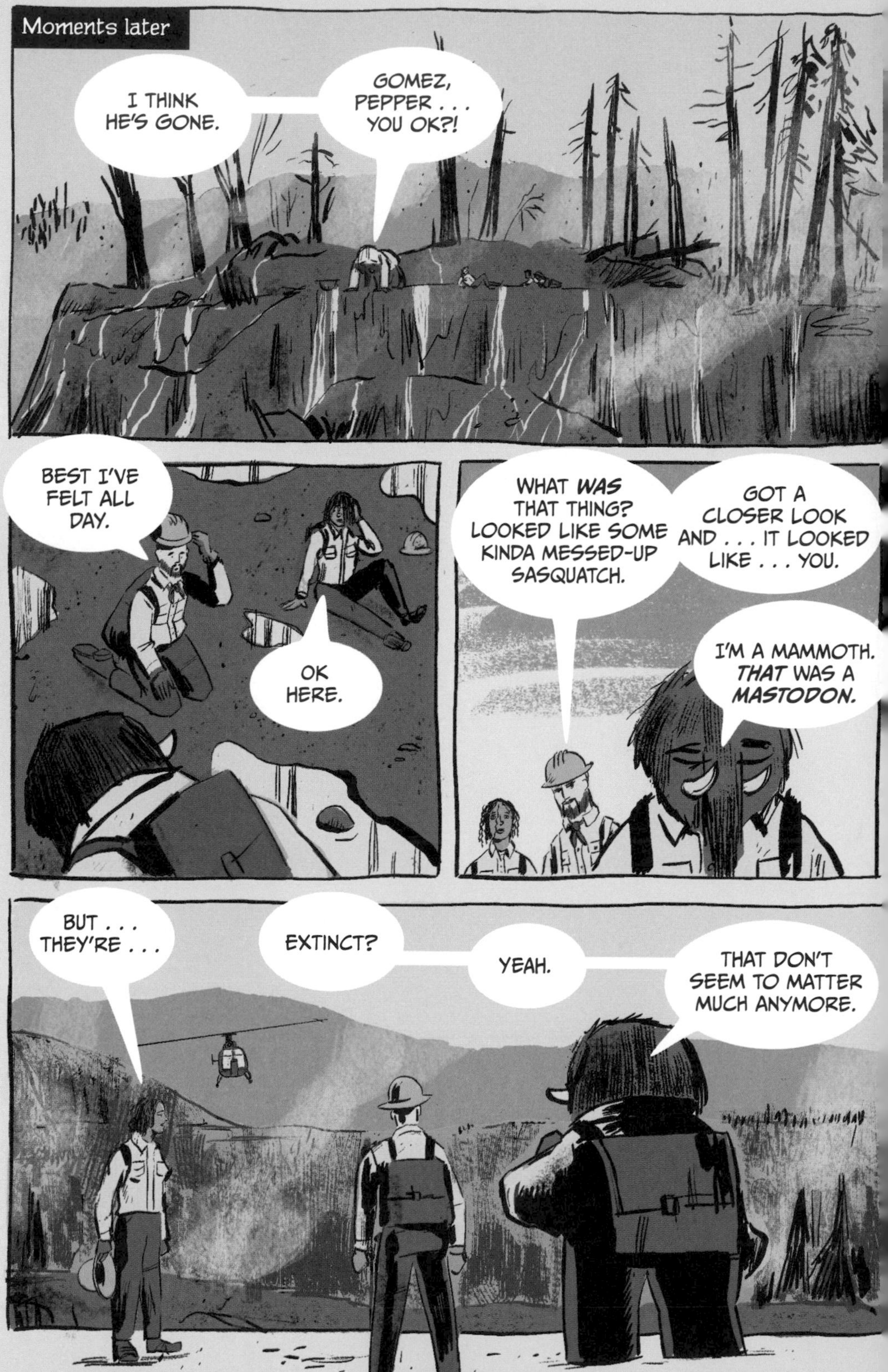
Moments later
I THINK HE'S GONE.
GOMEZ, PEPPER . . . YOU OK?!
BEST I'VE FELT ALL DAY.
OK HERE.
WHAT *WAS* THAT THING? LOOKED LIKE SOME KINDA MESSED-UP SASQUATCH.
GOT A CLOSER LOOK AND . . . IT LOOKED LIKE . . . YOU.
I'M A MAMMOTH. *THAT* WAS A *MASTODON.*
BUT . . . THEY'RE . . .
EXTINCT?
YEAH.
THAT DON'T SEEM TO MATTER MUCH ANYMORE.

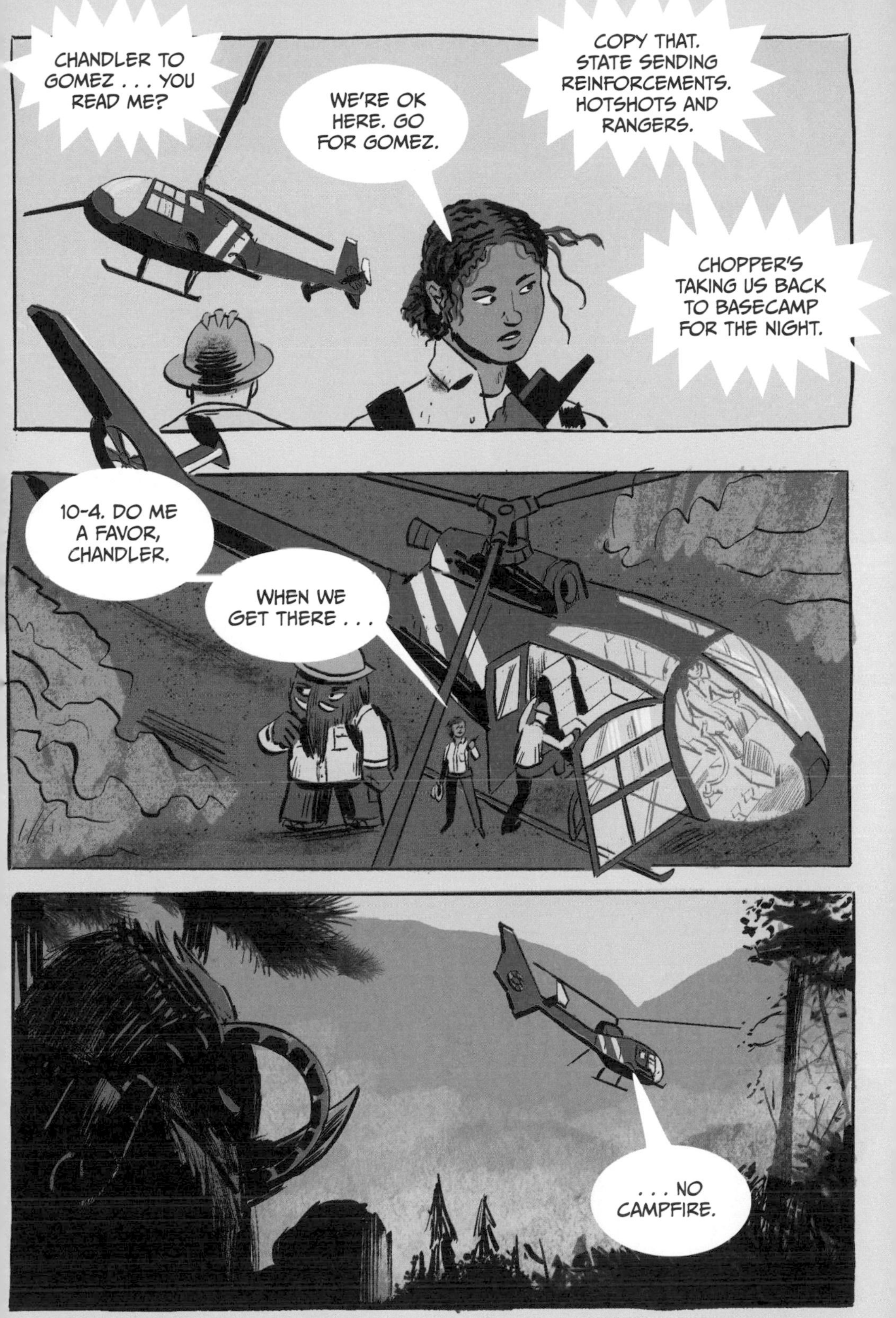
CHANDLER TO GOMEZ . . . YOU READ ME?
WE'RE OK HERE. GO FOR GOMEZ.
COPY THAT. STATE SENDING REINFORCEMENTS. HOTSHOTS AND RANGERS.
CHOPPER'S TAKING US BACK TO BASECAMP FOR THE NIGHT.
10-4. DO ME A FAVOR, CHANDLER.
WHEN WE GET THERE . . .
. . . NO CAMPFIRE.

Smokejumper basecamp, that night

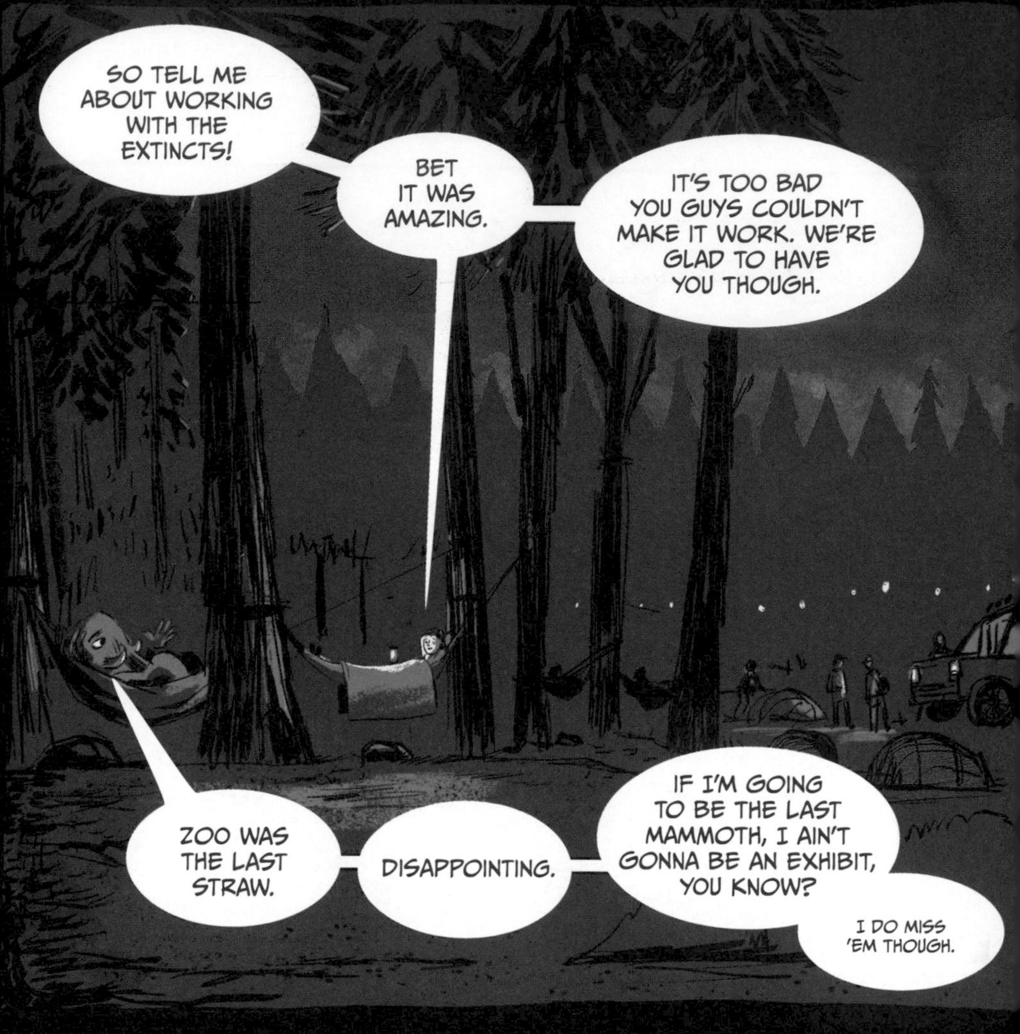
SO TELL ME ABOUT WORKING WITH THE EXTINCTS!
BET IT WAS AMAZING.
IT'S TOO BAD YOU GUYS COULDN'T MAKE IT WORK. WE'RE GLAD TO HAVE YOU THOUGH.
ZOO WAS THE LAST STRAW.
DISAPPOINTING.
IF I'M GOING TO BE THE LAST MAMMOTH, I AIN'T GONNA BE AN EXHIBIT, YOU KNOW?
I DO MISS 'EM THOUGH.

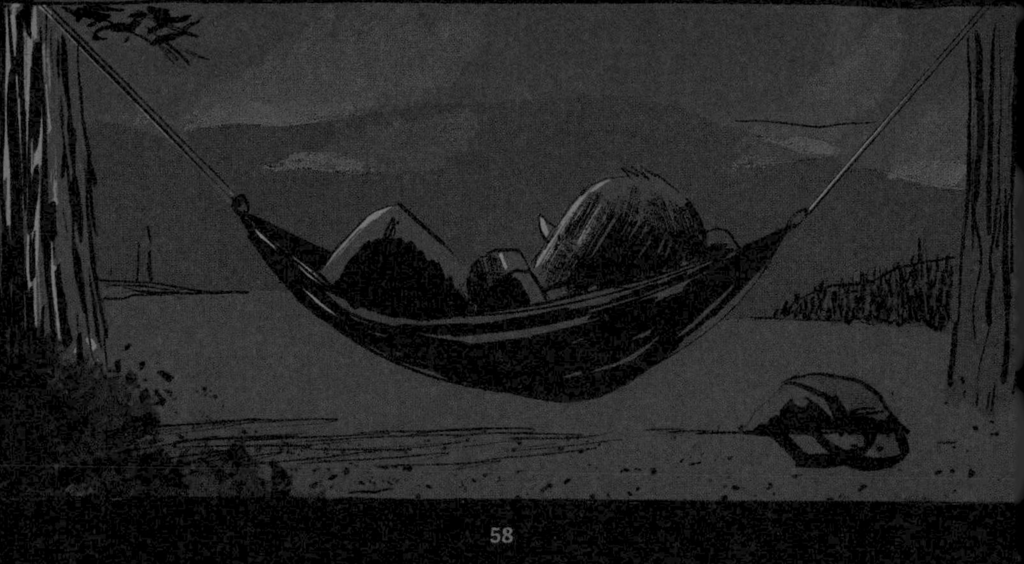

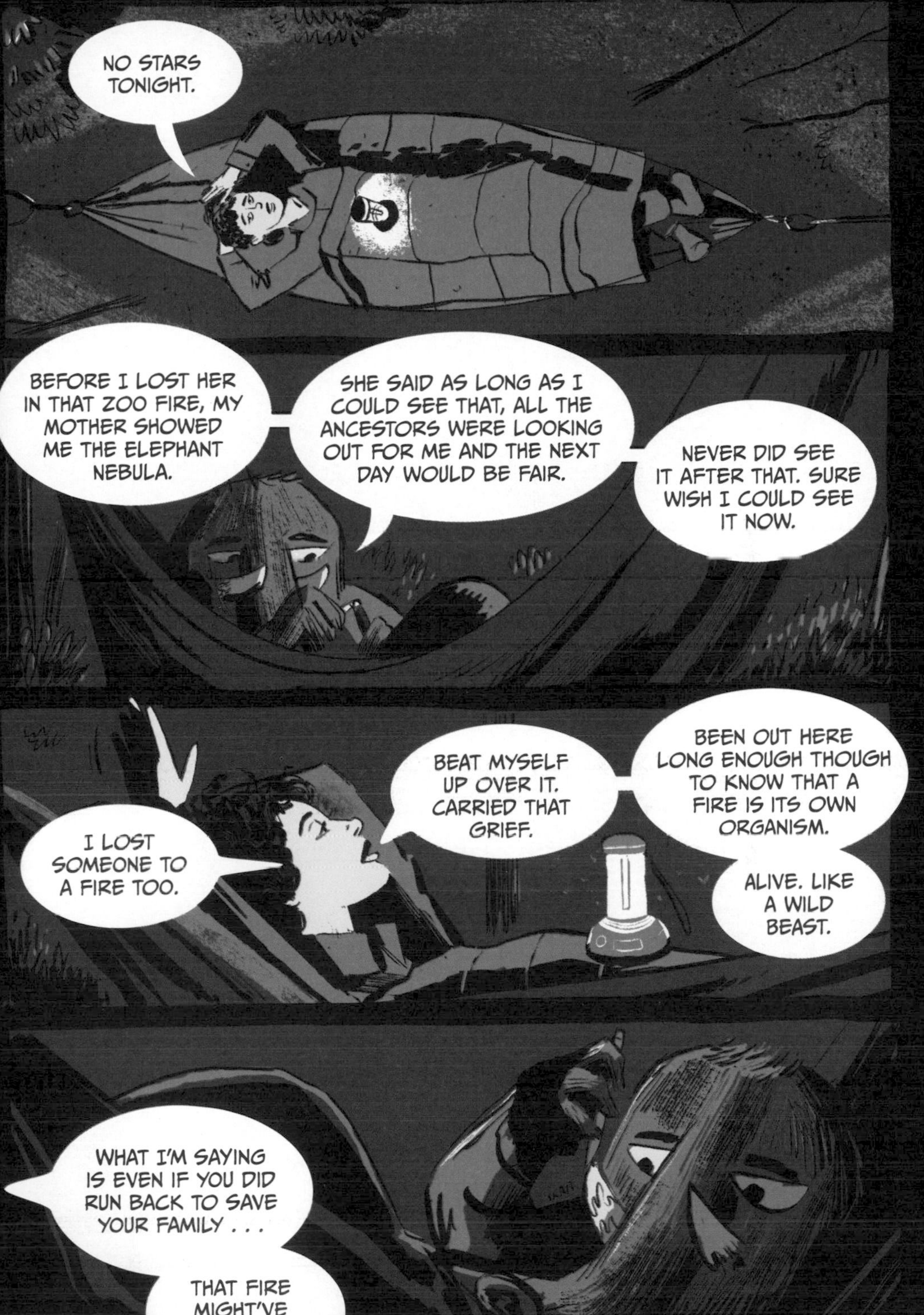
NO STARS TONIGHT.
BEFORE I LOST HER IN THAT ZOO FIRE, MY MOTHER SHOWED ME THE ELEPHANT NEBULA.
SHE SAID AS LONG AS I COULD SEE THAT, ALL THE ANCESTORS WERE LOOKING OUT FOR ME AND THE NEXT DAY WOULD BE FAIR.
NEVER DID SEE IT AFTER THAT. SURE WISH I COULD SEE IT NOW.
I LOST SOMEONE TO A FIRE TOO.
BEAT MYSELF UP OVER IT. CARRIED THAT GRIEF.
BEEN OUT HERE LONG ENOUGH THOUGH TO KNOW THAT A FIRE IS ITS OWN ORGANISM.
ALIVE. LIKE A WILD BEAST.
WHAT I'M SAYING IS EVEN IF YOU DID RUN BACK TO SAVE YOUR FAMILY . . .
THAT FIRE MIGHT'VE EATEN YOU TOO.

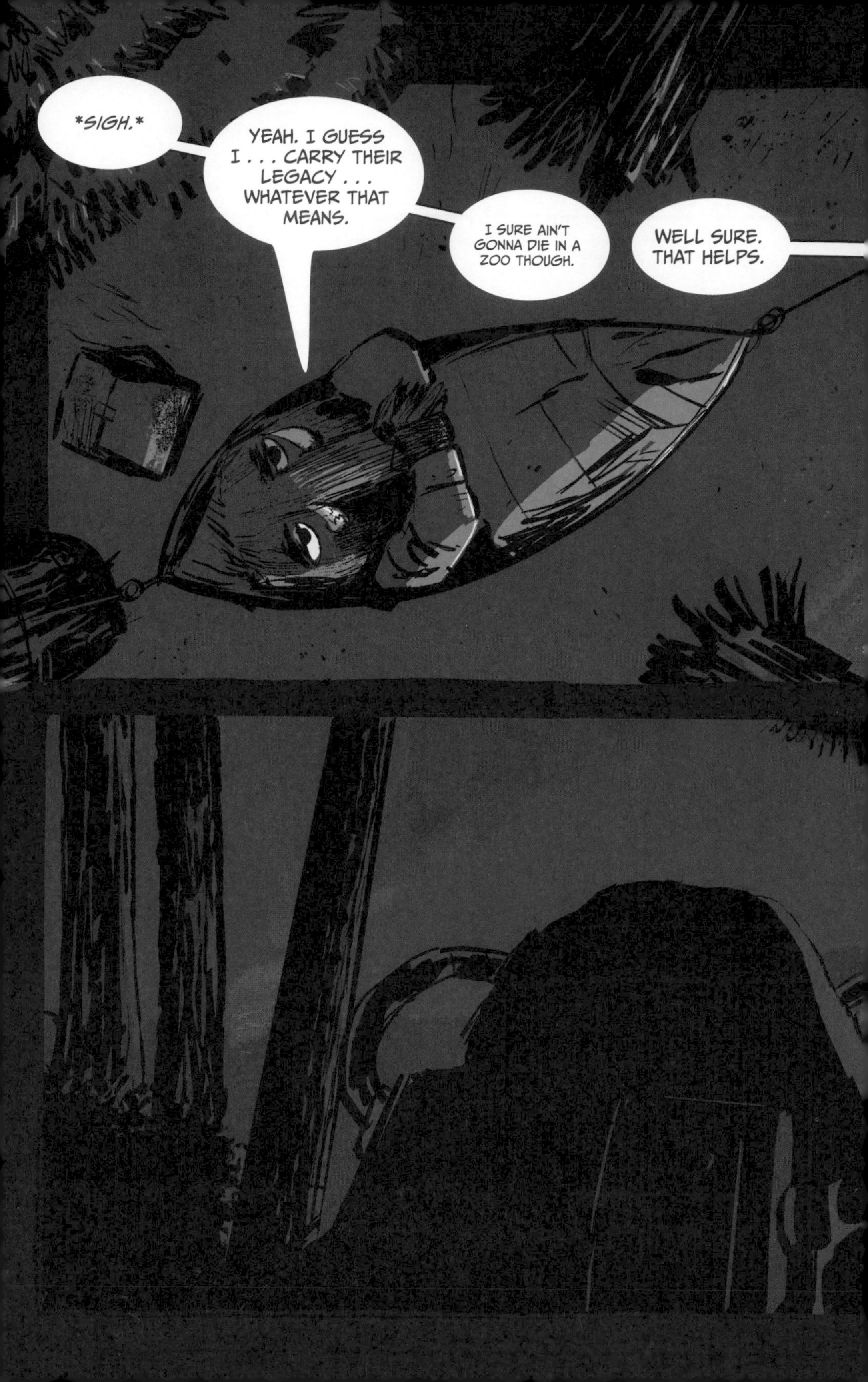
*SIGH.*
YEAH. I GUESS I . . . CARRY THEIR LEGACY . . . WHATEVER THAT MEANS.
I SURE AIN'T GONNA DIE IN A ZOO THOUGH.
WELL SURE. THAT HELPS.

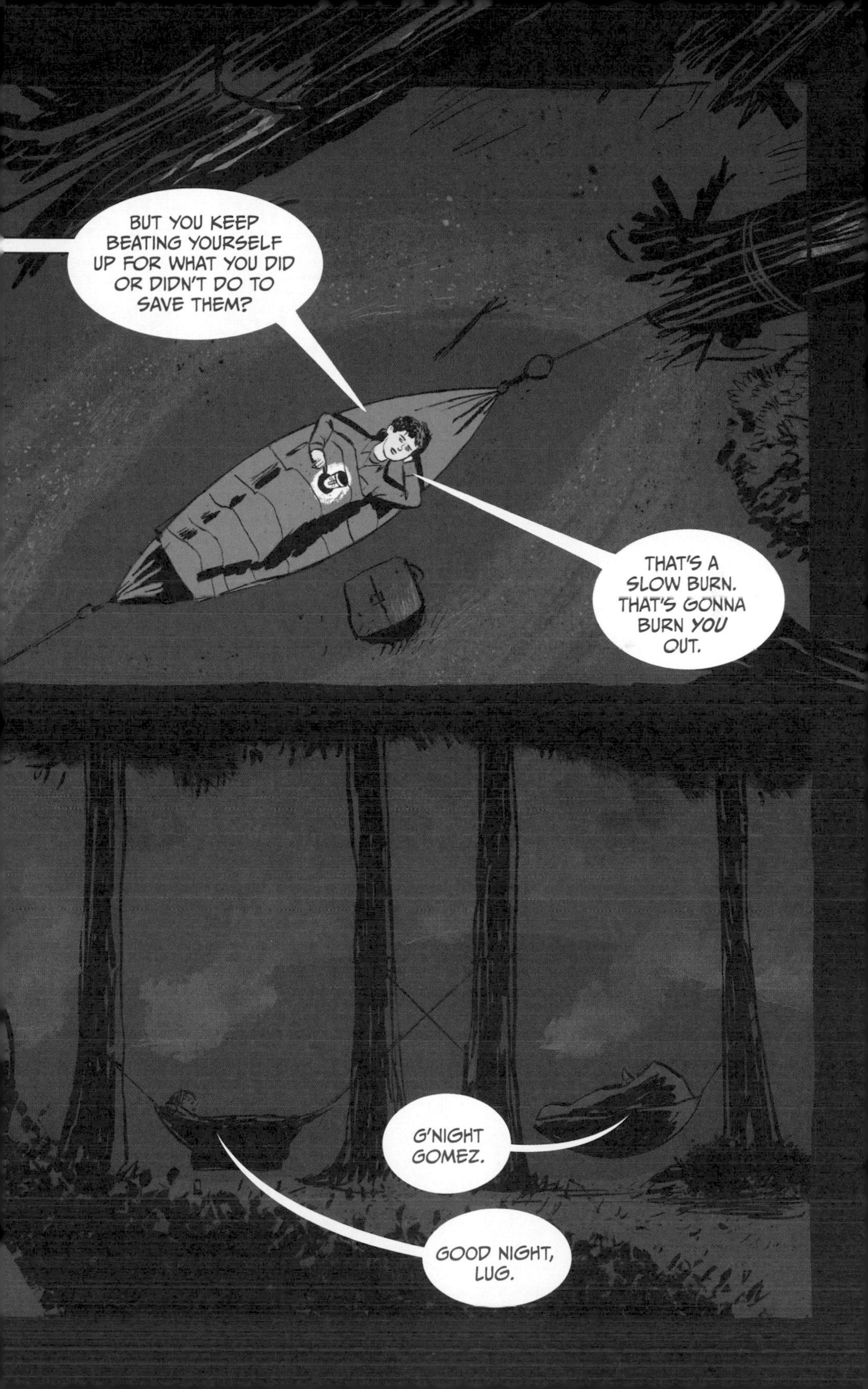
BUT YOU KEEP BEATING YOURSELF UP FOR WHAT YOU DID OR DIDN'T DO TO SAVE THEM?
THAT'S A SLOW BURN. THAT'S GONNA BURN *YOU* OUT.
G'NIGHT GOMEZ.
GOOD NIGHT, LUG.

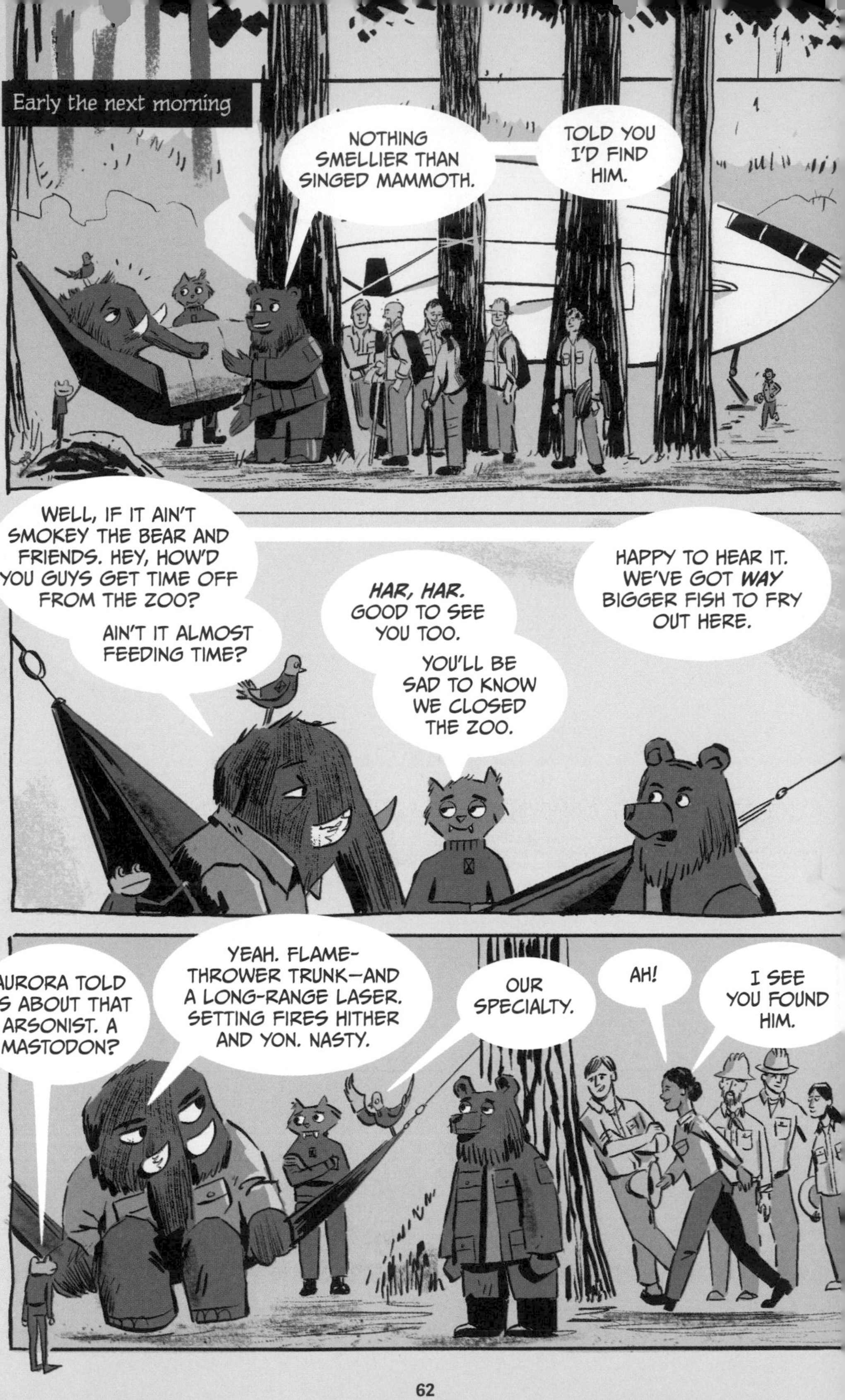
Early the next morning
NOTHING SMELLIER THAN SINGED MAMMOTH.
TOLD YOU I'D FIND HIM.
WELL, IF IT AIN'T SMOKEY THE BEAR AND FRIENDS. HEY, HOW'D YOU GUYS GET TIME OFF FROM THE ZOO?
AIN'T IT ALMOST FEEDING TIME?
HAR, HAR. GOOD TO SEE YOU TOO.
YOU'LL BE SAD TO KNOW WE CLOSED THE ZOO.
HAPPY TO HEAR IT. WE'VE GOT WAY BIGGER FISH TO FRY OUT HERE.
AURORA TOLD US ABOUT THAT ARSONIST. A MASTODON?
YEAH. FLAME-THROWER TRUNK—AND A LONG-RANGE LASER. SETTING FIRES HITHER AND YON. NASTY.
OUR SPECIALTY.
AH!
I SEE YOU FOUND HIM.

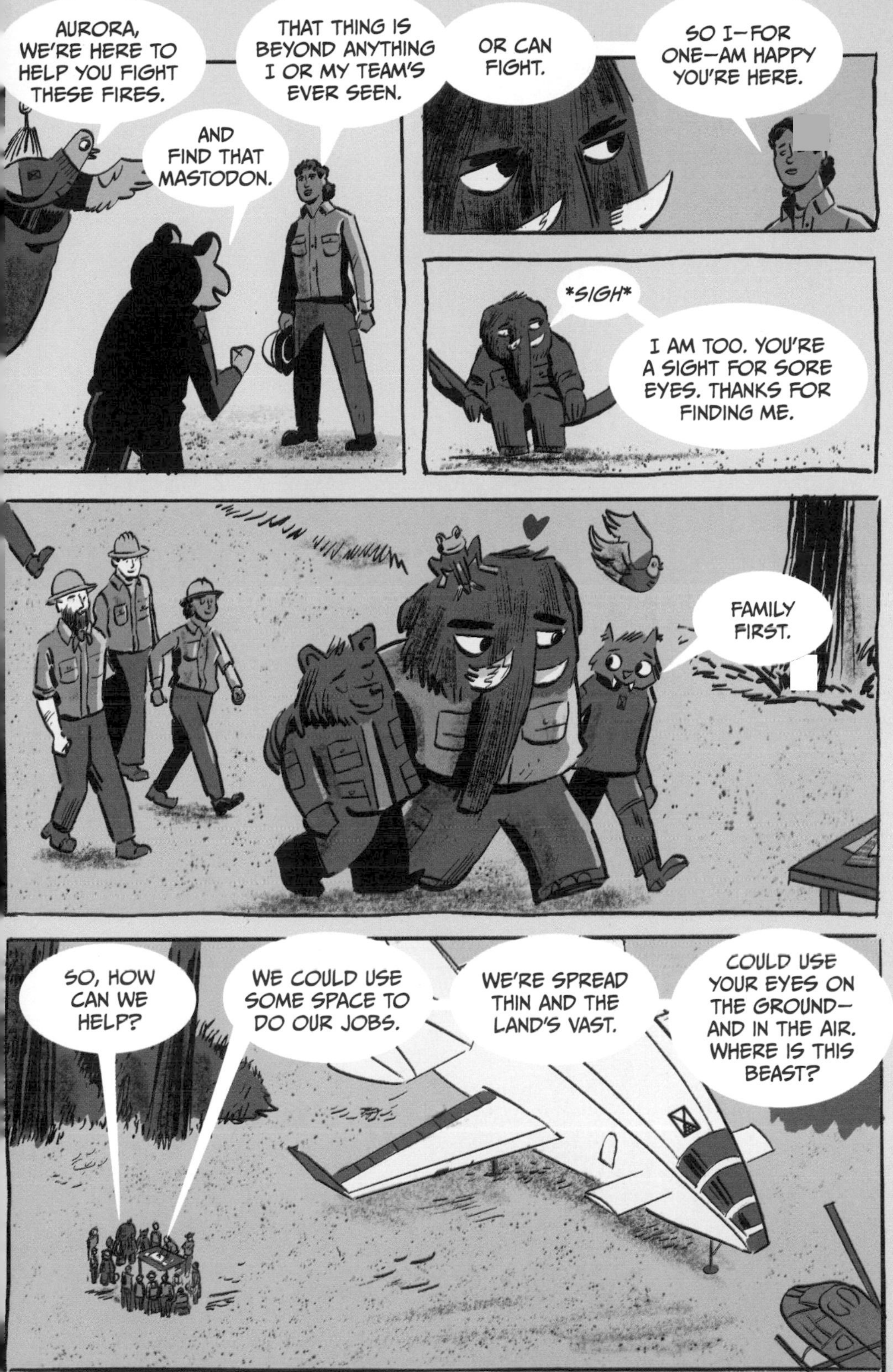
AURORA, WE'RE HERE TO HELP YOU FIGHT THESE FIRES.
AND FIND THAT MASTODON.
THAT THING IS BEYOND ANYTHING I OR MY TEAM'S EVER SEEN.
OR CAN FIGHT.
SO I—FOR ONE—AM HAPPY YOU'RE HERE.
*SIGH*
I AM TOO. YOU'RE A SIGHT FOR SORE EYES. THANKS FOR FINDING ME.
FAMILY FIRST.
SO, HOW CAN WE HELP?
WE COULD USE SOME SPACE TO DO OUR JOBS.
WE'RE SPREAD THIN AND THE LAND'S VAST.
COULD USE YOUR EYES ON THE GROUND—AND IN THE AIR. WHERE IS THIS BEAST?

I COLLECTED LIDAR DATA FOR THE WHOLE VALLEY. THE WINDAR'S COMPUTERS ARE ANALYZING IT NOW.

IT'S A FEW HOURS OLD BUT IT MIGHT YIELD SOME CLUES.

IF I CAN SNIFF OUT A MAMMOTH, I CAN SNIFF OUT A MASTODON.

TAP, TAP!

I'LL RECON . . . FLY THE UPDRAFTS HERE TO KEEP ME ALOFT FOR HOURS AND REPORT IN.

WE'RE GETTING NEW REPORTS OF SPOTTY RADIO SIGNALS IN THE VALLEY. THE CANYON KILLS RADIO SIGNALS.

IT'S TOUGH TO COMMUNICATE WITH ALL OUR CREWS.

I'LL TAKE THE WINDAR UP, CIRCLE OVERHEAD, AND CONVEY MESSAGES TO YOUR DISPATCH.

I COULD ALSO DIRECT YOUR CREWS TO SAFETY ZONES.

NOT TO MENTION KEEP AN EYE OPEN FOR THAT MASTODON.

OUR CAT ON THE HOT TIN ROOF. I LIKE IT.

EXCEPT . . .

SNIFF SNIFF . . .

WHAT IS THE PHRASE . . .

SNIFF SNIFF . . .

THE BEST LAID PLANS OF MICE AND MEN . . .

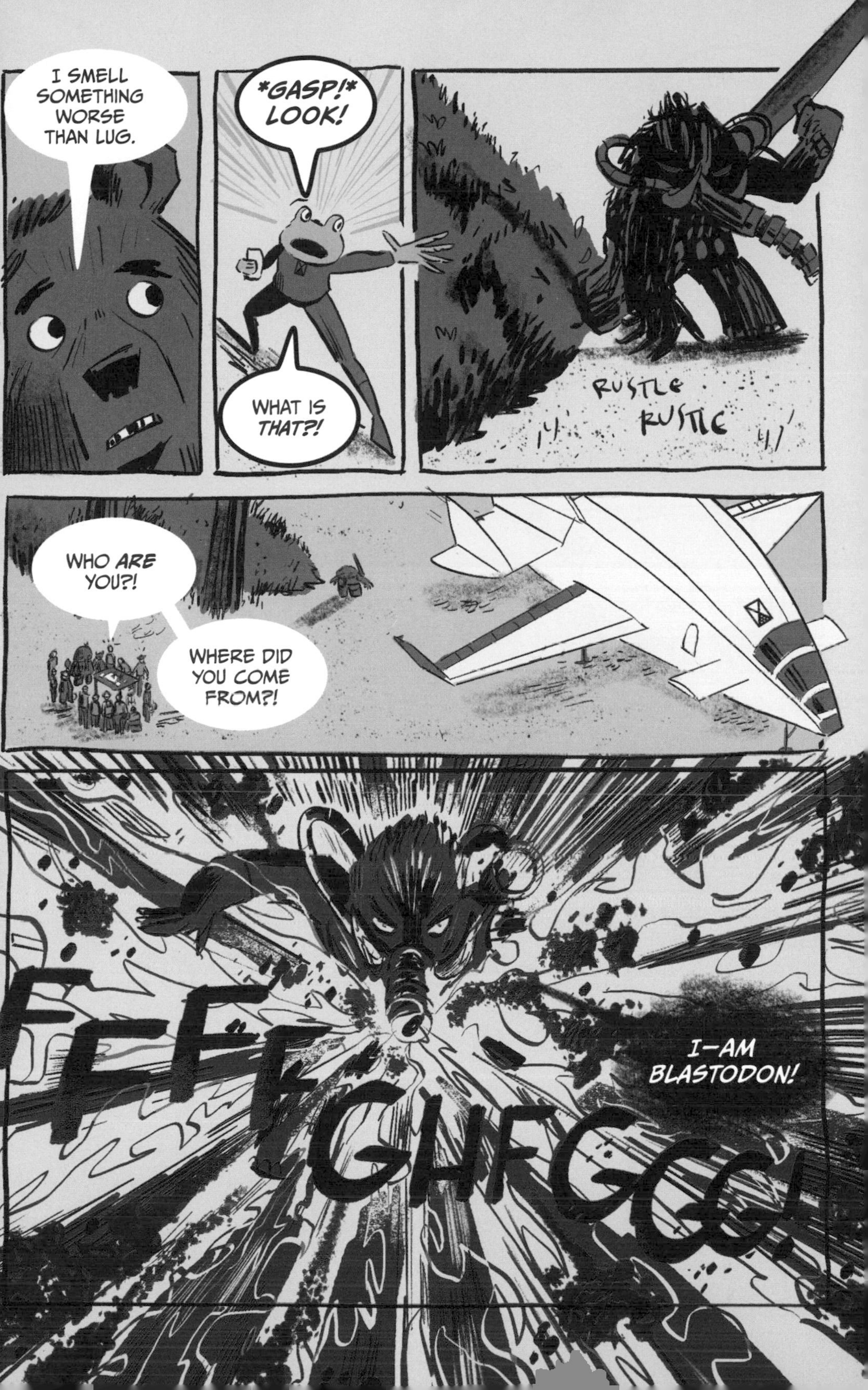

I SMELL SOMETHING WORSE THAN LUG.
*GASP!* LOOK!
WHAT IS THAT?!
RUSTLE RUSTLE
WHO ARE YOU?!
WHERE DID YOU COME FROM?!
FFFFGHFGGG!
I—AM BLASTODON!

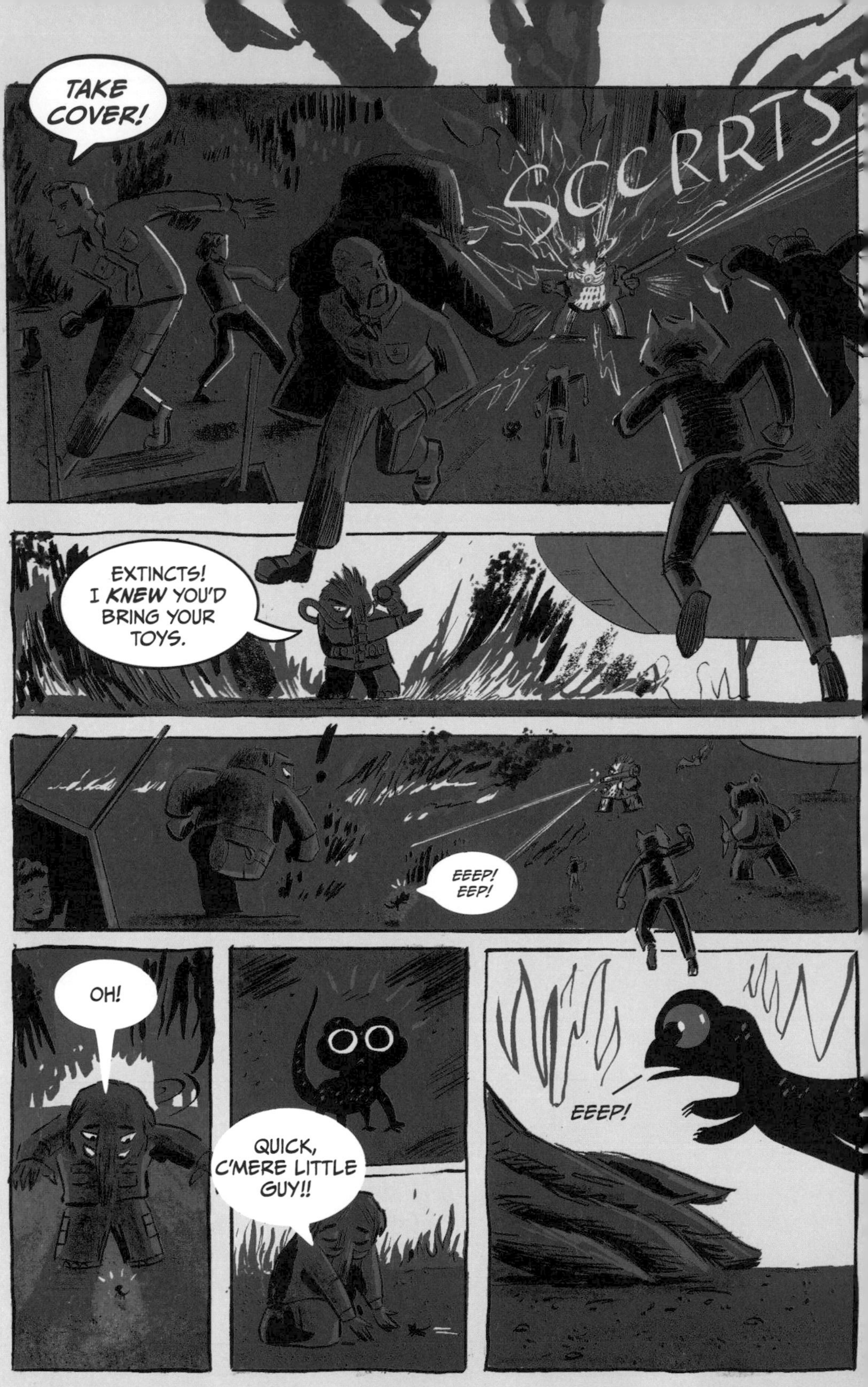
TAKE COVER!
SCCRRTS
EXTINCTS! I KNEW YOU'D BRING YOUR TOYS.
EEEP! EEP!
OH!
QUICK, C'MERE LITTLE GUY!!
EEEP!

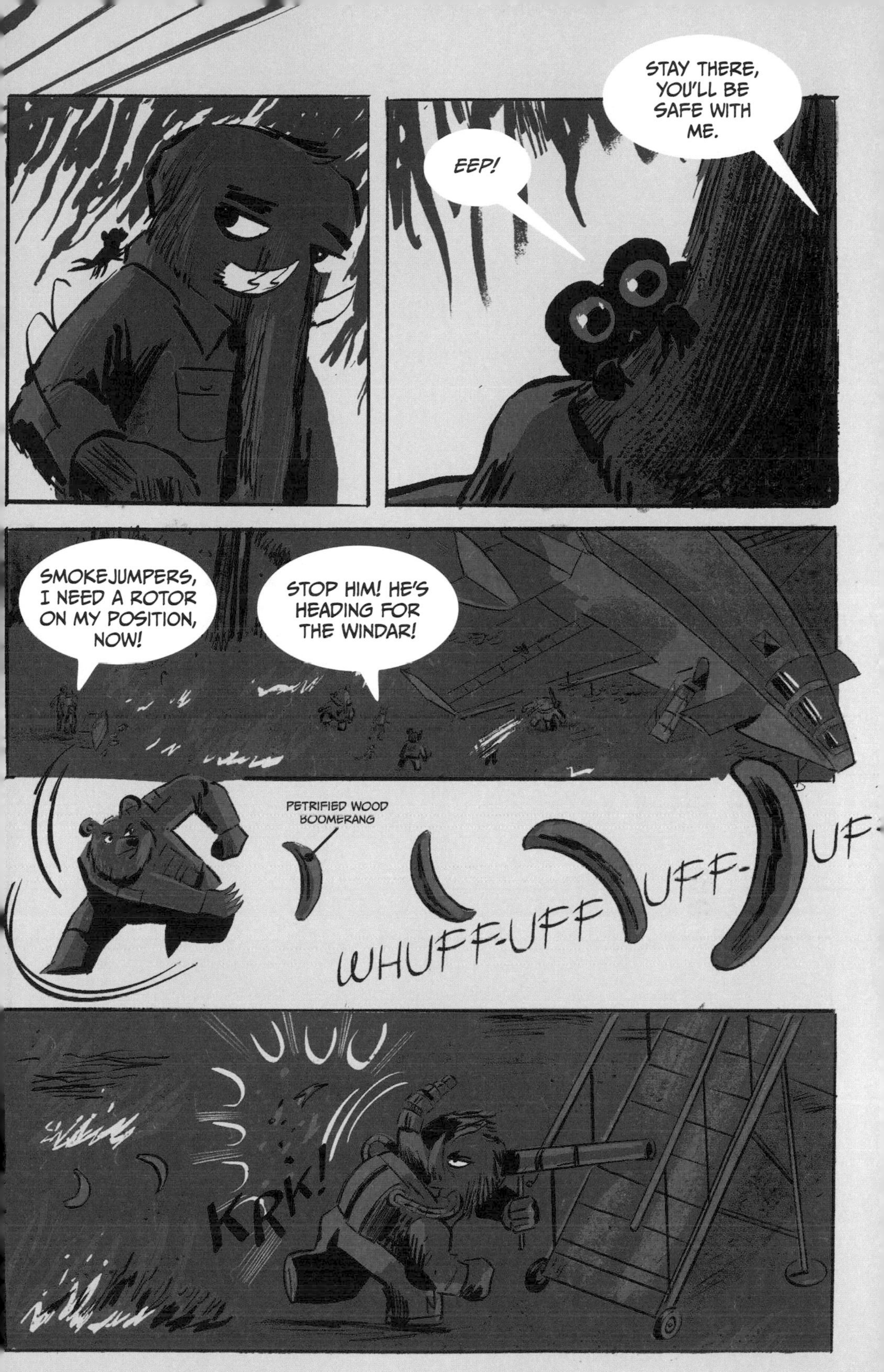
STAY THERE, YOU'LL BE SAFE WITH ME.
EEP!
SMOKEJUMPERS, I NEED A ROTOR ON MY POSITION, NOW!
STOP HIM! HE'S HEADING FOR THE WINDAR!
PETRIFIED WOOD BOOMERANG
WHUFF-UFF UFF- UF-
KRK!

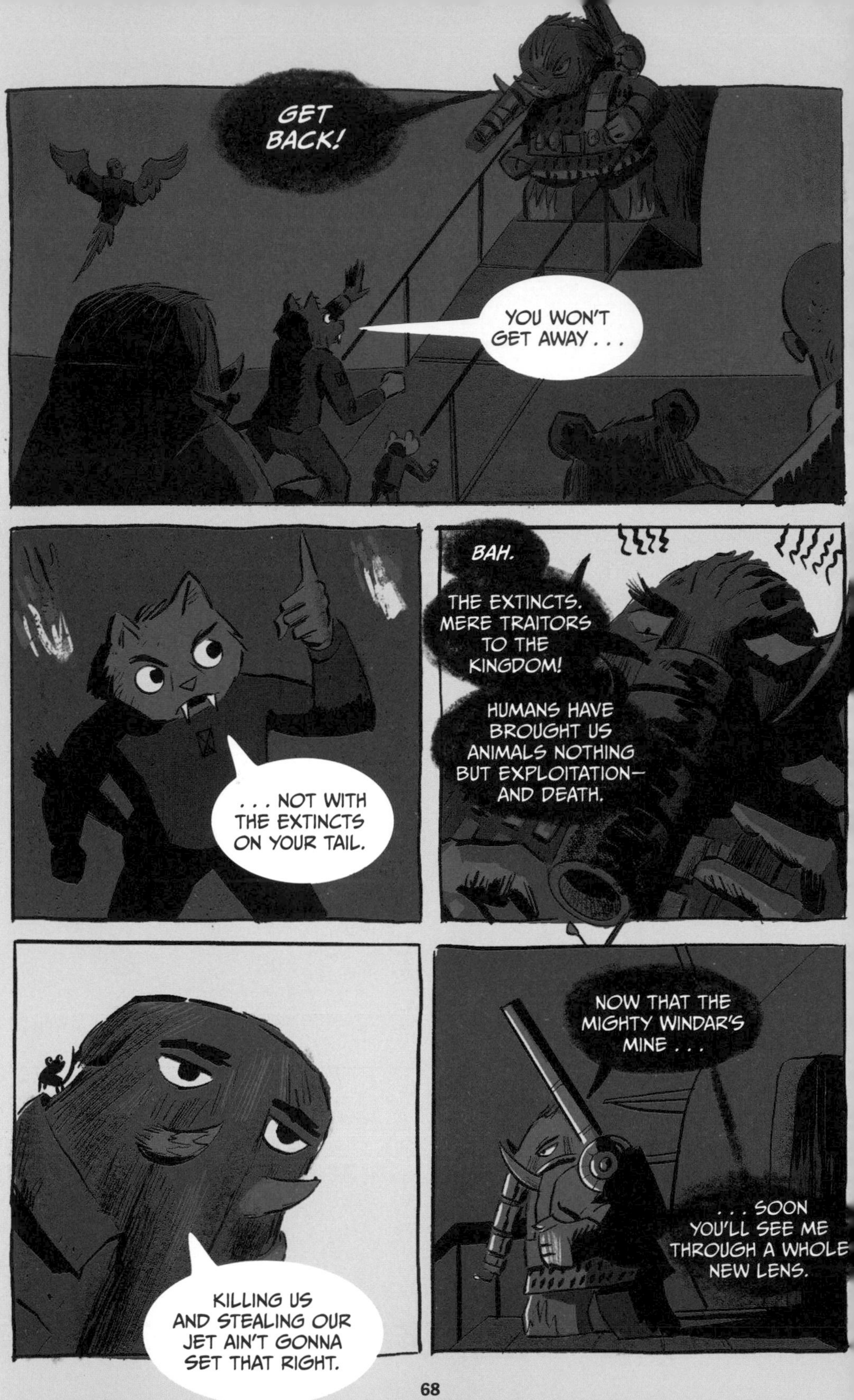
GET BACK!
YOU WON'T GET AWAY . . .
. . . NOT WITH THE EXTINCTS ON YOUR TAIL.
BAH.
THE EXTINCTS. MERE TRAITORS TO THE KINGDOM!
HUMANS HAVE BROUGHT US ANIMALS NOTHING BUT EXPLOITATION— AND DEATH.
KILLING US AND STEALING OUR JET AIN'T GONNA SET THAT RIGHT.
NOW THAT THE MIGHTY WINDAR'S MINE . . .
. . . SOON YOU'LL SEE ME THROUGH A WHOLE NEW LENS.

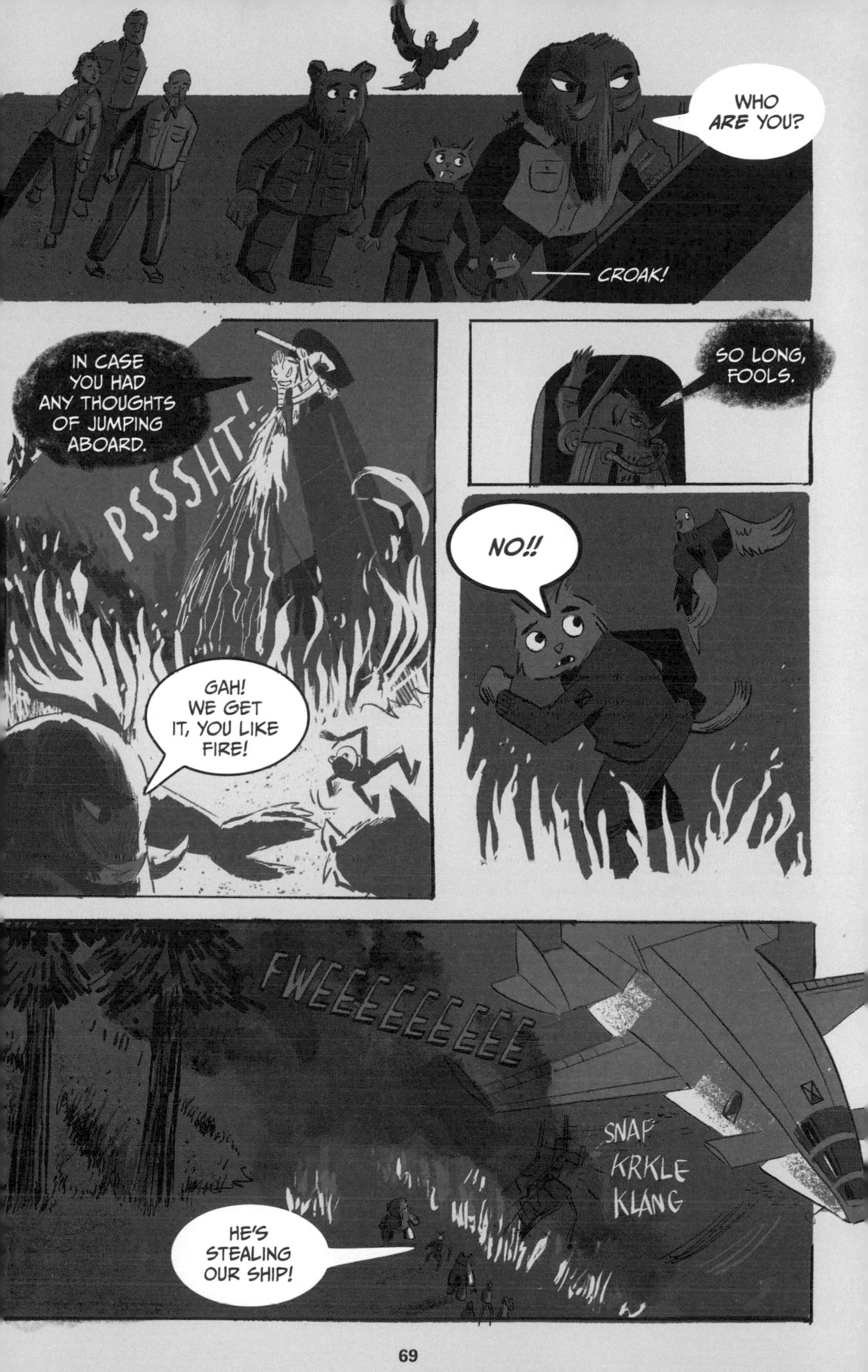
WHO ARE YOU?
CROAK!
IN CASE YOU HAD ANY THOUGHTS OF JUMPING ABOARD.
PSSSHT!
GAH! WE GET IT, YOU LIKE FIRE!
SO LONG, FOOLS.
NO!!
FWEEEEEEEEEE
SNAP
KRKLE
KLANG
HE'S STEALING OUR SHIP!

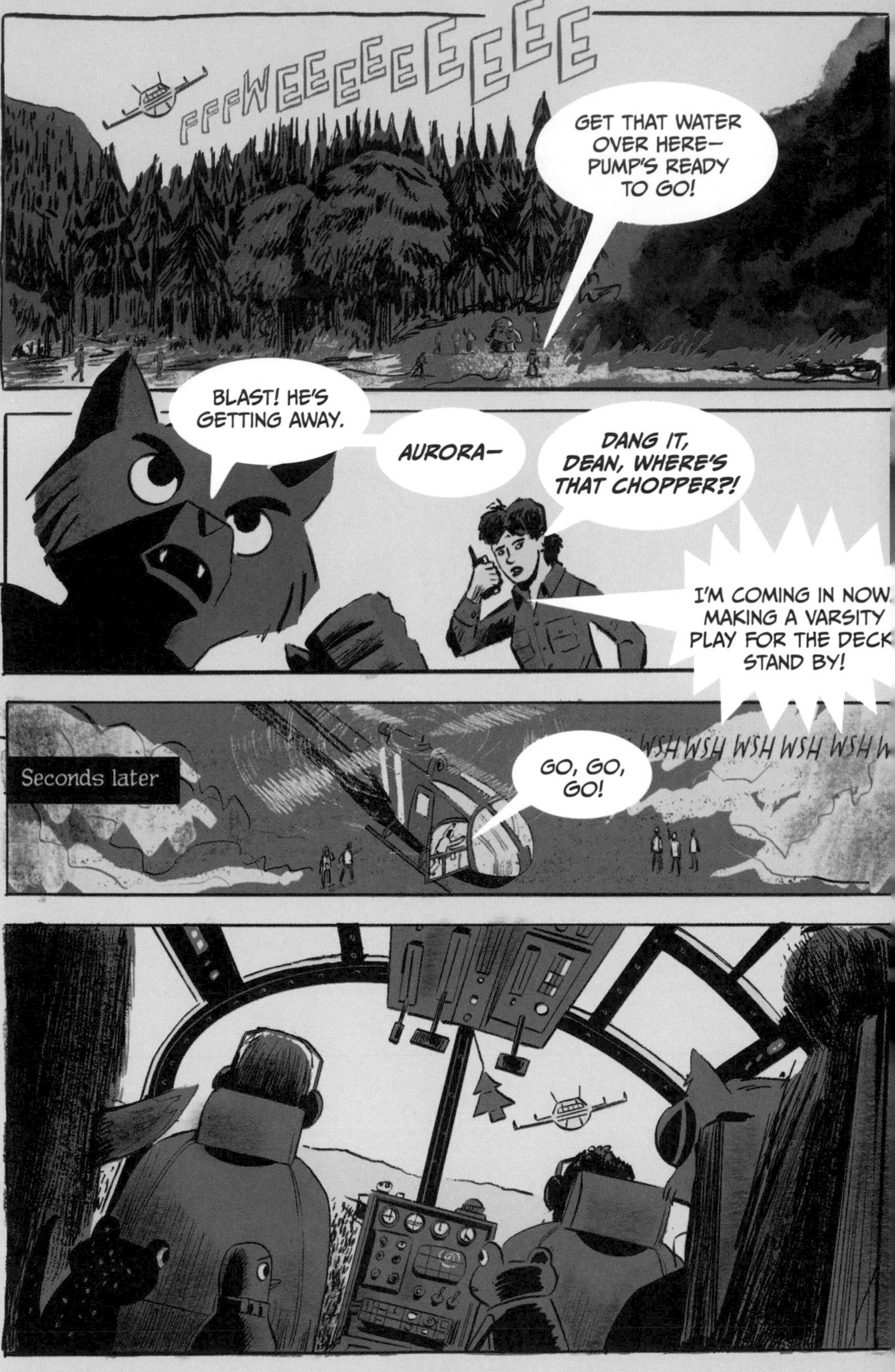
FFFWEEEEEEEEEE
GET THAT WATER OVER HERE— PUMP'S READY TO GO!
BLAST! HE'S GETTING AWAY.
AURORA—
DANG IT, DEAN, WHERE'S THAT CHOPPER?!
I'M COMING IN NOW. MAKING A VARSITY PLAY FOR THE DECK. STAND BY!
Seconds later
WSH WSH WSH WSH WSH
GO, GO, GO!

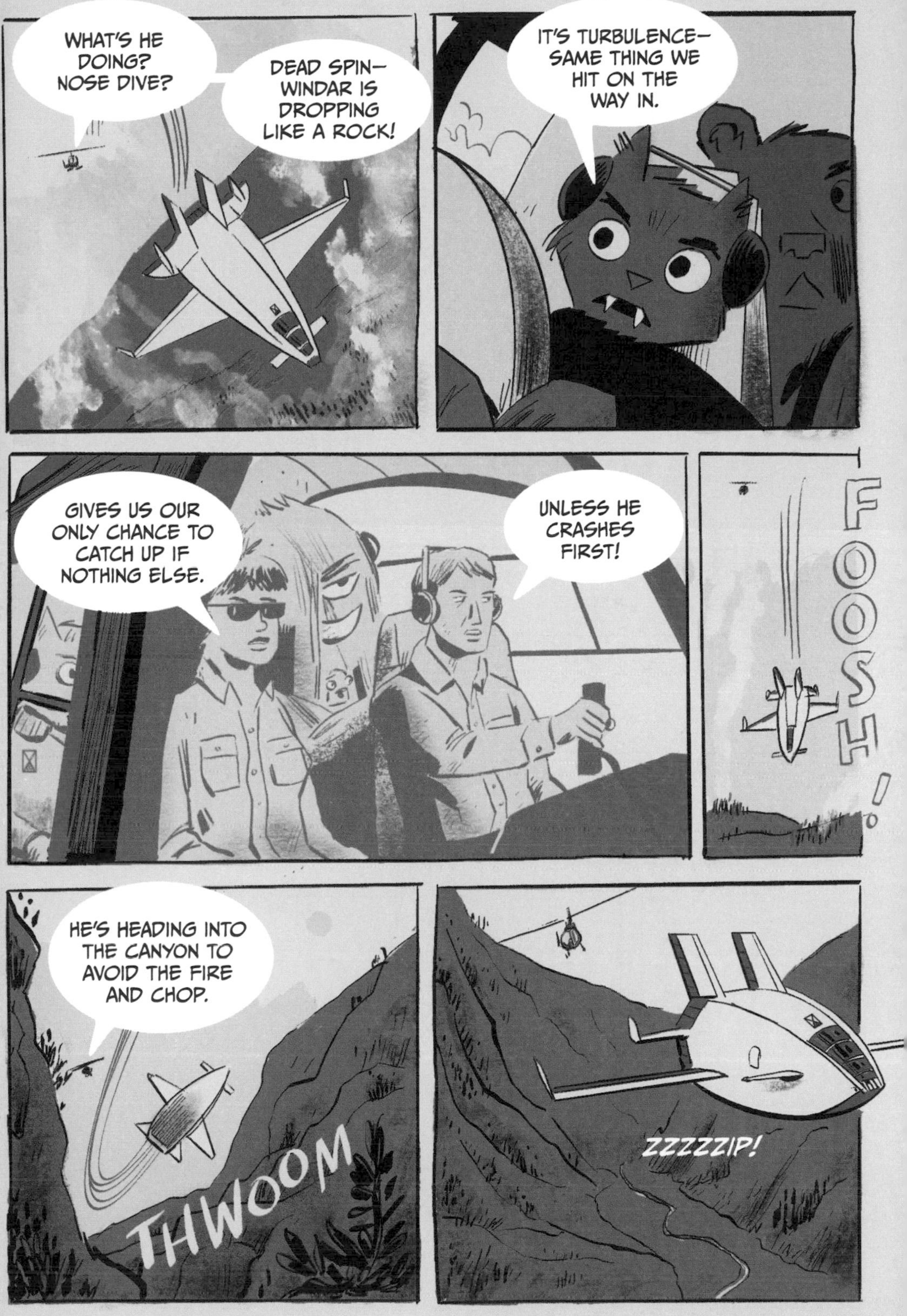
WHAT'S HE DOING? NOSE DIVE?
DEAD SPIN— WINDAR IS DROPPING LIKE A ROCK!
IT'S TURBULENCE— SAME THING WE HIT ON THE WAY IN.
GIVES US OUR ONLY CHANCE TO CATCH UP IF NOTHING ELSE.
UNLESS HE CRASHES FIRST!
FOOSH!
HE'S HEADING INTO THE CANYON TO AVOID THE FIRE AND CHOP.
THWOOM
ZZZZZIP!

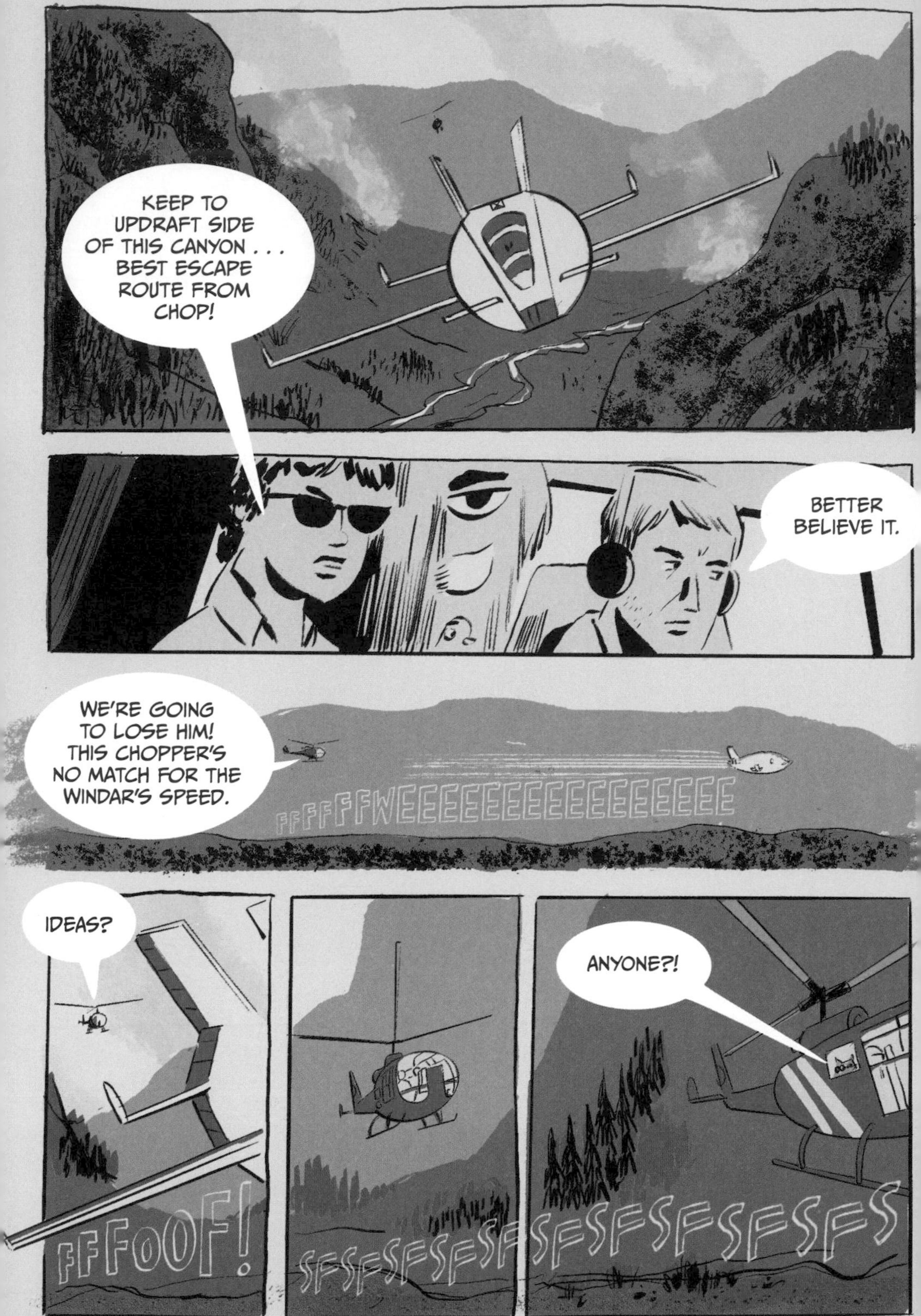
KEEP TO UPDRAFT SIDE OF THIS CANYON . . . BEST ESCAPE ROUTE FROM CHOP!
BETTER BELIEVE IT.
WE'RE GOING TO LOSE HIM! THIS CHOPPER'S NO MATCH FOR THE WINDAR'S SPEED.
FFFFFFWEEEEEEEEEEEEEEEEEEE
IDEAS?
FFFOOF!
SFSFSFSFSFSFSFSFSFSFSFS
ANYONE?!

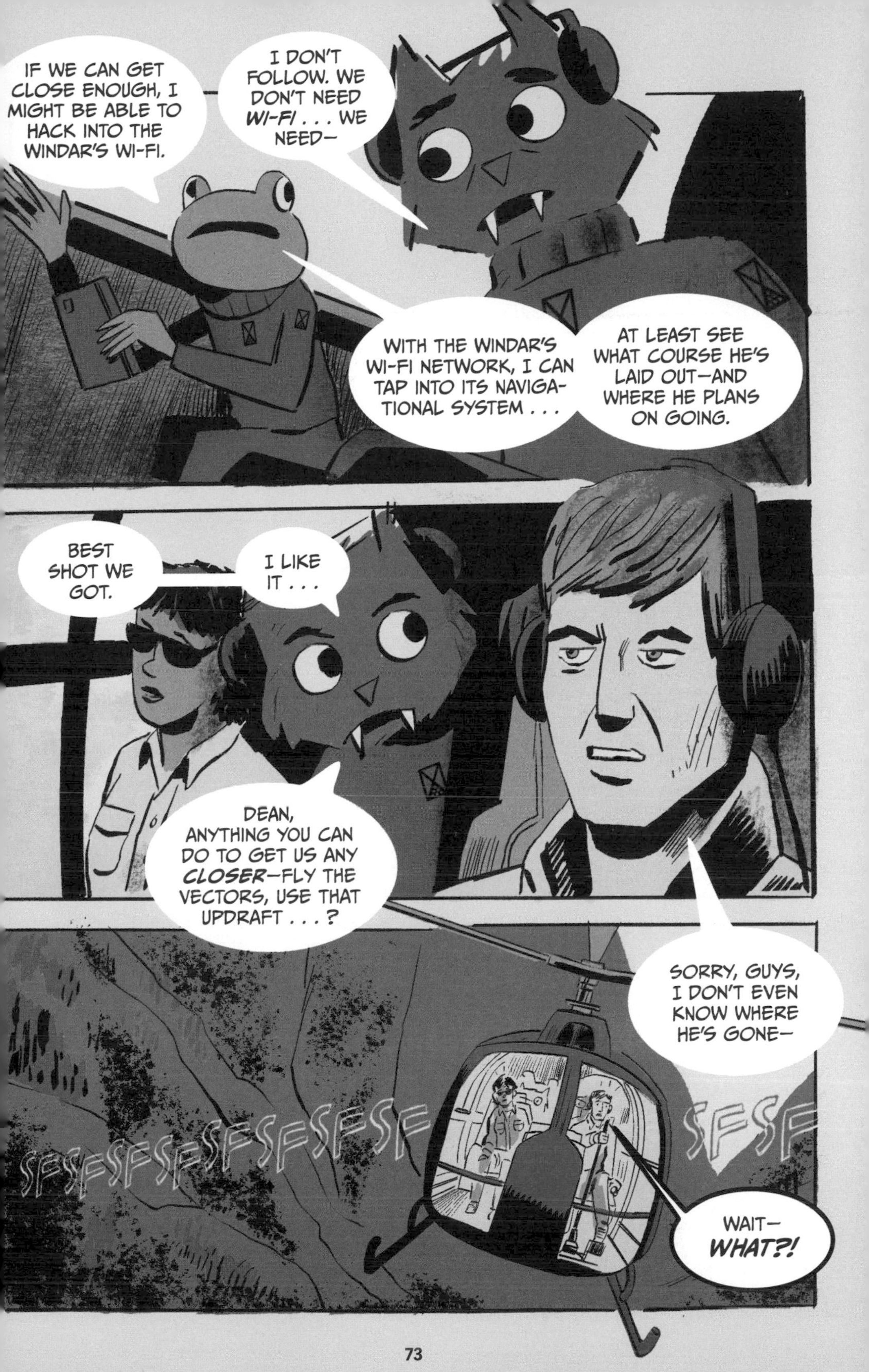
IF WE CAN GET CLOSE ENOUGH, I MIGHT BE ABLE TO HACK INTO THE WINDAR'S WI-FI.
I DON'T FOLLOW. WE DON'T NEED *WI-FI* . . . WE NEED—
WITH THE WINDAR'S WI-FI NETWORK, I CAN TAP INTO ITS NAVIGATIONAL SYSTEM . . .
AT LEAST SEE WHAT COURSE HE'S LAID OUT—AND WHERE HE PLANS ON GOING.
BEST SHOT WE GOT.
I LIKE IT . . .
DEAN, ANYTHING YOU CAN DO TO GET US ANY *CLOSER*—FLY THE VECTORS, USE THAT UPDRAFT . . . ?
SORRY, GUYS, I DON'T EVEN KNOW WHERE HE'S GONE—
SFSFSFSFSFSFSFSF
SFSF
WAIT— **WHAT?!**

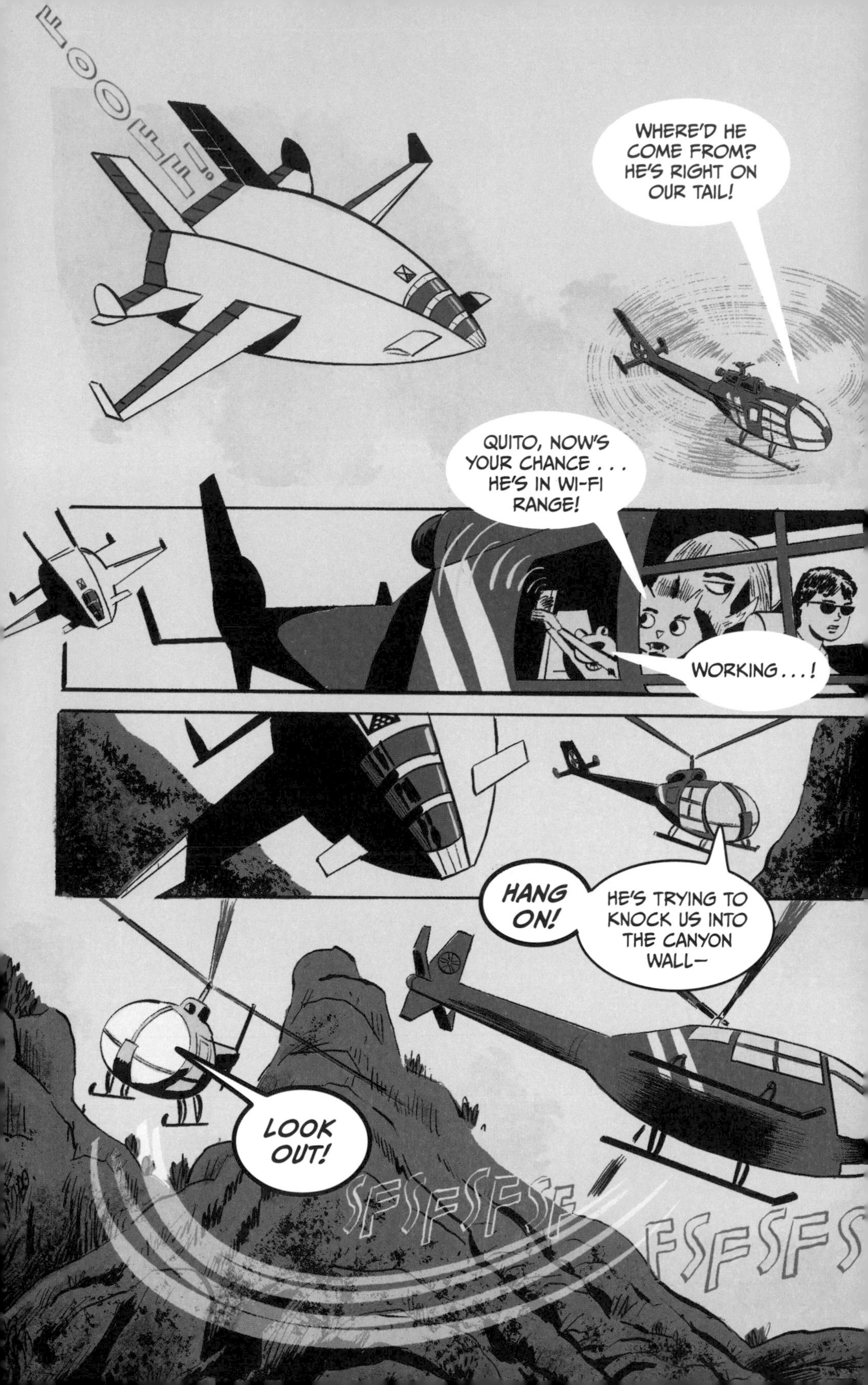
FOOSH!
WHERE'D HE COME FROM? HE'S RIGHT ON OUR TAIL!
QUITO, NOW'S YOUR CHANCE . . . HE'S IN WI-FI RANGE!
WORKING . . . !
HANG ON!
HE'S TRYING TO KNOCK US INTO THE CANYON WALL—
LOOK OUT!
SFSFSFSF
FSFSFS

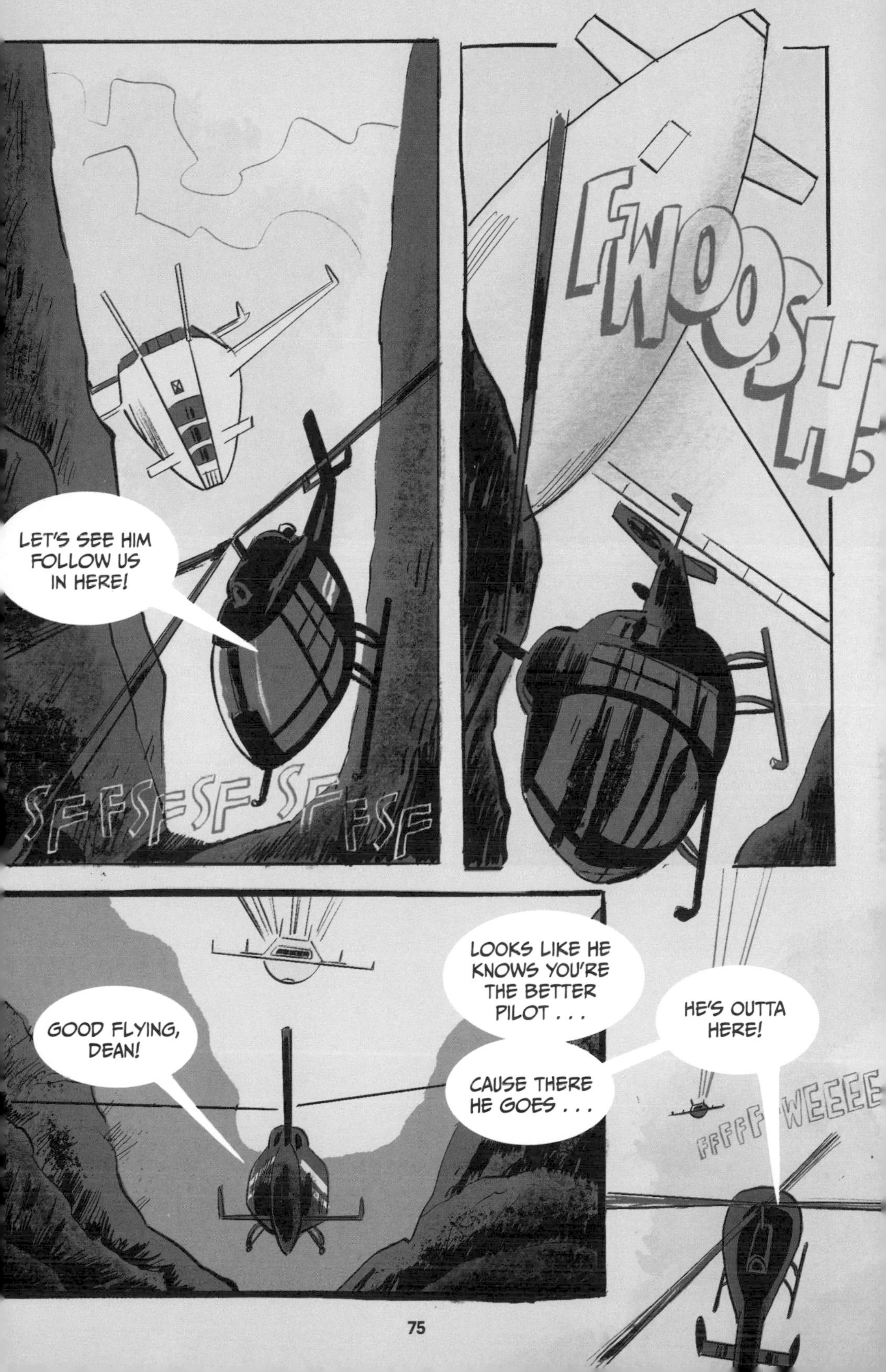

LET'S SEE HIM FOLLOW US IN HERE!
SFFSFSFSFFSF
FWOOSH!
GOOD FLYING, DEAN!
LOOKS LIKE HE KNOWS YOU'RE THE BETTER PILOT . . .
CAUSE THERE HE GOES . . .
HE'S OUTTA HERE!
FFFFF WEEEE

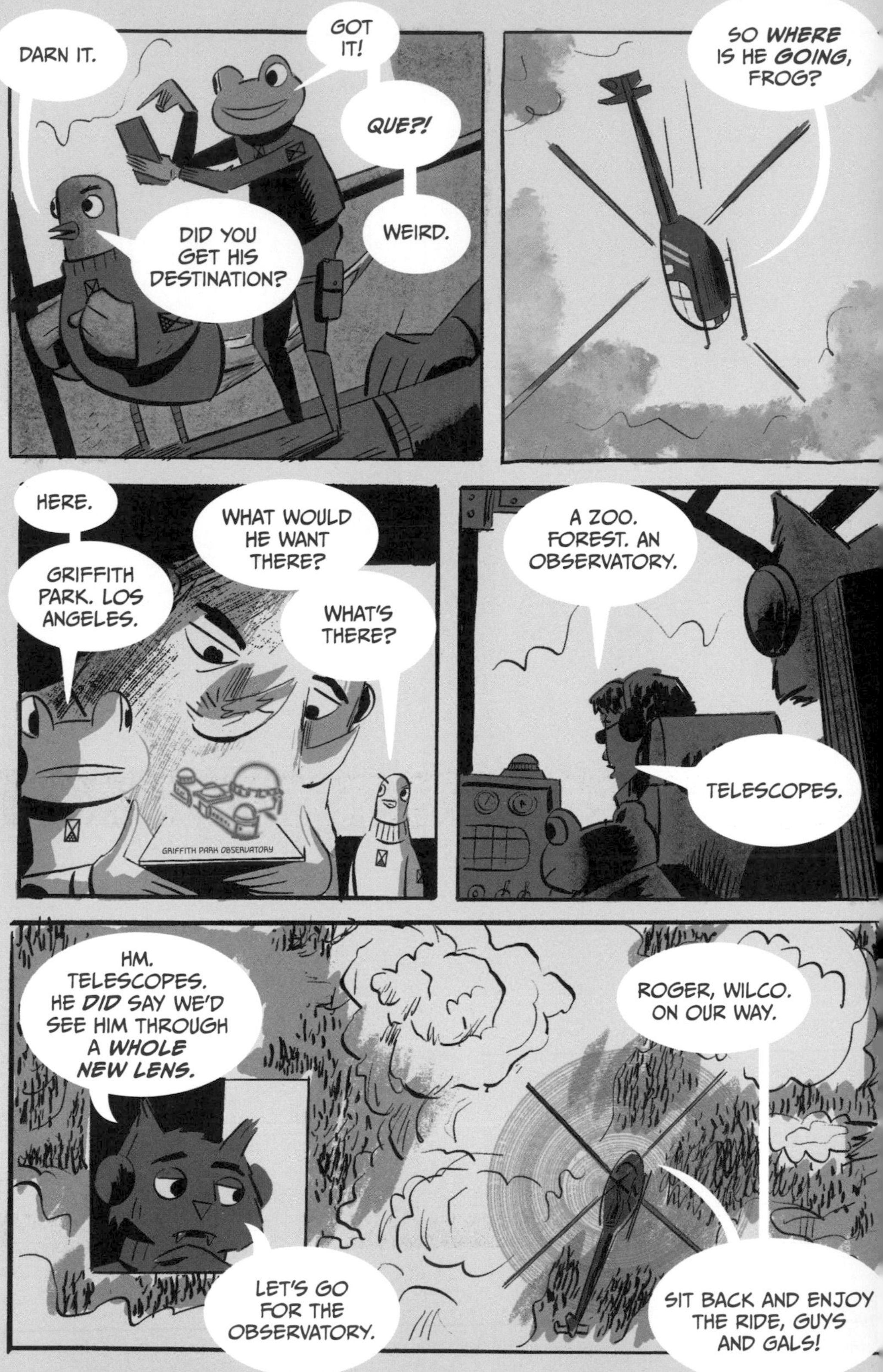
DARN IT.
GOT IT!
QUE?!
WEIRD.
DID YOU GET HIS DESTINATION?
SO *WHERE* IS HE *GOING*, FROG?
HERE.
GRIFFITH PARK. LOS ANGELES.
WHAT WOULD HE WANT THERE?
WHAT'S THERE?
GRIFFITH PARK OBSERVATORY
A ZOO. FOREST. AN OBSERVATORY.
TELESCOPES.
HM. TELESCOPES. HE *DID* SAY WE'D SEE HIM THROUGH A *WHOLE NEW LENS.*
LET'S GO FOR THE OBSERVATORY.
ROGER, WILCO. ON OUR WAY.
SIT BACK AND ENJOY THE RIDE, GUYS AND GALS!

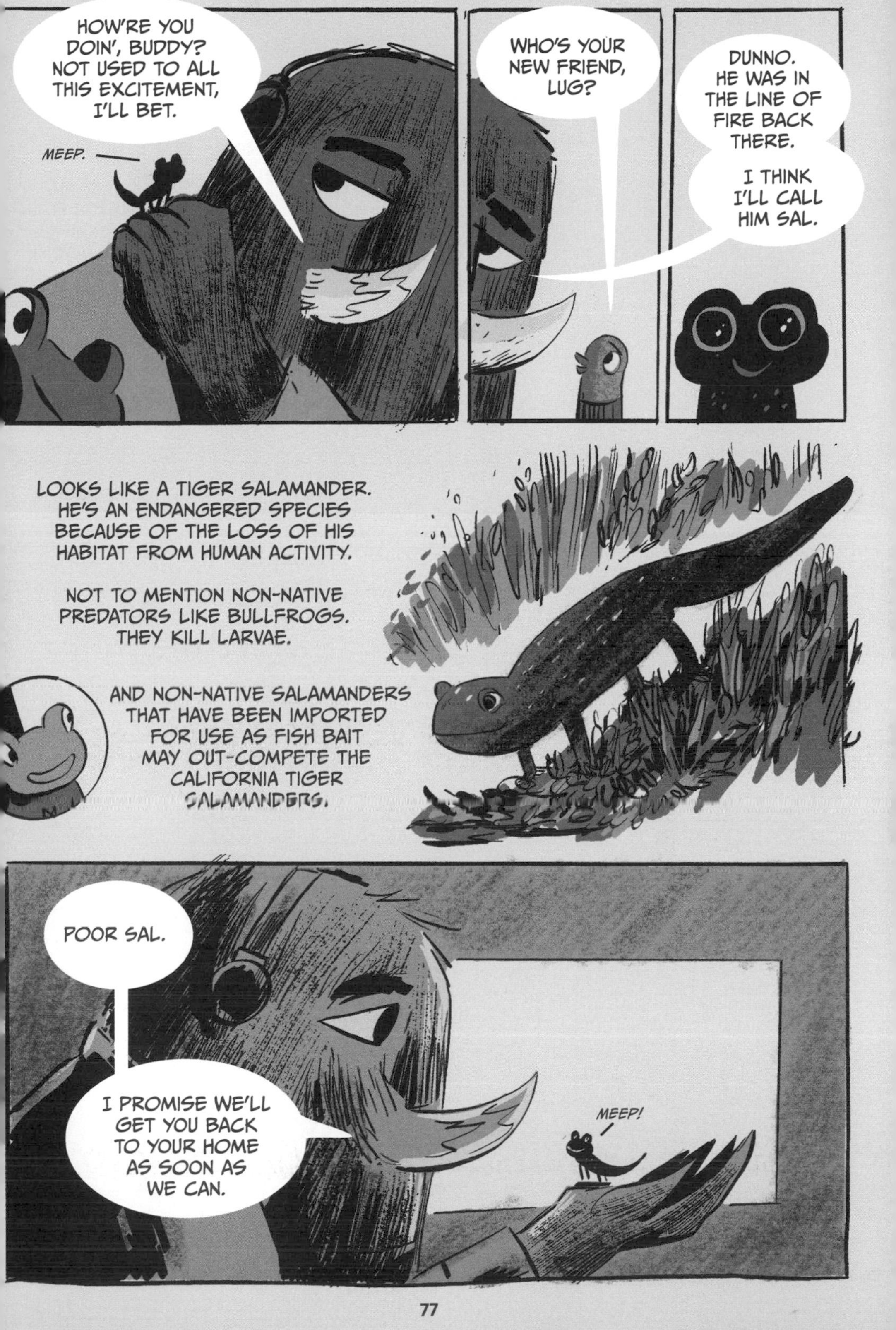
HOW'RE YOU DOIN', BUDDY? NOT USED TO ALL THIS EXCITEMENT, I'LL BET.
MEEP.
WHO'S YOUR NEW FRIEND, LUG?
DUNNO. HE WAS IN THE LINE OF FIRE BACK THERE.
I THINK I'LL CALL HIM SAL.
LOOKS LIKE A TIGER SALAMANDER. HE'S AN ENDANGERED SPECIES BECAUSE OF THE LOSS OF HIS HABITAT FROM HUMAN ACTIVITY.
NOT TO MENTION NON-NATIVE PREDATORS LIKE BULLFROGS. THEY KILL LARVAE.
AND NON-NATIVE SALAMANDERS THAT HAVE BEEN IMPORTED FOR USE AS FISH BAIT MAY OUT-COMPETE THE CALIFORNIA TIGER SALAMANDERS.
POOR SAL.
I PROMISE WE'LL GET YOU BACK TO YOUR HOME AS SOON AS WE CAN.
MEEP!

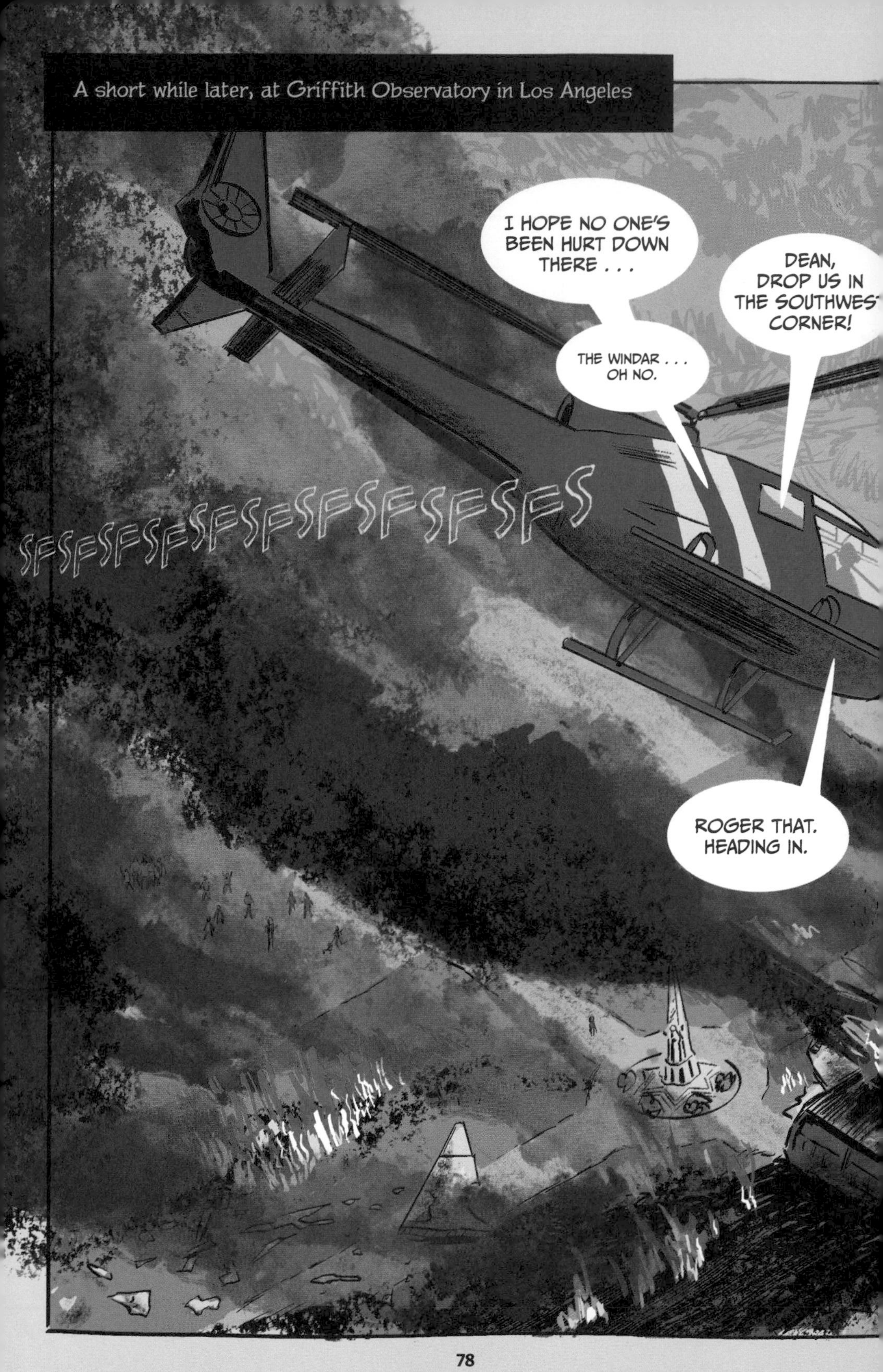
A short while later, at Griffith Observatory in Los Angeles
I HOPE NO ONE'S BEEN HURT DOWN THERE . . .
THE WINDAR . . . OH NO.
DEAN, DROP US IN THE SOUTHWES CORNER!
SFSFSFSFSFSFSFSFSFSFSFSFS
ROGER THAT. HEADING IN.

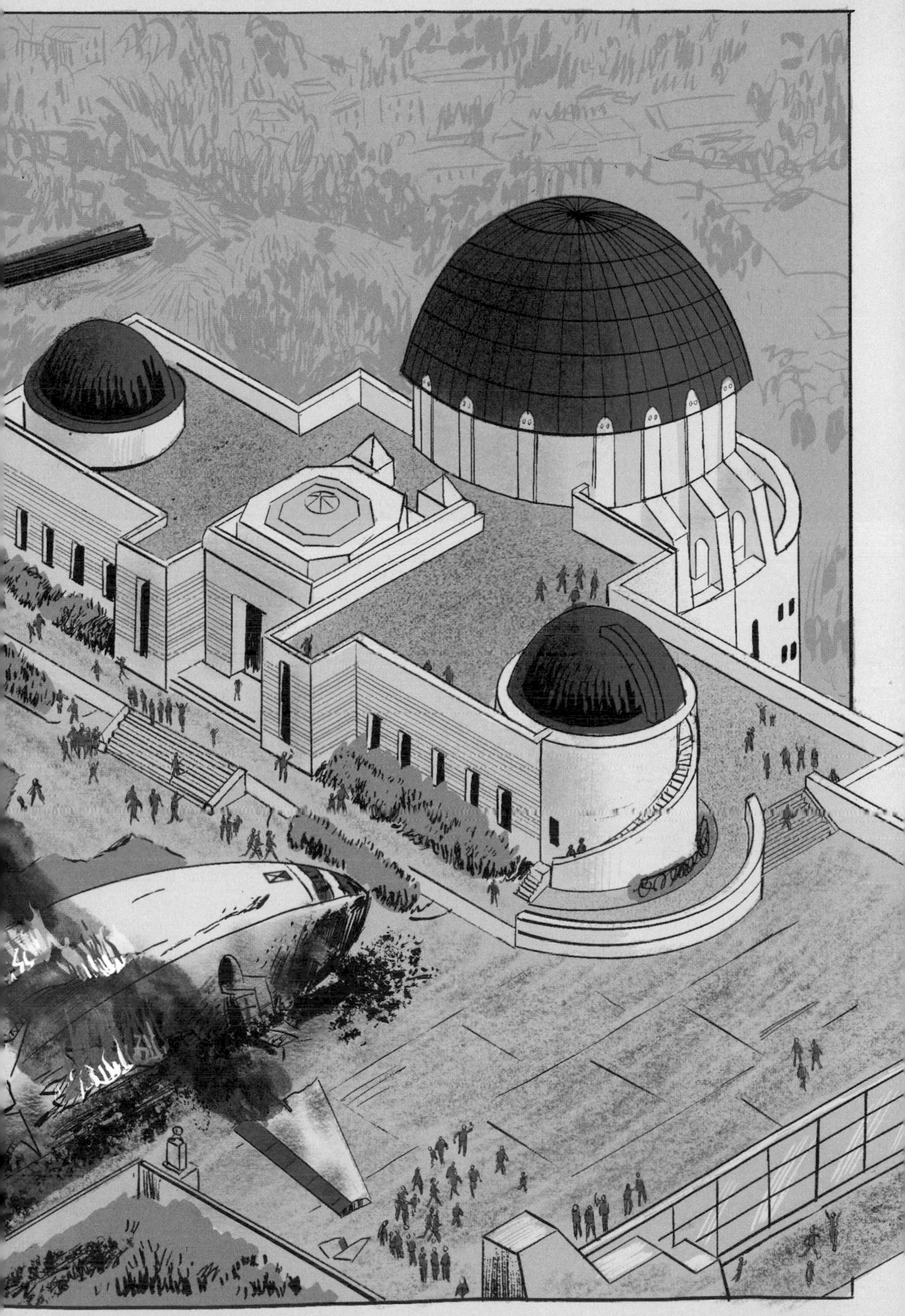

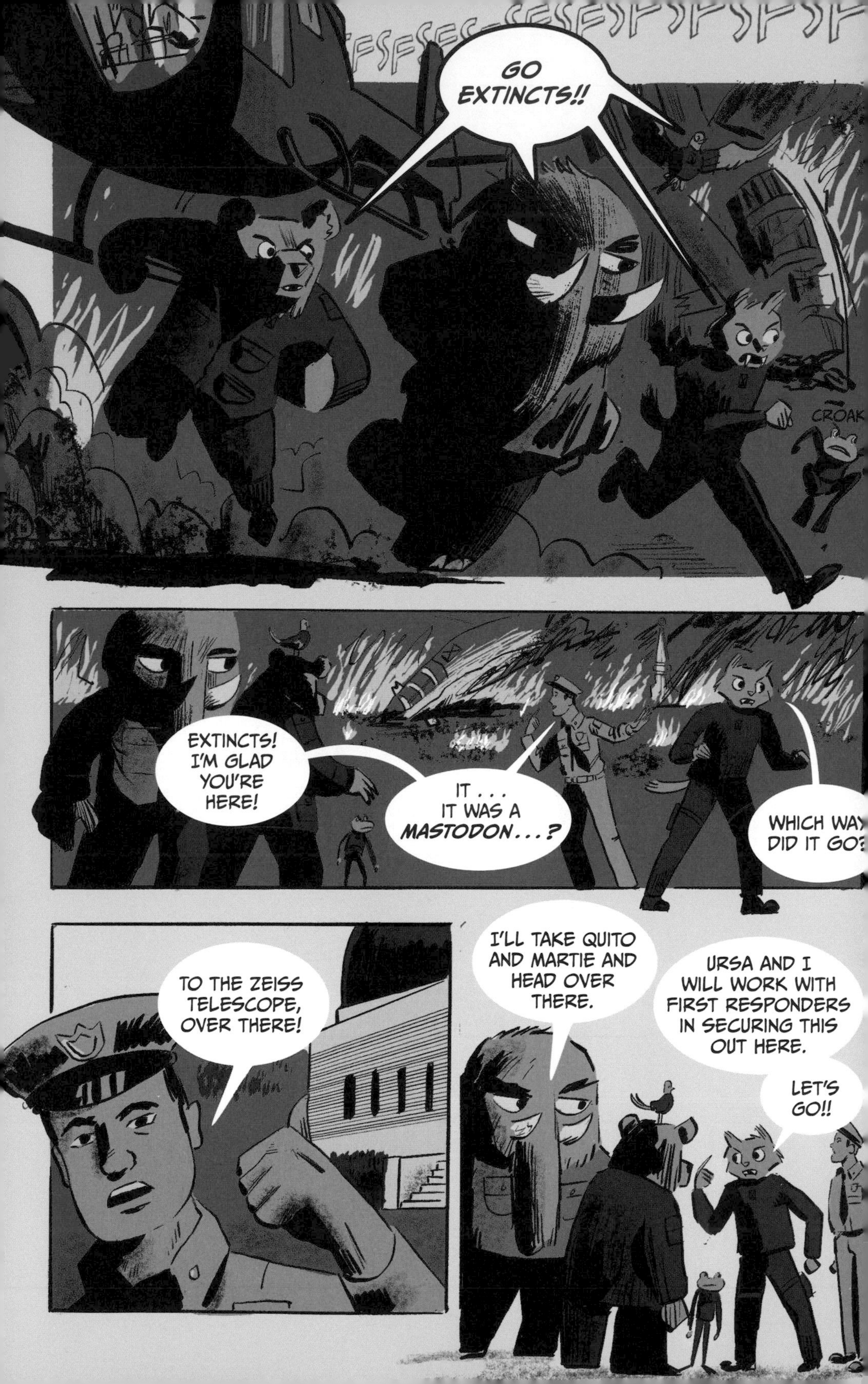
FSFSFSFS-SFSFSFSFSFSF
GO EXTINCTS!!
CROAK
EXTINCTS! I'M GLAD YOU'RE HERE!
IT . . . IT WAS A MASTODON . . . ?
WHICH WAY DID IT GO?
TO THE ZEISS TELESCOPE, OVER THERE!
I'LL TAKE QUITO AND MARTIE AND HEAD OVER THERE.
URSA AND I WILL WORK WITH FIRST RESPONDERS IN SECURING THIS OUT HERE.
LET'S GO!!

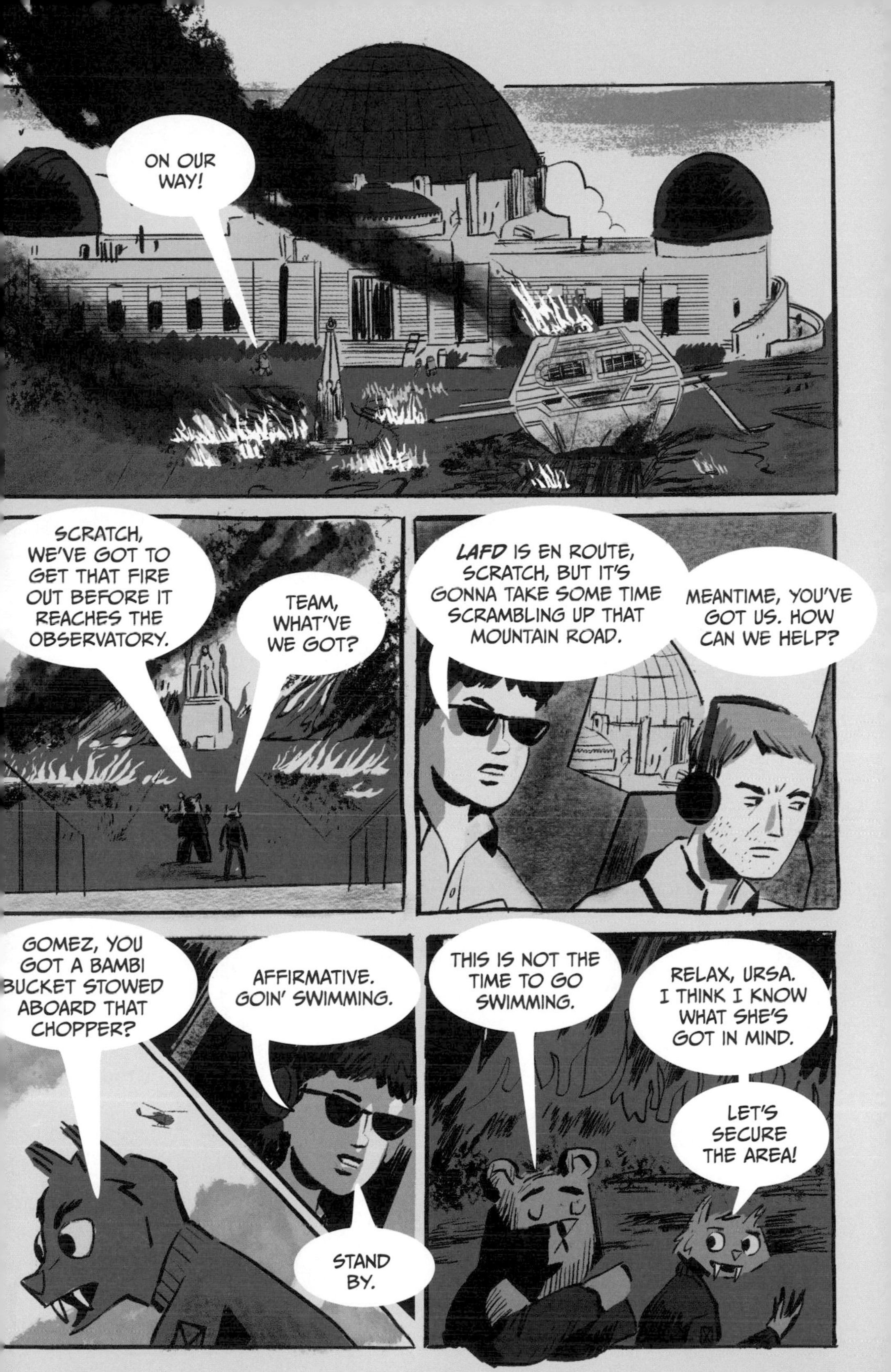
ON OUR WAY!
SCRATCH, WE'VE GOT TO GET THAT FIRE OUT BEFORE IT REACHES THE OBSERVATORY.
TEAM, WHAT'VE WE GOT?
*LAFD* IS EN ROUTE, SCRATCH, BUT IT'S GONNA TAKE SOME TIME SCRAMBLING UP THAT MOUNTAIN ROAD.
MEANTIME, YOU'VE GOT US. HOW CAN WE HELP?
GOMEZ, YOU GOT A BAMBI BUCKET STOWED ABOARD THAT CHOPPER?
AFFIRMATIVE. GOIN' SWIMMING.
STAND BY.
THIS IS NOT THE TIME TO GO SWIMMING.
RELAX, URSA. I THINK I KNOW WHAT SHE'S GOT IN MIND.
LET'S SECURE THE AREA!

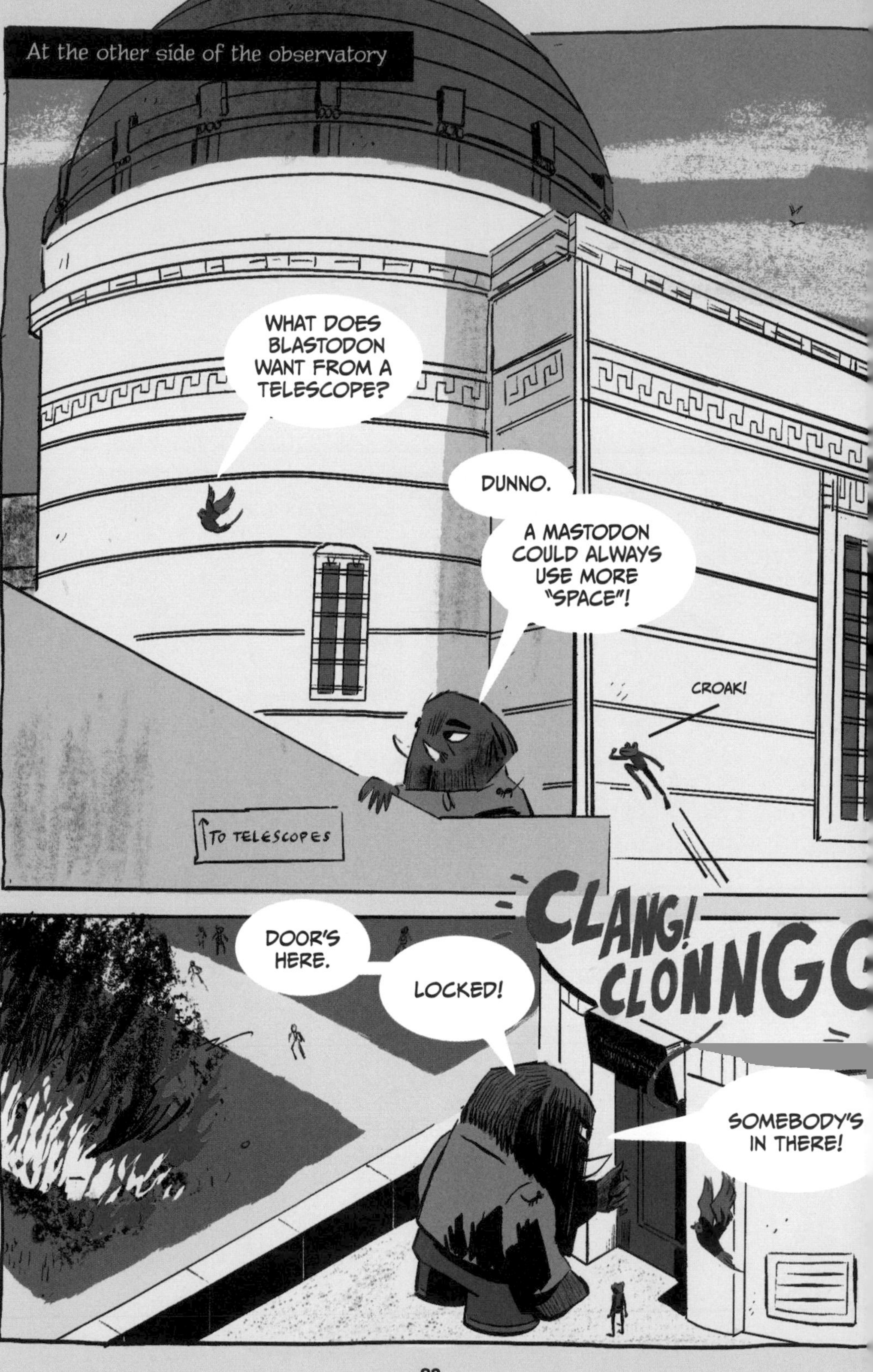
At the other side of the observatory
WHAT DOES BLASTODON WANT FROM A TELESCOPE?
DUNNO.
A MASTODON COULD ALWAYS USE MORE "SPACE"!
CROAK!
TO TELESCOPES
CLANG! CLONNGG
DOOR'S HERE.
LOCKED!
SOMEBODY'S IN THERE!

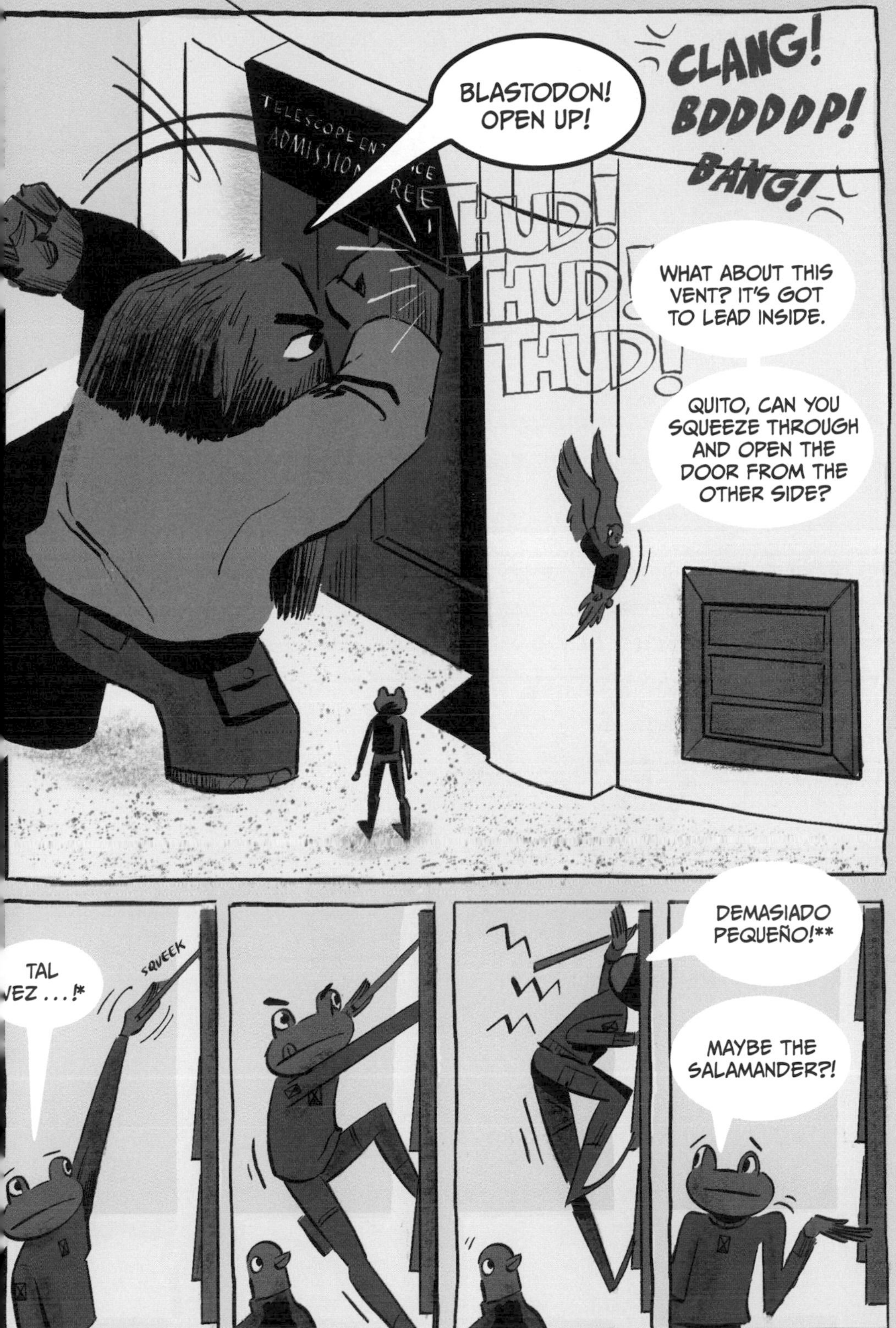
TELESCOPE ENTRANCE
ADMISSION FREE
BLASTODON! OPEN UP!
CLANG! BDDDDP! BANG!
THUD! THUD! THUD!
WHAT ABOUT THIS VENT? IT'S GOT TO LEAD INSIDE.
QUITO, CAN YOU SQUEEZE THROUGH AND OPEN THE DOOR FROM THE OTHER SIDE?
TAL VEZ . . . !*
SQUEEK
DEMASIADO PEQUEÑO!**
MAYBE THE SALAMANDER?!

* Maybe!

** Too small!

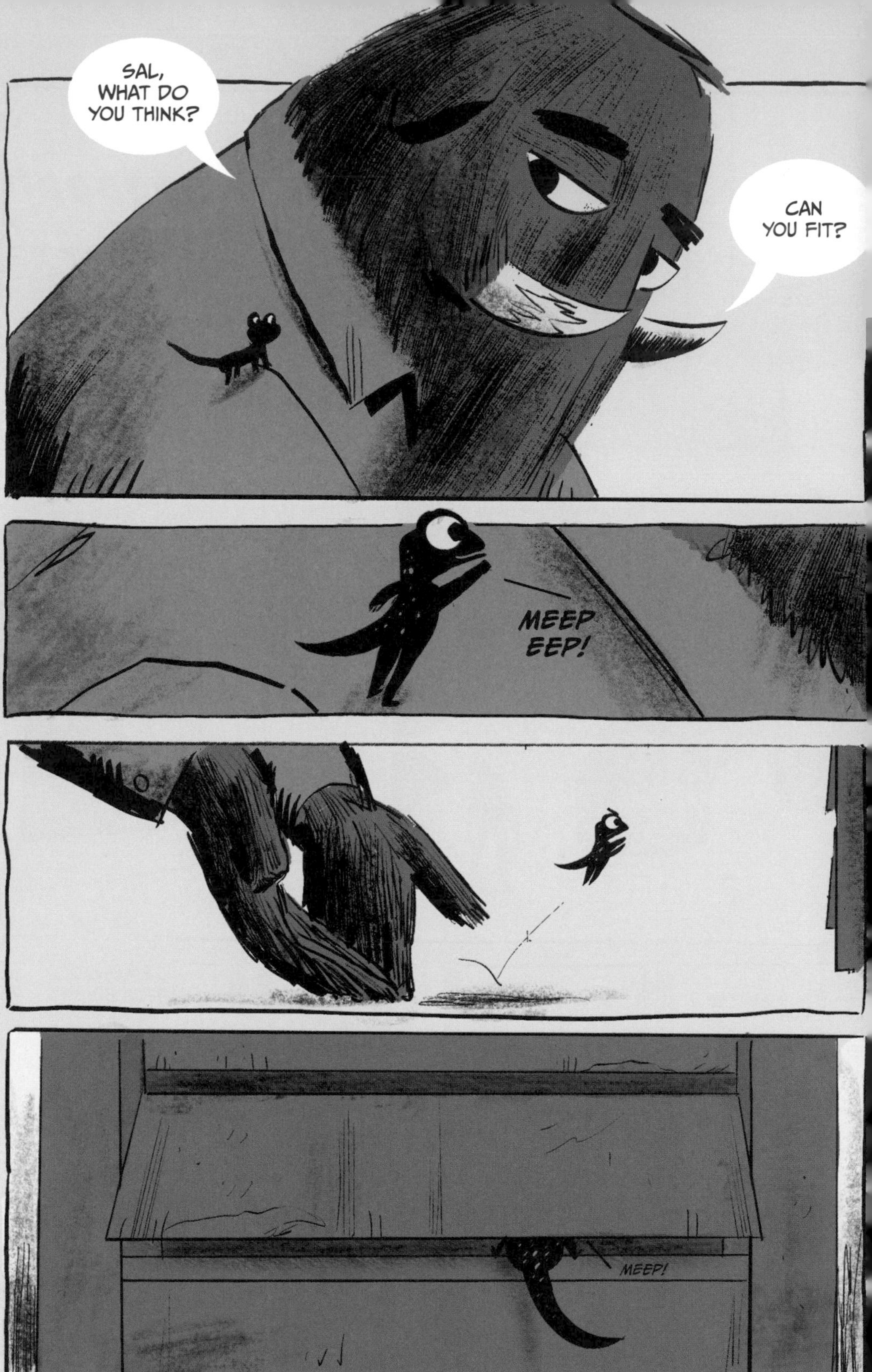
SAL, WHAT DO YOU THINK?
CAN YOU FIT?
MEEP EEP!
MEEP!

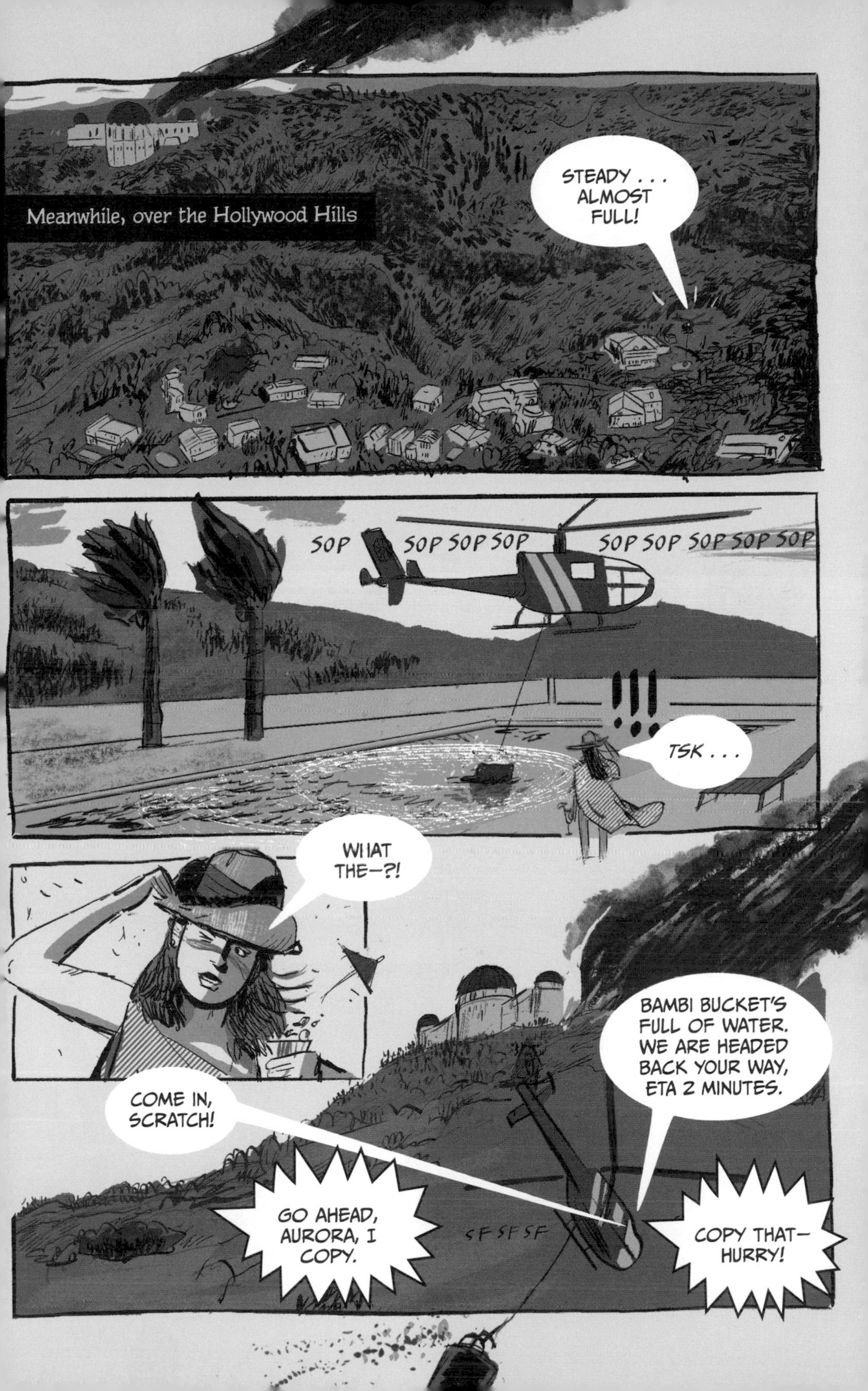
Meanwhile, over the Hollywood Hills
STEADY . . . ALMOST FULL!
SOP SOP SOP SOP SOP SOP SOP SOP SOP
!!!
TSK . . .
WHAT THE—?!
BAMBI BUCKET'S FULL OF WATER. WE ARE HEADED BACK YOUR WAY, ETA 2 MINUTES.
COME IN, SCRATCH!
GO AHEAD, AURORA, I COPY.
SF SF SF
COPY THAT— HURRY!

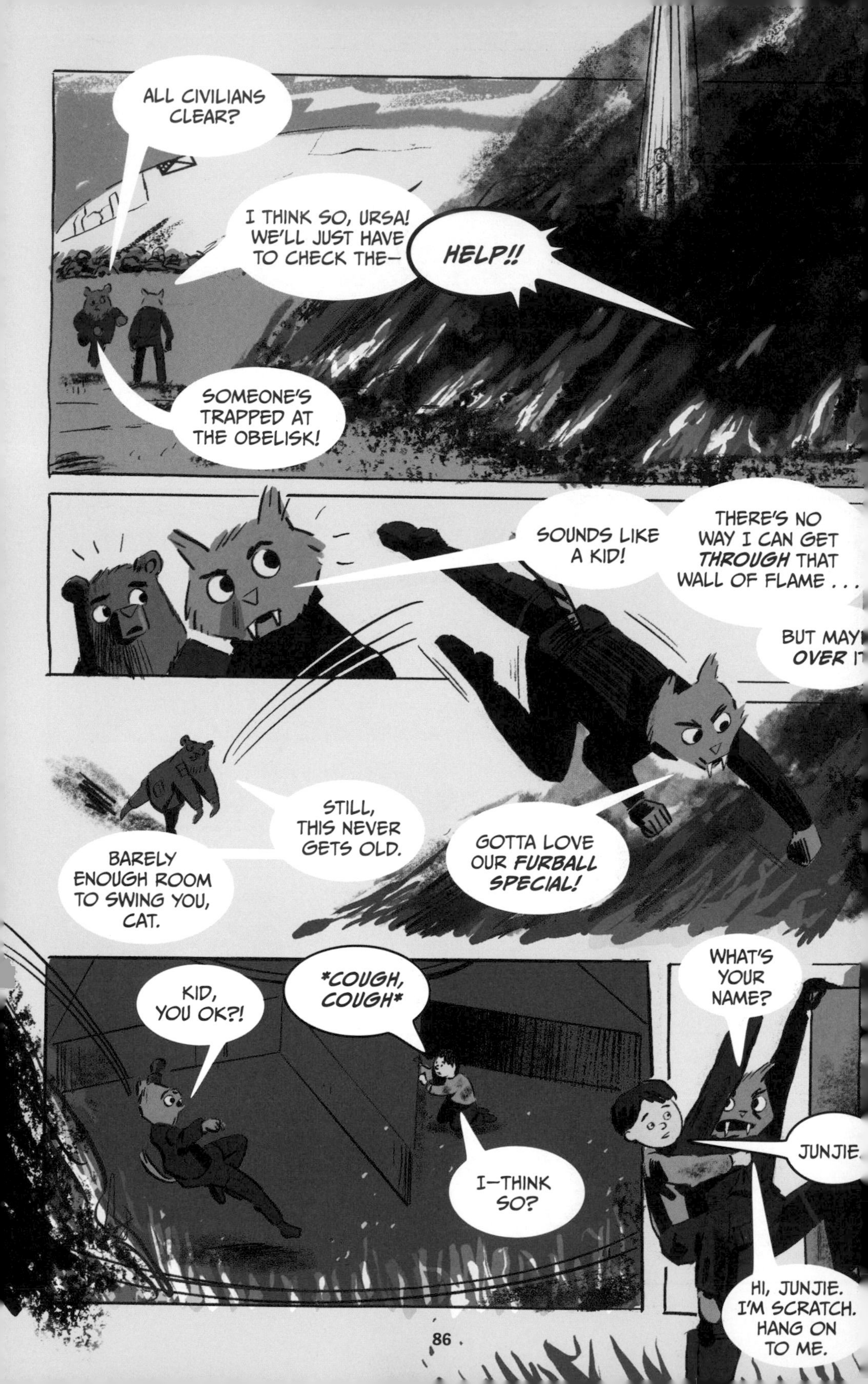
ALL CIVILIANS CLEAR?
I THINK SO, URSA! WE'LL JUST HAVE TO CHECK THE—
HELP!!
SOMEONE'S TRAPPED AT THE OBELISK!
SOUNDS LIKE A KID!
THERE'S NO WAY I CAN GET THROUGH THAT WALL OF FLAME . . .
STILL, THIS NEVER GETS OLD.
BARELY ENOUGH ROOM TO SWING YOU, CAT.
GOTTA LOVE OUR FURBALL SPECIAL!
KID, YOU OK?!
*COUGH, COUGH*
I—THINK SO?
WHAT'S YOUR NAME?
JUNJIE.
HI, JUNJIE. I'M SCRATCH. HANG ON TO ME.

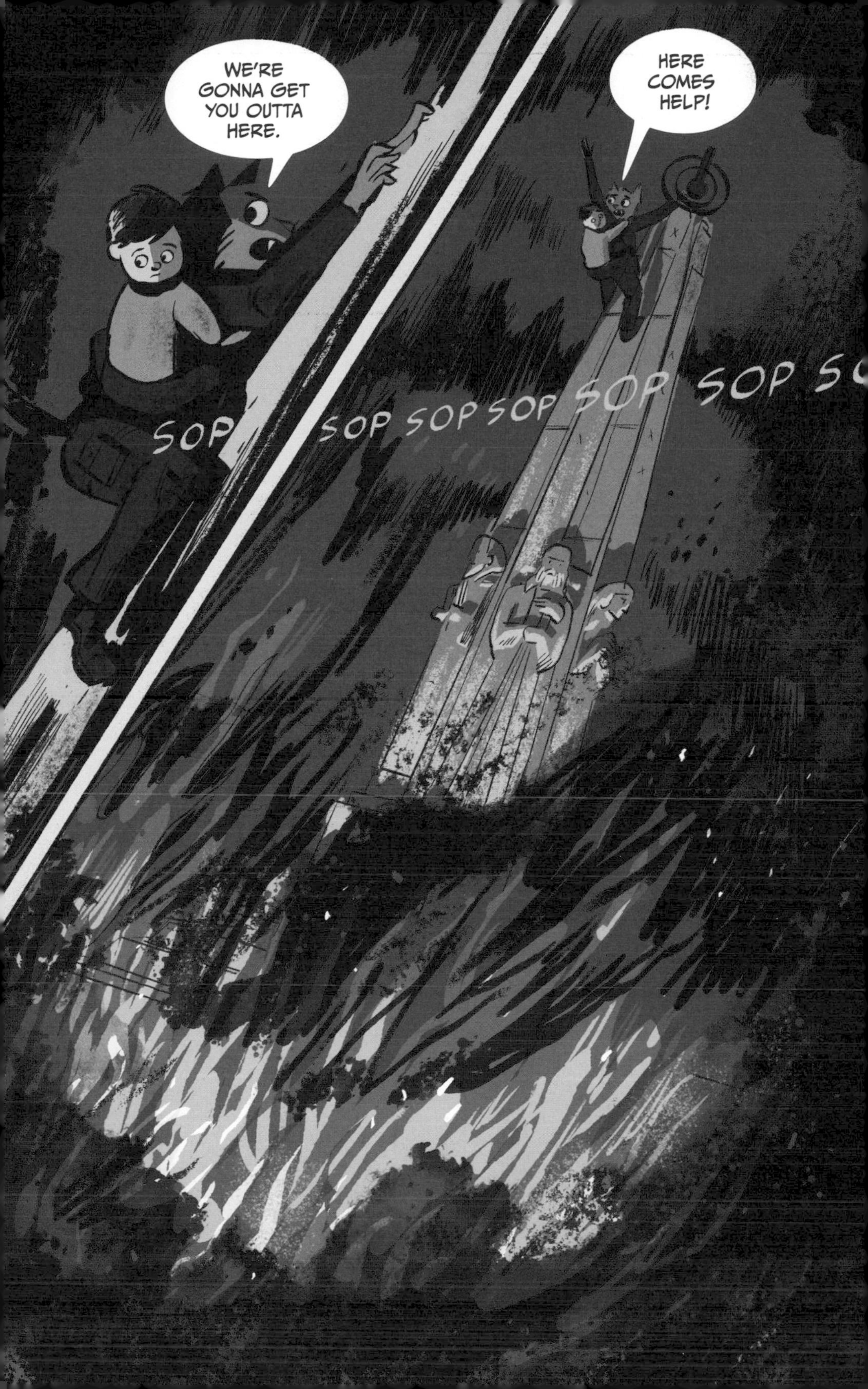
WE'RE GONNA GET YOU OUTTA HERE.
HERE COMES HELP!
SOP SOP SOP SOP SOP SOP

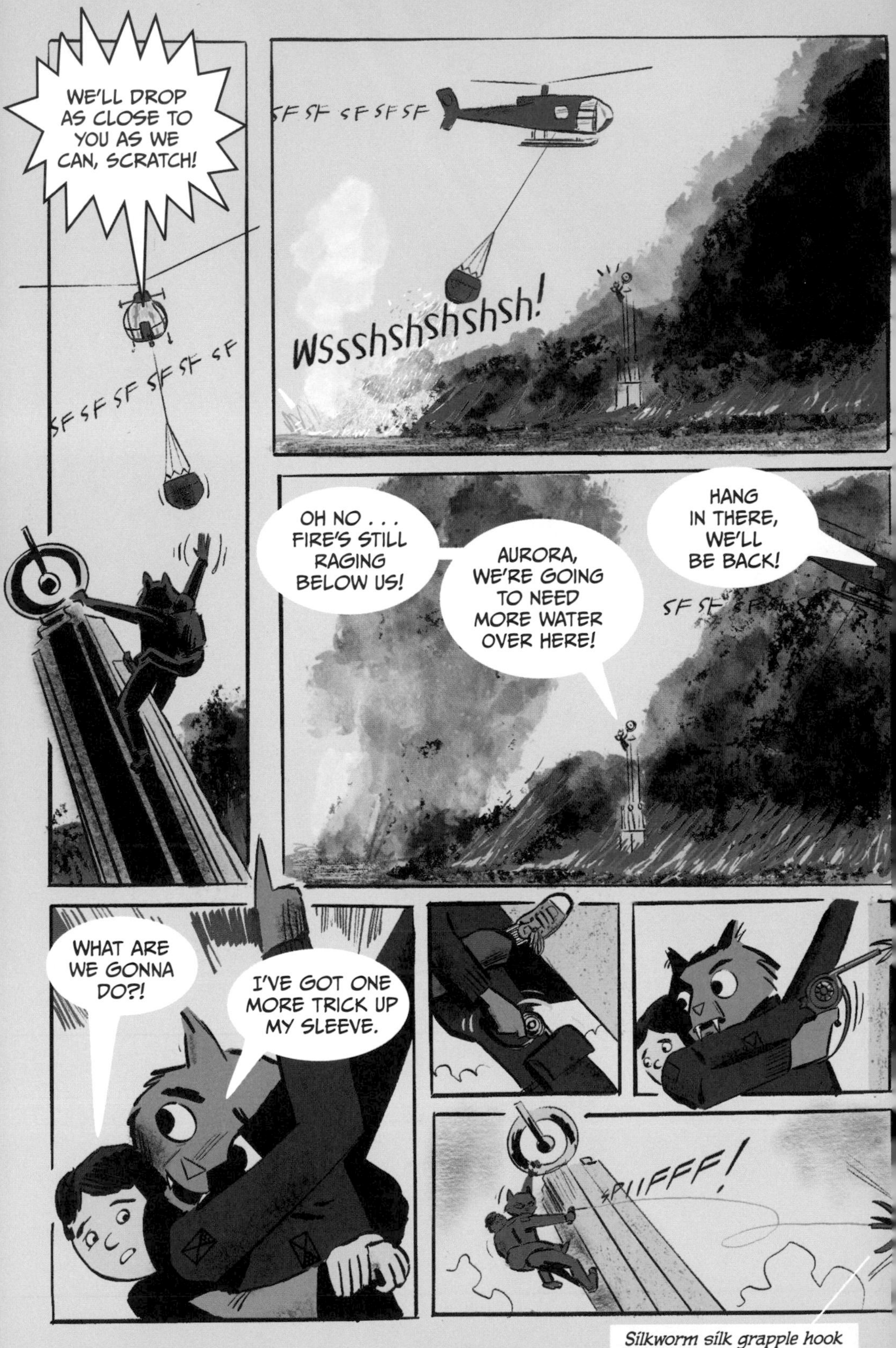
WE'LL DROP AS CLOSE TO YOU AS WE CAN, SCRATCH!
SF SF SF SF SF SF SF
SF SF SF SF SF
WSSSHSHSHSHSH!
OH NO . . . FIRE'S STILL RAGING BELOW US!
AURORA, WE'RE GOING TO NEED MORE WATER OVER HERE!
HANG IN THERE, WE'LL BE BACK!
WHAT ARE WE GONNA DO?!
I'VE GOT ONE MORE TRICK UP MY SLEEVE.
SPIIFFF!
Silkworm silk grapple hook

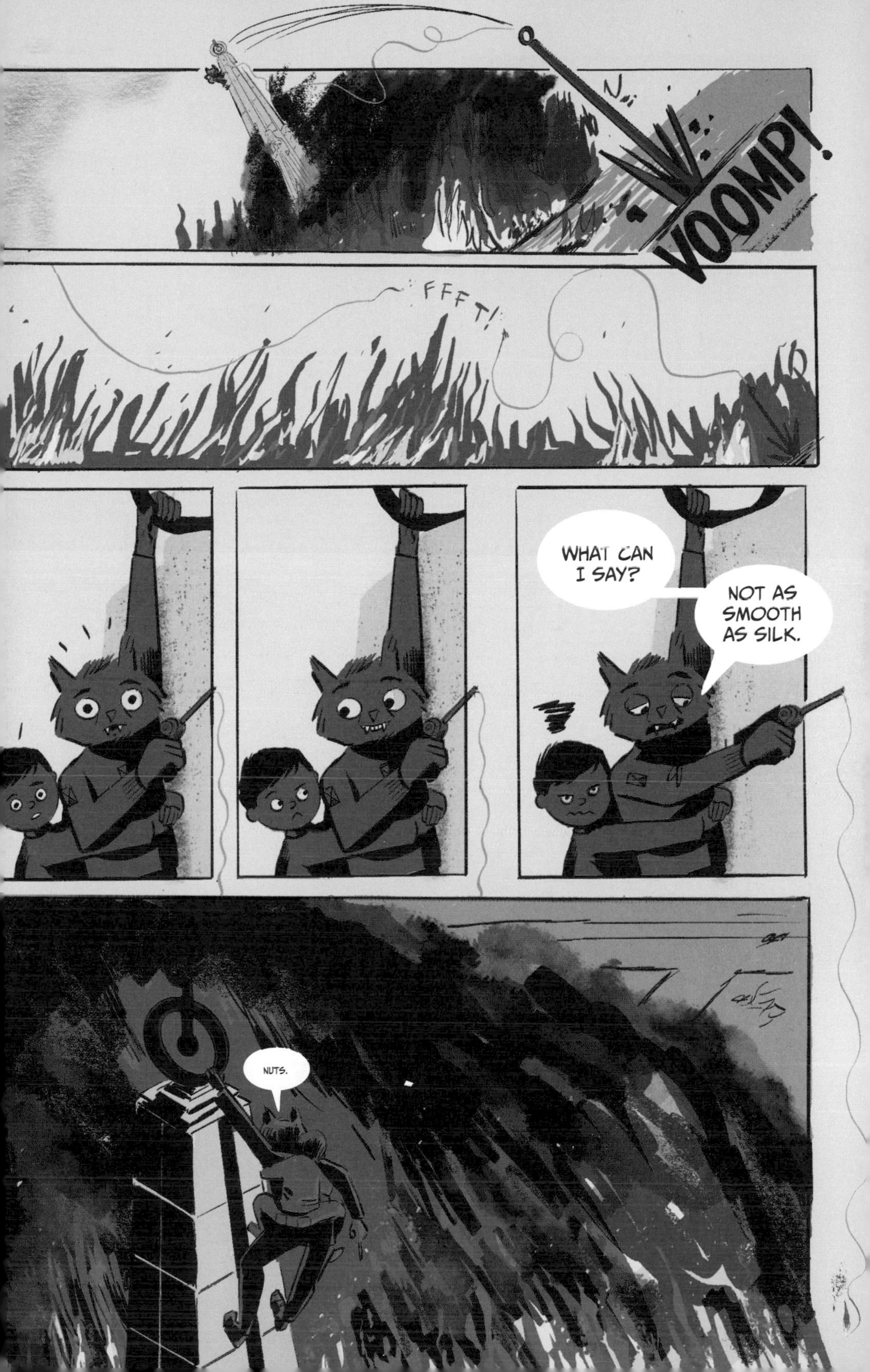
VOOMP!
FFFT!
WHAT CAN I SAY?
NOT AS SMOOTH AS SILK.
NUTS.

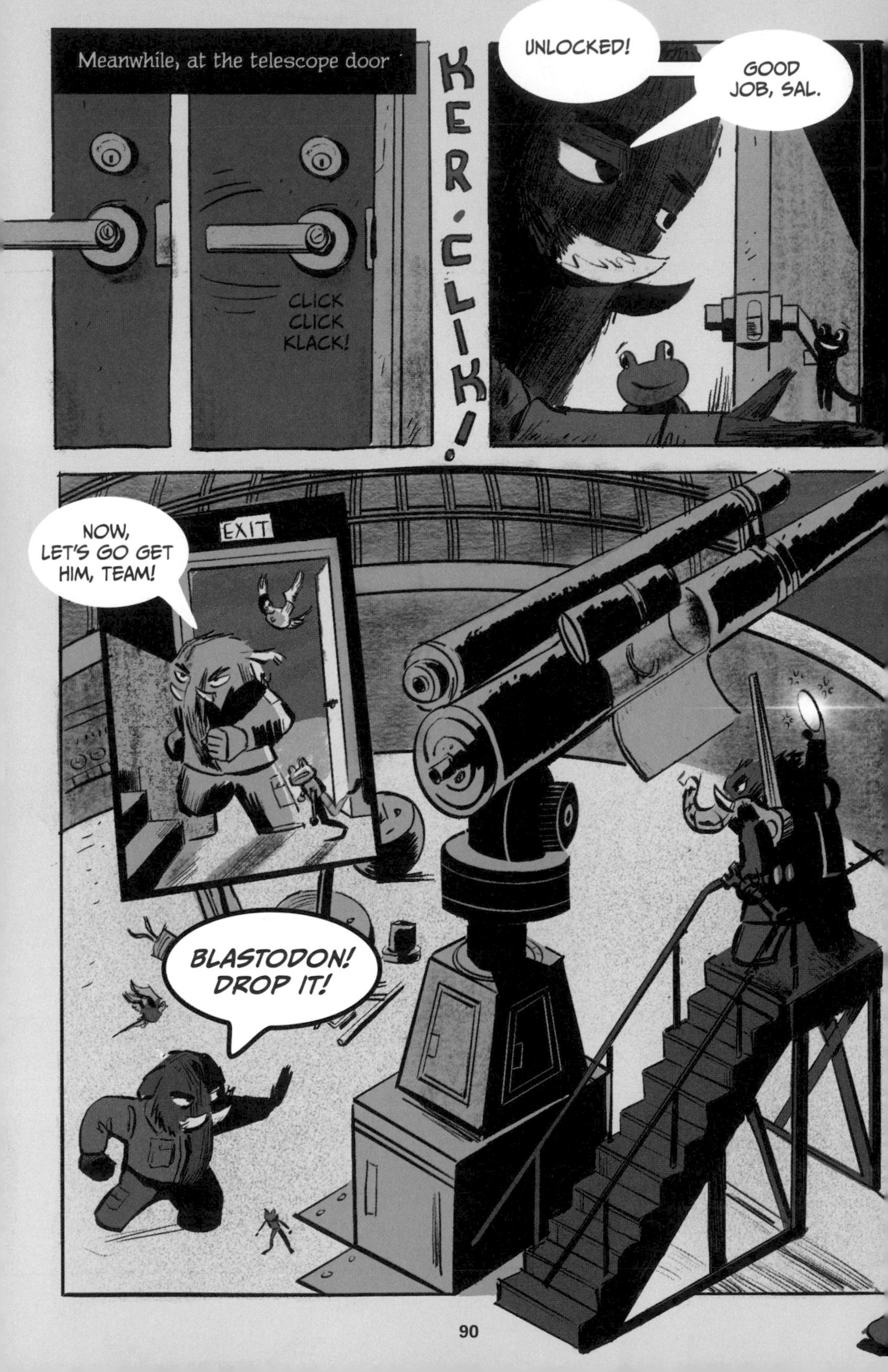
Meanwhile, at the telescope door
CLICK CLICK KLACK!
KER-CLIK!
UNLOCKED!
GOOD JOB, SAL.
NOW, LET'S GO GET HIM, TEAM!
EXIT
BLASTODON! DROP IT!

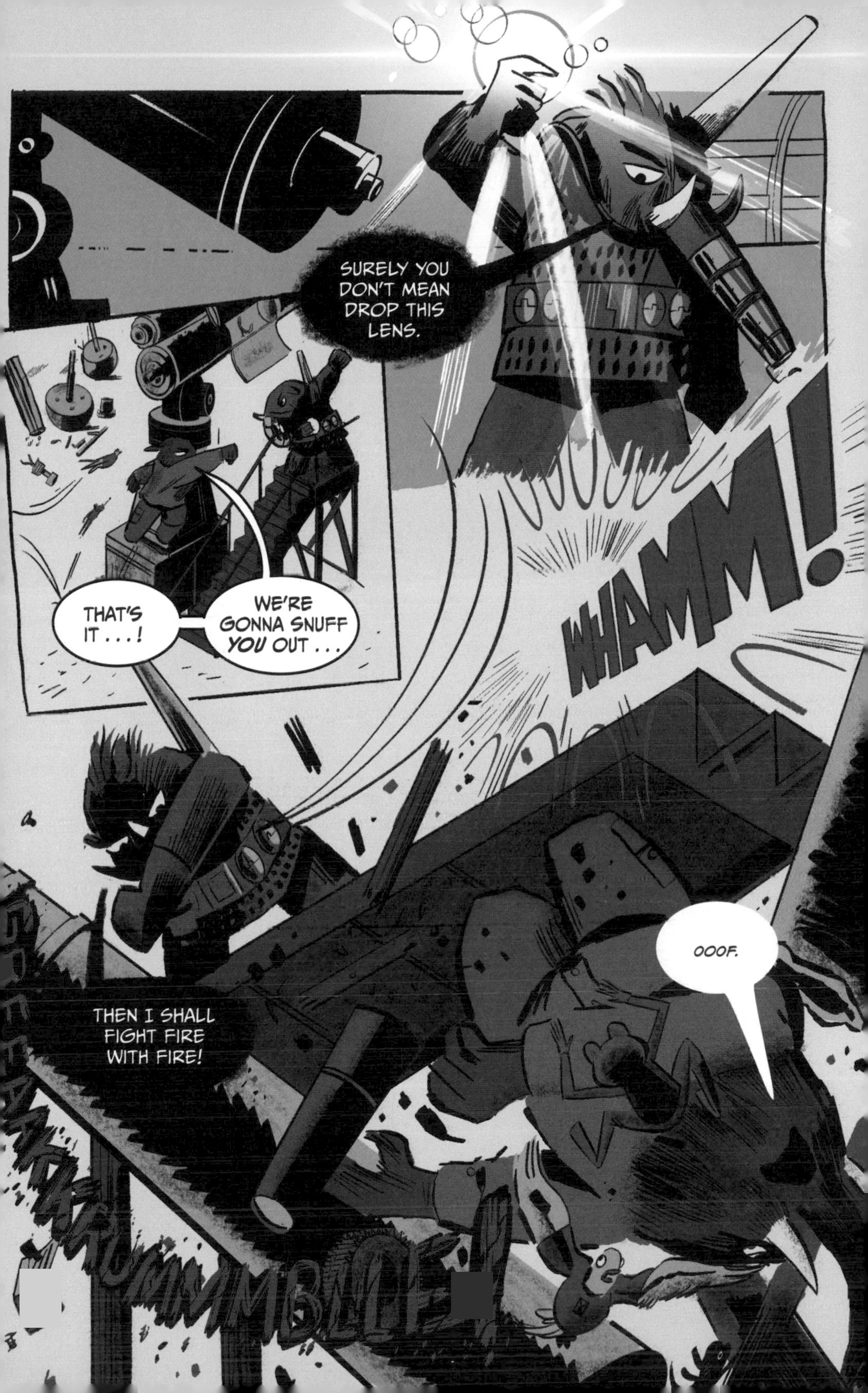
SURELY YOU DON'T MEAN DROP THIS LENS.
THAT'S IT . . . !
WE'RE GONNA SNUFF *YOU* OUT . . .
WHAMM!
THEN I SHALL FIGHT FIRE WITH FIRE!
OOOF.

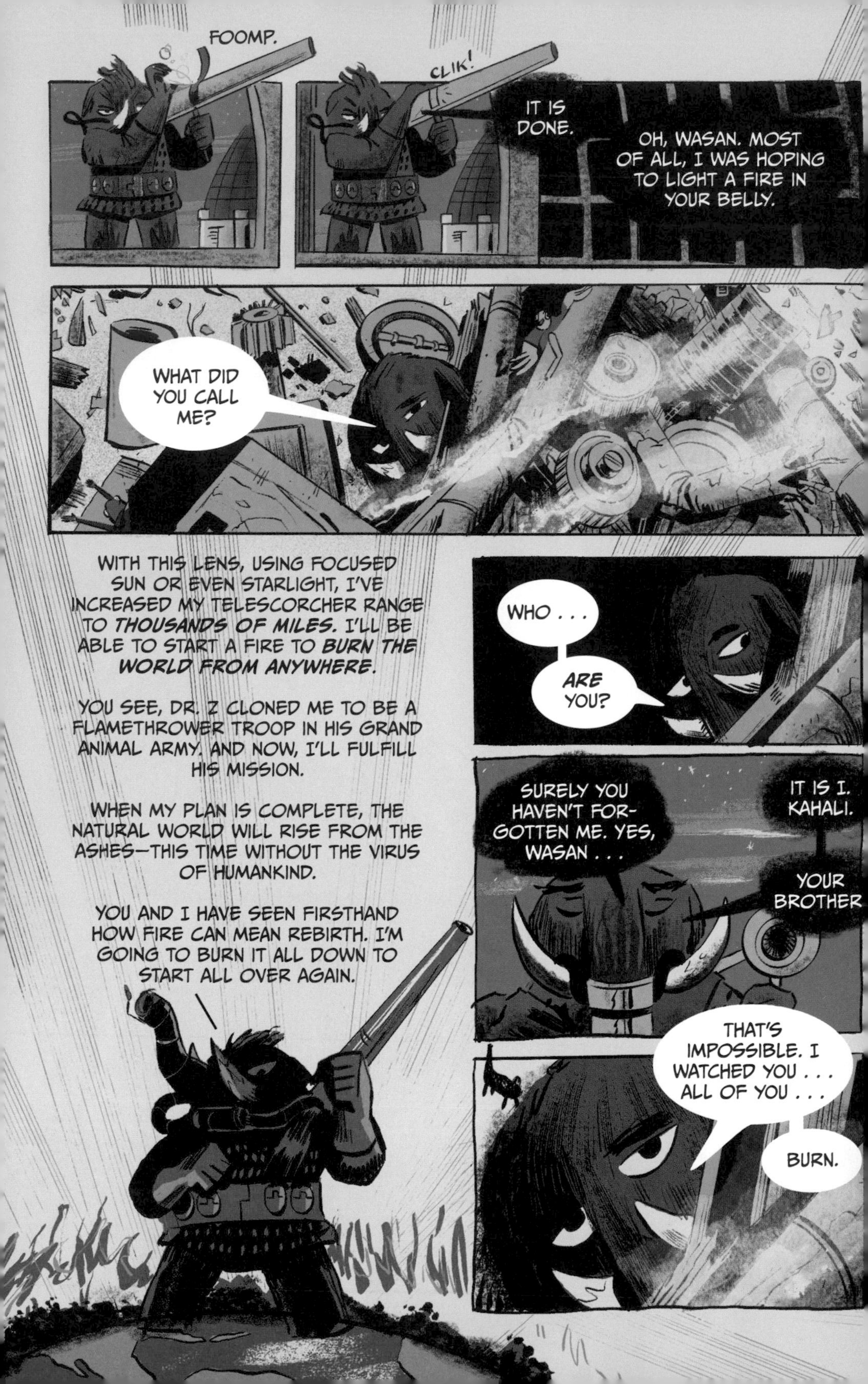
FOOMP.
CLIK!
IT IS DONE.
OH, WASAN. MOST OF ALL, I WAS HOPING TO LIGHT A FIRE IN YOUR BELLY.
WHAT DID YOU CALL ME?
WITH THIS LENS, USING FOCUSED SUN OR EVEN STARLIGHT, I'VE INCREASED MY TELESCORCHER RANGE TO *THOUSANDS OF MILES.* I'LL BE ABLE TO START A FIRE TO *BURN THE WORLD FROM ANYWHERE.*
YOU SEE, DR. Z CLONED ME TO BE A FLAMETHROWER TROOP IN HIS GRAND ANIMAL ARMY. AND NOW, I'LL FULFILL HIS MISSION.
WHEN MY PLAN IS COMPLETE, THE NATURAL WORLD WILL RISE FROM THE ASHES—THIS TIME WITHOUT THE VIRUS OF HUMANKIND.
YOU AND I HAVE SEEN FIRSTHAND HOW FIRE CAN MEAN REBIRTH. I'M GOING TO BURN IT ALL DOWN TO START ALL OVER AGAIN.
WHO . . .
*ARE* YOU?
SURELY YOU HAVEN'T FOR-GOTTEN ME. YES, WASAN . . .
IT IS I. KAHALI.
YOUR BROTHER
THAT'S IMPOSSIBLE. I WATCHED YOU . . . ALL OF YOU . . .
BURN.

KAHALI, DON'T DO THIS! THE FIRE YOU WANNA KINDLE FOR THE WORLD IS GONNA BURN YOU INSTEAD.

HA! YOU'RE A FOOL.

DROP THE WEAPON.

LET'S TALK.

THAT TIME HAS COME AND GONE.

BROTHER TO BROTHER.

TS TIME TO ROAST THE EXTINCTS!

FWEEEEE

SAL, NO, WAIT!

MEEEEP!

ZWOP!

FFFFGTT!

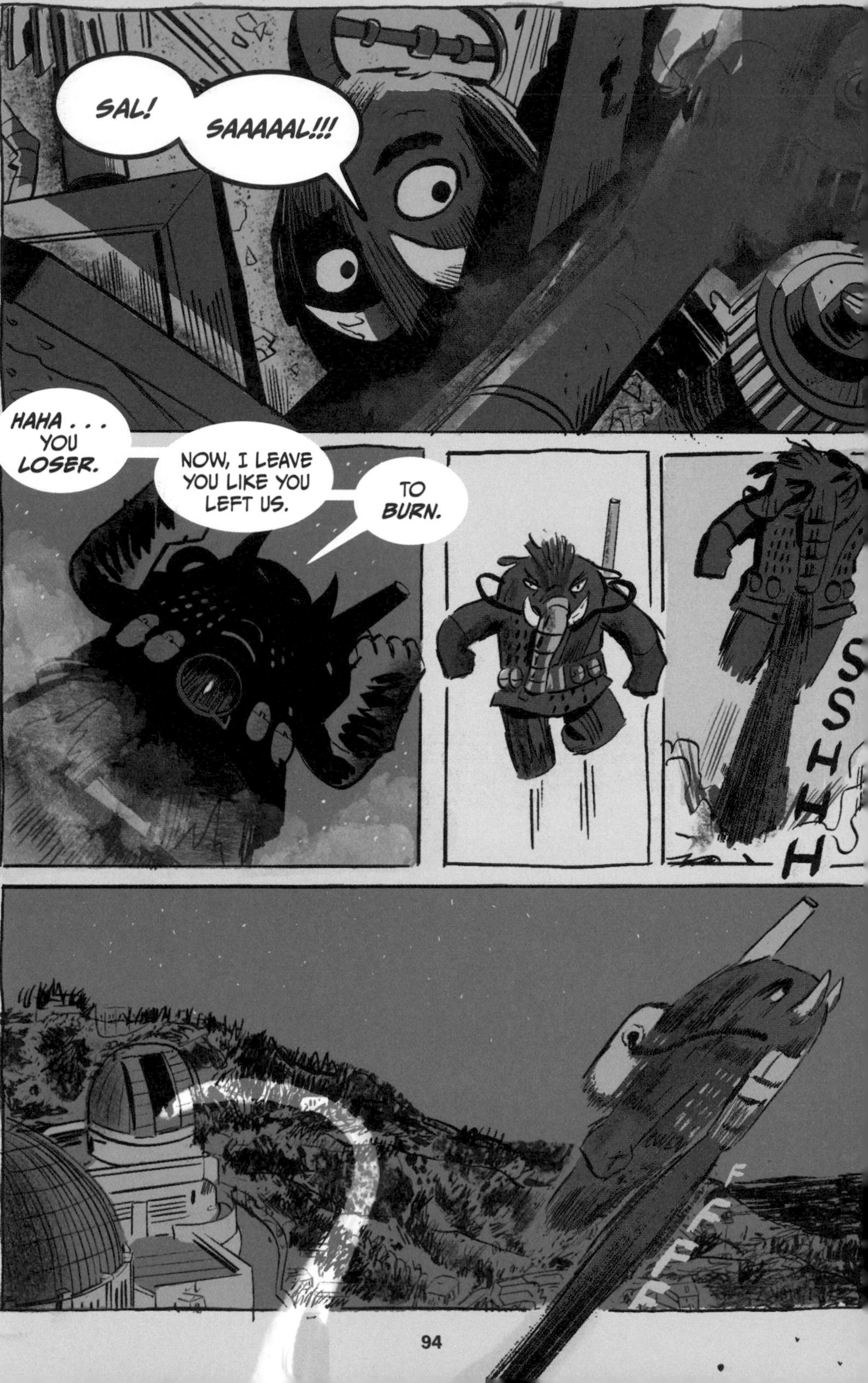
SAL!
SAAAAAL!!!
HAHA . . . YOU LOSER.
NOW, I LEAVE YOU LIKE YOU LEFT US.
TO BURN.
SSHHHH

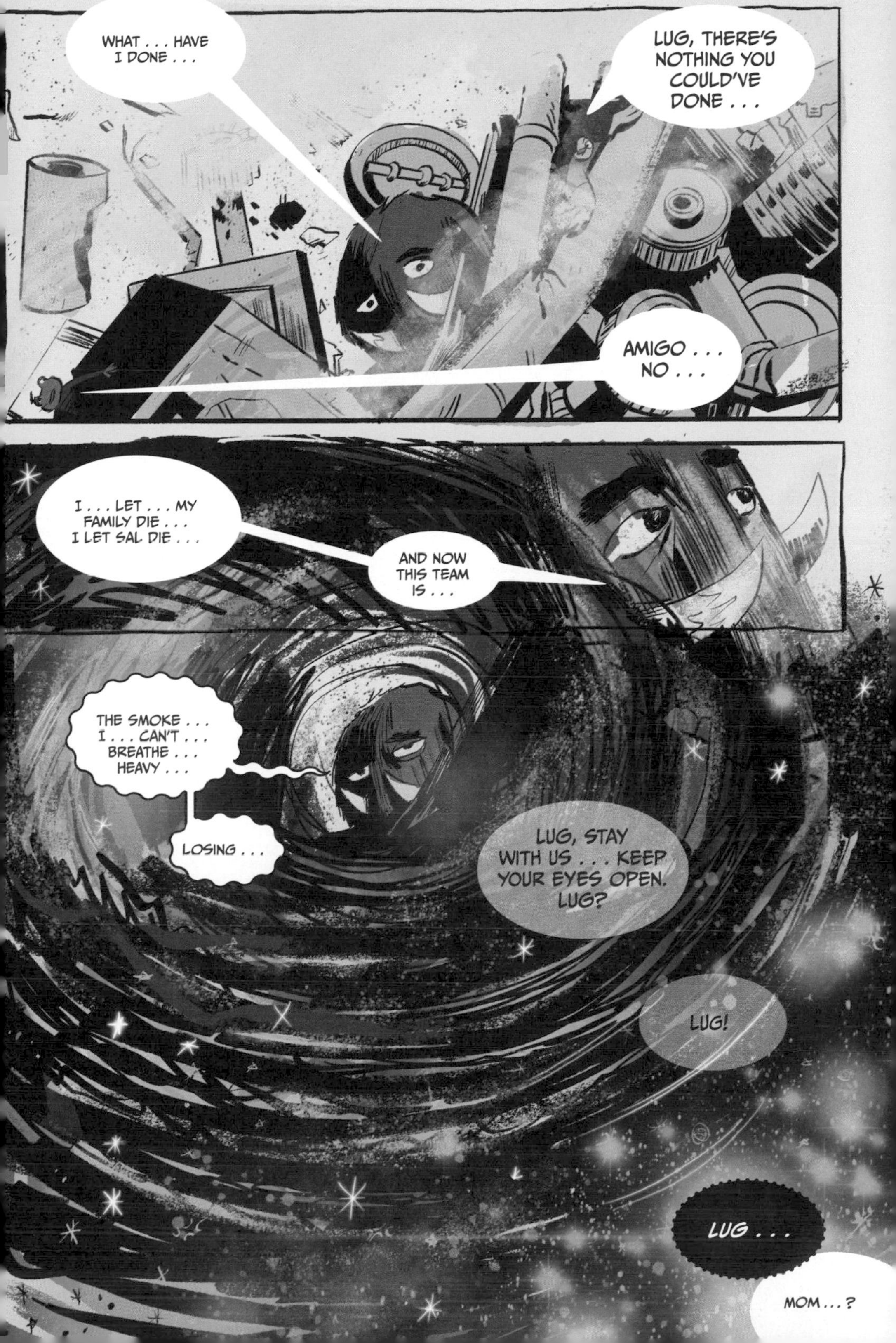
WHAT . . . HAVE I DONE . . .
LUG, THERE'S NOTHING YOU COULD'VE DONE . . .
AMIGO . . . NO . . .
I . . . LET . . . MY FAMILY DIE . . . I LET SAL DIE . . .
AND NOW THIS TEAM IS . . .
THE SMOKE . . . I . . . CAN'T . . . BREATHE . . . HEAVY . . .
LOSING . . .
LUG, STAY WITH US . . . KEEP YOUR EYES OPEN. LUG?
LUG!
LUG . . .
MOM . . . ?

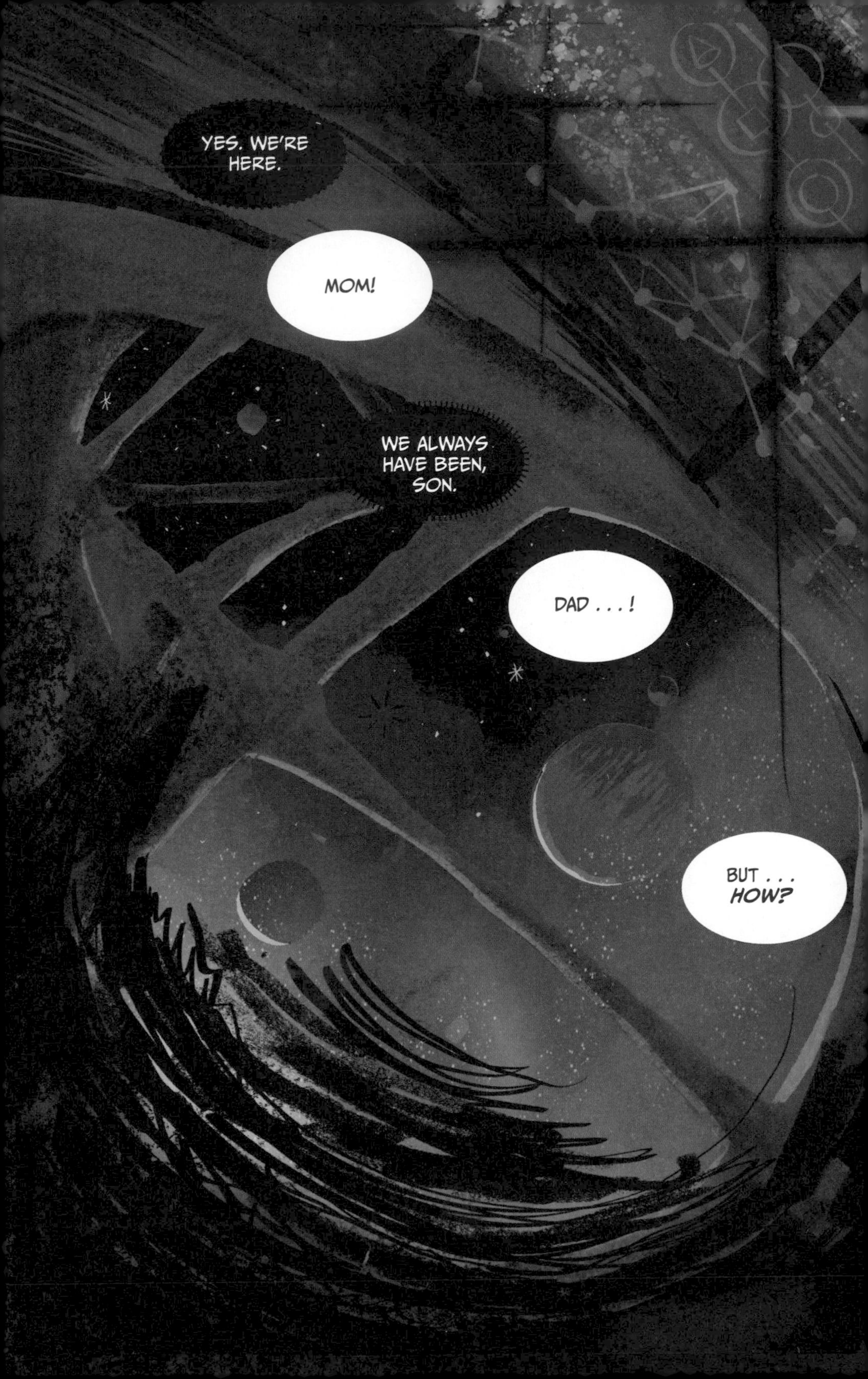
YES. WE'RE HERE.
MOM!
WE ALWAYS HAVE BEEN, SON.
DAD . . . !
BUT . . . *HOW?*

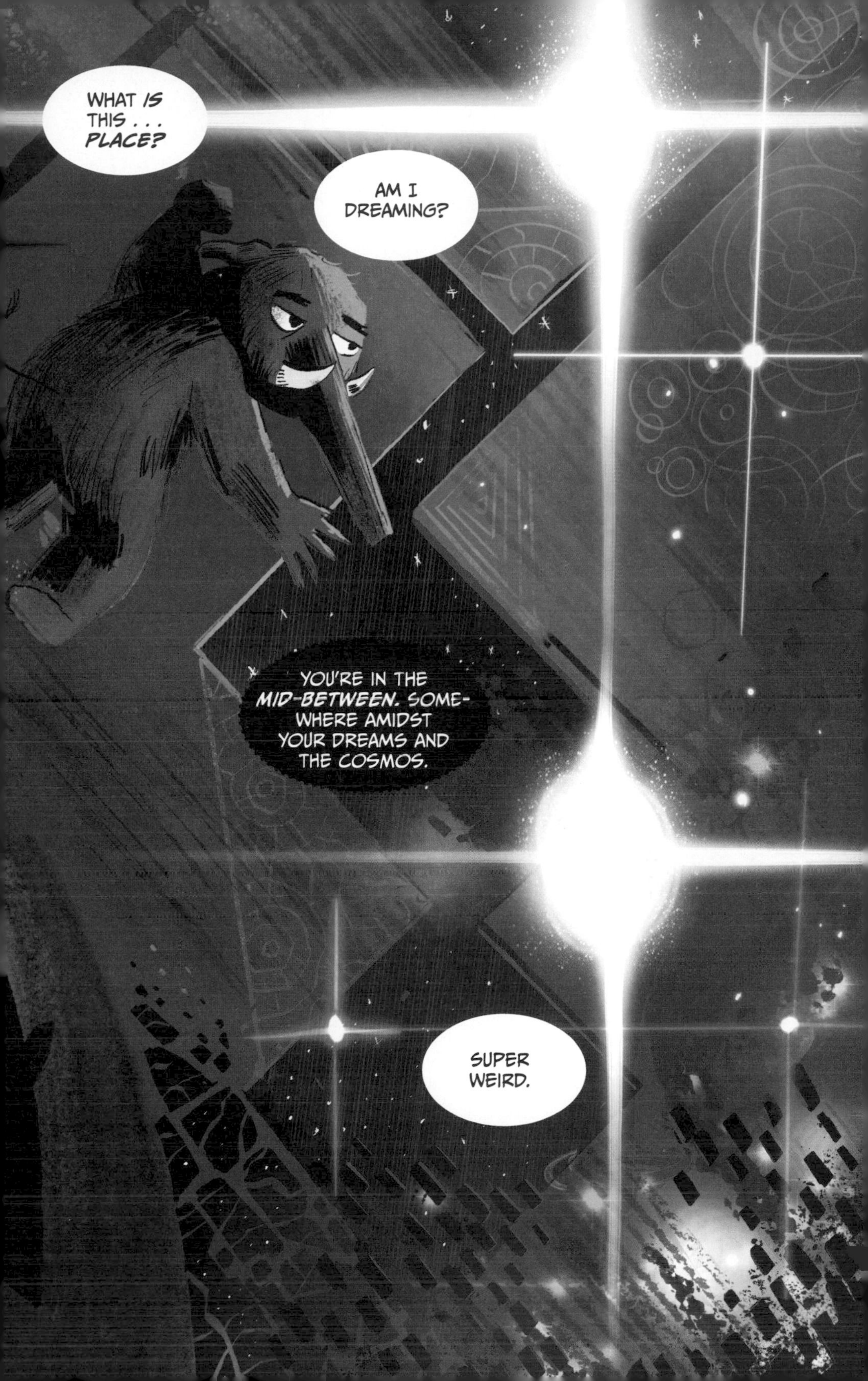
WHAT *IS* THIS . . . *PLACE?*
AM I DREAMING?
YOU'RE IN THE *MID-BETWEEN.* SOME-WHERE AMIDST YOUR DREAMS AND THE COSMOS.
SUPER WEIRD.

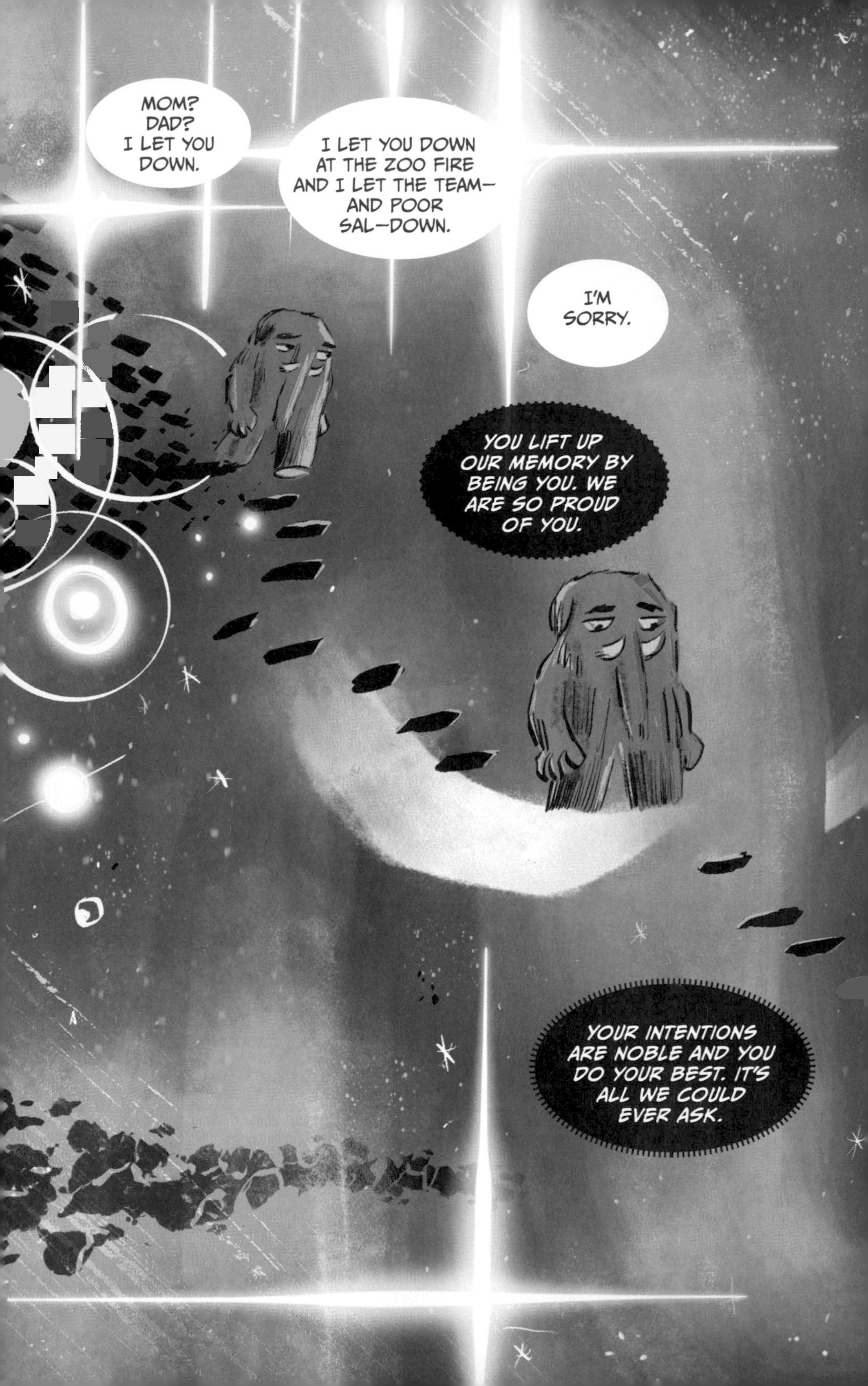
MOM? DAD? I LET YOU DOWN.
I LET YOU DOWN AT THE ZOO FIRE AND I LET THE TEAM—AND POOR SAL—DOWN.
I'M SORRY.
YOU LIFT UP OUR MEMORY BY BEING YOU. WE ARE SO PROUD OF YOU.
YOUR INTENTIONS ARE NOBLE AND YOU DO YOUR BEST. IT'S ALL WE COULD EVER ASK.

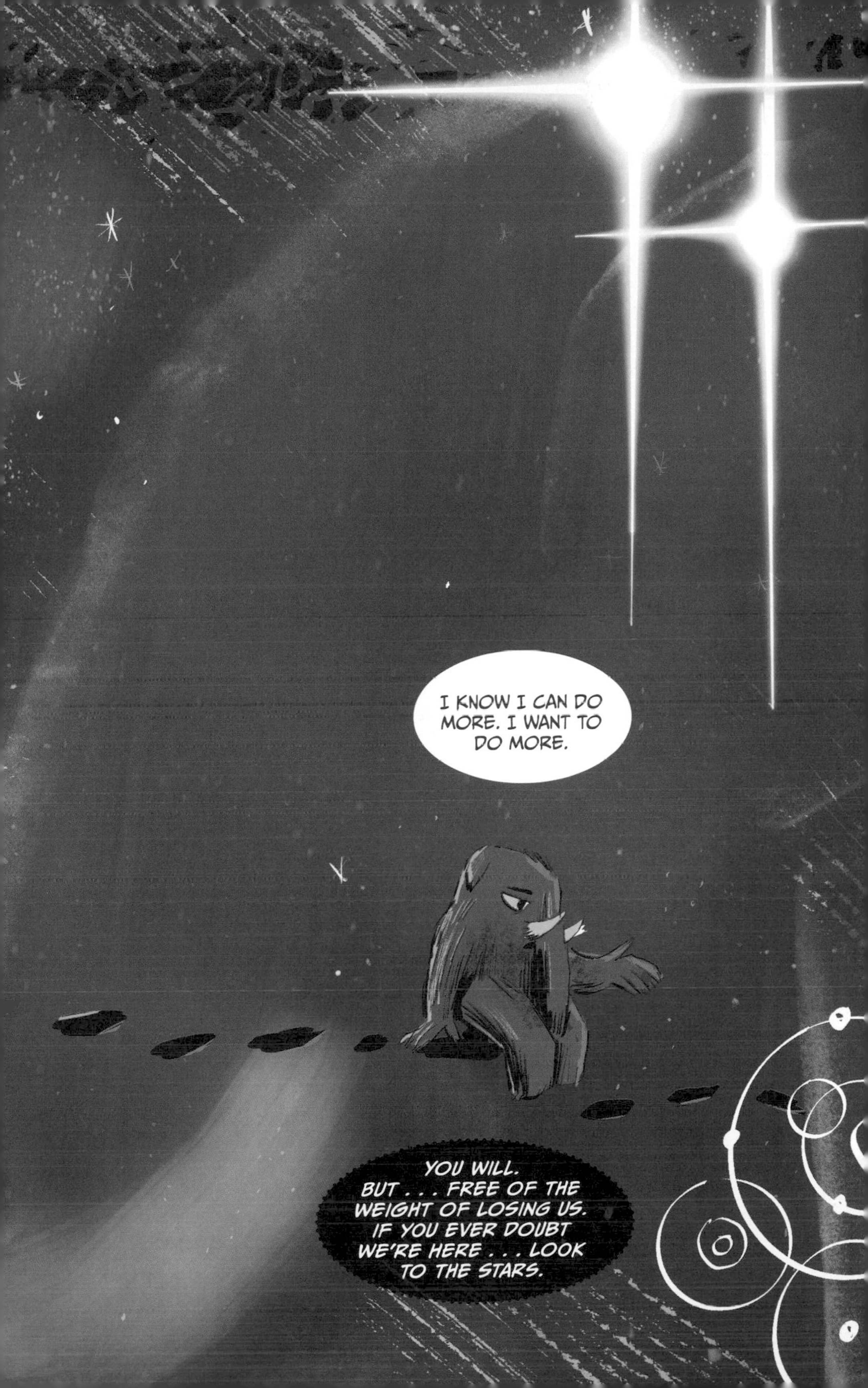
I KNOW I CAN DO MORE. I WANT TO DO MORE.
YOU WILL. BUT . . . FREE OF THE WEIGHT OF LOSING US. IF YOU EVER DOUBT WE'RE HERE . . . LOOK TO THE STARS.

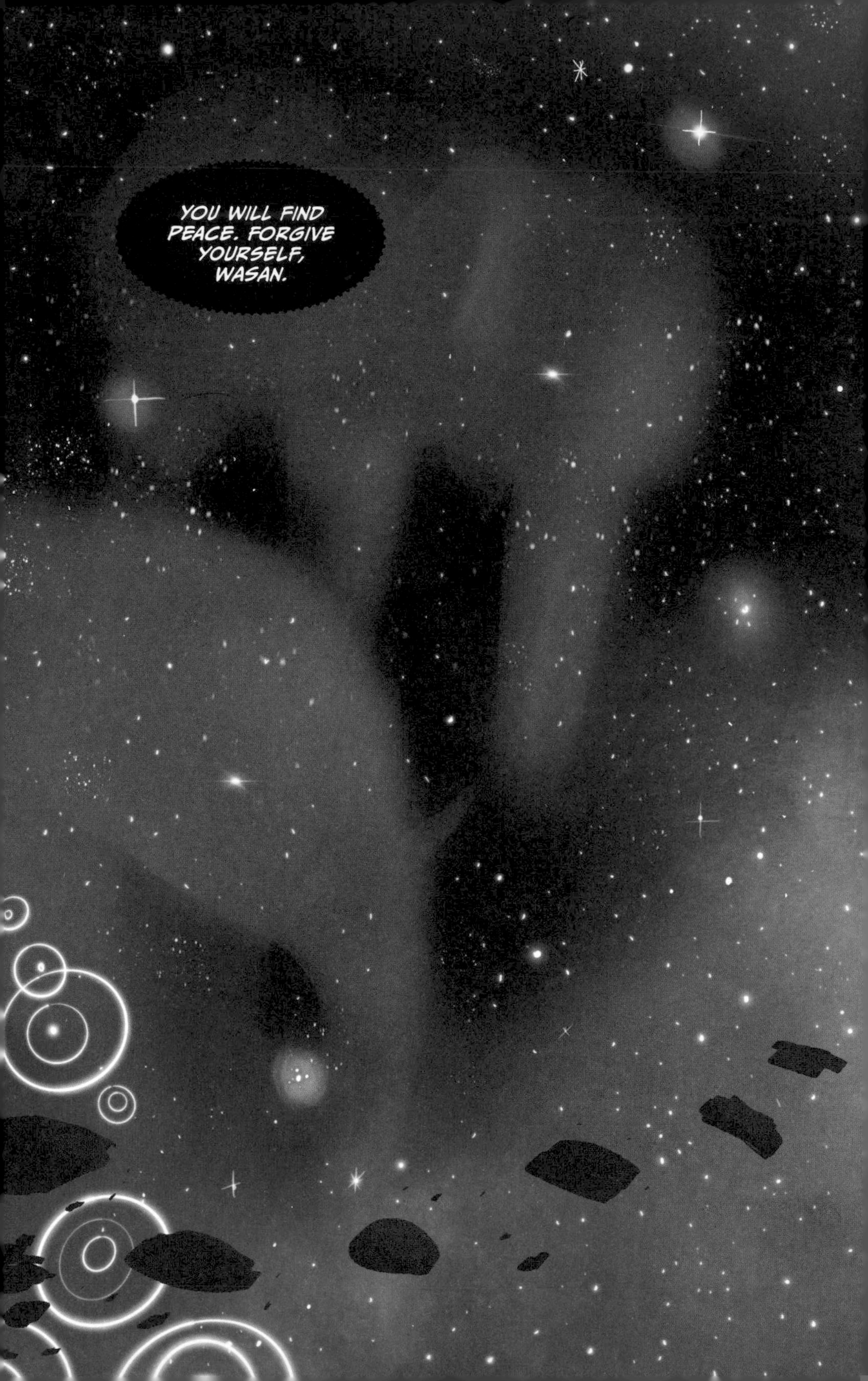
YOU WILL FIND PEACE. FORGIVE YOURSELF, WASAN.

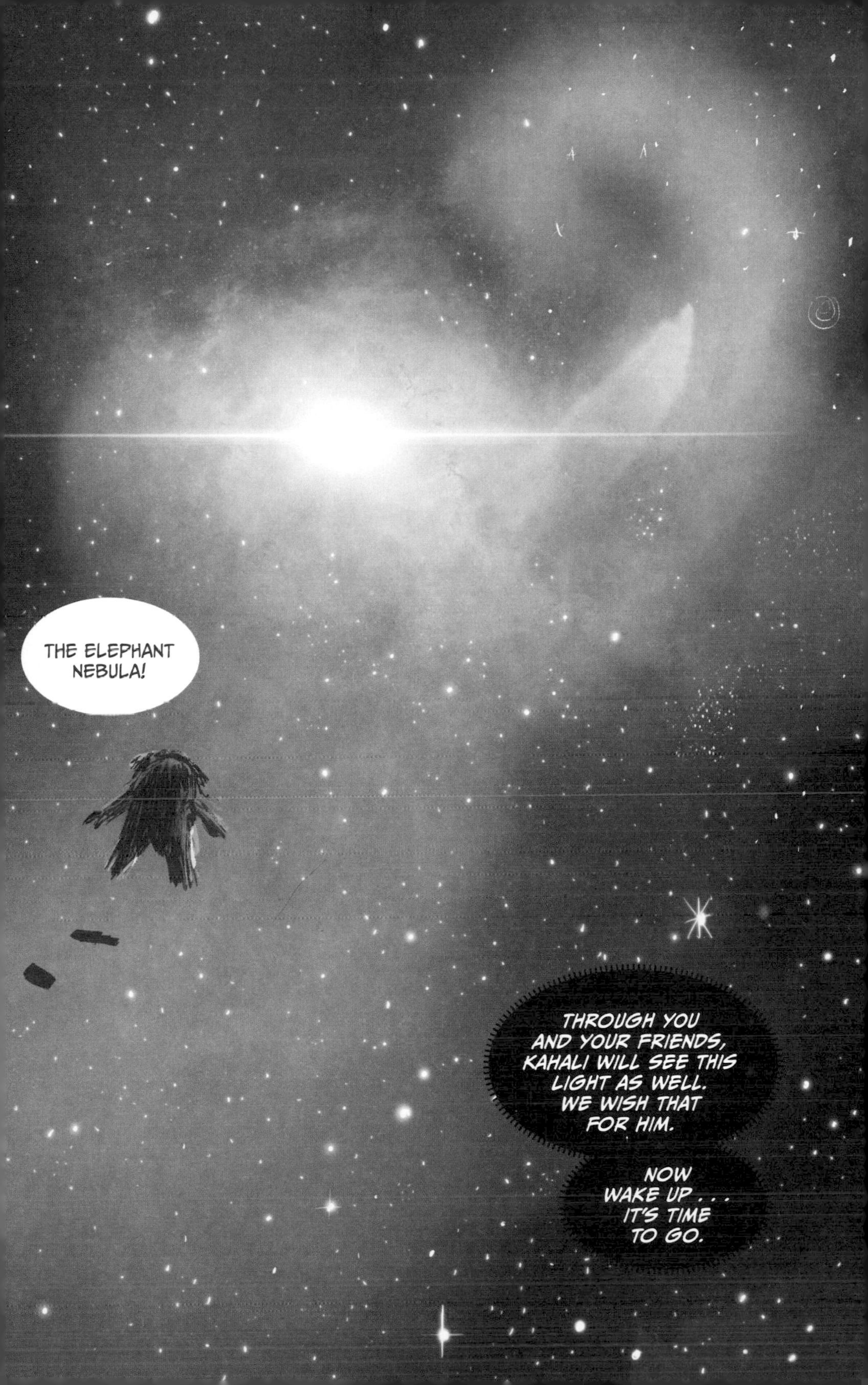
THE ELEPHANT NEBULA!
THROUGH YOU AND YOUR FRIENDS, KAHALI WILL SEE THIS LIGHT AS WELL. WE WISH THAT FOR HIM.
NOW WAKE UP . . . IT'S TIME TO GO.

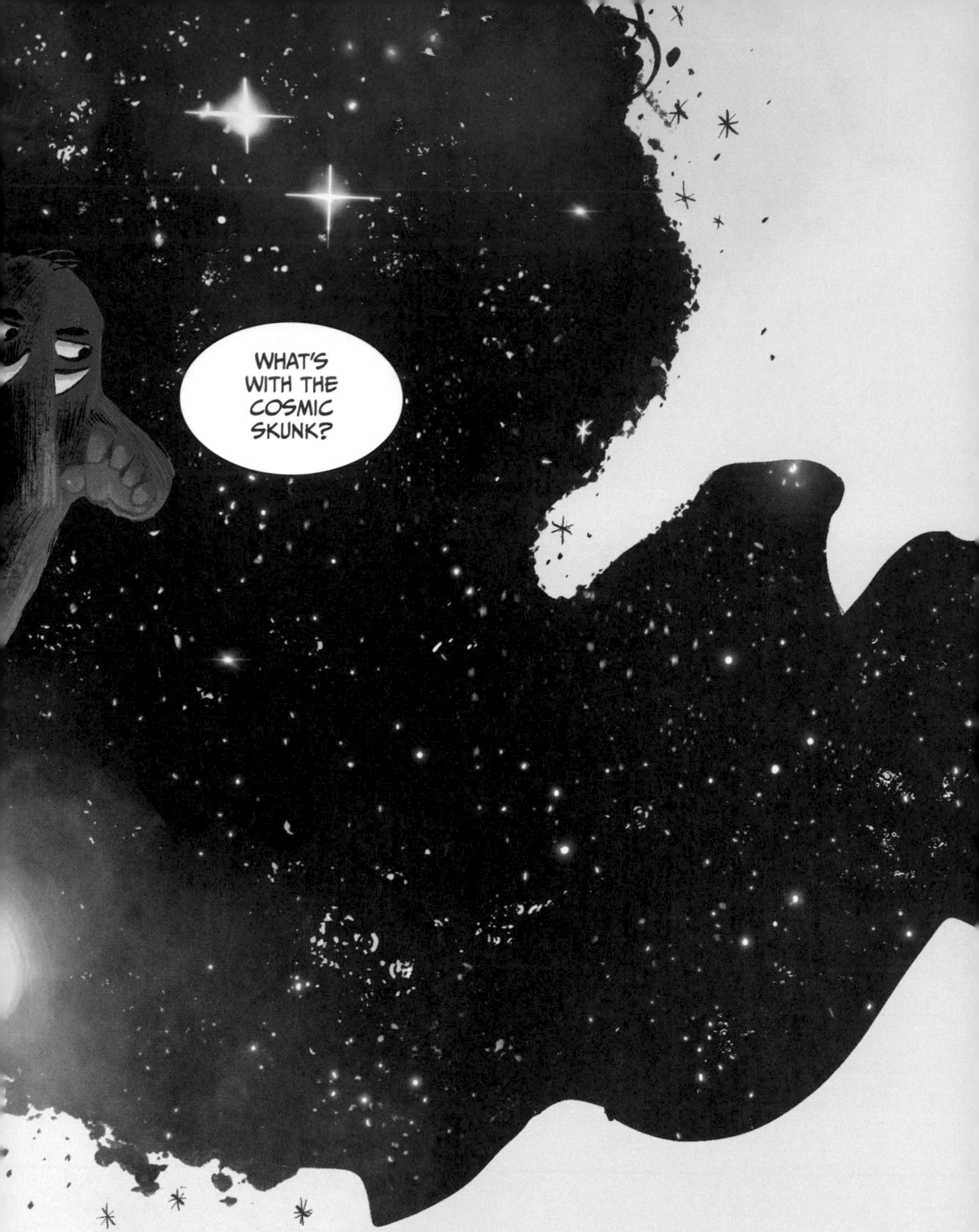
WHAT'S WITH THE COSMIC SKUNK?

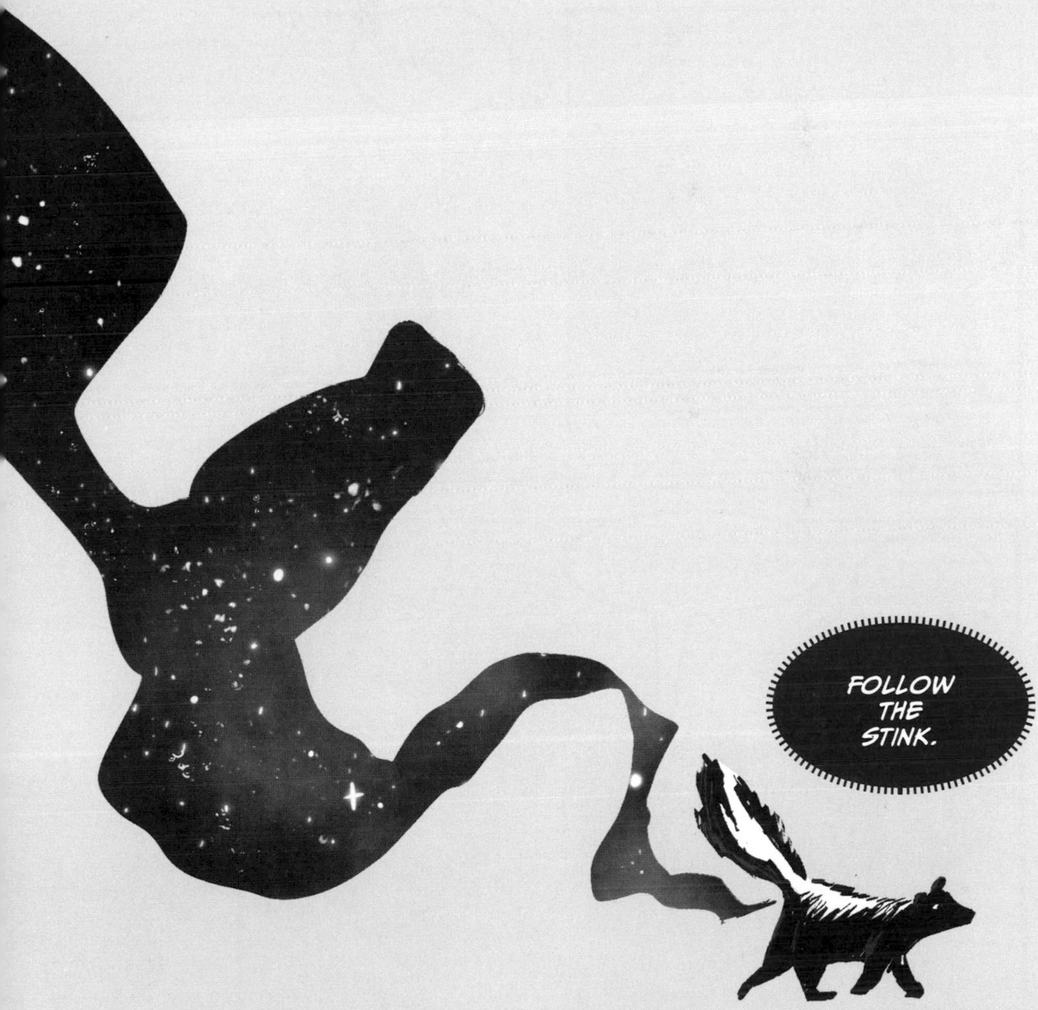
FOLLOW THE STINK.

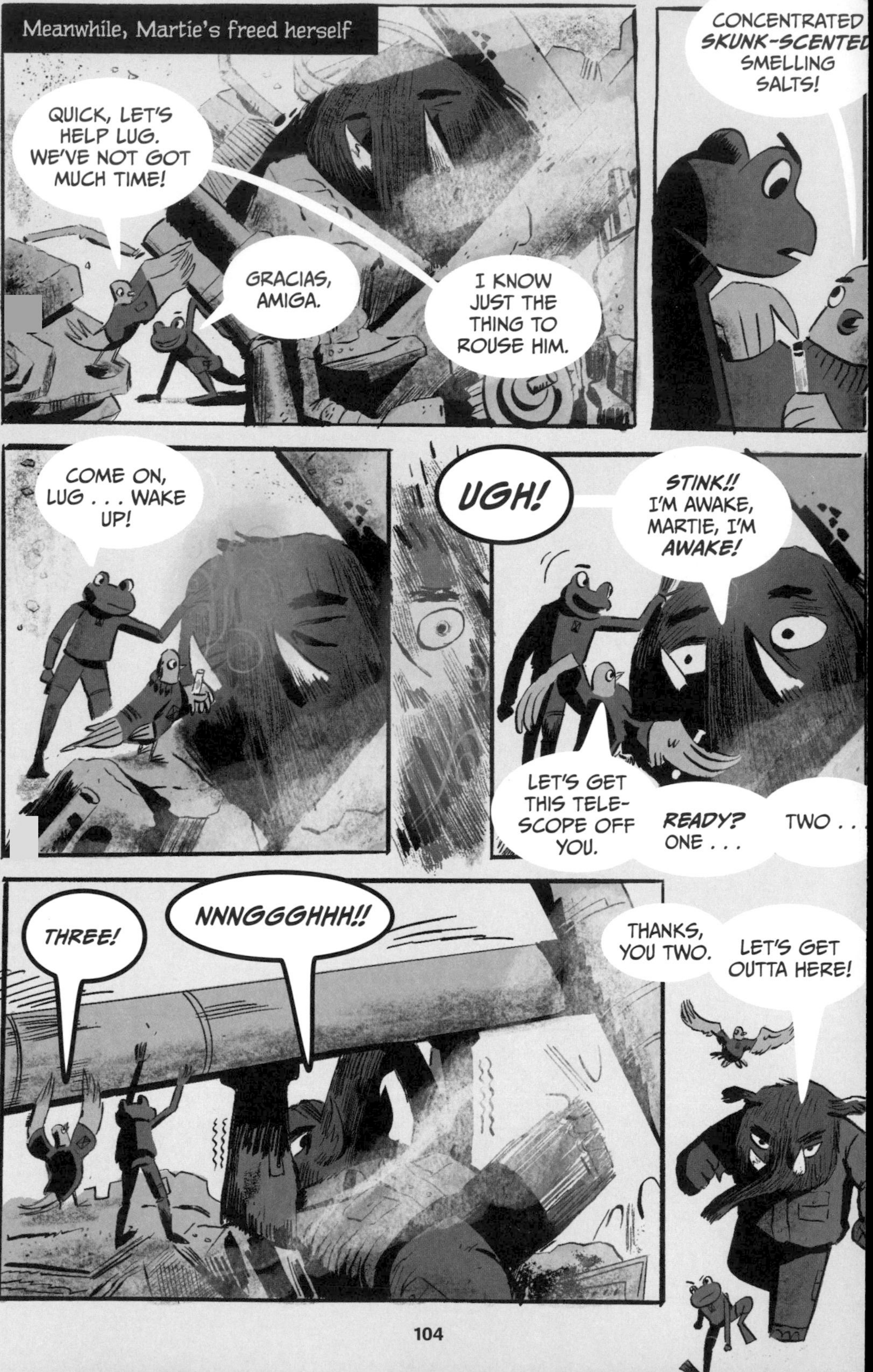
Meanwhile, Martie's freed herself
QUICK, LET'S HELP LUG. WE'VE NOT GOT MUCH TIME!
GRACIAS, AMIGA.
I KNOW JUST THE THING TO ROUSE HIM.
CONCENTRATED SKUNK-SCENTED SMELLING SALTS!
COME ON, LUG . . . WAKE UP!
UGH!
STINK!! I'M AWAKE, MARTIE, I'M AWAKE!
LET'S GET THIS TELE-SCOPE OFF YOU.
READY? ONE . . .
TWO . . .
THREE!
NNNGGGHHH!!
THANKS, YOU TWO.
LET'S GET OUTTA HERE!

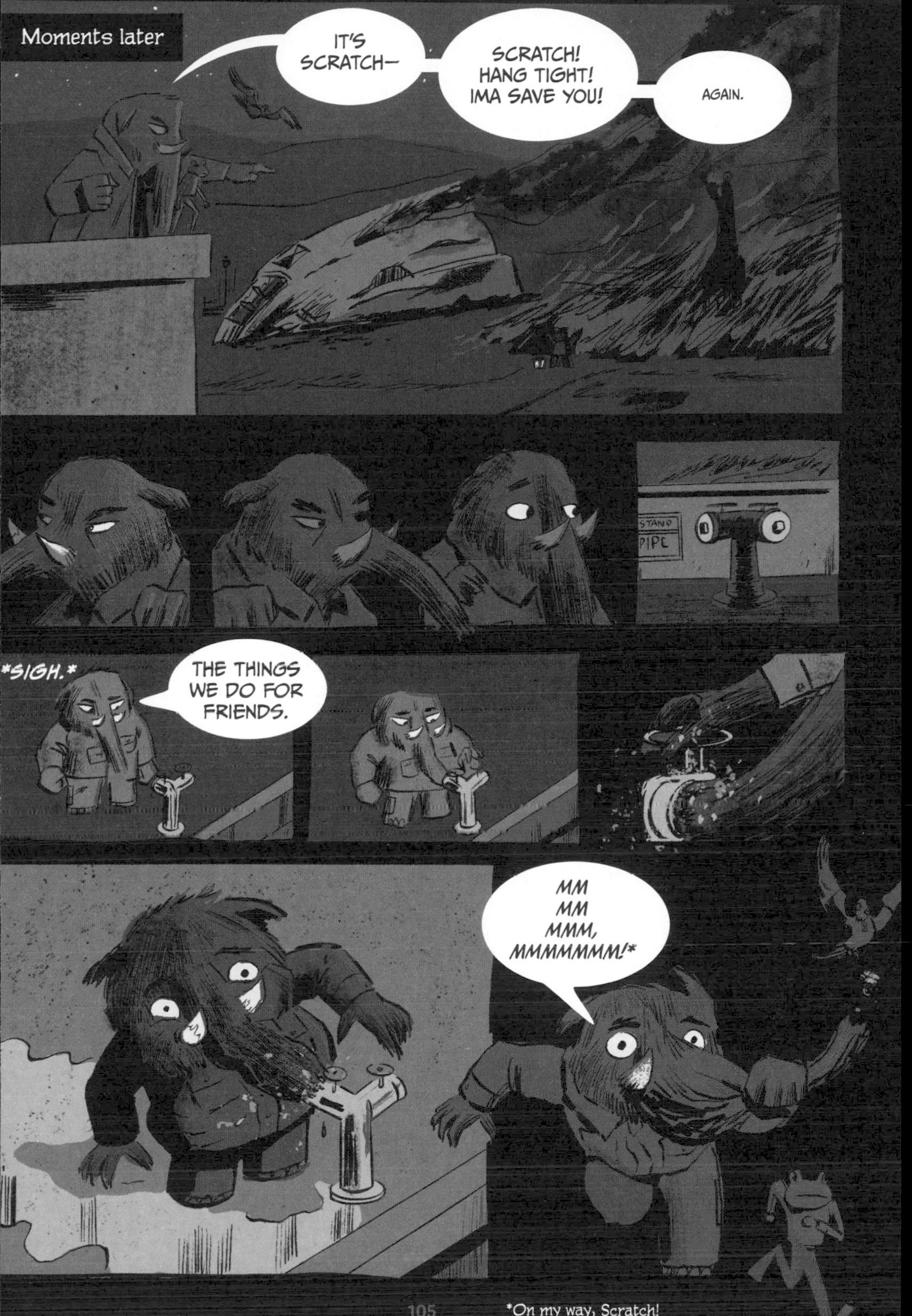
Moments later
IT'S SCRATCH—
SCRATCH! HANG TIGHT! IMA SAVE YOU!
AGAIN.
STAND PIPE
*SIGH.*
THE THINGS WE DO FOR FRIENDS.
MM MM MMM, MMMMMMM!*



*On my way, Scratch!

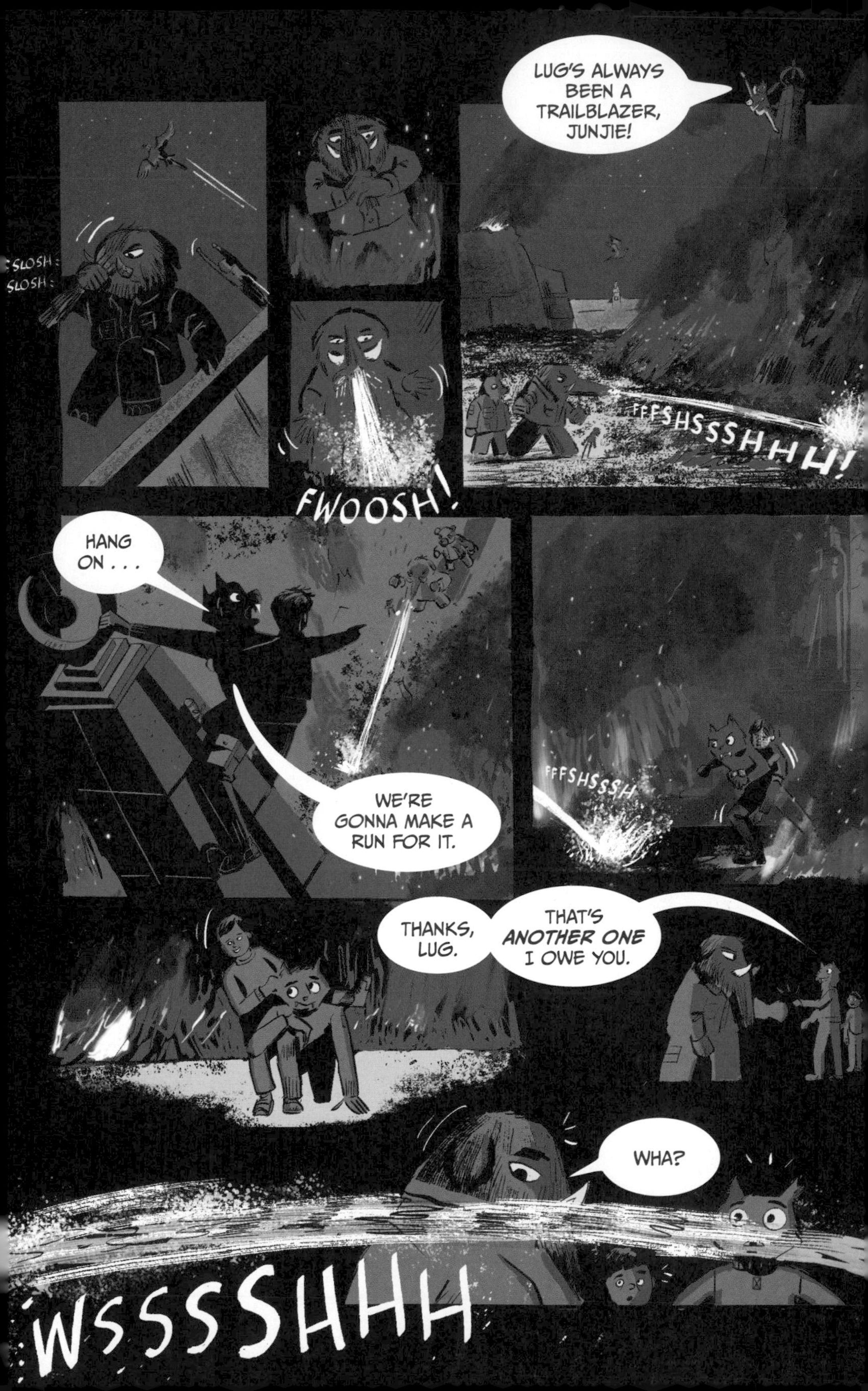
SLOSH
SLOSH
LUG'S ALWAYS BEEN A TRAILBLAZER, JUNJIE!
FWOOSH!
FFFSHSSSHHHH!
HANG ON . . .
WE'RE GONNA MAKE A RUN FOR IT.
FFFSHSSSH
THANKS, LUG.
THAT'S ANOTHER ONE I OWE YOU.
WHA?
WSSSSHHH

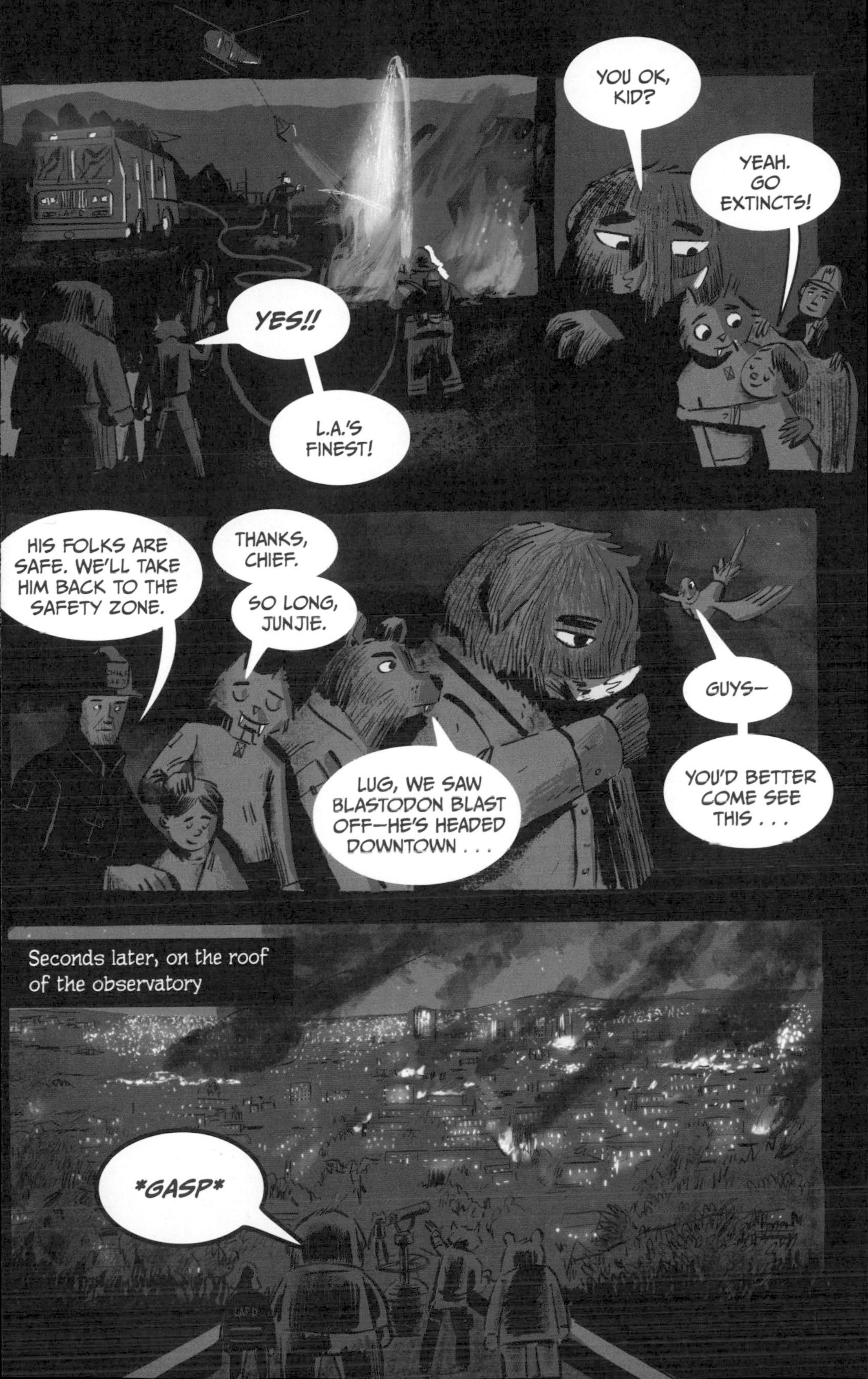
YES!!
L.A.'S FINEST!
YOU OK, KID?
YEAH. GO EXTINCTS!
HIS FOLKS ARE SAFE. WE'LL TAKE HIM BACK TO THE SAFETY ZONE.
THANKS, CHIEF.
SO LONG, JUNJIE.
LUG, WE SAW BLASTODON BLAST OFF—HE'S HEADED DOWNTOWN . . .
GUYS—
YOU'D BETTER COME SEE THIS . . .
Seconds later, on the roof of the observatory
*GASP*

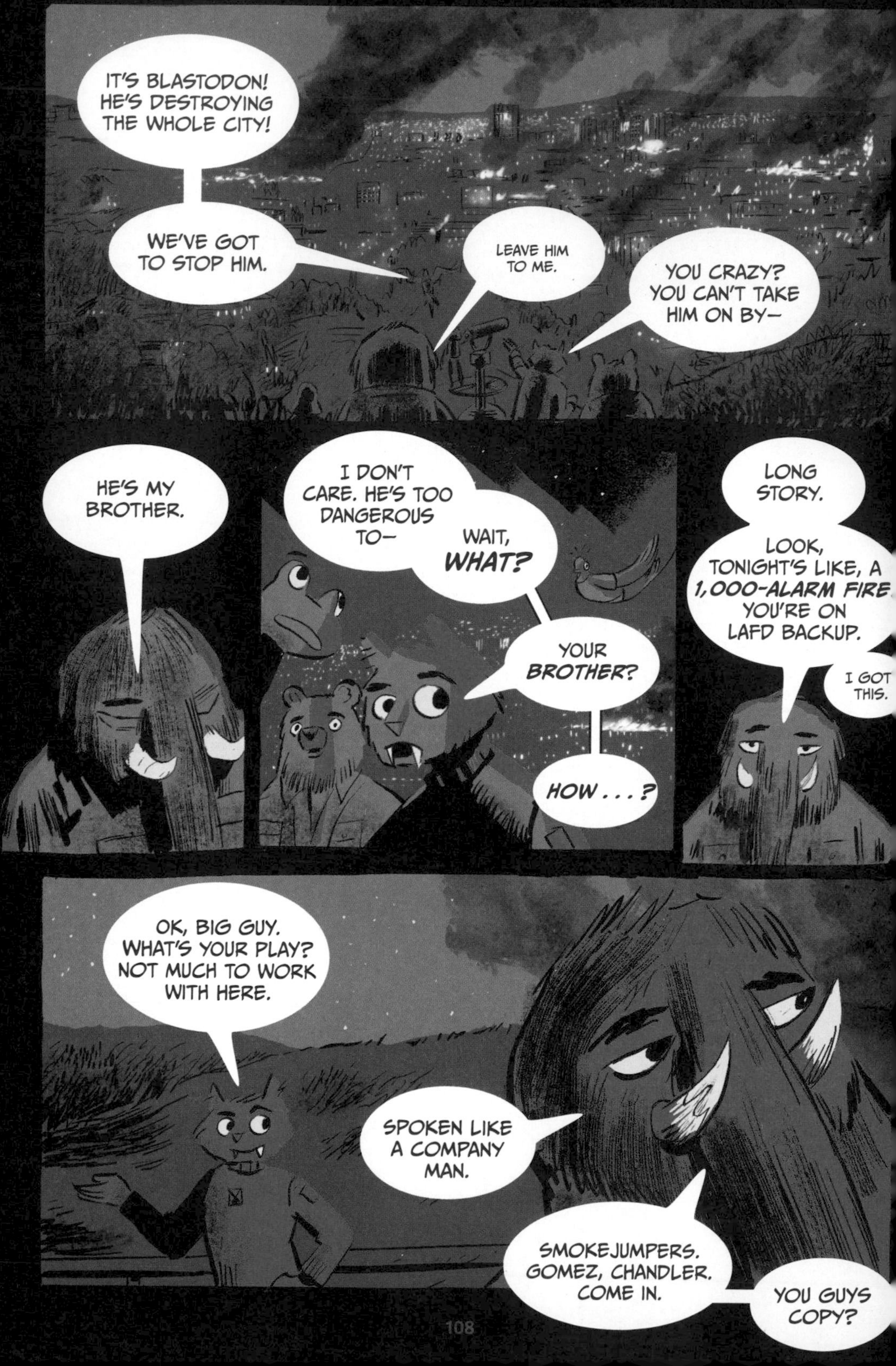
IT'S BLASTODON! HE'S DESTROYING THE WHOLE CITY!
WE'VE GOT TO STOP HIM.
LEAVE HIM TO ME.
YOU CRAZY? YOU CAN'T TAKE HIM ON BY—
HE'S MY BROTHER.
I DON'T CARE. HE'S TOO DANGEROUS TO—
WAIT, **WHAT?**
YOUR **BROTHER?**
**HOW . . . ?**
LONG STORY.
LOOK, TONIGHT'S LIKE, A ***1,000-ALARM FIRE.*** YOU'RE ON LAFD BACKUP.
I GOT THIS.
OK, BIG GUY. WHAT'S YOUR PLAY? NOT MUCH TO WORK WITH HERE.
SPOKEN LIKE A COMPANY MAN.
SMOKEJUMPERS. GOMEZ, CHANDLER. COME IN.
YOU GUYS COPY?

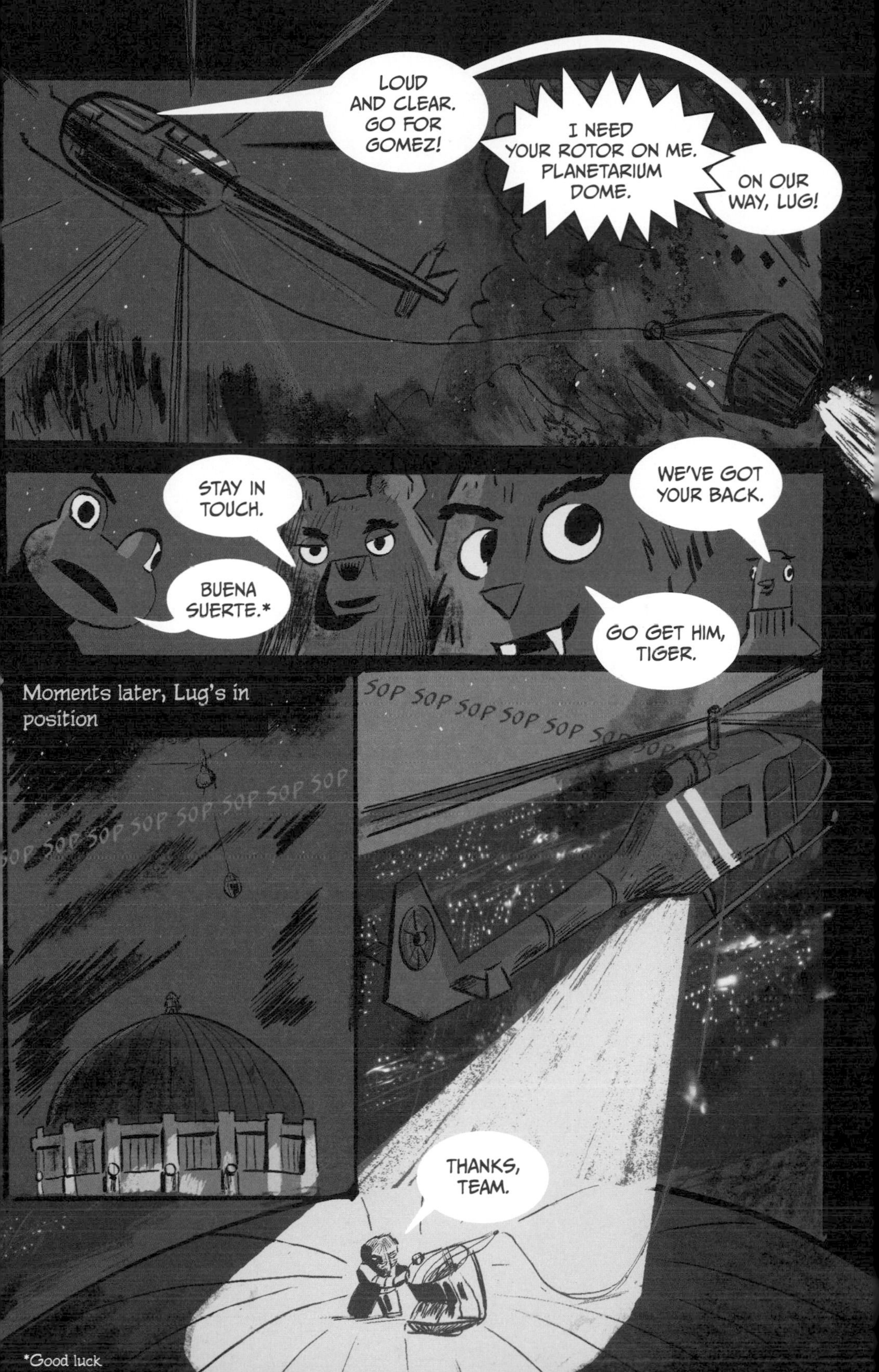
LOUD AND CLEAR. GO FOR GOMEZ!
I NEED YOUR ROTOR ON ME. PLANETARIUM DOME.
ON OUR WAY, LUG!
STAY IN TOUCH.
BUENA SUERTE.*
WE'VE GOT YOUR BACK.
GO GET HIM, TIGER.
Moments later, Lug's in position
SOP SOP SOP SOP SOP SOP SOP
SOP SOP SOP SOP SOP SOP SOP
THANKS, TEAM.

*Good luck

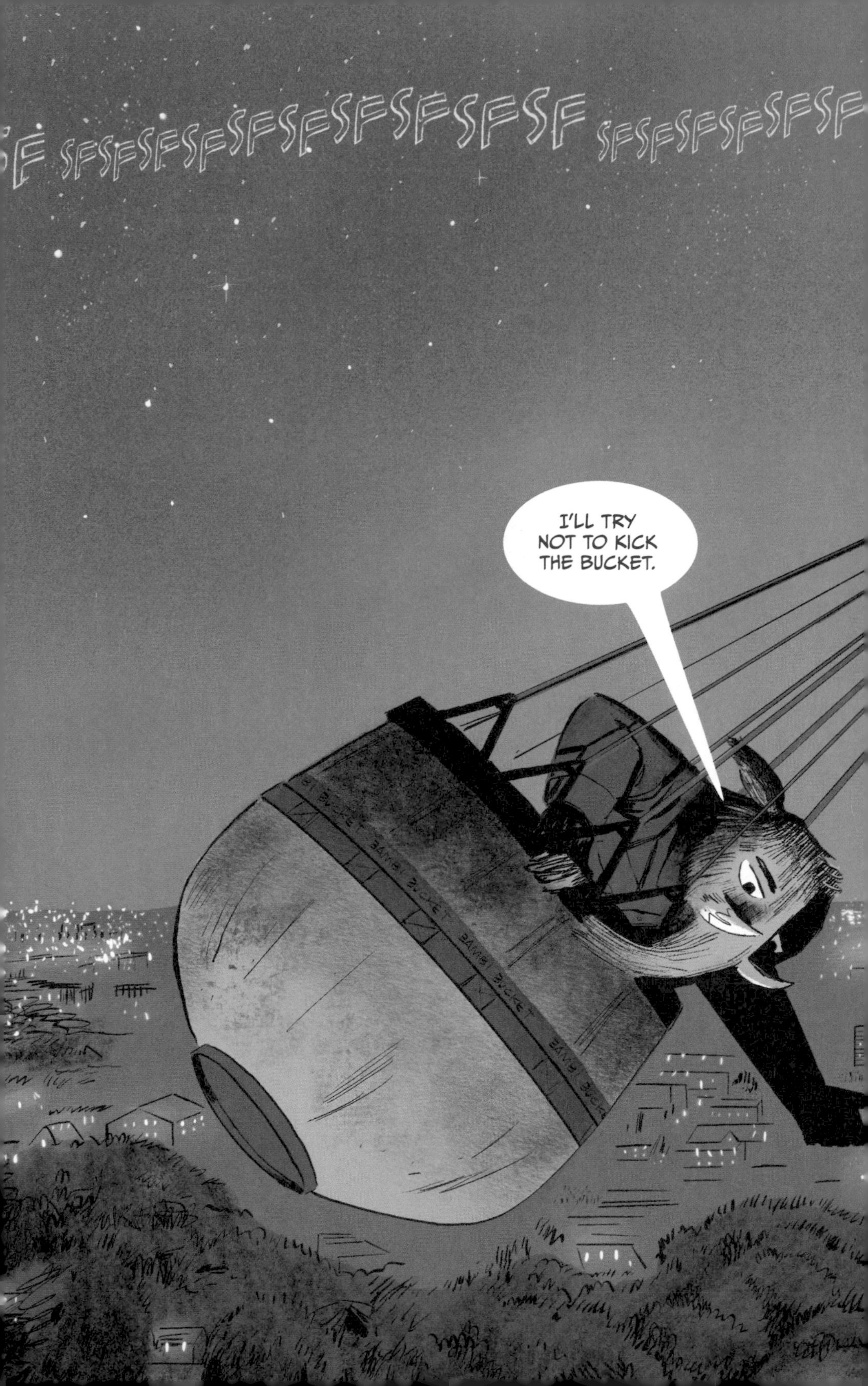
I'LL TRY NOT TO KICK THE BUCKET.
BAMBI BUCKET

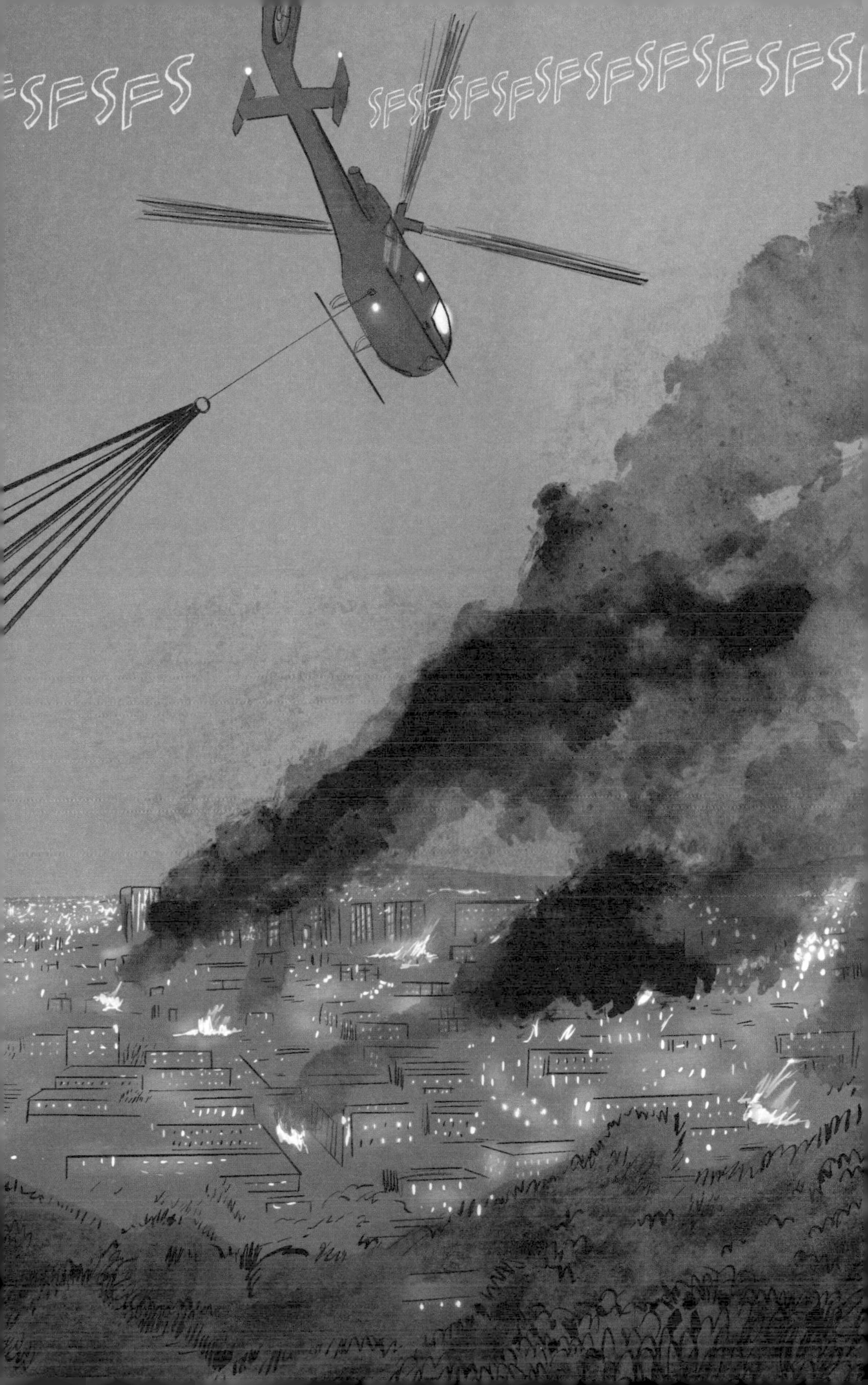

SFSFS
SFSFSFSFSFSFSFSFSFS

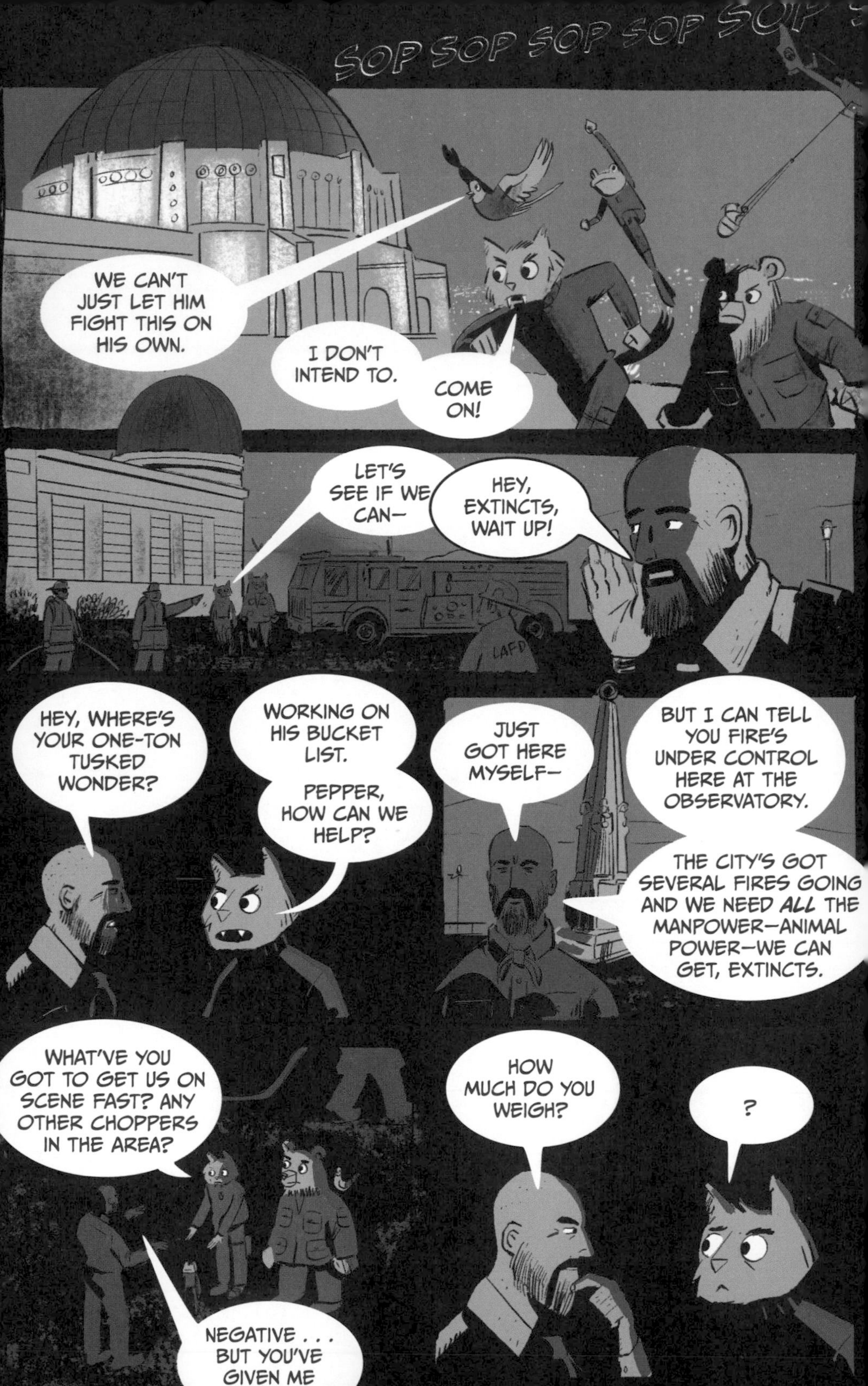
SOP SOP SOP SOP SOP
WE CAN'T JUST LET HIM FIGHT THIS ON HIS OWN.
I DON'T INTEND TO.
COME ON!
LET'S SEE IF WE CAN—
HEY, EXTINCTS, WAIT UP!
LAFD
HEY, WHERE'S YOUR ONE-TON TUSKED WONDER?
WORKING ON HIS BUCKET LIST.
PEPPER, HOW CAN WE HELP?
JUST GOT HERE MYSELF—
BUT I CAN TELL YOU FIRE'S UNDER CONTROL HERE AT THE OBSERVATORY.
THE CITY'S GOT SEVERAL FIRES GOING AND WE NEED ***ALL*** THE MANPOWER—ANIMAL POWER—WE CAN GET, EXTINCTS.
WHAT'VE YOU GOT TO GET US ON SCENE FAST? ANY OTHER CHOPPERS IN THE AREA?
NEGATIVE . . . BUT YOU'VE GIVEN ME AN IDEA.
HOW MUCH DO YOU WEIGH?
?

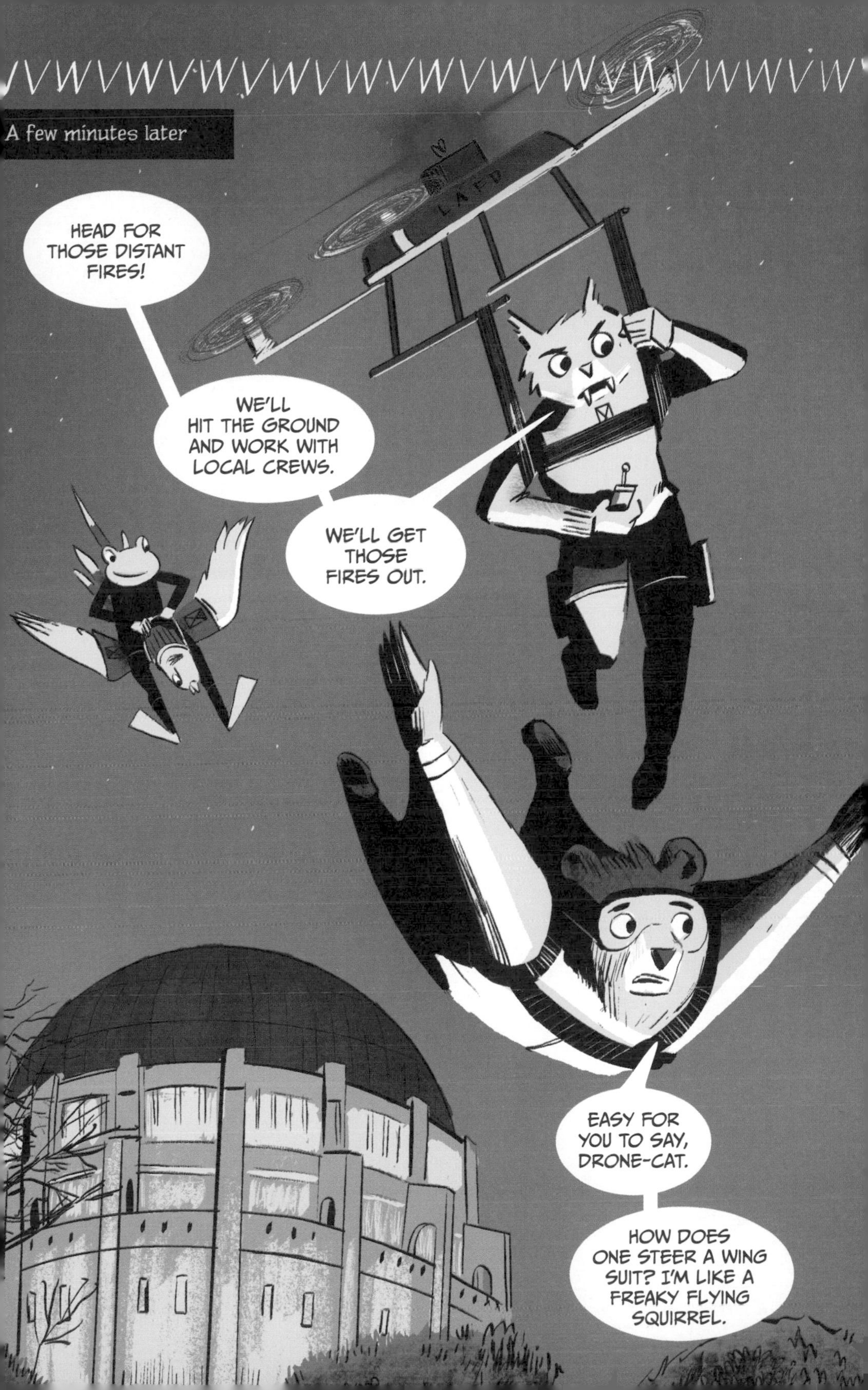
A few minutes later
HEAD FOR THOSE DISTANT FIRES!
WE'LL HIT THE GROUND AND WORK WITH LOCAL CREWS.
WE'LL GET THOSE FIRES OUT.
EASY FOR YOU TO SAY, DRONE-CAT.
HOW DOES ONE STEER A WING SUIT? I'M LIKE A FREAKY FLYING SQUIRREL.

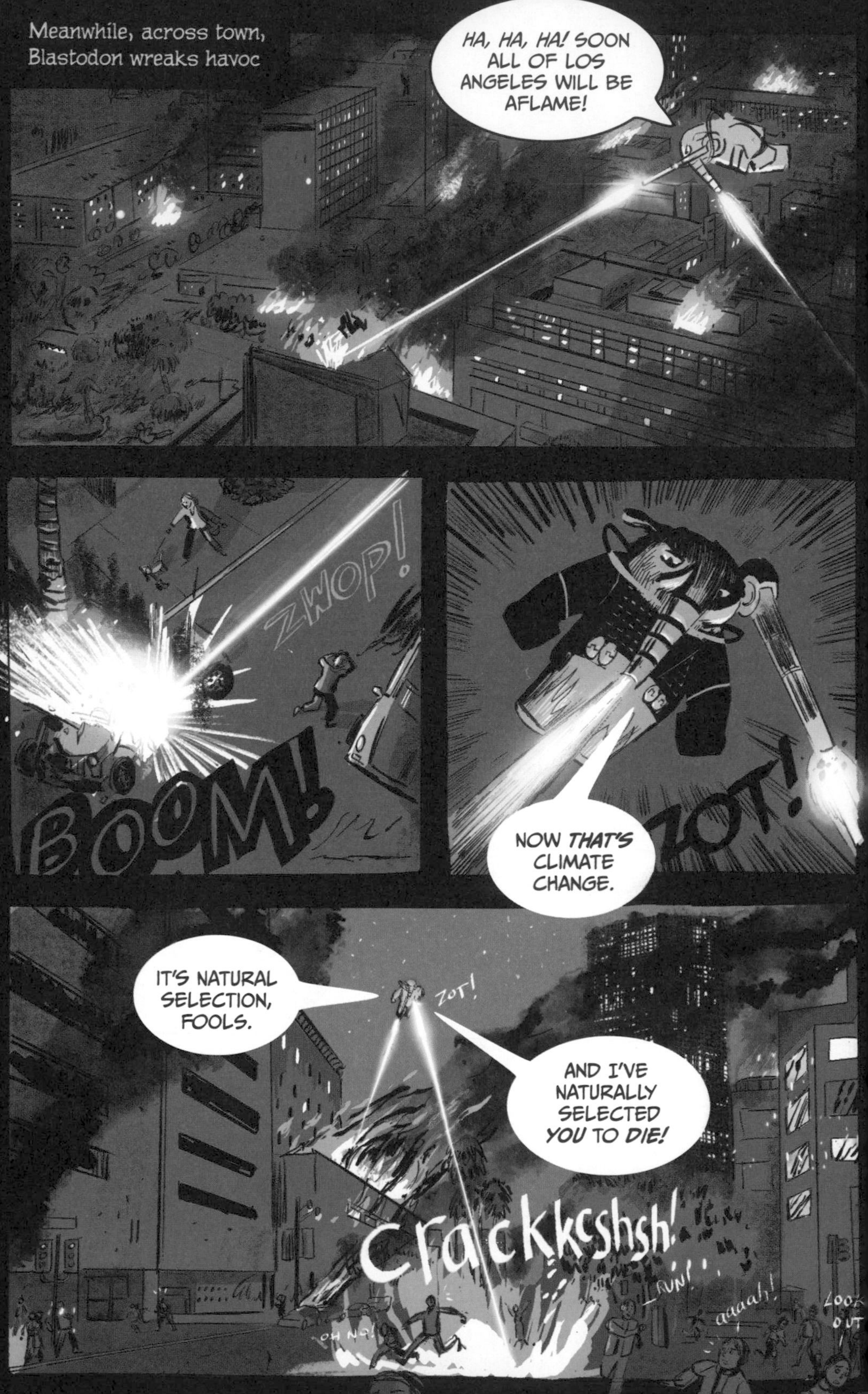
Meanwhile, across town, Blastodon wreaks havoc
HA, HA, HA! SOON ALL OF LOS ANGELES WILL BE AFLAME!
ZWOP!
BOOM!
ZOT!
NOW *THAT'S* CLIMATE CHANGE.
IT'S NATURAL SELECTION, FOOLS.
ZOT!
AND I'VE NATURALLY SELECTED *YOU* TO *DIE!*
Crackkcshsh!
RUN!
aaaah!
LOOK OUT!
OH NO!

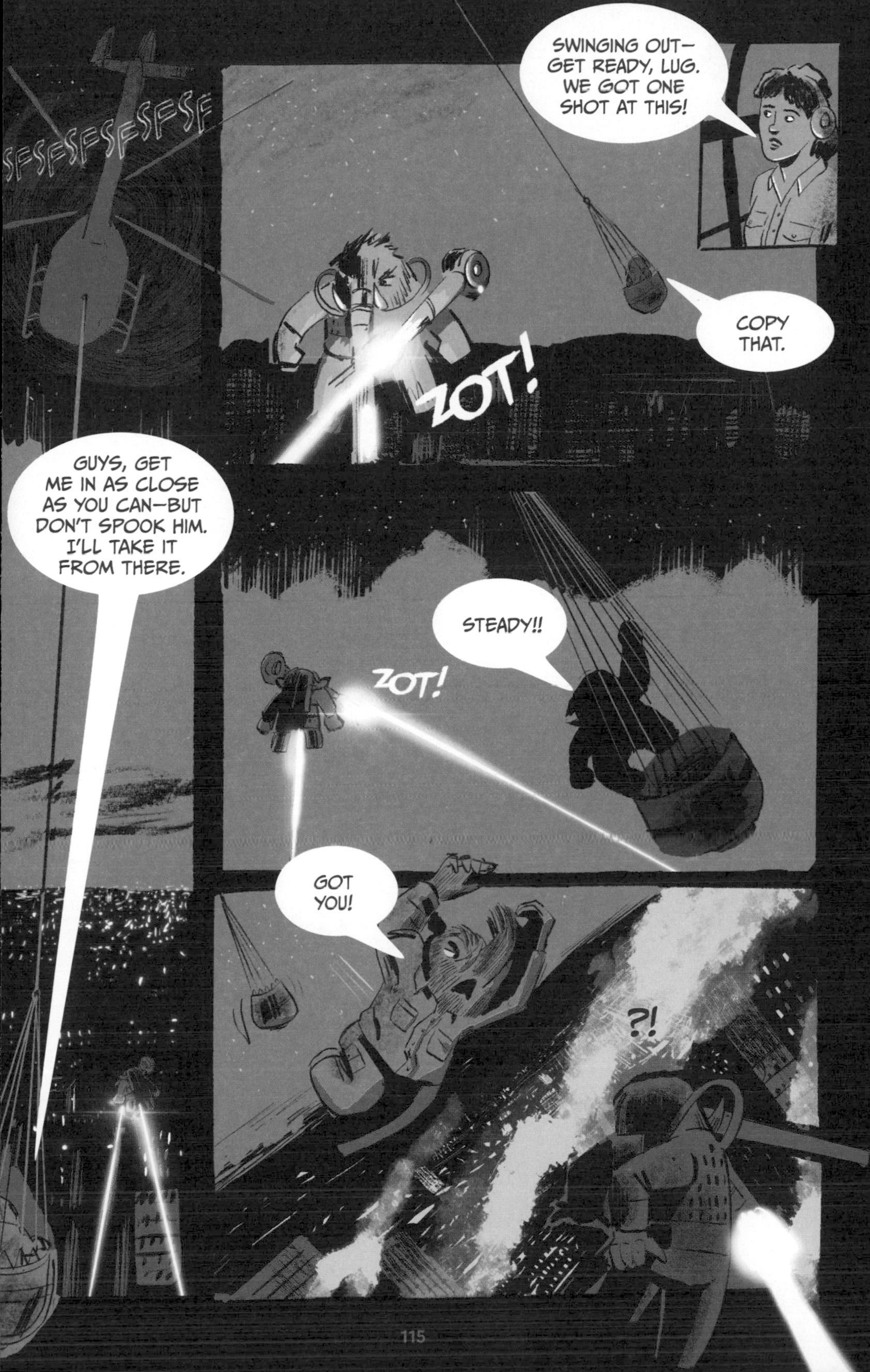
SFSFSFSFSFSFSF
SWINGING OUT—GET READY, LUG. WE GOT ONE SHOT AT THIS!
COPY THAT.
ZOT!
GUYS, GET ME IN AS CLOSE AS YOU CAN—BUT DON'T SPOOK HIM. I'LL TAKE IT FROM THERE.
STEADY!!
ZOT!
GOT YOU!
?!

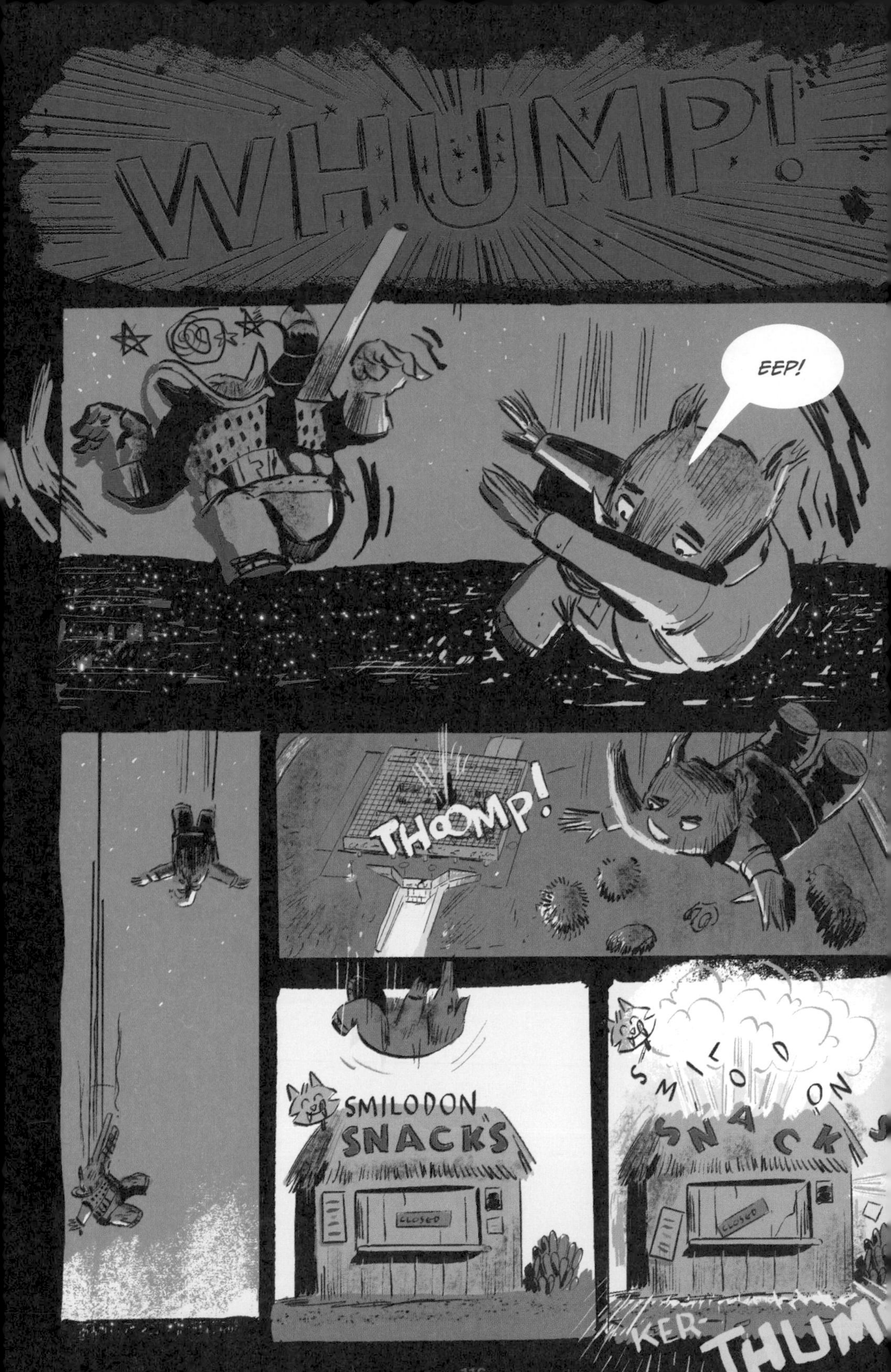
WHUMP!
EEP!
THOOMP!
SMILODON SNACKS
CLOSED
KER-THUM

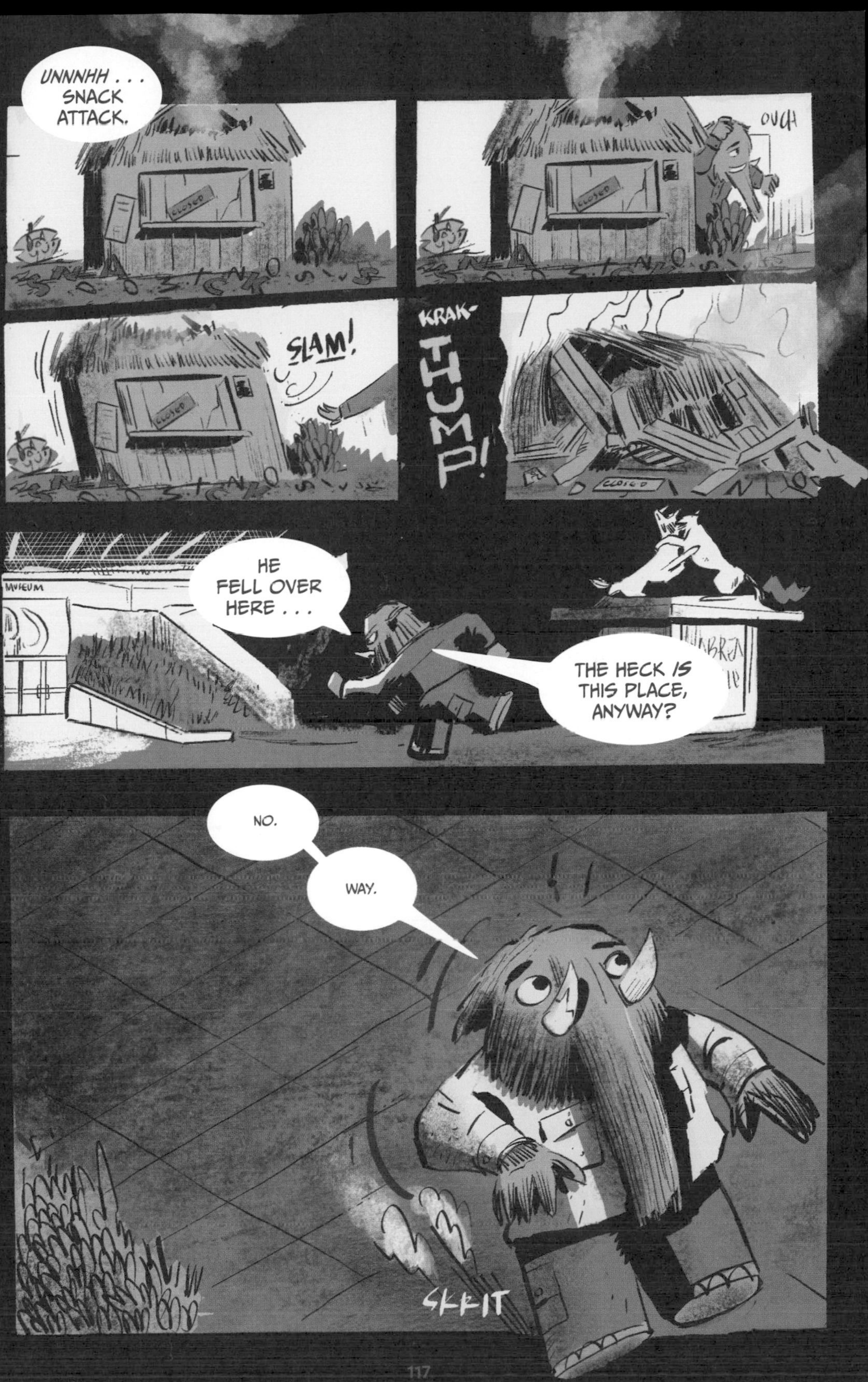
UNNNHH . . . SNACK ATTACK.
OUCH
SLAM!
KRAK-
THUMP!
HE FELL OVER HERE . . .
THE HECK IS THIS PLACE, ANYWAY?
NO.
WAY.
SKRIT

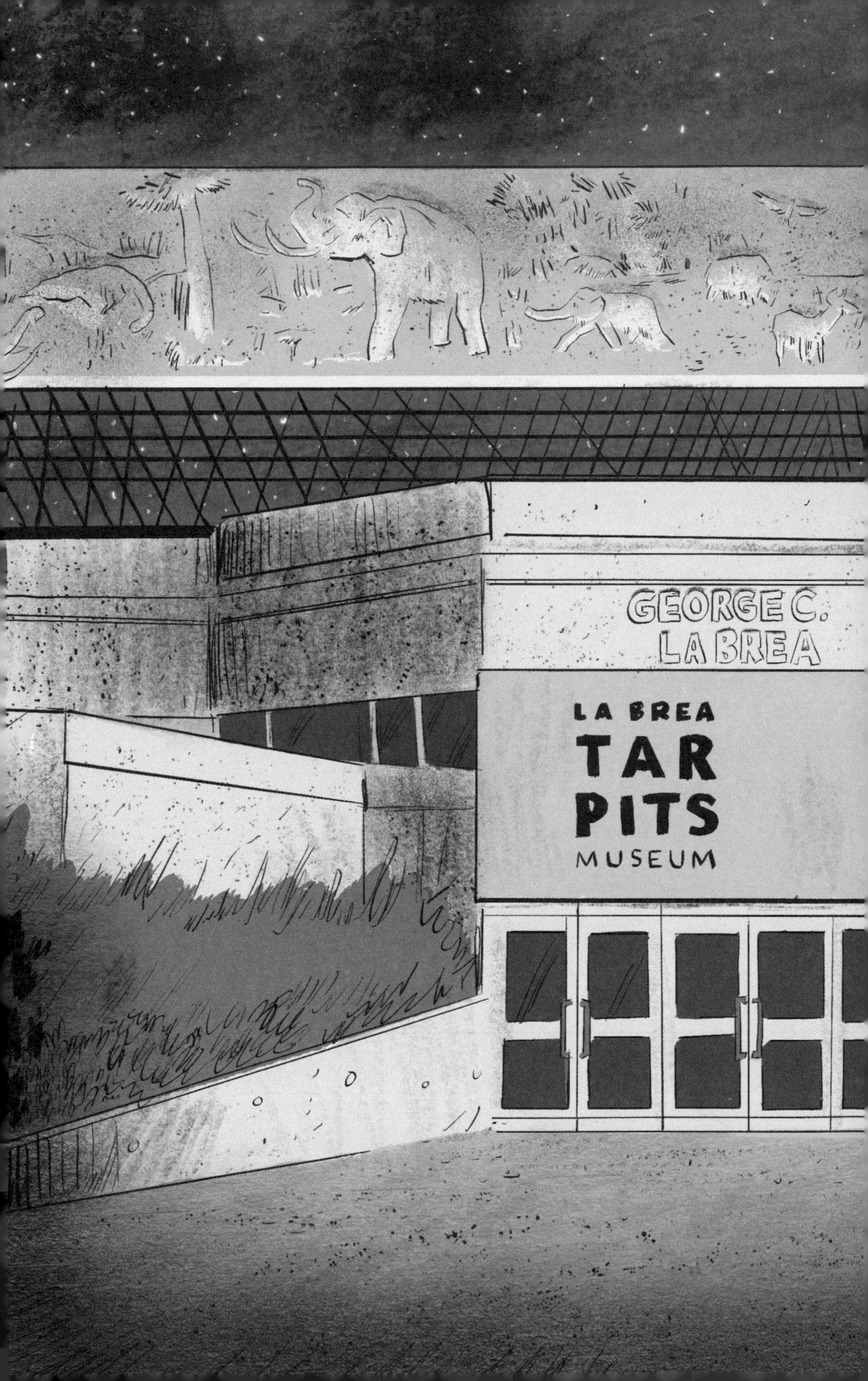
GEORGE C.
LA BREA
LA BREA
TAR
PITS
MUSEUM

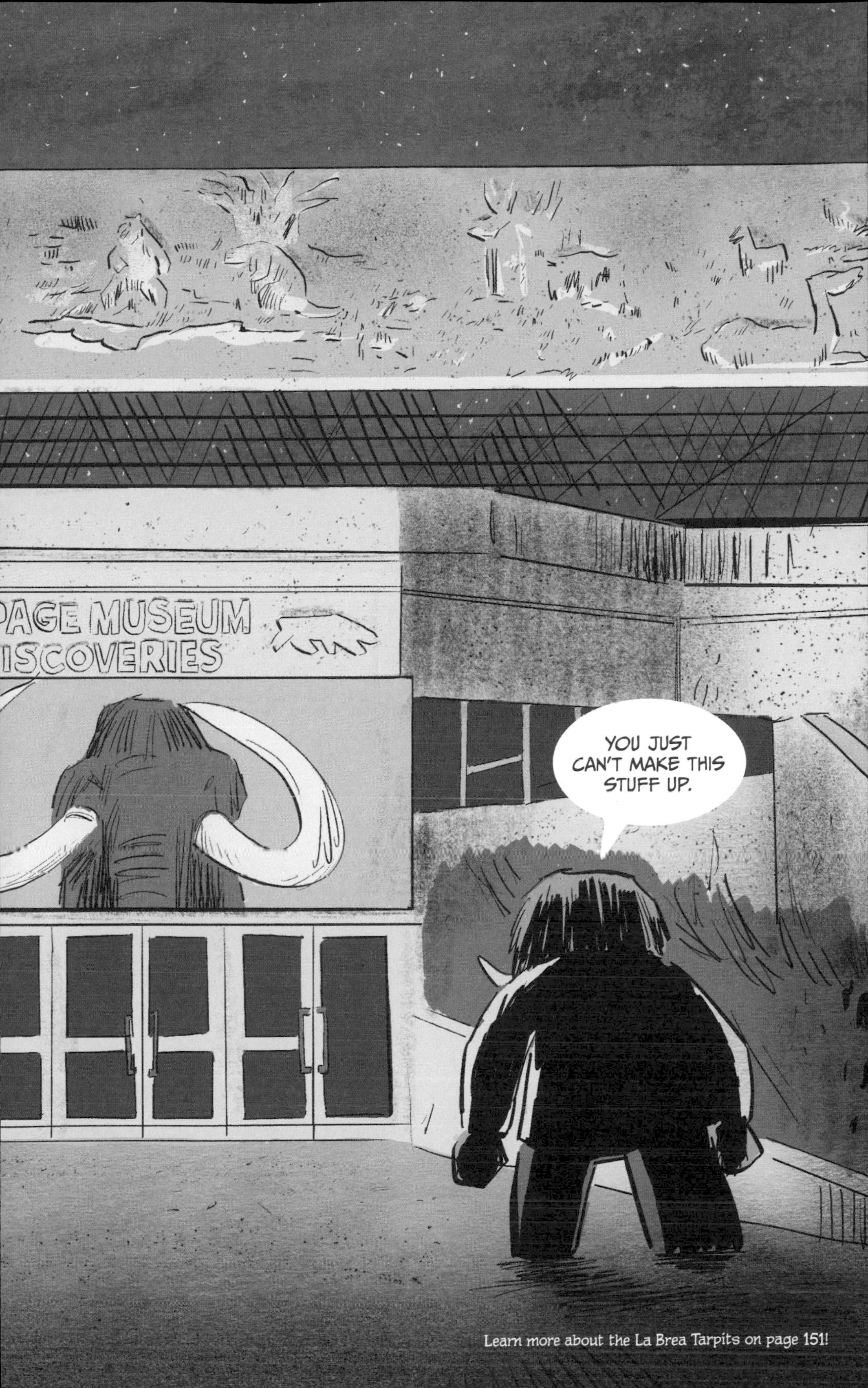
PAGE MUSEUM
ISCOVERIES
YOU JUST CAN'T MAKE THIS STUFF UP.
Learn more about the La Brea Tarpits on page 151!

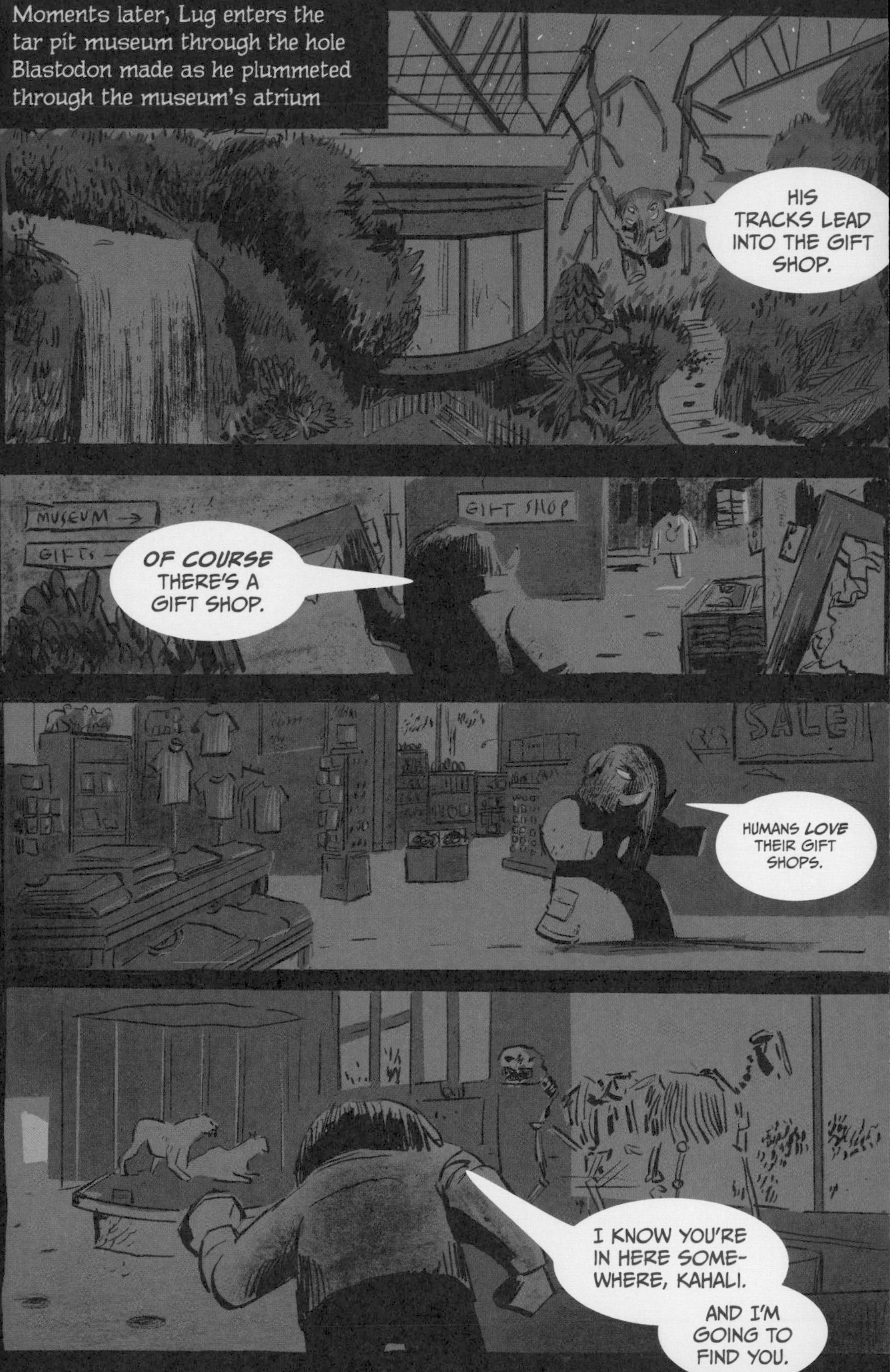
Moments later, Lug enters the tar pit museum through the hole Blastodon made as he plummeted through the museum's atrium
HIS TRACKS LEAD INTO THE GIFT SHOP.
MUSEUM
GIFT SHOP
OF COURSE THERE'S A GIFT SHOP.
SALE
HUMANS LOVE THEIR GIFT SHOPS.
I KNOW YOU'RE IN HERE SOMEWHERE, KAHALI.
AND I'M GOING TO FIND YOU.

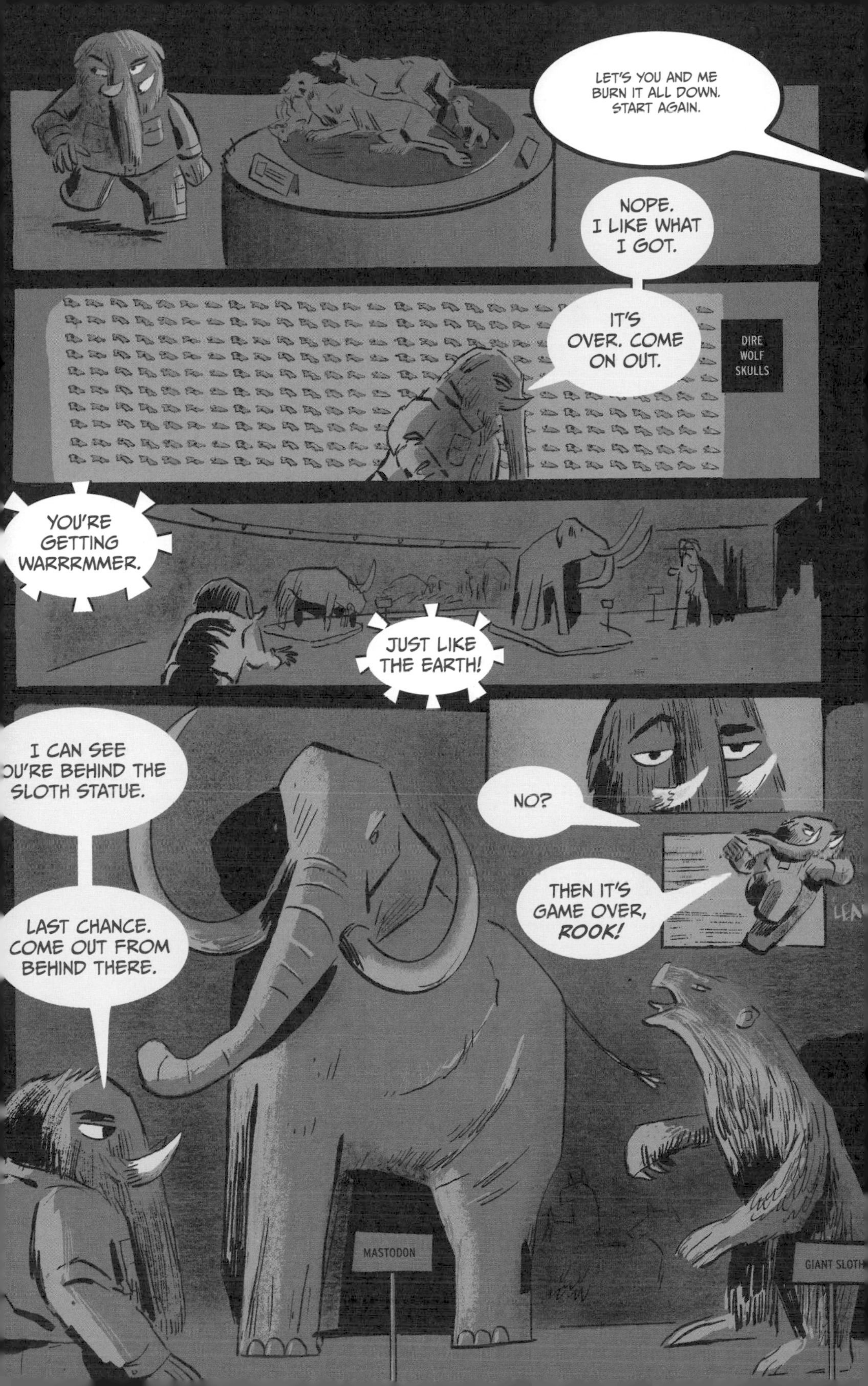
LET'S YOU AND ME BURN IT ALL DOWN. START AGAIN.
NOPE. I LIKE WHAT I GOT.
IT'S OVER. COME ON OUT.
DIRE WOLF SKULLS
YOU'RE GETTING WARRRMMER.
JUST LIKE THE EARTH!
I CAN SEE OU'RE BEHIND THE SLOTH STATUE.
LAST CHANCE. COME OUT FROM BEHIND THERE.
NO?
THEN IT'S GAME OVER, *ROOK!*
MASTODON
GIANT SLOTH

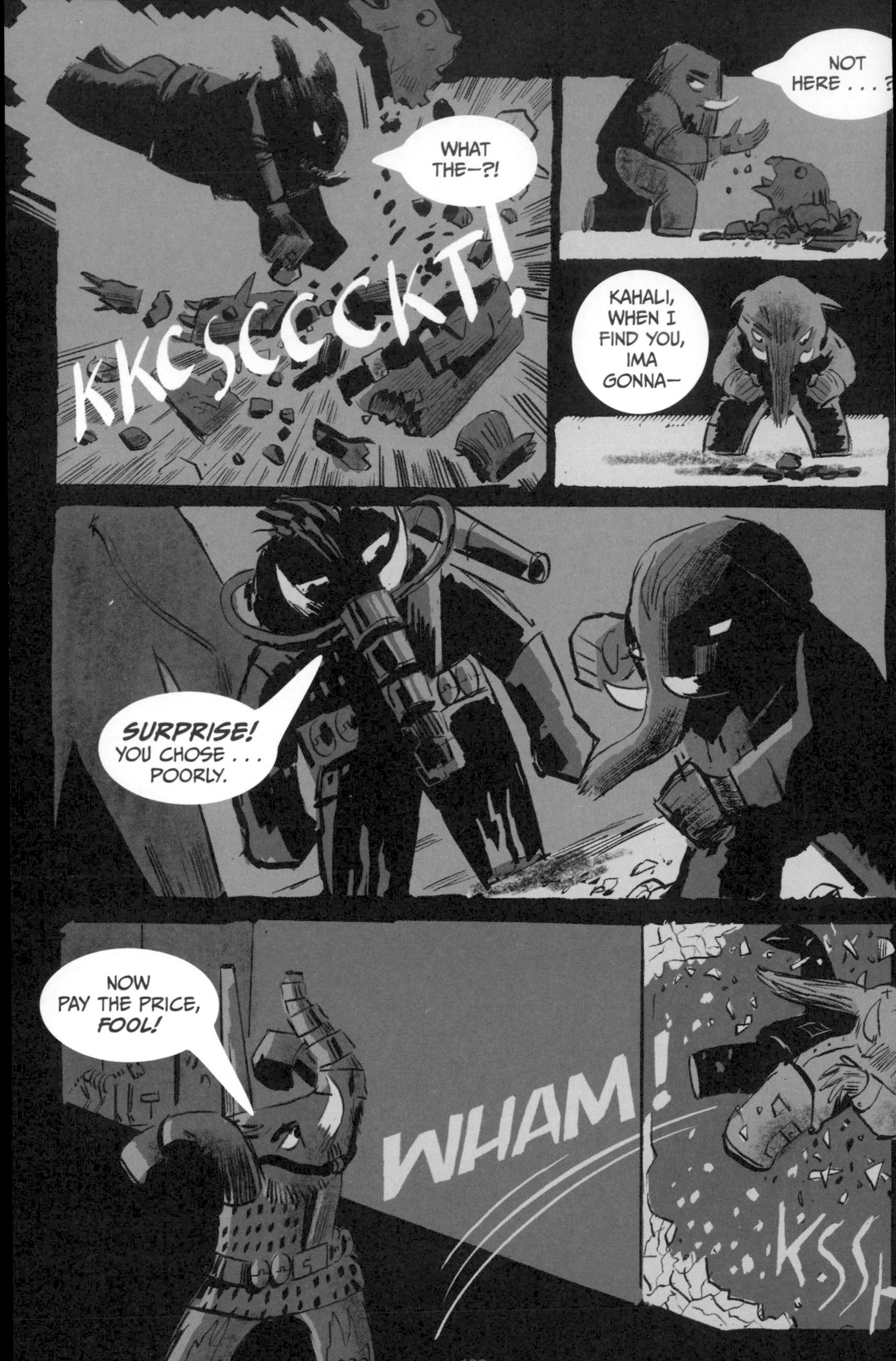
WHAT THE—?!
KKCSCCCKT!
NOT HERE . . . ?
KAHALI, WHEN I FIND YOU, IMA GONNA—
SURPRISE! YOU CHOSE . . . POORLY.
NOW PAY THE PRICE, FOOL!
WHAM!
KSS

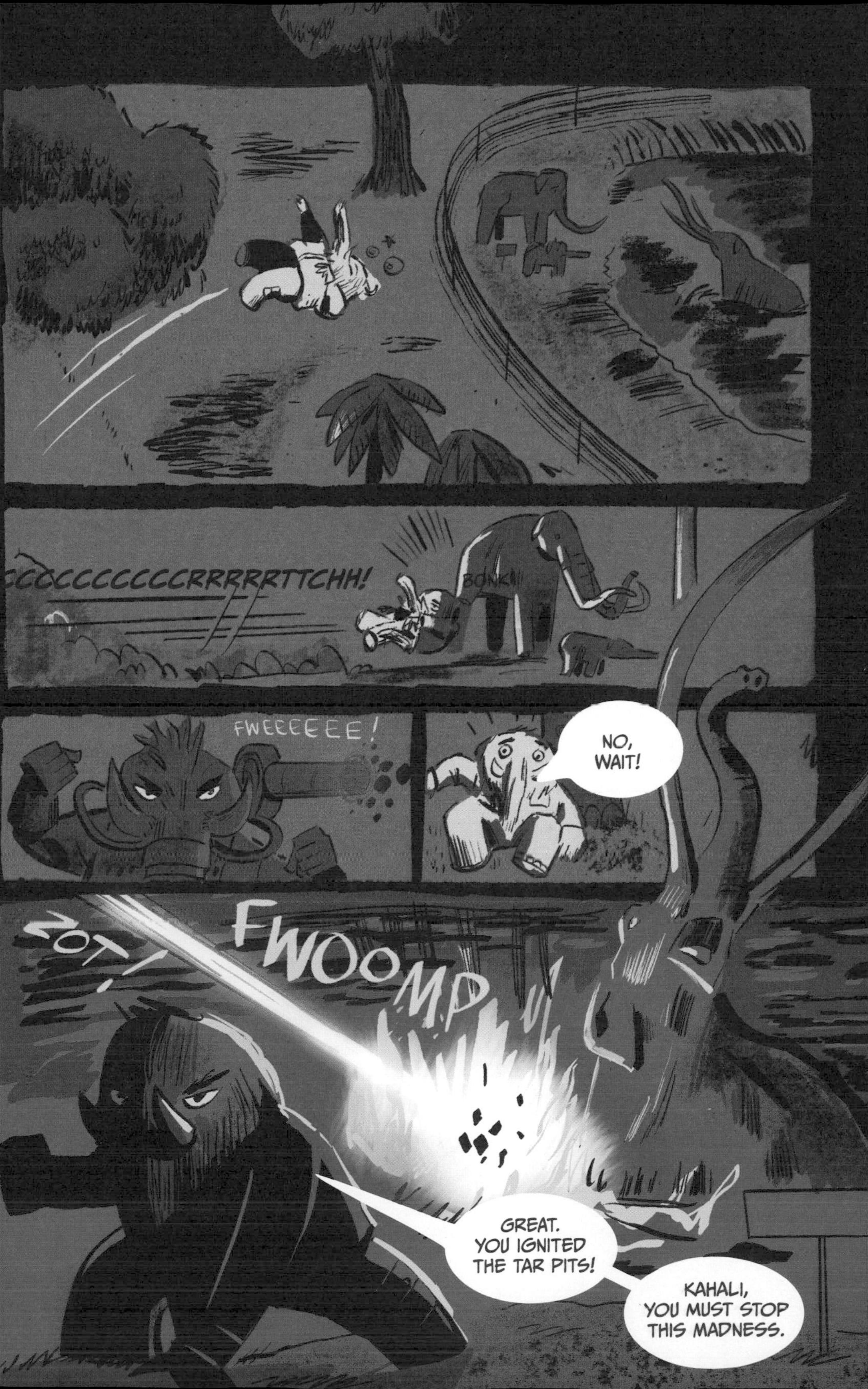
CCCCCCCCCCCCRRRRRRTTCHH!
BONK
FWEEEEEEE!
NO, WAIT!
ZOT!
FWOOMP
GREAT. YOU IGNITED THE TAR PITS!
KAHALI, YOU MUST STOP THIS MADNESS.

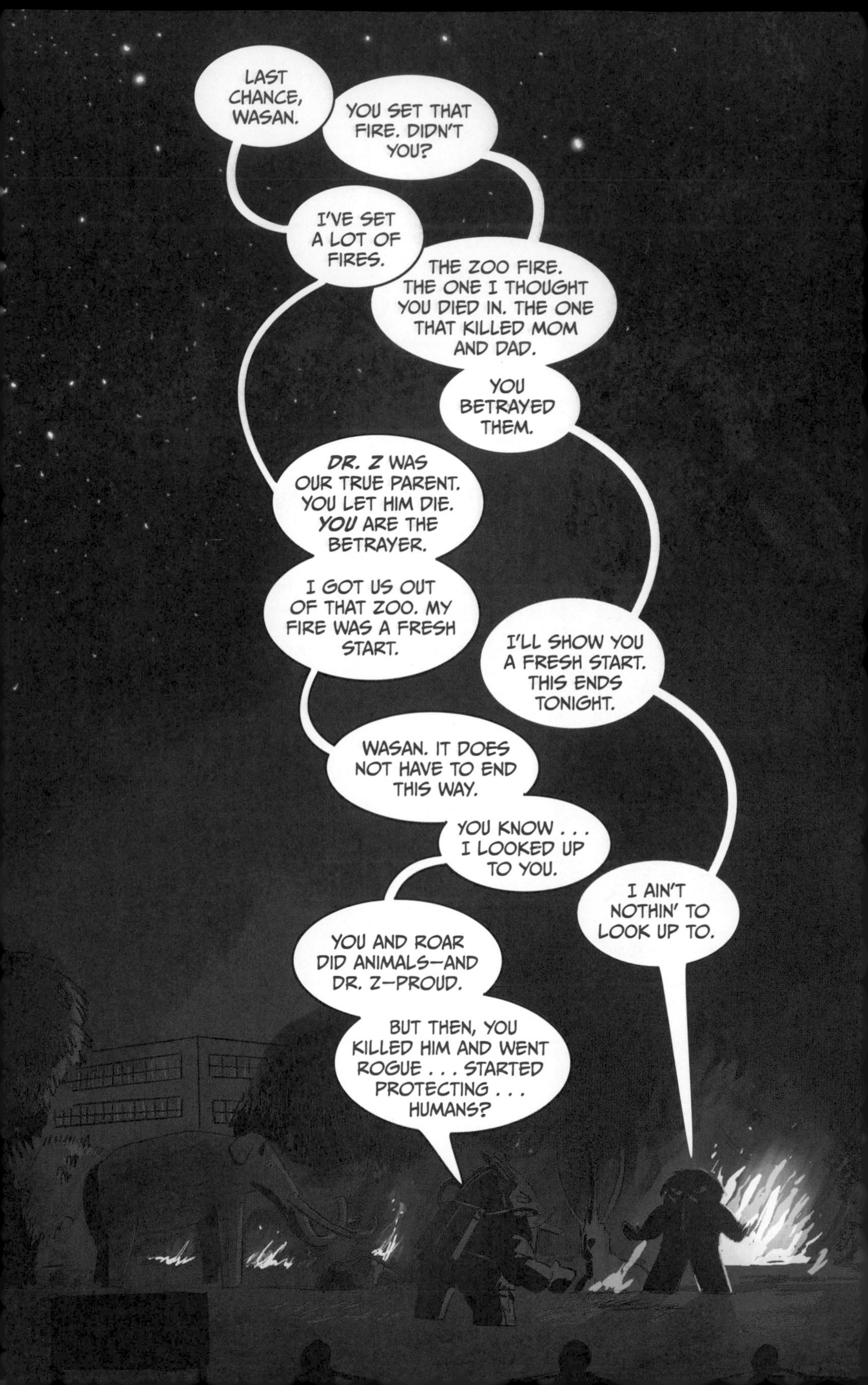
LAST CHANCE, WASAN.
YOU SET THAT FIRE. DIDN'T YOU?
I'VE SET A LOT OF FIRES.
THE ZOO FIRE. THE ONE I THOUGHT YOU DIED IN. THE ONE THAT KILLED MOM AND DAD.
YOU BETRAYED THEM.
*DR. Z* WAS OUR TRUE PARENT. YOU LET HIM DIE. ***YOU*** ARE THE BETRAYER.
I GOT US OUT OF THAT ZOO. MY FIRE WAS A FRESH START.
I'LL SHOW YOU A FRESH START. THIS ENDS TONIGHT.
WASAN. IT DOES NOT HAVE TO END THIS WAY.
YOU KNOW . . . I LOOKED UP TO YOU.
I AIN'T NOTHIN' TO LOOK UP TO.
YOU AND ROAR DID ANIMALS—AND DR. Z—PROUD.
BUT THEN, YOU KILLED HIM AND WENT ROGUE . . . STARTED PROTECTING . . . HUMANS?

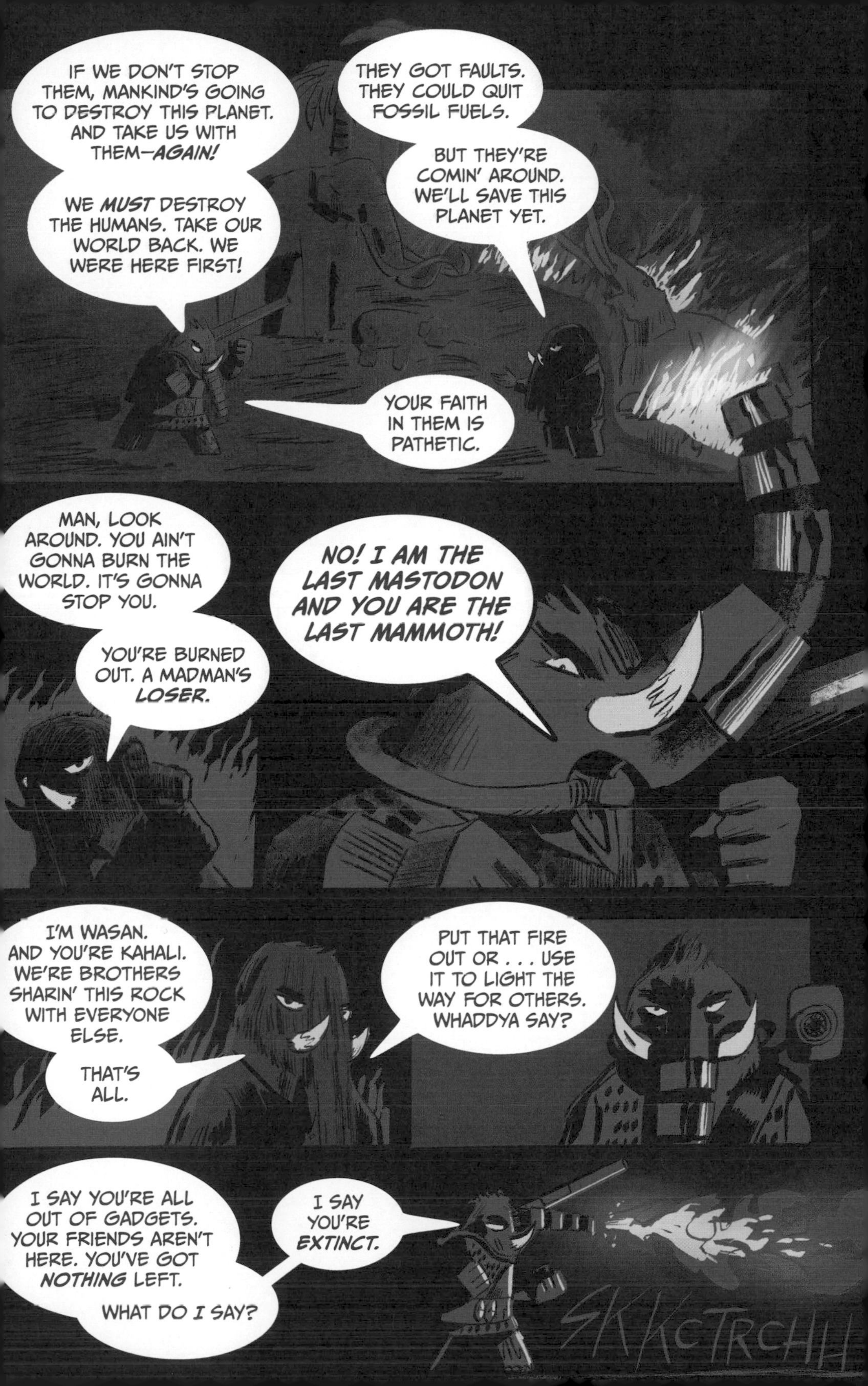
IF WE DON'T STOP THEM, MANKIND'S GOING TO DESTROY THIS PLANET. AND TAKE US WITH THEM—AGAIN!
WE MUST DESTROY THE HUMANS. TAKE OUR WORLD BACK. WE WERE HERE FIRST!
THEY GOT FAULTS. THEY COULD QUIT FOSSIL FUELS.
BUT THEY'RE COMIN' AROUND. WE'LL SAVE THIS PLANET YET.
YOUR FAITH IN THEM IS PATHETIC.
MAN, LOOK AROUND. YOU AIN'T GONNA BURN THE WORLD. IT'S GONNA STOP YOU.
YOU'RE BURNED OUT. A MADMAN'S LOSER.
NO! I AM THE LAST MASTODON AND YOU ARE THE LAST MAMMOTH!
I'M WASAN. AND YOU'RE KAHALI. WE'RE BROTHERS SHARIN' THIS ROCK WITH EVERYONE ELSE.
THAT'S ALL.
PUT THAT FIRE OUT OR . . . USE IT TO LIGHT THE WAY FOR OTHERS. WHADDYA SAY?
I SAY YOU'RE ALL OUT OF GADGETS. YOUR FRIENDS AREN'T HERE. YOU'VE GOT NOTHING LEFT.
WHAT DO I SAY?
I SAY YOU'RE EXTINCT.
SKKCTRCHH

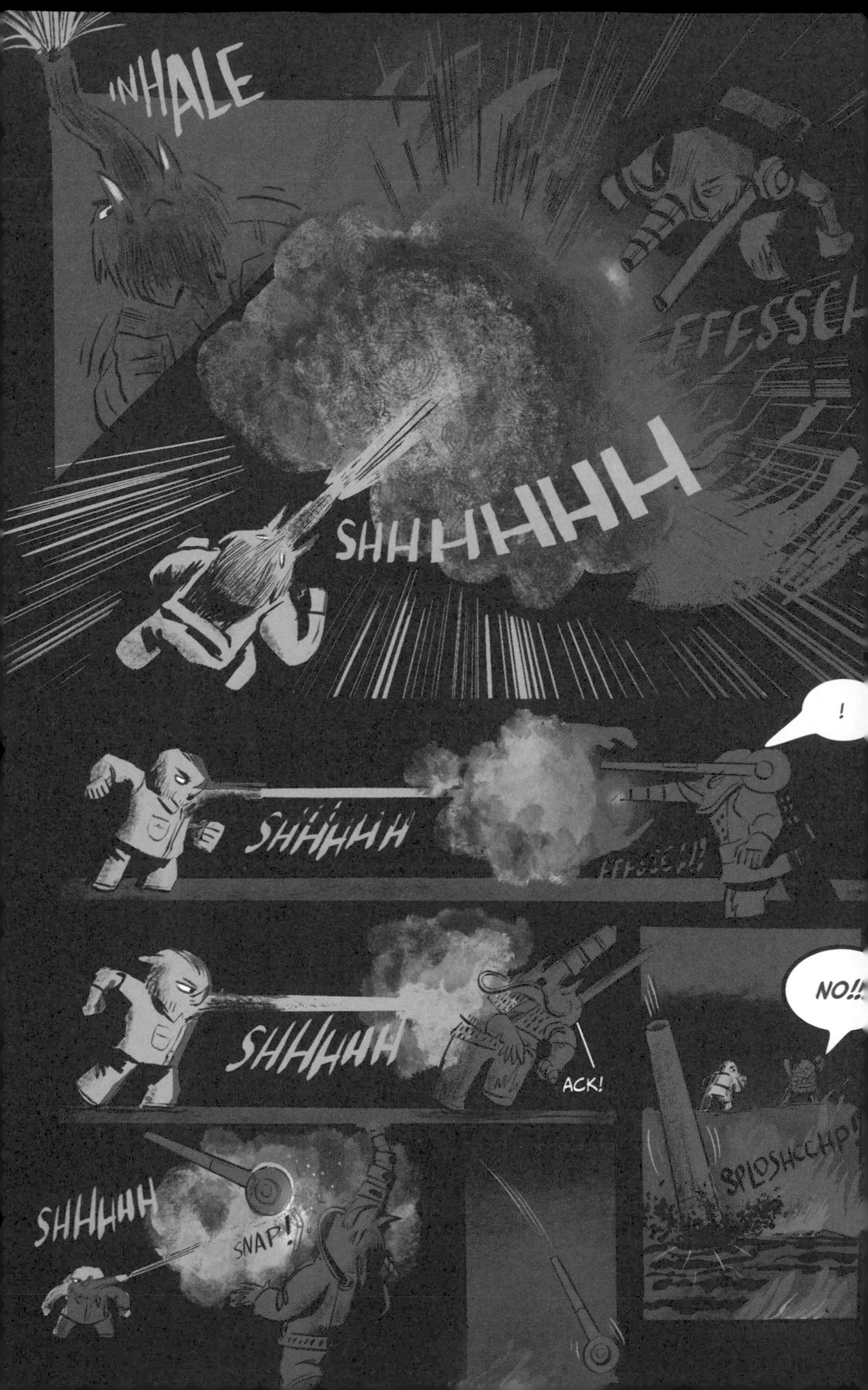
INHALE
FFESSCH
SHHHHHHH
!
SHHHHHH
SHHHHH
ACK!
NO!!
SHHHHH
SNAP!
SPLOSHCCHP

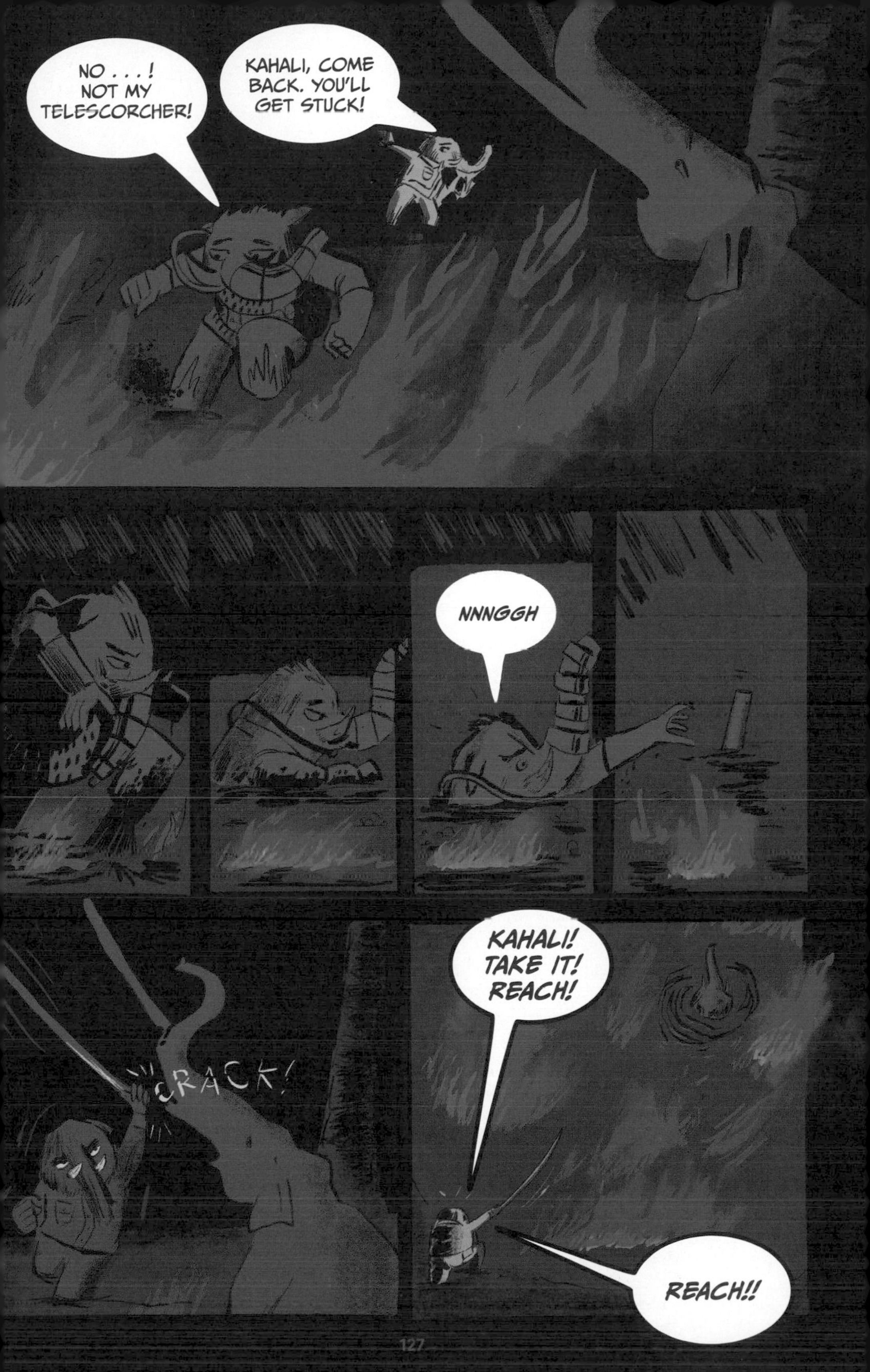
NO . . . ! NOT MY TELESCORCHER!
KAHALI, COME BACK. YOU'LL GET STUCK!
NNNGGH
CRACK!
KAHALI! TAKE IT! REACH!
REACH!!

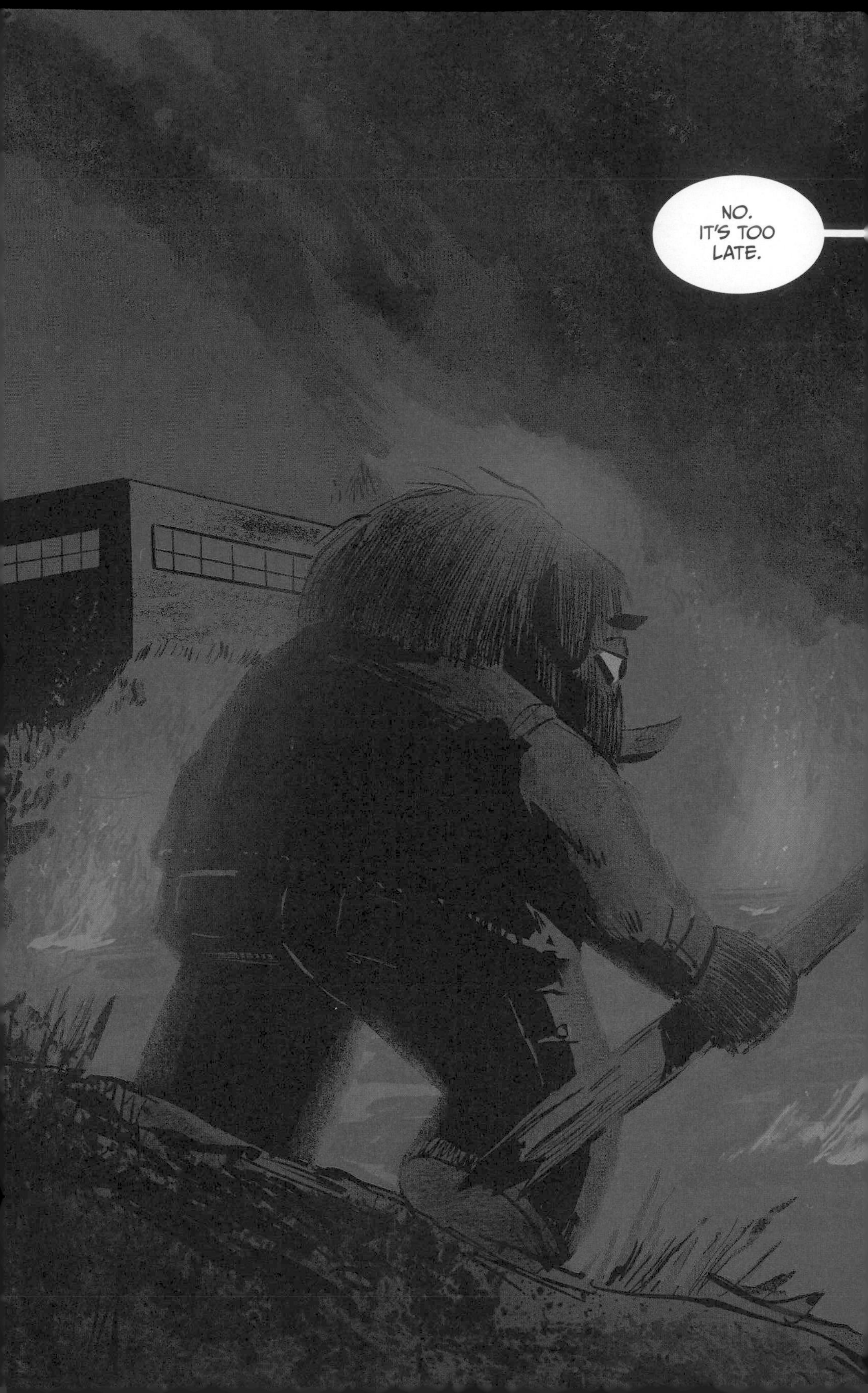
NO. IT'S TOO LATE.

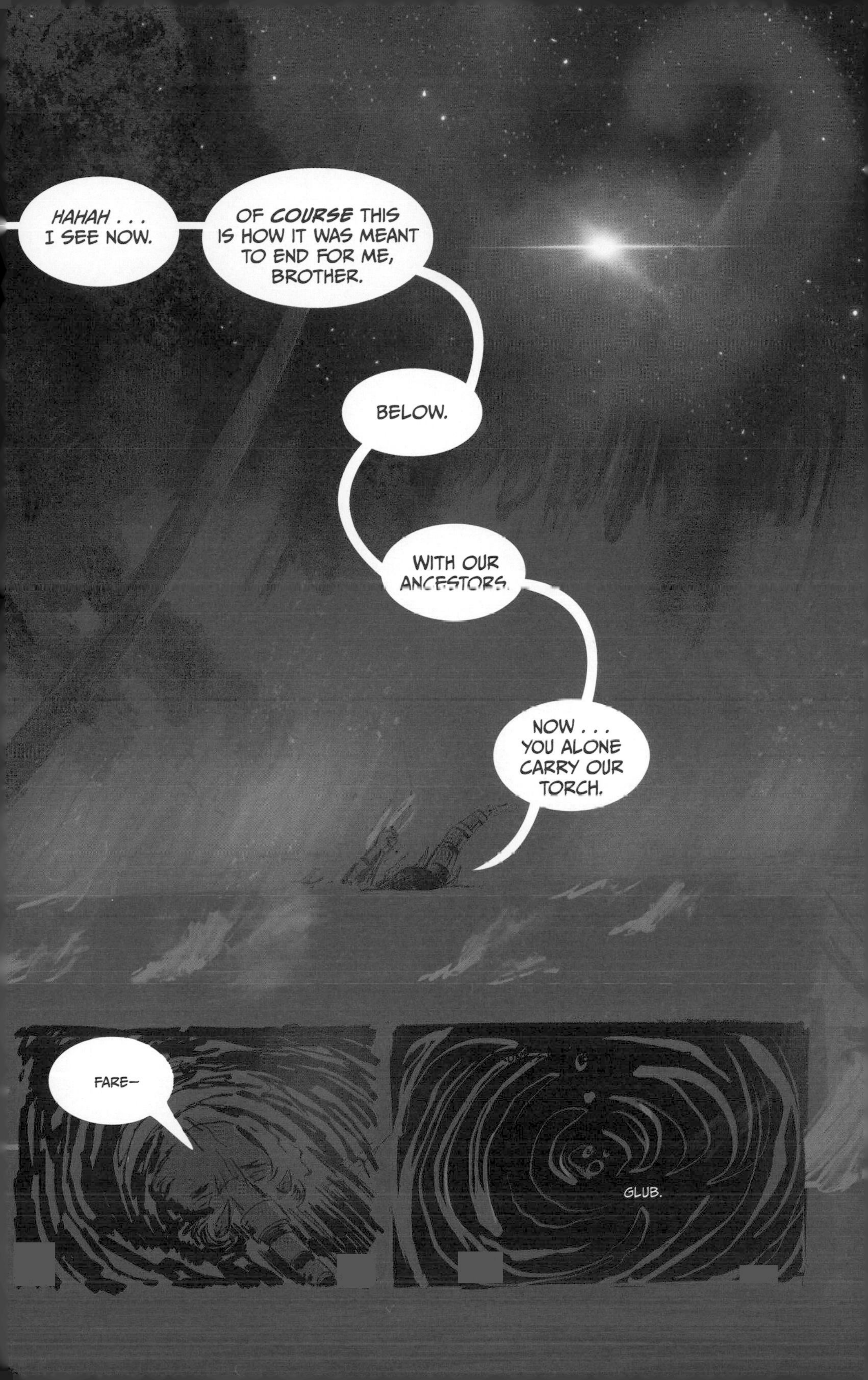
HAHAH . . . I SEE NOW.
OF COURSE THIS IS HOW IT WAS MEANT TO END FOR ME, BROTHER.
BELOW.
WITH OUR ANCESTORS.
NOW . . . YOU ALONE CARRY OUR TORCH.
FARE—
GLUB.

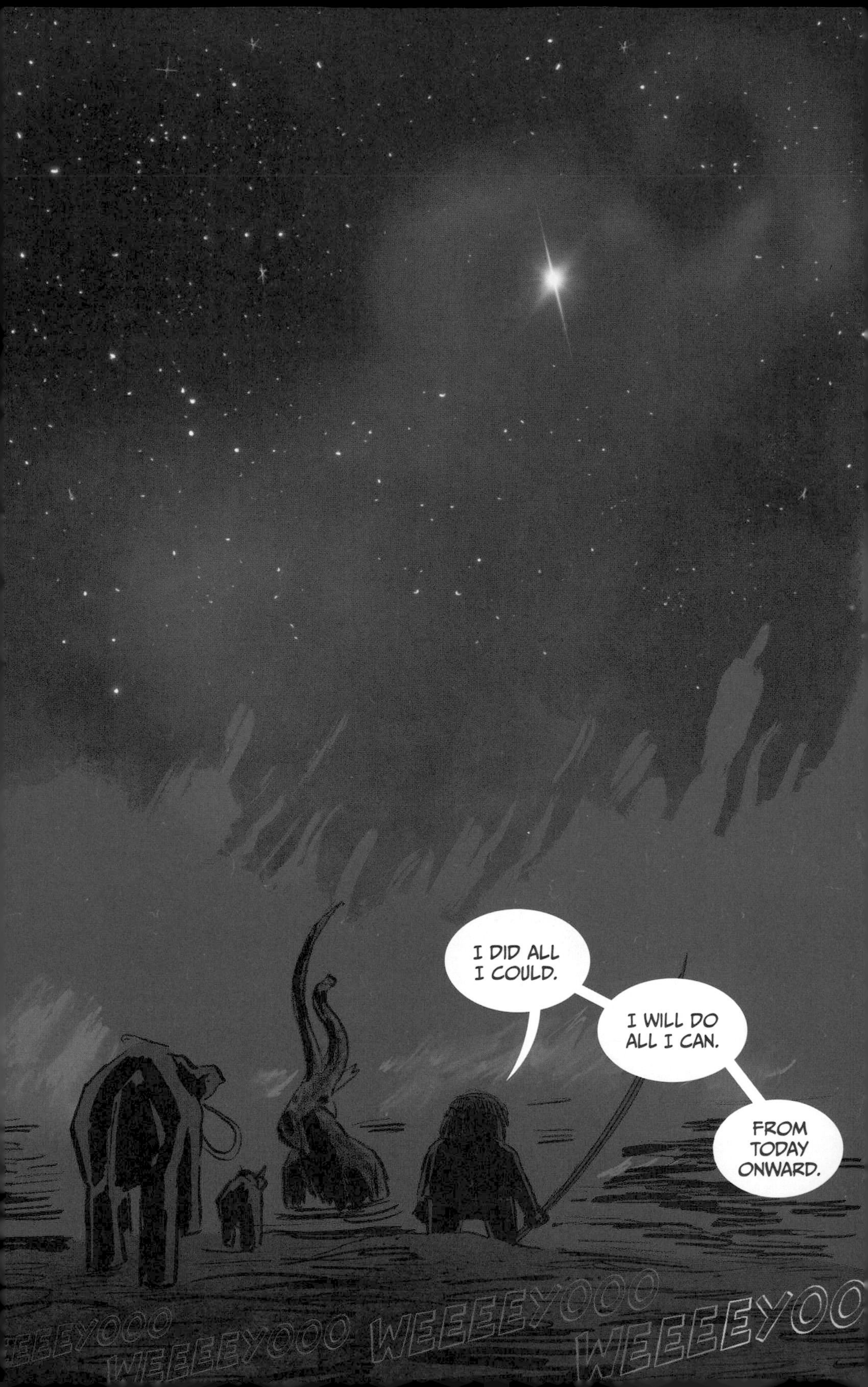
I DID ALL I COULD.
I WILL DO ALL I CAN.
FROM TODAY ONWARD.
EEEYOOO WEEEEYOOO WEEEEYOOO WEEEEYOO

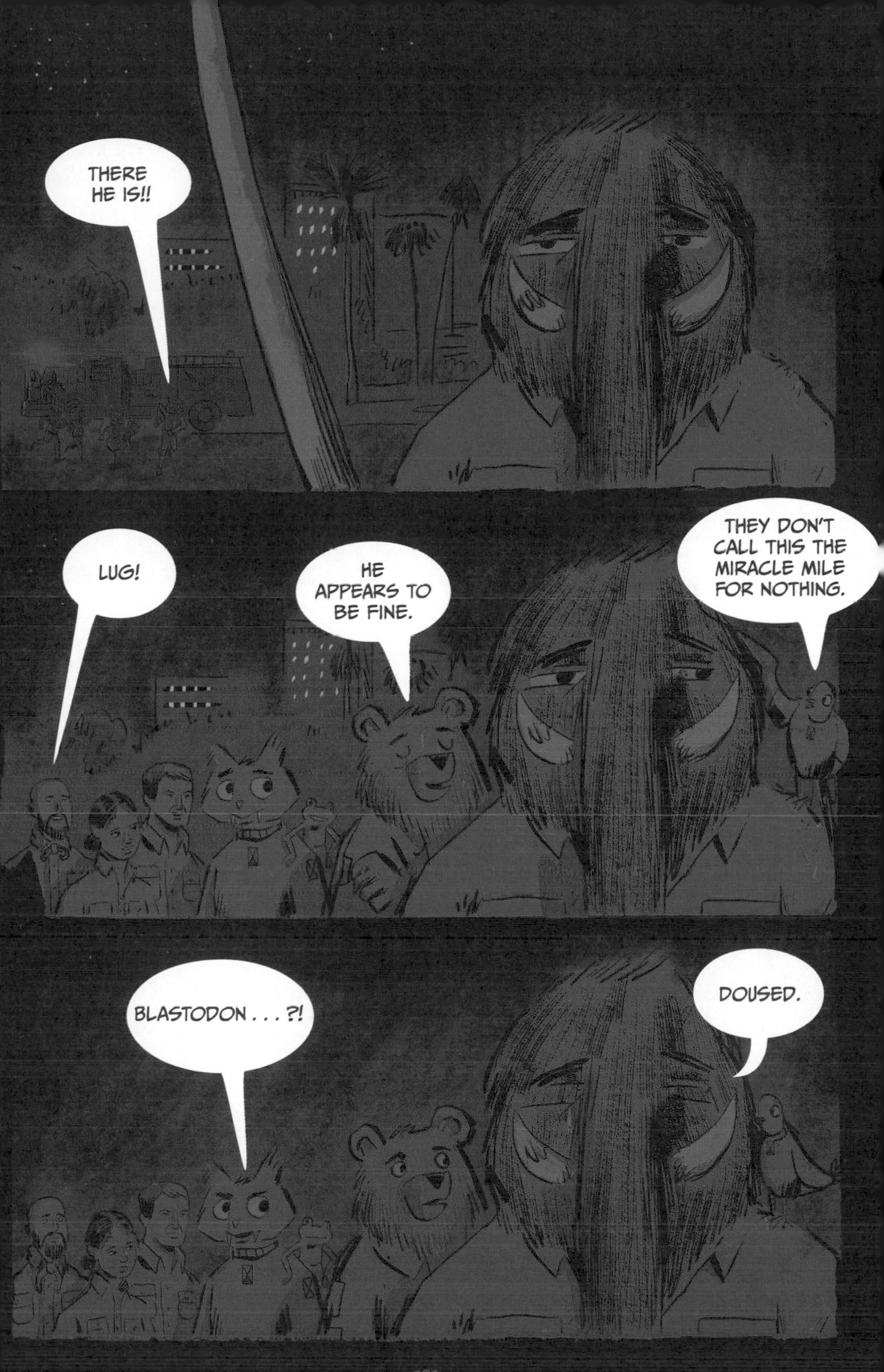
THERE HE IS!!
LUG!
HE APPEARS TO BE FINE.
THEY DON'T CALL THIS THE MIRACLE MILE FOR NOTHING.
BLASTODON . . . ?!
DOUSED.

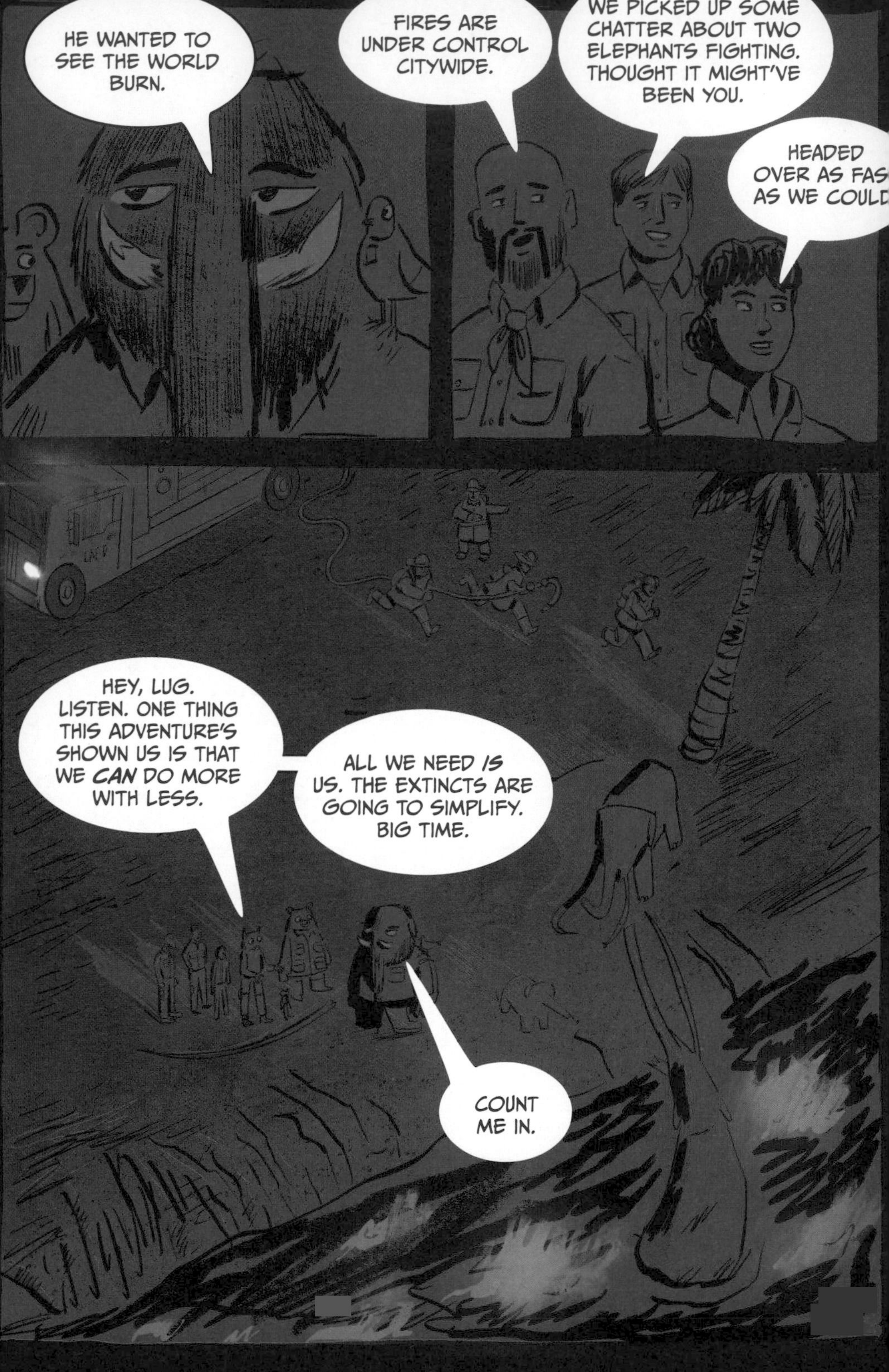
HE WANTED TO SEE THE WORLD BURN.
FIRES ARE UNDER CONTROL CITYWIDE.
WE PICKED UP SOME CHATTER ABOUT TWO ELEPHANTS FIGHTING. THOUGHT IT MIGHT'VE BEEN YOU.
HEADED OVER AS FAS AS WE COUL
HEY, LUG. LISTEN. ONE THING THIS ADVENTURE'S SHOWN US IS THAT WE *CAN* DO MORE WITH LESS.
ALL WE NEED *IS* US. THE EXTINCTS ARE GOING TO SIMPLIFY. BIG TIME.
COUNT ME IN.

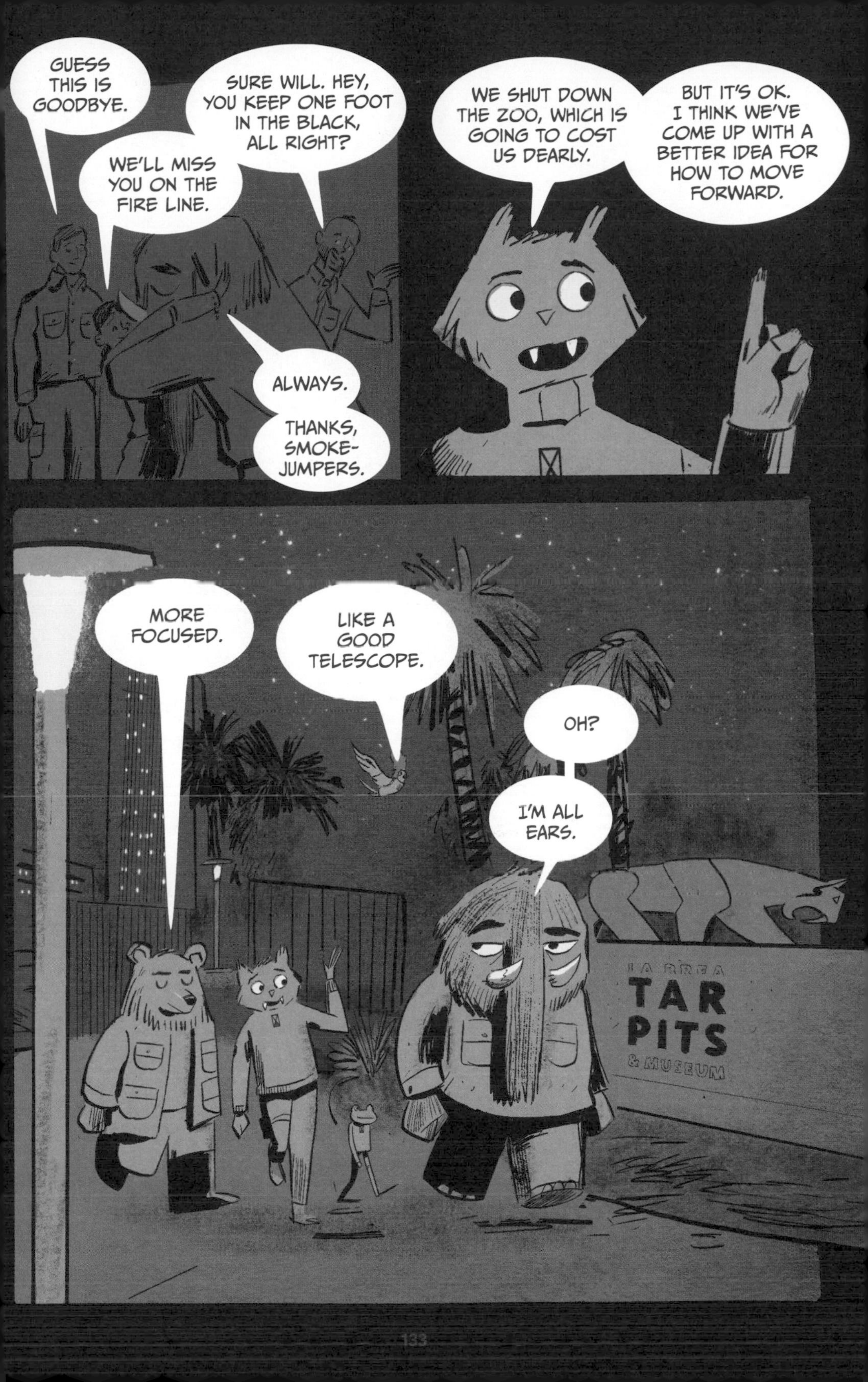
GUESS THIS IS GOODBYE.
WE'LL MISS YOU ON THE FIRE LINE.
SURE WILL. HEY, YOU KEEP ONE FOOT IN THE BLACK, ALL RIGHT?
ALWAYS.
THANKS, SMOKE-JUMPERS.
WE SHUT DOWN THE ZOO, WHICH IS GOING TO COST US DEARLY.
BUT IT'S OK. I THINK WE'VE COME UP WITH A BETTER IDEA FOR HOW TO MOVE FORWARD.
MORE FOCUSED.
LIKE A GOOD TELESCOPE.
OH?
I'M ALL EARS.
LA BREA
TAR PITS
& MUSEUM

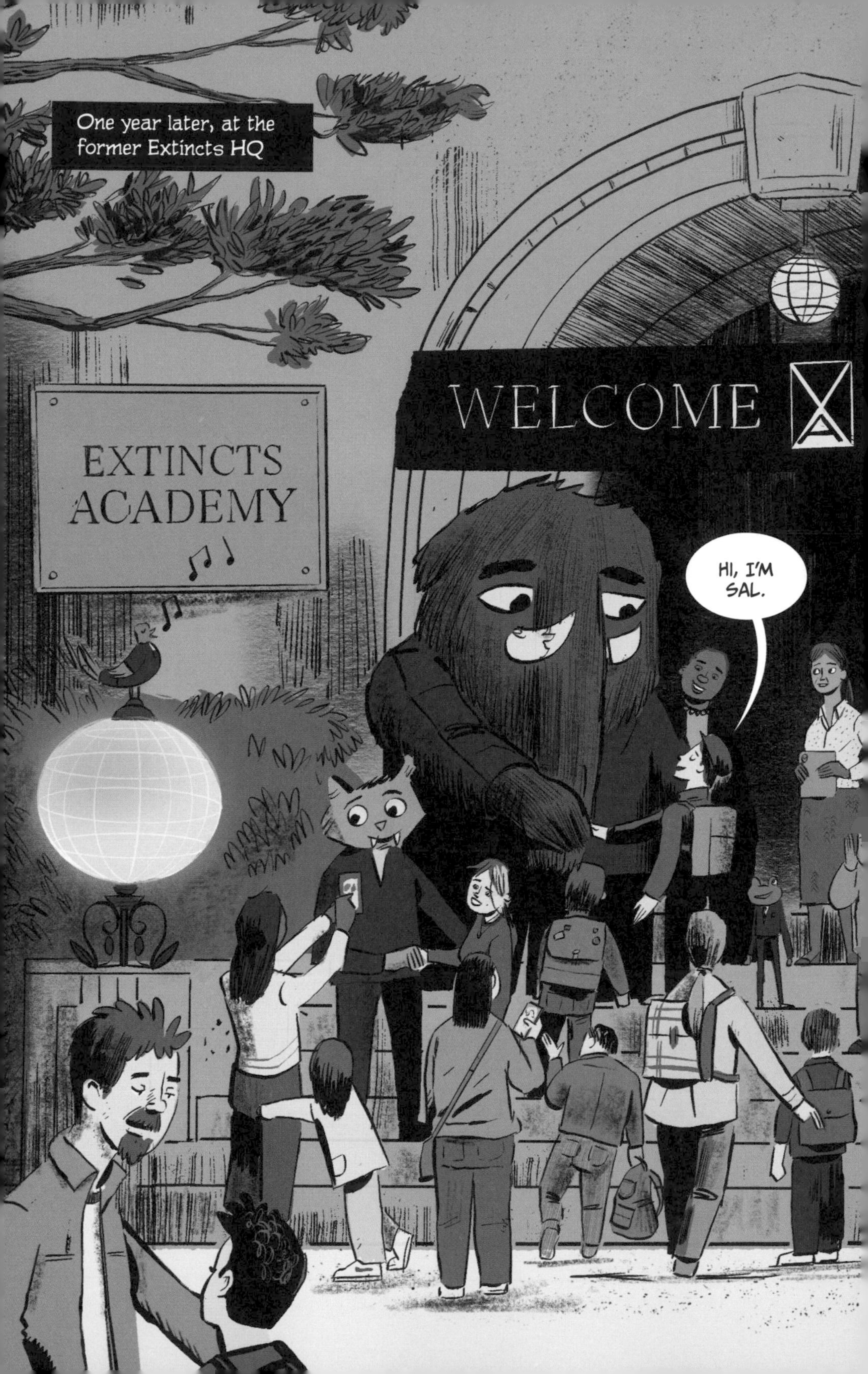
One year later, at the former Extincts HQ
EXTINCTS ACADEMY
WELCOME
HI, I'M SAL.

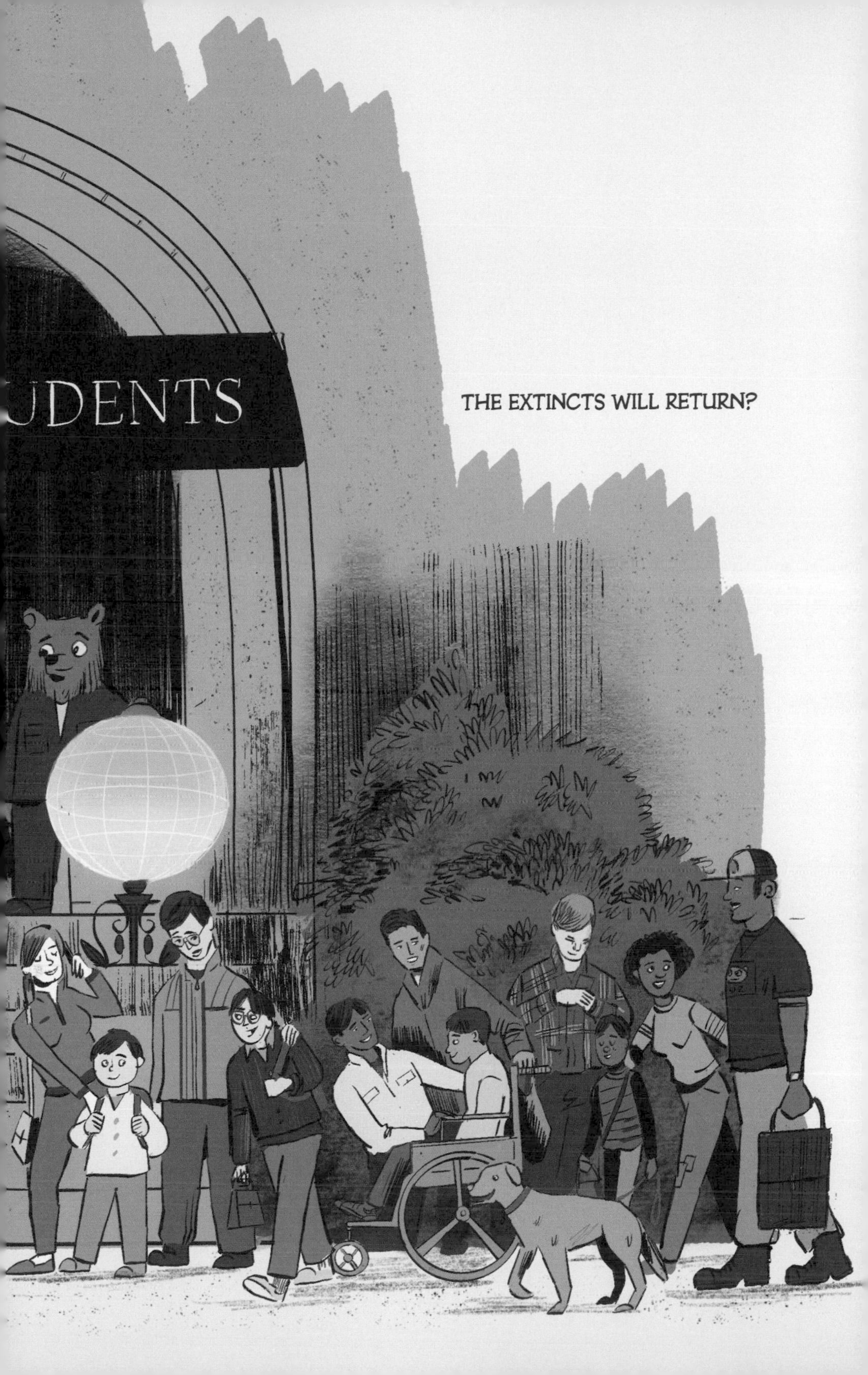
UDENTS
THE EXTINCTS WILL RETURN?

# THE EXTINCTIARY

Your field guide to select creatures & concepts found in this book

# ASIAN ELEPHANT *Elephas maximus*

**HABITAT:** Forests, scrublands, and grasslands
**TEMPORAL RANGE:** Pliocene to Holocene
(about 2.5 million years ago–present day)
**DISTRIBUTION:** South Asia
**SIZE:** 6.5–9' at shoulder, 3–4 tons
**LIFE SPAN:** Around 45 years
**WHY ENDANGERED:** Human encroachment of
habitat; poaching for ivory tusks and skin by humans
**FUN FACT:** Their trunk contains 40,000 muscles.

## ELEPHANT IN NO ROOM

The Asian elephant is the largest creature on the Asian continent, but there are three subspecies of these creatures: *Elephas maximus* from Sri Lanka, *Elephas maximus indicus* from mainland Asia, and *Elephas maximus sumatranus* from the island of Sumatra.

Asian elephants are social animals and live in groups of six to seven related females. The elder female, called a matriarch, leads the group. They live close to water to satisfy their enormous thirst, and their daily routine includes a lot of eating—mostly grass, but also tree bark, leaves, roots, and stems. They also like rice, bananas, and sugarcane.

The International Union for Conservation of Nature (IUCN) first listed the elephant as endangered in 1986. At that time, the creature's population had declined by fifty percent over the previous seventy-five years, or about three elephant generations. Today, there are about fifty thousand individuals occupying a rapidly shrinking wild habitat. The biggest threats to these creatures are habitat loss and fragmentation, caused by development by humans. Poaching also threatens these large mammals. Despite a Geneva Convention outlawing the harvesting of elephant tusks in 1989, ivory remains a precious commodity in illegal trading. Most ivory originates from the tusks of African elephants, but hunters also poach tusked male Asian elephants (females do not have tusks). Elephant skin, tail hair, and meat are also in demand. Humans capture elephants to appear in zoos and for riding, which presents another significant threat to wild populations. India, Myanmar, and Vietnam banned trapping years ago, but illegal trapping continues today.

The Asian elephant appears as deities in various religious traditions. For instance, the Hindu religion represents Wisdom in the form of the elephant deity Ganesh.

The Asian elephant is the closest living relative to the Woolly Mammoth.

**SEE A SPECIMEN**
American Museum of Natural History, New York, NY (life-size model)
Michigan State University Museum, East Lansing, MI (skeleton)
Natural History Museum, London (life-size model)

**FURTHER READING**
Blewett, Ashlee Brown, and Daniel Raven-Ellison. *Mission: Elephant Rescue: All about Elephants and How to Save Them.* Washington, D.C.: National Geographic, 2014.
Desmond, Jenni. *The Elephant.* New York, NY: Enchanted Lion Books, 2018.
Hurt, Avery Elizabeth. *Elephants.* Washington, D.C.: National Geographic, 2016.
O'Connell, Caitlin, Donna M. Jackson, and T. C. Rodwell. *The Elephant Scientist.* Boston, MA: Houghton Mifflin Harcourt, 2016.

# MASTODON/MAMMUT *Elephas americanum and others*

**HABITAT:** Forests
**TEMPORAL RANGE:** Early Pliocene to
Upper Pleistocene (About 5.3 million–
11,000 years ago)
**DISTRIBUTION:** North America, Eurasia
**SIZE:** 7.7' at shoulder, 9' tall, 6 tons
**LIFE SPAN:** Around 60 years
**WHY EXTINCT:** Food loss due to climate
change; hunted by humans; disease
**FUN FACT:** Their tusks grew 8' long, sometimes longer.

## THE BIRTH OF EXTINCTION

Today, extinction lives. Signs of it are everywhere. Skeletons of extinct animals stand in museum exhibit halls. Dinosaurs roar on our movie screens. Kids play with saber-toothed cat toys and learn about extinction from a young age.

But this wasn't always the case.

In fact, it wasn't until 1796 that scientists recognized species could be wiped from the face of the earth—and it was the close examination of a mastodon's tooth that changed all that. This tooth was unlike that of any known creature, even an elephant. It was French naturalist Georges Cuvier who first asked what had happened to this huge animal that we no longer see. That question led to what we know today about the mastodon—as well as about extinction as a valid scientific concept.

Were they alive today, mastodons might be confused for modern elephants, given their trunk, tusks, and size. But they were a different species. They were also similar to woolly mammoths but varied from them as well. In addition to tooth differences, mastodons were shorter and stockier than mammoths, and their tusks grew straighter and longer (up to eight feet!) than those of their mammoth cousins.

Mastodons lived in herds and ate leaves, soft branches, and high-growing fruits of woody plants. Males abandoned their herd once they reached maturity and lived alone or in male groups.

There are a number of theories about how the mastodon went extinct, including being caused by climate change and overhunting by humans. A study linking mastodons to tuberculosis has recently produced a new theory that disease contributed to their extinction. Of 113 skeletons, scientists found signs of the disease in 59—some 52 percent—of them.

### SEE A SKELETON
American Museum of Natural History, New York, NY
Field Museum of Natural History, Chicago, IL
Houston Museum of Natural Science, Houston, TX
La Brea Tar Pits and Museum, Los Angeles, CA

### FURTHER READING
Bardoe, Cheryl. *Mammoths and Mastodons: Titans of the Ice Age.* New York, NY: Abrams Books for Young Readers, 2010.
Lowell, Barbara, and Antonio Marinoni. *My Mastodon.* Mankato, MN: Creative Editions, 2020.

# SLOTH, GIANT *Megalonyx jeffersonii*

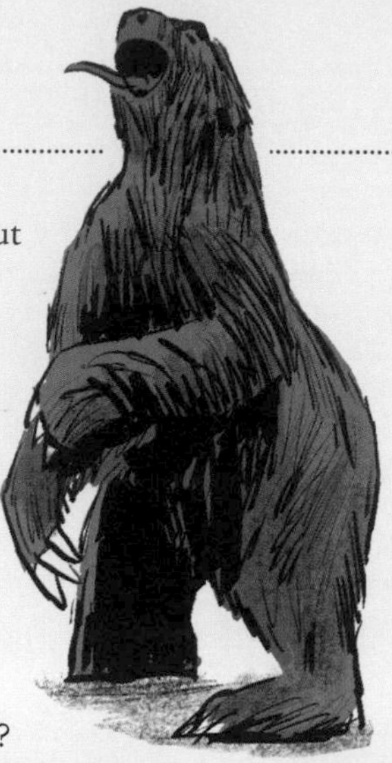

**HABITAT:** Woodlands and forests
**TEMPORAL RANGE:** Pliocene to Late Pleistocene (About 5.5 million–11,000 years ago)
**DISTRIBUTION:** North and Central America
**SIZE:** 9' long, maximum weight 1.1 tons (2,200 lbs.)
**LIFE SPAN:** 30–40 years
**WHY EXTINCT:** Human hunting and/or climate change
**FUN FACT:** In Greek, *megalonyx* means "giant claw."

## "QUADRUPED OF THE CLAWED KIND"

It's 1796 and then–Vice President Thomas Jefferson is studying mysterious bones. They are unlike any bones he or anyone has ever seen. What creature did they belong to? Perplexed, all the future president could definitively say was that these bones were three times as large as those of a lion and once belonged to a "quadruped of the clawed kind."

Years later, when Jefferson dispatched Lewis and Clark, he asked Meriwether Lewis to keep an eye out for this mysterious creature. He hoped they would find them living in the West. Unknown to Jefferson, the bones belonged to *Megalonyx*, an extinct genus of giant ground sloth. Not without some irony, scientists named *Megalonyx jeffersonii* after Thomas Jefferson.

In Jefferson's defense, the *Megalonyx* was unlike most animals known in his time—or, for that matter, in ours. Standing on its hind legs, the creature was more than ten feet tall, allowing it to use its forepaws and huge claws to tear off branches and leaves to eat. Massively built, it could weigh more than two thousand pounds—and other giant ground sloths were even heavier. It had a large bony jaw and peg-like teeth and lived throughout North and Central America.

For many years, scientists speculated that climate change and early humans, who would have found the huge, slow creatures easy prey, might have sped up the sloth's demise. Yet there was no physical evidence to support this idea until 2008. Then, archaeologists discovered telltale marks on the femur of an Ohio *Megalonyx* specimen. The thirteen-thousand-year-old fossil had forty-one unusual cuts that appeared to be the work of human-made tools.

### SEE A SKELETON

Illinois State Museum, Springfield, IL
University of Iowa Museum of Natural History, Iowa City, IA (life-size model)
Orton Geological Museum, Columbus, OH
Ancient Ozarks Natural History Museum, Ridgedale, MO
Natural History Museum of Utah, Salt Lake City, UT

### FURTHER READING


Frisch-Schmoll, Joy. *Ground Sloths.* North Mankato, MN: Capstone, 2015.
Prothero, Donald R., and Mary Persis Williams. *The Princeton Field Guide to Prehistoric Mammals.* Princeton, NJ: Princeton University Press, 2017.
Zoehfeld, Kathleen Weidner, and Franco Tempesta. *Prehistoric Mammals.* Washington, DC: National Geographic Kids, 2015.

## CALIFORNIA TIGER SALAMANDER *Ambystoma californiense*

**Habitat:** Grasslands and foothills
**Temporal Range:** Middle Jurassic to Holocene (About 164 million years ago–present day)
**Distribution:** California
**Size:** Males 8" long; females approx 7"
**Life span:** 14 years or more
**Why Endangered:** Loss of habitat; competition from invasive species, pesticides, and cars.
**Fun Fact:** This salamander is unable to hear sounds but can sense sound vibrations.

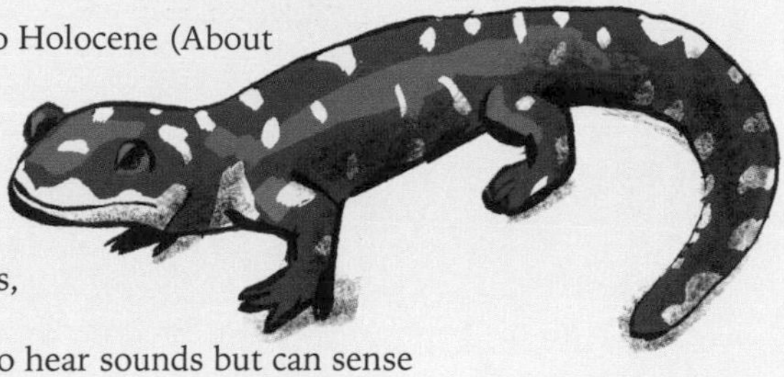

## BORROWS BURROWS

If you're out and about on a rainy November night in central California, watch your step! An endangered tiger salamander might be making a trip out of its burrow, headed back to its birthplace pond to spawn.

It's rare for these creatures to be out and about. California tiger salamanders are a type of mole salamander and, as such, spend most of their adult lives underground. But since they are poorly equipped to dig, they will sometimes use burrows made by squirrels and other burrowing mammals as homes.

They're called tiger salamanders because of the white or yellow stripes on their black bodies. Their bellies can be white or a pattern of a pale yellow on black.

Adult salamanders eat mostly insects. Larvae also eat insects in addition to algae, mosquito larvae, and even tadpoles. They live in grasslands and low foothills with the ponds and pools they require for breeding.

The California tiger salamander is not extinct, but it is threatened. Encroaching suburban and farmland development destroy its habitat. Invasive species such as bullfrogs and imported salamanders used for bait compete with it for food and eat its larvae. Widespread rodent control efforts have reduced the availability of burrows, with pesticides also reducing prey populations, like mosquitoes. Cars and all-terrain vehicles also kill migrating salamanders. With so many threats, these salamanders are proven survivors—but their time could be running out.

**See A Specimen**
Los Angeles Zoo, Los Angeles, CA (tiger salamander)
Maryland Zoo, Baltimore, MD (Eastern tiger salamander)
Smithsonian National Zoo, Washington, DC (Japanese giant salamander)

**Further Reading**
Guillain, Charlotte. *Life Story of a Salamander.* Chicago, IL: Heinemann Library, 2015.
Hughes, Catherine D. *Little Kids First Big Book of Reptiles and Amphibians.* Washington, DC: National Geographic Partners, 2020.
Mazer, Anne, and Steve Johnson. *The Salamander Room.* New York, NY: Knopf, 1991.
Nelson, Robin. *Salamanders.* Minneapolis, MN: Lerner, 2009.

# GLOSSARY

**ANCHOR POINT** A strategic spot from which to start digging a fire line; used to minimize the chances of flames surrounding the firefighters as they work.

**BAMBI BUCKET** A collapsible bucket, invented by Don Arney in 1982, that hangs from a helicopter and drops water on a fire.

**BURNOUT** Intentionally setting a fire inside a control line so that the fire will burn fuel between the oncoming fire and the fire line. *See also* Control Line.

**BURNOVER** Occurs when a fire overpowers firefighters or their equipment, removing their chance to use escape routes and reach safety zones.

**CHAIN** A unit of measurement equal to sixty-six linear feet.

**CLIMATE CHANGE** A long-term change in the average weather patterns of Earth's established local, regional, and global climates.

**CONTROL LINE** A man-made or naturally occuring barrier used to control a fire. *See also* Fire Line.

**DE-EXTINCTION** The process of creating an organism of an extinct species or one that looks like an extinct species. Also known as species revivalism or resurrection biology.

**DRIP TORCH** A handheld device used to intentionally set fires by dripping a flaming mixture of diesel and regular gasoline onto the ground.

**ELEPHANT TRUNK NEBULA** A mass of interstellar gas and dust within a larger gas area found in the Cepheus constellation. Located about 2,400 light-years away from Earth. Likely a site of star formation, the nebula contains several very young stars (less than one hundred thousand years old) that were discovered in 2003.

**ESCAPE ROUTE** A preplanned exit firefighters take to a safety zone. *See also* Safety Zone.

**EXTINCTION** The end of a member of a species or a group of species. Scientists consider the moment of extinction to be the death of the last individual of the species. However, the species may have lost the ability to reproduce and rebuild itself before that point.

**FIRE LINE** A trench or other linear barrier dug or scraped down to mineral soil to remove the presence of fire fuel and keep fire from spreading.

**FIRE SHELTER** A rapidly deployable foil tent that reflects radiant heat and offers a firefighter a small pocket of breathable air. Used only in extreme situations as a last resort.

**FUEL** Flammable material that feeds a fire; examples include grass, sticks, leaves, and trees.

**GLOBAL WARMING** A continual rise in the average temperature of Earth's climate. It is a significant component of climate change. In addition to climbing global surface and atmospheric temperatures, the term *global warming* can also be used to include its effects, such as rising ocean levels. *See also* Climate Change.

**GREENHOUSE EFFECT** The process by which radiation from the sun is absorbed and, unable to return to space, is re-radiated by greenhouse gases. While some energy radiates back into space, some is sent toward Earth's surface. This warms the planet's atmosphere and surface to a temperature higher than what it would be if no radiation were being trapped.

**GREENHOUSE GASES** Like the glass of a greenhouse, a greenhouse gas absorbs and then radiates energy. Greenhouse gases cause the greenhouse effect on planets. Greenhouse gases in Earth's atmosphere include water vapor, carbon dioxide, methane, nitrous oxide, and ozone.

**HOTSHOT** Firefighters who work the hottest part of wildfires mainly by building fire lines. Well-trained and held to high physical standards, these women and men also assume difficult missions in fighting fires.

**MICROCLIMATE** A local group of atmospheric conditions different from those in the immediate surrounding area. Often, the difference is only slight, but it can also be substantial.

**MINERAL SOIL** Dirt with little combustible material, usually lying below organic layers of soil.

**NATURAL SELECTION** A process by which populations of living creatures adapt and change over generations; a key component of evolution.

**NOMEX** Brand name for fire-resistant material used in clothing worn by firefighters.

**ON STATION** Over the drop zone in smokejumper parlance.

**PULASKI** A combination chopping and trench-digging tool, with an axe blade on one side and an adze-like digging blade on the other. Mounted on a straight handle.

**RELATIVE HUMIDITY** The ratio of actual moisture in the air to the maximum amount of moisture in the air if it were saturated.

**SAFETY ZONE** An area in which to take refuge without being burned. Examples include an already burned area, a field that won't burn, rocky terrain, or a previously built safety perimeter.

**SAWYER** A worker who cuts down trees, brush, and undergrowth to clear a path for a fire line or to otherwise remove fuel from the path of fire. Also known as a feller.

**SMOKEJUMPER** A firefighter who travels to fight fires by aircraft and parachute.

**SWAMPER** A worker who assists fellers by clearing away brush, limbs, and small trees.

**TAR PITS** Pools of crude oil that seep to the surface. As hydrocarbons evaporate from this seeping oil into the atmosphere, the oil becomes asphalt. This sticky substance traps animals and can sink around them, like quicksand. Predators see these trapped animals and walk into the pits, thinking to catch an easy meal. They too become trapped and die. To this day, scientists find the entangled remains of predators and prey in excavation projects.

# HELP THE EXTINCTS SAVE THE WORLD

HERE ARE SOME WAYS YOU CAN GET INVOLVED TO HELP PREVENT WILDFIRES AND—IF YOUR AREA IS AT RISK—BE PREPARED FOR THEM.

## ON YOUR OWN

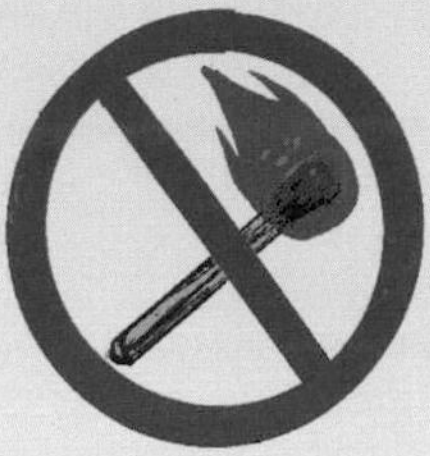

• Never, ever play with matches or lighters.

• Remember, only humans can prevent wildfires. It's up to us to be safe and do no harm.

• Always be careful around fire.

## WITH YOUR PARENTS

### WHILE IN THE GREAT OUTDOORS

• Be aware of your home area's risk of wildfires. If you live in rural areas, near forests, or in a dry climate, the risks are higher. Contact your local fire department if you have questions about this.

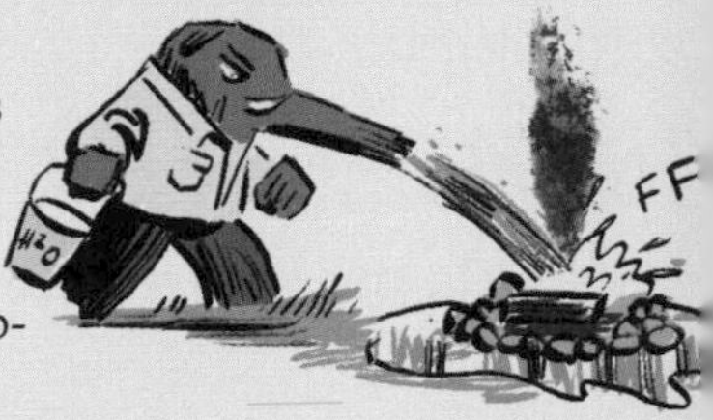
FF

• When you're around a campfire, always make sure it's under adult supervision.

• Have a grown-up completely extinguish your campfire before leaving it. Douse it with water until the campfire is cold.

### IN YOUR OWN BACKYARD (TO PREPARE AHEAD OF TIME)

• Keep gas cans, propane tanks, and wood piles at least thirty feet away from the house at all times.

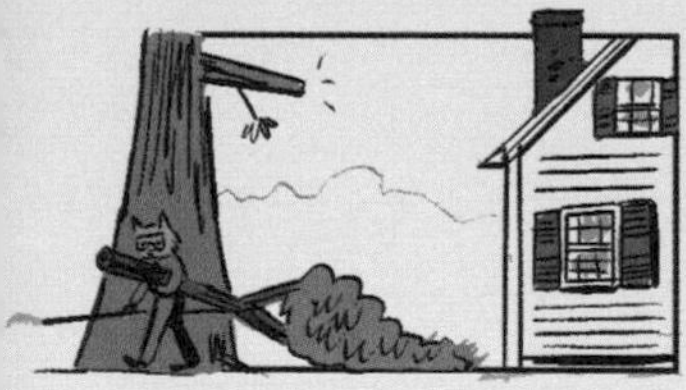

• Always keep your roof, gutter, and patios clear of leaves, pine needles, and other flammables.

• Remove flammable vegetation and mulch material within five feet of your house. Substitute these with nonflammable materials.

• Remove shrub, tree, or plant branches that overhang within ten feet of your house, roof, or chimney.

• Keep emergency phone numbers handy by all the phones in your home.

• Clearly mark driveway entrances and make sure your house number or address is visible. This allows emergency personnel to find your house in case of emergency.

• Locate and maintain an adequate water source outside your home. This could be a swimming pool, a pond, a cistern, or a well. Firefighters can draw water from these sources to extinguish a fire.

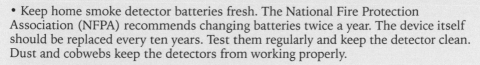

• Pick a place for family members to meet outside your neighborhood in case you cannot get home or need to evacuate.

• Identify someone who is not local to contact in case local phone lines go down.

• Keep home smoke detector batteries fresh. The National Fire Protection Association (NFPA) recommends changing batteries twice a year. The device itself should be replaced every ten years. Test them regularly and keep the detector clean. Dust and cobwebs keep the detectors from working properly.

## IF THERE ARE REPORTS OF WILDFIRES IN YOUR AREA

• Be ready to leave immediately.

• Tune in to local radio and television stations for up-to-date emergency information.

• Have an adult park the car facing the direction of escape. Backing up and turning around takes time and space you may not have later.

• Confine pets to one room so that you can find them if you need to evacuate in a hurry.

## AND WHAT TO DO AFTER

• Do not return to or enter your home until fire officials say it is safe.

• Use caution when entering burned areas. Embers and hot spots can flare up without warning.

• Stay clear of fallen or damaged power lines, poles, and downed wires.

• Watch for ash pits and stay away from them. Have a grown-up mark them for safety. Warn family and neighbors to stay away from of the pits.

• Keep pets under your direct control. Hidden embers, ash pits, and other hotspots could burn their paws or hooves.

• Consult local public health guidance on the safe cleanup of ash and the safe use of masks.

• Water down debris as you clean up to minimize breathing in dust particles.

• Wear leather gloves and heavy-soled shoes to protect hands and feet.

Source: www.redcross.org/get-help/how-to-prepare-for-emergencies/types-of-emergencies/wildfire.html

# ABOUT WILDFIRES

Climate change–fueled wildfires are becoming more common, intense, destructive, and costly—and they are contributing to further climate change. One thing is certain: Time is running out and our world's survival hangs in the balance.

## CAUSES

There are many causes of forest fires, but we humans are responsible for most of them. According to the U.S. Department of the Interior, careless cigarette handling, campfires, arson, and other activities cause about 90 percent of wildfires each year, while lava and lightning strikes account for 10 percent.

It's true that wildfires can be good for a forest. Fires make way for new growth, return nutrients to the soil, and reduce the buildup of fire fuel, such as dead branches, fallen trees, dry leaves, and so on. After all, Mother Nature has been burning forests for millennia. But by fighting fires, humans can actually increase wildfire risk because the unburned dry fuel unnaturally accumulates, worsening current and future fires in terms of their size and destructive power.

In addition to all that, climate change is a major cause of the heating and drying out of forests, turning them into powder kegs and exposing them to dangers posed by fires.

Some studies reveal that warming is the main driver of more fires, doubling the area burned across the United States' West between 1984 and 2015. The year 2021 saw the hottest summer ever recorded in California, Nevada, and Oregon. Arizona and Washington had their second-hottest summer in 2021. Researchers warn that continued warming and drought will lead to bigger blazes. In fact, in 2020, California alone saw its largest wildfire season on record. That year, more than ten thousand wildfires destroyed more than 4.2 million acres. That's close to 5 percent of the state's 100 million acres of land. In 2021, California saw 2.5 million acres burned in over 8,600 fires—among them the Dixie Fire, the second-largest single wildfire in state history. In fact, eight of the largest fifteen wildfires in California occurred in the last two years. Other states face similar devastation. In 2021, Texas experienced 5,576 wildfires, Arizona more than 1,100, and Montana more than 2,111. Unfortunately, those numbers are expected to rise in coming years not only in the United States but around the globe. South America, Australia, Europe, Russia, and China are all seeing a dramatic increase in wildfire frequency and destructive force.

To make matters worse, wildfire season is starting sooner and ending later each year. A severe multiyear drought resulting from a lack of soaking rains or appreciable snowfall in the American West lead to fires earlier in 2021 than usual. For instance, by mid-2021, Arizona had experienced 311 fires compared to 127 in the same period in 2020. Fifteen thousand acres burned in that time, whereas 1,290 acres burned in the same time frame the previous year.

## IMPACT

Wildfire's damage to the environment, property, and life is so massive that we cannot fully measure it. Researchers estimate that more than 33,000 people die each year because of wildfire pollution, with more than three thousand of them in the United States. The estimated 2021 fire season in California alone resulted in more than $4.4 billion in property damage. Costs for the U.S. 2021 wildfire season could total between $70 and $90 billion.

Plants and wildlife are threatened too. Wildfires destroy habitats for birds and small mammals. Even fish are threatened as ash from the fires flows into streams. And climate change complicates forests' ability to reestablish themselves after big fires. The Windy Fire and the KNP Complex fires burned California's Sequoia and Kings Canyon national parks and destroyed up to 3,637 mature sequoia trees—a species that has survived fires for centuries.

Forest fires affect our planet's climate. Fires send greenhouse gases into the atmosphere that contribute to global warming and destroy trees that would otherwise capture carbon. This cycle makes the effects of climate change even worse and its associated problems bigger, including a fire season that starts earlier in the year and runs later.

With resources stretched thin, climate change forces the National Park Service to make choices about what to protect in the country's national parks. They warn, "It will not be possible to safeguard all park resources, processes, assets, and values in their current form or context over the long term."

## SOLUTIONS

For all that is spent on fighting fires, only a fraction is spent on preventing them. Some experts believe that if governments dedicated more resources to stopping the fires before they began or adopted new measures that limited a fire's capacity to destroy property and life, we'd see less destruction and potentially fewer fires. Outfitting older homes with fire-resistant materials, community protection plans, and fuel reduction/prescribed burn programs would also be effective in limiting fires and their damage. These measures should be used while also adopting greener practices that benefit the environment and reduce the effects of climate change.

The winds of change might be blowing. In 2021 California invested $1.5 billion in wildfire response and forest resilience. This move represents a policy shift in a state that historically has focused on putting fires out rather than stopping them before they start. The Biden Administration's 2022 budget takes a similar approach to reducing the risks and impacts of catastrophic wildfires by improving the health, resilience, and recovery of wildland ecosystems.

Want more to change? That's up to you and me.

# ABOUT SMOKEJUMPERS

Smokejumpers might be the most specialized and elite teams in the entire firefighter service. Not that they'd tell you—smokejumpers shun the spotlight—but theirs is a long, storied, and brave history, composed of diverse teams in the Pacific Northwest. For seventy-five years, they've served the public and Mother Nature alike.

## WHAT IN BLAZES

Blackwater Fire, 1937 Wyoming. Forest firefighters find themselves battling a wildfire and become entrapped by it. Ultimately, fifteen of them would perish fighting the blaze. An investigation would later find that a faster response to the fire would've saved their lives. Within two years, the smokejumper program was under development.

The concept of smokejumping dates to the 1930s, when people were thinking of new ways to use airplanes, still a fairly new invention at that time. The first smokejump was made in the summer of 1940 in Idaho's Nez Perce National Forest.

## HOW THE—?

It's up to these airborne firefighters to knock down extremely remote wildfires before they spread. Smokejumpers load their gear into fixed-wing aircraft, then fly to and leap in pairs near the fire, but not into it. Because they parachute directly to the fire, they are rested and ready for the hard work of fighting fires in rugged and remote terrain. Smokejumper planes have a spotter on board and circle above the fire, relaying vital information about wind speed, fire activity, and terrain. Depending largely on their own arms, legs, and brains, smokejumpers must be in excellent physical shape. They also must maintain a certain body weight, as their aircraft can lift only so much weight per mission.

## WHO WOULD?

There have been six thousand smokejumpers in the program's seventy-five-year history, with roughly three hundred currently on active duty. Trailblazers include the first female smokejumper, Deanne Shulman, in 1981. In 1945 the first all-Black paratrooper unit, the 555th Parachute Infantry Battalion, called the "Triple Nickles," retrained as smokejumpers. Their presence made smokejumping one of the first racially integrated jobs in the United States. Currently, there are nine smokejumper crews in the country, seven operated by the U.S. Forest Service (USFS) and two by the Bureau of Land Management (BLM).

## WHY THE—?

Even though the job is treacherous, deaths are infrequent. The most widely known fatalities occurred in the 1949 Mann Gulch Fire, with twelve smokejumper deaths, and in 1994 in the South Canyon Fire, with three deaths. Their five-to-six-week intensive training is grueling and only the toughest make it. Once aboard, smokejumpers are in charge of their own gear and even sew their own parachutes.

Why do they do it? They don't do it for the glory or the glamour. They earn around $31,000 a year and 25 percent for overtime and hazard pay. Smokejumpers do their job to serve the public and a proud legacy. Plus, there's camaraderie, beautiful scenery, and the chance to make a difference. Public service is really what it's all about. Smokejumpers take the constitutional oath.

## MAKING A DIFFERENCE

The smokejumper program is in trouble. Some think they are a relic of the past—like cavalry on a battlefield. There's not as much remote backcountry anymore, and it's easier to get to historically remote locations, reducing the need for parachuting in. Smokejumpers contend they can also support search and rescue operations and collect wildlife data to more fully round out their critical firefighting service. Their record of safety and effectiveness speaks for itself.

# GEAR

Smokejumpers rely on a small but rock-solid kit in their missions in the remote wilderness.

## JUMP SUIT

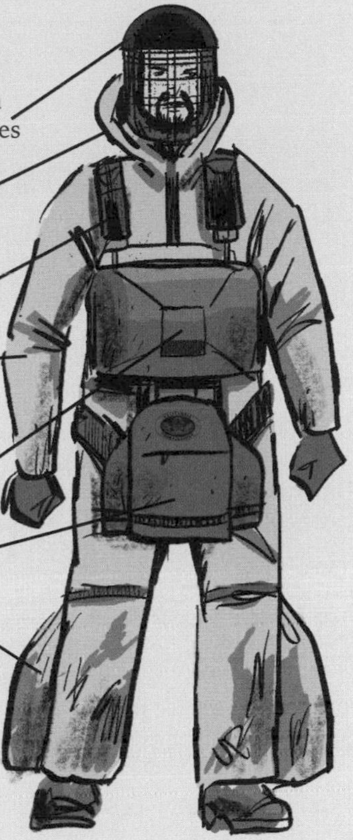

Helmet with wire mesh to keep out tree branches
Padded Kevlar high collar for tree landings
Parachute harness
Jumpsuit
Reserve parachute
Personal gear bag
Huge pockets for more personal gear including rope to lower themselves down in case of tree landing


## WILDLAND FIRE GEAR

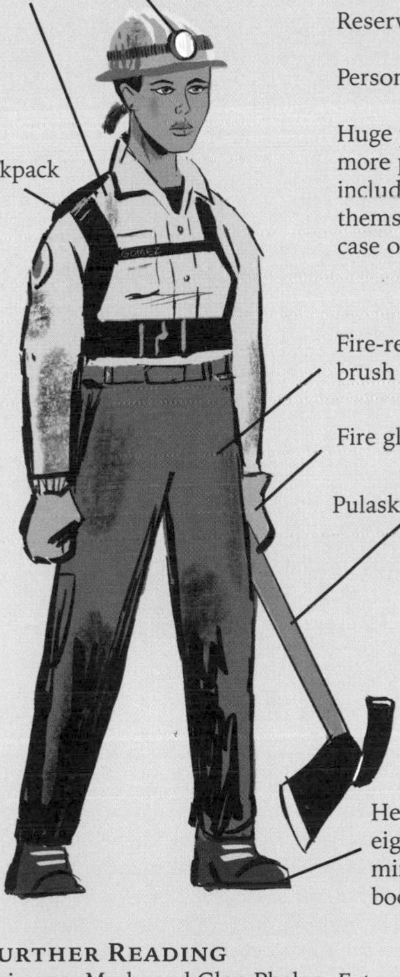

Helmet with head light
Nomex shirt
Backpack
GOMEZ
Fire-resistant brush pants
Fire gloves
Pulaski tool
Heat-resistant eight-inch minimum boots


### THE FIGHT STUFF

The minimum required physical fitness standards for smokejumpers include being able to haul 110 pounds for three miles within ninety minutes, as well as run 1.5 miles and complete twenty-five push-ups, forty-five sit-ups, and seven pull-ups, all in less than eleven minutes.


**Further Reading**

Thiessen, Mark, and Glen Phelan. *Extreme Wildfire: Smoke Jumpers, High-Tech Gear, Survival Tactics, and the Extraordinary Science of Fire.* Washington, DC: National Geographic, 2016.

# THE ELEPHANT'S TRUNK NEBULA

Located over 2,400 light-years away from Earth in the Cepheus constellation, the Elephant's Trunk Nebula is, in fact, a small part of a much larger nebula. The "trunk" itself is a twenty-light-year-long concentration of stars and ionized gas. Stellar radiation and wind compress this dust and gas into clumps to form new stars. Scientists determined some to be younger than one hundred thousand years old, far fewer than the hundreds of millions years (or longer) stars are known to exist. The massive Mu Cephei is the brightest star in the area but many more—over 250 stars—also shine in this region. Astronomers discovered the Elephant's Trunk (designated IC 1396A) as part of the larger IC 1396 emission nebula.

To find the Elephant's Trunk Nebula in the Northern Hemisphere's night sky, first look for the Cepheus constellation, then for Mu Cephei, or "Hershel's Garnet Star." Mu Cephei is one of the largest and reddest stars in the sky and exists on the outer edges of the nebula. The larger nebula (1396) is faintly visible with the naked eye in only *very* dark skies, away from cities, suburbs, and other sources of light pollution. The trunk (1396A) is visible only with a telescope. Who knew elephants were light?

# THE GRIFFITH OBSERVATORY

Once, observatories sat alone on remote mountaintops, available only to scientists.

But Griffith J. Griffith changed all that when he donated funding and land on which to build an observatory, museum, and planetarium. Completed in 1935, Griffith Observatory makes astronomy accessible to everyone. Admission is free to all exhibits, including a twelve-inch Zeiss refracting telescope, a coelostat (a kind of solar telescope), a Foucault pendulum, and many other attractions. More than seven million people have looked through the Zeiss telescope, which is thought to be the most people to have viewed through any telescope.

The observatory's dramatic white Greek and Beaux-Arts building sits on Mount Hollywood in Los Angeles's Griffith Park. On the grounds, there are sunset and moonset lines that point toward a notable sunset or moonset point on the horizon. On the front lawn, there's a scale model of our solar system and a monument in tribute to six great astronomers: Hipparchus, Nicolaus Copernicus, Galileo Galilei, Johannes Kepler, Isaac Newton, and William Herschel. Incidentally, George Stanley, the sculptor of the Academy Award's Oscar statuette, sculpted Sir Isaac Newton.

Wildfires have plagued the observatory over the years. In 2007 a fire in the Hollywood Hills came close to the building, and then in July 2018 officials evacuated the observatory after a wildfire burned twenty-five nearby acres. Firefighters were able to extinguish the blaze before it damaged any buildings.

**Visit the Griffith Observatory**
2800 East Observatory Road, Los Angeles, CA 90027
(213) 473-0800
griffithobservatory.org

# THE LA BREA TAR PITS

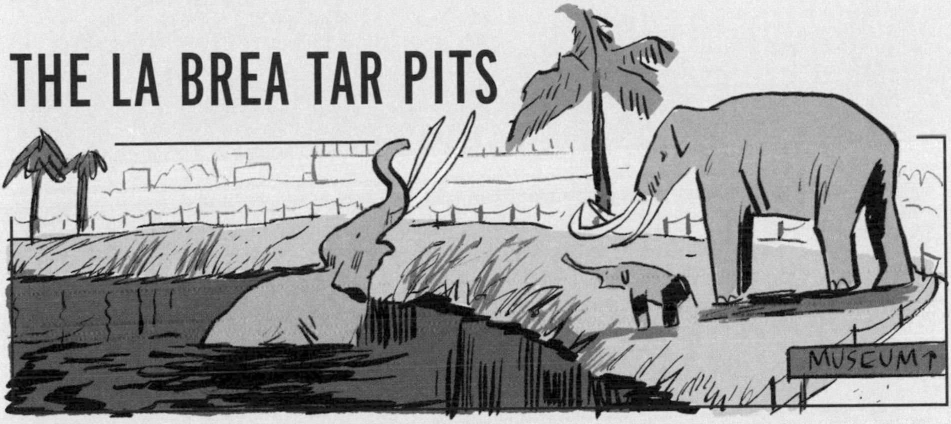
MUSEUM↑

The La Brea Tar Pits are a group of tar pits in Los Angeles's Hancock Park. Today, as it has for thousands of years, tar—*brea* in Spanish—oozes from the ground. Over the millennia, animals, unaware of the danger posed by the gooey tar, stepped into the pits and slowly sank until they become trapped. Predators, sensing an easy lunch, also wandered into the pit, only to themselves become trapped and die. The bones of these once-unfortunate animals gradually sank and were preserved by the tar. Among the animal bones found in the pit are those belonging to dire wolves, bison, horses, Jefferson's ground sloth, an American lion, saber-toothed cats, and mammoths. Scientists found only one set of human remains in the pit, those of a woman who lived and died ten thousand years ago.

Humans created the visible tar pits we see today. In fact, the lake pit in which Blastodon and Lug have their battle was originally an asphalt mine. Fossil hunters excavated others.

In 1977, entrepreneur George Page opened the museum that bears his name. The museum presents the story of the pits and displays the specimens taken from them. There are life-sized models of animals in and around the pits. He took great care in designing the exhibits so that they were attractive and could be toured in about an hour. Of more than one hundred pits, pit 91 remains regularly excavated and visitors can observe this activity from a museum viewing station.

**Visit The La Brea Tarpits**
5801 Wilshire Blvd., Los Angeles, CA 90036
(213) 763-3499
tarpits.org

# MAKE YOUR OWN TELESCOPE

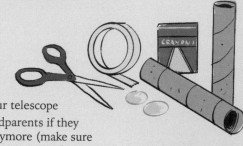

## WHAT YOU'LL NEED

- Two empty paper towel tubes
- Scissors
- Masking tape
- Crayons, paint, or markers to decorate your telescope
- 2 convex lenses. Ask your parents or grandparents if they have old reading glasses they don't use anymore (make sure the glasses are reading glasses and not glasses to see distant objects). Remove the lenses from the frames. Convex lenses are also available online.

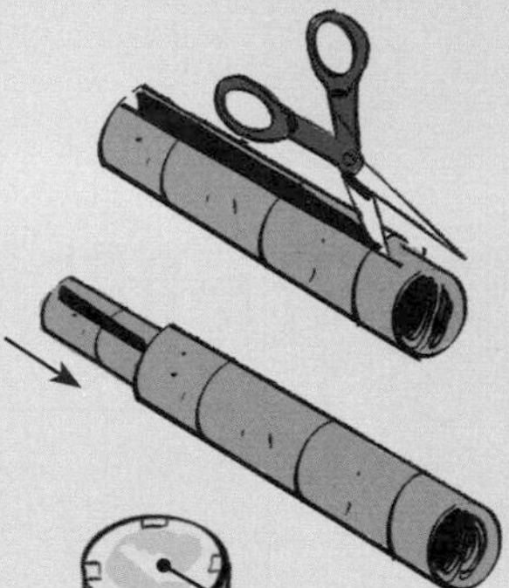

## HOW TO MAKE YOUR TELESCOPE

1. Cut one tube all the way up the side. Wrap one edge of the cut side slightly over the other edge and hold it in place with one hand.

2. Put the cut tube inside the other tube. When you release the inner tube, it should expand to fit inside the outer tube—but it should still be movable inside. If not, remove the inner tube and roll it tighter, then reinsert into the outer tube.

3. Tape one lens to the outer edge of the inner tube so that the curve of the lens faces inside the tube.

*eyepiece lens' curve faces inside tube*

4. Tape the second lens to the outside edge of the outer tube. This time, the curve of the lens points toward the outside of the tube. Don't block the lens with the tape—keep the tape on the edge of the lens.

*other lens' curve faces outside*

5. Look through the lens of the inner tube. Aim your telescope at faraway objects (but never use a telescope to look at the sun). You can focus by sliding the inner tube in and out.

6. Decorate your telescope! Stars, planets, trees, animals, and words are some graphic ideas. Have fun and happy looking!

## HEY, QUITO, WHY DOES IT DO THIS?

YOU MADE A REFRACTING TELESCOPE! FIRST, THE LENSES GATHER MORE LIGHT THAN YOUR EYE CAN. THE TWO LENSES THEN BEND THE LIGHT, MAKING AN OBJECT APPEAR CLOSER THAN IT REALLY IS. THE SIZE OF THE IMAGE PRODUCED BY THE TELESCOPE DEPENDS ON THE CURVE OF ITS LENSES. LENSES WITH DIFFERENT CURVATURES WILL CHANGE THE MAGNIFICATION POWER OF THE TELESCOPE.

# FURTHER READING

## BOOKS FOR YOUNG READERS

Furgang, Kathy. *Wildfires*. Washington, DC: National Geographic, 2015.
Marrin, Albert. *When Forests Burn: The Story of Wildfire in America*. New York, NY: Alfred A. Knopf, 2022.
Philbrick, W. R. *Wildfire: A Novel*. New York, NY: Scholastic, 2021.
Potenza, Alessandra. *All About Wildfires: Discovering How They Spark, Burn, and Spread*. New York, NY: Children's, an imprint of Scholastic, 2022.
Simon, Seymour. *Wildfires*. New York, NY: Harper, 2016.
Tarshis, Lauren, and Scott Dawson. *I Survived the California Wildfires, 2018*. New York, NY: Scholastic, 2020.

## BOOKS FOR OLDER READERS

Egan, Timothy. *The Big Burn: Teddy Roosevelt and the Fire That Saved America*. Boston, MA: Houghton Mifflin Harcourt, 2011.
Maclean, John N. *Fire on the Mountain: The True Story of the South Canyon Fire*. New York, NY: Harper Perennial, 2009.
MacLean, Norman. *Young Men and Fire*. Chicago, IL: Univ. of Chicago Press, 2017.
Santos, Fernanda. *The Fire Line: The Story of the Granite Mountain Hotshots*. New York, NY: Flatiron, 2017.
Simard, Suzanne W. *Finding the Mother Tree: Discovering the Wisdom of the Forest*. New York, NY: Alfred A. Knopf, 2021.

## WEBSITES

smokejumpers.com
smokeybear.com
livingwithfire.com
nfpa.org
stateforesters.org/where-we-stand/wildfire/
goextincts.com

# BIBLIOGRAPHY

McDonough, Brendan, and Stephen Talty. *Granite Mountain*. New York, NY: Hachette, 2016.
Ramos, Jason A., and Julian Smith. *Smokejumper: A Memoir by One of America's Most Select Airborne Firefighters*. New York, NY: William Morrow, 2015.
Wray, Britt, and George M. Church. *Rise of the Necrofauna: The Science, Ethics, and Risks of De-Extinction*. Vancouver, BC: Greystone, 2019.

# ACKNOWLEDGMENTS

This book is in your hands because of my brave and beautiful wife, Christy, and stouthearted sons, Owen and Daniel. How many times they must've seen me hunched over my iPad writing or drawing this book. As with book 1, I hope book 2 is worthy of all that time we were apart. I thank my parents for instilling in me a deep appreciation for nature and for their support as I worked on this book. Thank you, I love all of you.

To my agent, Paul Rodeen—we did it! I appreciate the pep talks and your behind-the-scenes wizardry. To my editor, Maggie Lehrman, always there, thank you. To Andrew Smith, for this amazing opportunity. To the whole team at Amulet Books, for bringing the Extincts to life. Heather, Megan, Mary, Patricia—thanks to all of you and your respective teams.

I thank Matt Tavares, Ryan Higgins, Dan Santat, and Victoria Jamieson for their early support of the first book. I am so grateful. Bob Shea, Zach Ohora, and Samantha Berger, I thank you for your early support as well.

Thank you, Jerry Jamowski! Your 79.9 WFUZ internet radio program made every Thursday night a Saturday night. I drew more than a few pages herein while listening to your tunes.

Librarians and teachers everywhere, thank you for what you do every day. Thank you independent booksellers for your support of the Going Extincts tour, especially Whitelam Books, The Silver Unicorn, An Unlikely Story, Inkwood Books, Children's Book World, Word Play, Curious Iguana, Once Upon A Time Bookstore, G. Willikers! Books and Toys, The Blue Bunny, and Newtonville Books.

Gracias Carlos Caprioli por el español!

For smokejumpers, hotshots, and firefighters everywhere. We are in your debt.

And a special thank YOU for reading my words and looking at my pictures.

# AUTHOR/ILLUSTRATOR *Scott Magoon*

**HABITAT:** New England
**TEMPORAL RANGE:** Late Holocene
**DISTRIBUTION:** Worldwide
**SIZE:** 6'1", approx. 190 lbs.
**AGE:** Late 40s
**FUN FACT:** Collects vintage Star Wars
and GI Joe action figures—and jazz records

## WRITING AND DRAWING FOR AGES

Scott was born back in the 1900s. He earned a BA in English literature from Northeastern University sometime before the dawn of the twenty-first century. More recently, he was a children's book art director at major American publishers. Now he writes and illustrates books full-time. He's a lefty and, like his ancestors, enjoys running long distances, good food, and good music. He and his nomadic family travel to new places together from their Boston-area home.

He's illustrated thirty-one picture books and written five. This is his second graphic novel.

Visit scottmagoon.com to learn more about him and his books and to get in touch. Sign up for his newsletter, the Magoon Tribune, while you're there, for quarterly updates on all the latest and greatest.

You can also visit goextincts.com to find out more about extinct and endangered creatures, access a teacher's guide, and get behind-the-scenes stuff from the Extincts, free downloads, and special Extincts merchandise—the profits of which benefit environmental causes.

CATCH UP WITH BOOK 1 IN THE SERIES,

**QUEST FOR THE UNICORN HORN!**

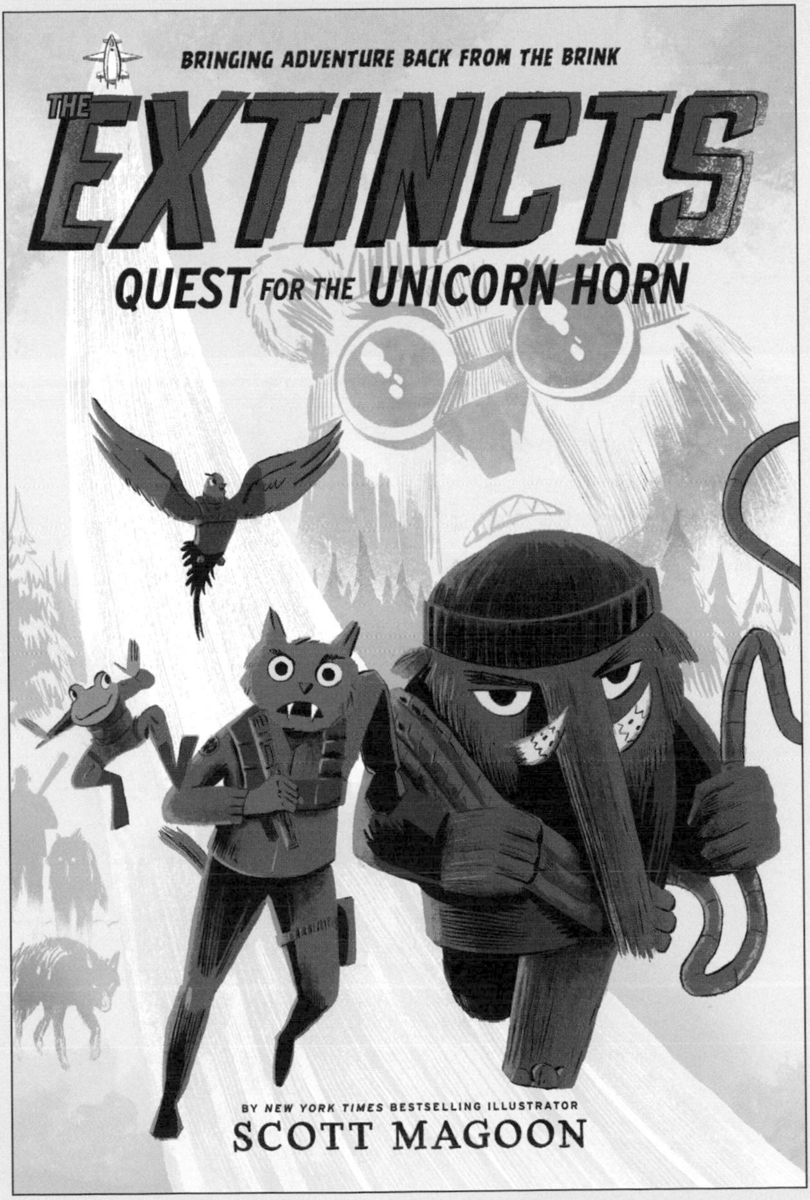
BRINGING ADVENTURE BACK FROM THE BRINK
THE EXTINCTS
QUEST FOR THE UNICORN HORN
BY NEW YORK TIMES BESTSELLING ILLUSTRATOR
SCOTT MAGOON

Fire that's closest kept burns most of all.

–William Shakespeare

For smokejumpers, hotshots, and firefighters everywhere
—S.M.

Library of Congress Control Number for the hardcover edition 2022940922

Hardcover ISBN 978-1-4197-5252-0
Paperback ISBN 978-1-4197-5253-7

Text and illustrations © 2023 Scott Magoon
Book design by Heather Kelly

The interiors of this book were printed with soy inks on FSC-certified paper. Approximately 3% of the power used at the facility where this prints comes from solar energy.

Nomex is a trademark of the DuPont Corporation.
Bambi bucket is a trademark of SEI Industries, LTD.

Printed and bound in China
10 9 8 7 6 5 4 3 2 1

Amulet Books are available at special discounts when purchased in quantity for premiums and promotions as well as fundraising or educational use. Special editions can also be created to specification. For details, contact specialsales@abramsbooks.com or the address below.

Amulet Books® is a registered trademark of Harry N. Abrams, Inc.

**ABRAMS** The Art of Books
195 Broadway, New York, NY 10007
abramsbooks.com